P9-CFB-845

MONROE COLLEGE LIBRARY NR

3784P 01089001 7
Monroe Coll

Music of the Heart

Katie Ashley

To all my readers and fans who have exceeded all my wildest writing dreams. From the bottom of my heart, I send you love, and give you immense hugs. God bless you for your support.

"Music is the literature of the heart; it commences where speech ends."

~Alphonse de Lamartine

Chapter One

Abby

My cowboy boots clomped across the pockmarked pavement as I weaved in and out of the rows of tour buses. Screamo rock music blared around me, echoing through the cramped parking lot. Roadies and technicians brushed past me with scratchy conversations emitting from their headsets and walkie-talkies. Once they swept their gaze over the dangling authorized pass around my neck, they didn't ask what I was doing, nor did they ask if they could give me a hand.

Intense June heat beat against my back and singed the bare flesh above my thin sundress straps. I grunted and gave a tug on the rolling suitcase behind me while the guitar case I carried at my right side felt like it was weighed down with lead.

Rock Nation was one of the biggest music festivals in the country. A hundred bands performed over three days, and the shows lasted around the clock. Music fanatics camped out in the middle of the desert and somewhat recreated Woodstock. Well, that's just what I'd been told. It wasn't like I'd spent the last two days with thousands of stinky, mud-caked strangers. I'd just come off a 737 from Austin, Texas, and hopped the closest cab to the arena.

My only real interest in being at Rock Nation was seeing Jacob's

Ladder—the chart topping, Christian rock cross-over band. The three members, Gabe, Eli, and Micah, just happened to be my older brothers, and the reason I was wandering around a parking lot in the middle of the desert.

Sweating profusely, lost, and frustrated was not quite what I had envisioned when my brothers asked me to join them on their summer tour. It wasn't the first time I had gone around the country with them since they had burst into the limelight two years ago. But it was the first time I had to decide if the rootless existence of a musician was really for me. After singing my ass off, as my brother Eli claimed, for the label executives, I had been offered the role as lead singer. The role was available because my oldest brother, Micah, was exiting the band to get married and join the seminary.

After rolling my suitcase to a halt, I sat my guitar case down. Shielding my hand over my eyes from the glaring sun, I peered at the buses. Trust me, when you've seen one tour bus, you've seen them all. Very few boasted the band's name who called them their home away from home. Right now, I was faced with row after row of them compressed together so tight you could barely move between them.

Peering at the windshields, I looked for the usual multicolored paper with the bus number. For the life of me, I couldn't remember what number I was supposed to be looking for. I dug my phone out of my purse and gazed at Micah's text. *Can't come to meet you like we planned. Crashing after the 4am show. Pass will be at the box office. Come on to the bus. It's 419. We take off at 9am with or without you.*

With a frustrated grunt, I shoved my phone back into my purse.

4

Most of the time, the boys were a lot more considerate of me. I guess they thought since this wasn't my first time at the rodeo, so to speak, I should be able to take care of myself. Usually, they tried to treat me like I was still ten, instead of twenty-one.

"Where the heck is bus 419?" I growled.

"Yeah, just how much do you wanna see Blaine Bennett?" a voice asked over my shoulder.

I whirled around to see a roadie grinning wickedly at a very scantily clad girl. At the mention of getting closer to her idol, she pressed herself against him. "Really bad," she purred.

Oh, ew. It was way too early for this kinda crap. "Um, excuse me?" I questioned.

While the girl acknowledged me, the roadie tuned me out. "Hello, I'm talking to you! I mean, I may not be rubbed up against you, but I am speaking."

The roadie gave a grunt of frustration before turning around. His irritation faded a little as he did a pervy head to toe appraisal of me. "And just what can I do for you, sugar?"

The girl must've thought she was losing her chance to see Blaine whoever he was because she stepped around the roadie and tried blocking his view of me.

Craning my neck, I said, "Listen, I *really* need to find bus 419. I've got to find Jacob's Ladder."

The roadie's eyes rolled back in his head, and I didn't even want to guess what Miss Thing was doing to him. I glanced away and let the waves of disgust roll over me. I was so going to give the boys a piece of my mind when I finally found them. Realizing I was getting nowhere with the roadie, I stomped my boot on the pavement like the irritated child I felt like. "Look, I have a pass, and if I don't get to Jacob's Ladder's bus ASAP, they're going to be epically pissed, and I'm going to give them a full-on description of you so they can totally get your useless ass fired!"

The roadie momentarily jolted back into reality and pushed the girl back a little. "Hang on just a second, babe. She's going to irritate the hell out of me until I get her to the bus."

The girl's lips curved down in a pout. "You promise you'll come back and take me to see Blaine?"

He bobbed his head enthusiastically. "As long as you keep doing what you were doing."

She grinned as he turned and trudged over to me. "If I don't get Jake's prize piece of ass to him, he really will fire me," the roadie mumbled.

"Huh?" I questioned, as he jerked me by the elbow.

We wove in-between several more buses. When we arrived at one, he banged on the door. The driver appeared in the doorway with a biscuit in one hand and a headset in the other. "Yeah?"

"She's supposed to be on the bus," the roadie replied.

The driver eyed my luggage and guitar case. "You sure?"

I huffed exasperatedly as I waved the pass around my neck at him. "Um, yeah, the guys are going to be really ticked if you leave without me," I snapped.

The roadie snorted. "Guess she's their entertainment for the road."

"I'm their sister, thank you very much."

"Whatever ya say, babe. No judgment from me," the driver replied. He put down his biscuit and headset and leaned forward to take my guitar case. "The guys are—"

"Still asleep. Yeah, I know, and trust me, I also know better than to disturb them!" I replied as I climbed up the stairs. I turned around as the roadie shoved my suitcase at me. "Thanks. You've been *so* much help."

He grumbled something under his breath before stalking away. The driver closed and locked the door before easing back down in his seat.

Motioning towards the living area, I said, "I'll just go make myself comfortable until the guys wake up."

"Fine," he muttered before putting on his headset. I guess he was more than ready to tune me out.

I walked down the aisle and flopped into one of the captain's chair. Ugh, what an absolutely shitty morning. Rubbing my temples, I tried soothing the headache that was already forming. Not only was it brought on by the stressful morning, but I hadn't eaten anything yet, which was a huge no-no for me with my hypoglycemia. I'd overslept and been in such a rush to get to the airport that I had forgotten to grab the snack bag my mom, who still couldn't grasp I was twenty-one not twelve, had packed for me. I didn't dare take a peek in the cabinets to see what sustenance the boys might have. I was pretty sure they lived from one fast food joint to the next.

Instead, I leaned back and closed my eyes, hoping a quick nap might get rid of my headache. It wasn't long before the gentle sway of the bus rolling along the highway lulled me to sleep.

When I woke up, my neck and head ached from banging against the large picture window. Raising my hands over my head, I stretched and yawned. The view outside boasted wheat fields spanning as long and far as I could see. Jeez, how long had I been out? A glance at my phone showed almost an hour. I whirled around in the captain's chair to find the living area of the bus still empty and quiet as a tomb.

The boys must've been on one of their coma binges after an adrenaline-sucking weekend. Sometimes they could go for forty-eight straight hours without sleep, but then they would crash and burn for a whole day.

I picked up my phone and texted Gabe. *Wake up, sleepyhead! Feelin' lonely. My bros suck at welcoming their baby sister!*

It was only a second before my phone buzzed. *Hey Little Girl. Come on back to the bedroom. I'm just chillin'*

I smiled and texted, *B right there*

Pulling myself out of the chair, I made my way past the bunks where Eli and Micah snored. I eased the bedroom door open, finding the room bathed in darkness. "Gabe?"

I was surprised not to find the television on or him playing Xbox. "I just texted you, so don't think you're going to pretend you're asleep or something."

8

A mound of clothes caused me to stumble forward, and I pitched onto the side of the bed. "Gabriel Andrew Renard, if this is your idea of a joke, it isn't funny!"

A long moan erupted from underneath the covers as a body shifted toward me. When I was little, the boys, Gabe especially, used to love to scare me. I had a feeling where this was heading, and after the morning I'd had, I wasn't in the mood. "Okay, fine. If you're going to be a jerk, then I'm going back outside." I grunted with frustration and started to hoist myself off the bed.

An arm snaked around my waist, jerking me down further onto the mattress. "What—" I started before the warm flesh of a man's body pushed me onto my back and covered me with his weight. It took all of one second to realize this was *so* not Gabe.

Scorching hot lips met my own, and I shuddered. They pressed eagerly and with intense longing while fingers wrapped and tangled their way through my hair. When I opened my mouth to protest, a tongue darted inside, dancing tantalizing against my own.

For a moment, my traitorous body enjoyed the sensations pulsing through me. Then I realized I was allowing a stranger some heavy first base action while his hand started to round second. With all the strength I had, I pushed against him.

"Get off me!" I screeched.

He ignored me as his fingers fisted the hem of my dress. A lazy chuckle erupted from him. "Bree, babe, what the hell are you doing wearing clothes to bed?"

Bree? This jerk was mauling me because he thought I was someone else. I gritted my teeth and smacked his bare, and very sculpted, chest. "I'm not Bree!"

The hands left my body, and I heard fumbling above me. The light on the bedside table flicked on. I sucked in a breath at the drop-dead gorgeous face hovering over mine. His dark hair was buzzed short, and he had several piercings in his ears. Blue eyes, hazy with a mixture of sleep deprivation and desire, stared down at me. He drank in my appearance, stopping to linger on my heaving chest and how my dress had bunched up my thighs. A seductive grin stretched across his face. "No, you're definitely not Bree. You put her to shame, Angel."

When he started to lean over to kiss me again, I brought my hand in front of his face. "Look, if Gabe put you up to this, the joke is up. You got me. Ha, ha."

His brows furrowed, and I noticed the silver hoop in one of them. "Who the hell is Gabe?"

My heart shuddered a little, and I tried to still the fear prickling over my body. "My brothers didn't put you up to this?"

"No, babe, I don't think so."

"Oh God," I moaned, bringing my hand over my eyes.

"So you're telling me you didn't sneak into my bed on purpose?"

I snatched my hand away and glared up at him. "Of course I didn't! I don't even know you."

"Well, give me a chance to get to *know* you better." He pressed into me again, and for a brief instant, I fought the longing crisscrossing

10

over my body. After all, I'd never kissed a strange guy or been in a stranger's bed. I'd never even been in a boyfriend's bed. My experience with guys was pretty much non-existent.

"No, I have to go," I murmured against his urgent lips.

"You don't have to fight it. I promise I won't think bad of you later on. And I'll make you feel so fucking good, you won't be thinking bad of yourself either, Angel."

When it was very clear he wasn't going to let me up, my desire got doused with anger. Who the heck did he think he was pinning me down and trying to get to *know* me better? Drawing all the strength I could muster, I brought my knee up against his groin.

"FUCK!" he groaned, rolling off of me.

Seizing the opportunity, I scrambled out of the bed. I threw open the bedroom door and stomped out into the hallway. "Okay, boys, you've had your fun, so cut the crap! You better get your sorry asses up right now!" I screamed.

Three pairs of legs dangled out of the bunks. Almost in unison, they hopped out onto the floor. Three bleary eyed, heavily tattooed rockers in various states of undress, stared at me with bewildered expressions.

"Oh shit," I murmured before I pitched forward and everything went black.

***

Chapter Two

JAKE

Scorching pain ripped through my crotch, and I groaned in agony. One minute I'd been making out with an angel straight out of Heaven and the next a hellish wildfire raged through my junk.

In my haze, I heard the angel screaming her fucking head off and then I heard a loud thump. Once I could see straight again, I gritted my teeth and staggered out of bed. I cupped my aching balls through my boxers and stumbled to the bedroom doorway.

The angel, turned raging bitch, lay in a heap in the hallway. AJ sat beside her, cradling her head in his lap, while my other bandmates, Brayden and Rhys, knelt down, staring at her in silent wonder.

When Brayden caught sight of me in the doorway, he narrowed his dark eyes. He rose up and took a step towards me, his jaw clenched tight. His 6'1, muscled form might have been threatening if I didn't know him for the total tenderhearted pansy he was. "Dude, what the fuck is going on?"

I threw up my hands. "How the hell should I know? I woke up to find her in my bed and then she nailed me in the balls!"

AJ shook his dark head of hair and snickered. "You gotta work on your game, man."

I flipped him off before grinding the sleep out of my eyes with my fists. "I thought it was Bree—I mean, she's always sneaking in my bed along tour stops. But then the chick was saying something about a dude named Gabe and her brothers putting me up to it."

"That makes total sense. I mean, what sweet, straight-laced girl like this is going to be getting in your bed," Rhys remarked, his blue eyes twinkling with amusement as he twirled the diamond stud in his ear.

We all gazed down at the girl. Nope, she was definitely not groupie material like Bree. She reminded me of Brayden's wife, Lily. They'd been high school sweethearts, and somehow their relationship had survived the last eight years of craziness as our band moved from the garage to the biggest arenas in the country.

Scratching the dark stubble on his chin, AJ grinned wickedly. "Hmm, with the sundress and headband, she's kinda got a Sookie Stackhouse/*True Blood* look going on. Pure but sexy as hell."

Rhys wrinkled his nose and shook his dirty blonde head. "Oh hell no. She's a hundred times hotter in the face than Sookie!" He motioned to the angel's cleavage. "And damn, look at that rack."

Brayden grunted in frustration. "Guys, could you stop thinking with your dicks for one minute, and focus on the fact we've got a poor, helpless girl passed out on the floor!"

"You've been married too long, Bray," I mused, continuing to take in the blonde's features. She had felt like heaven pressed up against me. Well, until she'd cock-blocked me rather painfully.

At her moan, we all jumped back like we'd been caught doing something we shouldn't have. She blinked her eyes a few times, bringing her hand to her forehead. Her brows furrowed as she rubbed

13

her fingertips into her hairline. Then her eyes flew open, and she stared up at us. Her face crumpled with mortification. "Oh God, it wasn't a nightmare."

AJ laughed. "Ya know, chicks are usually a lot more stoked about meeting us than you are."

Her dark blue eyes widened. "Oh, I'm sorry if I sounded rude. I didn't mean that how it came out."

I crossed my arms over my chest. "Kneeing me in the junk was rude, babe."

She cocked her head to the side and gave me a death glare before pulling herself into a sitting position. "You wouldn't stop molesting me. What else was I supposed to do?" she snapped.

Brayden bristled as he closed the gap between us. "Somehow you managed to leave that tidbit out of your story."

AJ extended his hand. "Come on, Sookie, let's get you up off that dirty floor."

She gave him a puzzled look. "But my name's not Sookie. It's Abigail—well, Abby."

Once AJ pulled her up, she fell against his chest, trying to steady herself. I rolled my eyes when he seemed to get a little too much enjoyment out of her pressed against him as her hands fisted his shirt for balance.

Brayden must've realized it too because he took Abby by the arm. "Come on over here and have a seat." He motioned toward one of the captain's chairs.

"Did you have fun feelin' her up, dickhead?" I hissed to AJ.

He grinned. "It was a little piece of Heaven right here." He closed his eyes and swept his hand to his heart. *"Diablo linda, esas tetas se sienten increible. Me gustaria metertelo hasta que estes gritando."*

Abby froze in front of us. She jerked away from Brayden and whirled around. "¡Ni te lo pienses sucio!"

AJ's eyes popped open, and his brows shot up in shock. "How the hell do you know Spanish?"

"My parents were missionaries. I spent most of my early years abroad—Mexico, Central America, and Brazil. My Portuguese isn't as good as my Spanish though." She cocked her head at AJ. "¡Pendejo!"

"Ha! I am an asshole for saying that!" He roared with laughed. "My apologies, Sookie—I mean, Abby." He then thrust out one of his hands. "I'm Alejandro Joaquin Resendiz, otherwise known as AJ—drummer extraordinaire of Runaway Train and your potential Latin lova."

Abby grinned as she reached out to shake his hand. "Abby Renard."

AJ's dark eyes widened. "No shit—Renard, like Renard Parish in *True Blood*? See you could *totally* be Sookie!"

"Quite a charmer, aren't you AJ?" Abby questioned with a giggle.

"Anything for you, mi amor. I mean, do you know what a fucking turn-on it is to hear fluent Spanish coming off a pair of lips like yours?" His eyes rolled back in his head with delight.

"No, but I'm sure you're going to elaborate for me, right?"

I couldn't help snickering. The more Abby/Hell's Angel spoke the more I started to dig her. She wasn't star-struck by us, and she gave as

15

good as she got—my sore balls were testimony of that.

Rhys stepped forward and offered Abby his hand. "I'm Rhys McGowan—bassist and if you're looking for a real man, a much better choice than that douchebag." He jerked his thumb at AJ.

AJ brought Abby's hand to his lips. "Just remember. Latin men are the best."

"I'll try to remember that," she murmured. As she took her hand from AJ, she brought it to her head. "Ugh, why am I still so dizzy?"

AJ dove into the fridge for a bottle of water and gave it to Abby while Brayden knelt down beside her. "Maybe put your head between your knees?" he suggested, in a calm, soothing voice. At the same time, Rhys snatched up a paper towel and ran it under the tap before handing it to Abby. I glanced around at my bandmates with a mixture of disbelief. They were falling all over themselves to impress Abby with their thoughtfulness. That never, *ever* happened with a woman on the bus. The chicks were there to wow and impress us with their sexual talents. As soon as they were done, they were sent unceremoniously off the bus.

Well, I guess, Brayden's motives were different. He was the father figure and caretaker of the band as well as being the father to four-year-old, Jude, and eight-month-old, Melody. And regardless of the tits and ass thrown in his face twenty-four seven, he remained true to his wife. Although I gave him shit about it, I really did admire him for being loyal.

Abby gave a ragged sigh. "I'm okay. Really, you don't have to fuss over me." She smoothed her hair back and wiped a few dust bunnies off her dress. "I'm hypoglycemic so sometimes I pass out when I don't eat…that coupled with the adrenaline rush of being in a stranger's bed and seeing you all instead of my brothers made me faint."

After taking a hesitant sip of water, Abby patted her cheeks down with the paper towel. When she glanced up, she found all of us staring at her. "So, um, I guess you're wondering how I ended up here, huh?"

Brayden motioned to the authorized pass nestled in her ample cleavage. "I'm going to take a wild guess and say you got on the wrong bus."

Abby nodded. She then launched into a story about why she was even at Rock Nation. When she explained about the roadie and Jacob's ladder, I sucked in a breath. "He thought you were looking for me."

"Huh?" she asked.

"I'm Jake Slater. He probably wasn't paying much attention, right?"

She nodded.

"I mean, Jake Slater and Jacob's Ladder running together kinda sound similar—if the asshat even heard anything past J. He just assumed you were coming to see me."

Abby's eyebrows shot up. "And you often have random chicks coming to your bus with luggage and a guitar case?" she countered.

The grin I gave her caused pink splotches on Abby's cheeks. "Never mind," she muttered, looking away from me.

The sound of her phone vibrating on the table interrupted us. She grabbed it and frantically brought it to her ear. "Gabe, oh my God, it's so good to hear from you!"

The voice on the other line spoke frantically. She shook her head. "No, no, I didn't get cold feet about the tour. It's just...I, um, I got on the wrong bus."

At his response, her face clouded over with fury. "Oh really? Well, maybe one of you assholes should have come to meet me!" With his next words, she sputtered with indignation. "Don't you chastise me about cussing! I'm a grown woman, and I'll say whatever I want to! I can't believe you have me on speakerphone. Eli, if you don't stop laughing, I'm going to beat the shit out of you the moment I see you! And if you think I can't, just remember Costa Rica!"

I couldn't help laughing at her fiery personality. The other guys were equally amused at the spitfire in front of us.

"How did this happen? There were over a hundred buses out there, Gabe. When I asked about Jacob's Ladder, they thought I meant Jake Slater."

Gabe's voiced screeched on the other end so loud we all could hear it. "You're on Runaway Train's bus?!!!"

"Yes," she replied. At his next statement, she snorted. "Well, I've only managed to do the drummer and the bassist so far, but I'm thinking I could get a threesome going and knock out the others. Maybe I'll gang-bang with the roadies when we stop for dinner!"

Rhys made a strangled noise in his throat while AJ muttered, "Fuck me," under his breath. Even I couldn't stop the below-the-belt stirring at her imaginative suggestion.

She rolled her eyes. "Gabe, would you give me a little credit? I've held on to my virginity this long. I think it'll hold for a while."

18

We all exchanged wild glances. Rhys tugged so hard on his stud it came out of his ear and fell to the ground. AJ fumbled for the beer next to him and drained it in a long guzzle—his chest heaving hard as he stared at Abby. Even Brayden appeared shell-shocked by her declaration. All of us had to be thinking the same thing. How was it possible for a smokin' hot girl like the one before us to be a…virgin?

Abby whirled around and saw our expressions. A flush entered her cheeks, and she ducked her head. She sank back down into her chair and buried her head between her knees. "I can't believe I just admitted that in a room full of men," she whispered. When Gabe said something else, her voice broke with emotion. "Look, I just need to know how we're going to fix this." After sniffling for a few seconds, she raised her head and scanned our faces. "Yeah, one sec." She handed the phone to Brayden. "He wants to know your tour schedule, so I'll be able to get off the bus and onto a plane as soon as possible."

He nodded as he took the phone and stepped away from us. "Hey Gabe, this is Brayden Vandenburg, and don't worry, man, I'm gonna take good care of Abby until we can get her back to you guys—" He jerked back like he had been stunned. "That was *so* not what I meant. Besides, I'm a married man. Now here's where we are…" His voice trailed off as he walked down the aisle.

Rhys patted Abby's back reassuringly. "Hey, don't worry. It's going to be okay."

With her head buried in her hands, she mumbled. "Thanks. I hope so."

Edging Rhys out of the way, I knelt down beside Abby. Taking her chin in my hands, I pulled her head up to meet my gaze. "Don't sweat it, Angel. Your brother and Bray will figure it out. I promise we'll have you back to your civilized little world as soon as possible and before you can get too traumatized by being in our presence."

She smacked my hand away. "What do you mean civilized?"

I shrugged. "I just meant that it's obvious you're used to a certain way of life."

Her blonde brows shot up so far I thought they might reach her white headband. "Are you insinuating that I'm some spoiled little brat who is used to having everyone bow to her every whim?"

"Maybe."

Abby narrowed her eyes at me. "My parents were missionaries. Do you even understand what that means?"

A smirk curved at my lips. "I know all about the missionary position, Angel. In fact, I believe I was trying to acquaint you with it earlier when you cock blocked me."

"You're seriously disgusting!" she cried popping up out of her chair. She almost toppled me over before I could stand up. She poked her finger into my chest. "I'll have you know that I'm not some prima donna who can't survive without someone taking care of me. The lives of missionaries and their families are very simplistic, so trust me when I say, I've seen a lot of hard shit. Yeah, we lived in major cities like Rio in Brazil and Guadalajara in Mexico, but I've also tromped through the jungles and gone days without showers, least of all cell phones and WiFi. So I can assure you that there's nothing you and your band of merry miscreants can do that would shock or scare me!"

I rolled my eyes. "Oh please. You fucking passed out at the sight of the guys, not to mention that you flipped and got your lacy panties all in a twist when I made out with you."

"Are you trying to say that I couldn't make it on this bus?" she countered.

I cocked my head at her. "Come on, Angel. You would die a thousand deaths if you even had to stay one night on here with us and our raging sex drives, atrocious language, and bad table manners."

"You seem to forget I have three older brothers. I'm well acquainted with unruly guys."

Crossing my arms over my chest, I smirked down at her. "So you're saying if you had the chance to get off the bus in the next few hours, you wouldn't?"

She inched forward, standing toe to toe with me. "Are you saying I don't have the courage to stay?"

"Yeah, I am."

AJ held up his hands. "Whoa, what the fuck do you two think you're doing?"

"What are the terms for me to prove myself to you?" Abby asked.

Without even thinking, I blurted, "One week on the bus."

Her tough-as-nails resolve wavered a little. "One week?" she squeaked, her voice cracking.

Rhys tried pushing us apart. "Okay, that's really funny, but you two can stop now," he argued. When neither of us backed down, he said, "Let me remind you that Abby has a tour she needs to be on, and we have one as well. No one has to prove anything to anyone, okay?"

I tore my gaze from Abby's to glare at him. "This isn't anything to you, man. This is between me and Angel."

"It's Abby," she growled.

I arched my brows at her. "So what's it gonna be, *Angel*?"

Fury flashed in her blue eyes before she whirled around. She stomped over to Brayden and snatched the phone away from him. "Gabe, there's been a change of plans."

***

Chapter Three

Abby

"Are you insane?" Gabe sputtered into my ear. His voice had risen an octave since I had taken the phone from Brayden and informed him about the bet. I edged away from the guys to where I was practically back in the bedroom I had fled from not twenty minutes before.

Once I felt I was sufficiently out of earshot, I replied, "No, I'm perfectly sane, thank you very much."

I was on speaker phone with all the boys again because Eli came at me next. "Look, Abster, we all know when your temper gets the better of you and when you're doing the spoiled baby girl 'I'm used to getting my way' act. But this isn't one of us you're fighting with—this is a mega rockstar douchebag! Trust me, you don't owe Jake Slater a damn thing. You won't ever see him again after today, so I would advise you to get over this dumbass bet notion and get the hell off the bus! *Now!*"

"Why Matthew Elijah Renard, don't tell me you're cussing at me now? And with some of your infamous exploits with girls on and off tour how is that any different than with Jake? I mean, whatever would Mom and Dad say?" I chided into the phone.

"Don't get sassy with me, Abigail Elizabeth!" he countered.

I exhaled noisily and leaned back against the wall. "Come on guys. A tour is a tour. This is all a learning experience, so in the end, I think this would be a good opportunity for me."

Eli groaned. "An opportunity for what? To be degraded, ogled, and potentially seduced into one or more of their STD infested beds?"

Rolling my eyes, I replied, "No, I think it would be good to see the inner-workings of another band. And I think you're being very unfair and judgmental about the guys." Okay, so maybe he was right on the mark about all of them but Brayden thinking that way, but I wouldn't give in and let Eli know that—I would never hear the end of it.

"Abby, you're a twenty-one-year-old virgin who has no experience with men outside the two relationships you've had with youth group leaders who probably never got past first base with you."

"Ha, I'll have you know it was second with Paul!" The moment the words left my lips, I cringed. The last thing I needed was my brothers knowing my sexual past...or lack thereof.

"I think my eyes need bleaching with the mental image I just got," Gabe moaned.

"Whatever," I grumbled.

Eli snorted into the phone. "Regardless of what you've done or not done, since we are guys and have dicks, I think we know a little more about what Runaway Train is thinking about you right now, and all of them, but maybe the married one, wants to screw you!" he snapped.

I gasped at the same time I heard a smack on the other line. "Don't talk like that in front of her," Micah admonished. I was glad to finally hear his voice. He was the shyest of boys, the deep thinker, and the

24

one with a tender heart and soul as deep as the ocean. "What about you, Mike?" I asked.

He sighed deeply. "While I share some of the boys' apprehension, I also try to look at this through a greater scheme of events. You're a bright light, Abby, and who knows the good you might do with those guys in the short time you have with Runaway Train."

"Exactly. I mean, Mom and Dad brought us up to give people from all walks of life and circumstances a chance, right?"

Before Micah could reply, Eli laughed manically. "If you think for one minute that *Dad* is going to be okay with you on a bus with four hard-core rockers, you have lost your freakin' mind."

The mention of our father doused my confidence. Oh jeez, what had I done? He was going to kill me. Twenty-one or not, overprotective fathers never seem to fully realize that their daughters were grown adults.

At my silence, Micah said, "Don't worry, Abby. I'll talk to him and try to smooth things over. At the end of the day, we all know your true character. We know that you're capable of doing this and not succumbing to temptation. Right?"

"Well, duh, of course."

"Then I look forward to seeing you in a week."

"Me too, Mike."

He exhaled noisily into the phone. "But don't think for a minute I won't be calling in to check on you every day—maybe twice."

I laughed. "I wouldn't expect any less of you."

"Love ya, Baby Girl."

"Love you, too." When the other guys were silent, I added, "And I love you too, Gabe and Eli even though you're being jerkfaces!"

A deep chuckle came from Eli. "You know we love you, Abster. You've been a sweet pain in the ass since the moment Mom brought you home from the hospital."

"Thanks a lot," I grumbled.

"If one of those douchebags dares to lay even a finger on you, I'm totally forgetting the turn the other cheek message, and I'll pound his ass, got it?" Gabe growled.

I grinned as I shook my head. "Yeah, I'll be sure to pass on your message."

"I'm glad to hear it."

"Okay then. I guess this is goodbye for now."

A deep chorus of "Byes" echoed around me before I hung up the phone. Cradling it to my chest, a tremble went through me when the enormity of what I had done finally crashed over me. I had made a bet with the notorious womanizing lead singer of Runaway Train to stay on their bus for an entire week. What the hell had I been thinking? I blew out a frustrated breath. Well, no time for worrying about it now. As my mom would say, I'd made my bed, and I had to lie in it.

I moaned at the thought of bed and sleeping arrangements. I mean, where was I going to sleep? I hoped to goodness it wasn't going to have to be with one of the guys. I gazed around the roosts, counting them in my head. There were two extra ones if one of the guys slept in the bedroom. Phew, okay, at least I wouldn't be sharing a bed with Mr. Octopus Arms Slater.

Taking a deep breath, I pushed myself off the wall and headed back down the hallway. The guys were lounging around the table when I came back up the aisle. "Is everything okay?" Brayden asked, his expression one of deep concern.

"Um, well, as good as it can be considering my brothers think I've lost my mind for consenting to a bet to stay on a bus with a group of absolute strangers, not to mention they're pretty hard-core rockers." I forced a smile to my lips. "But besides that, I'm peachy."

Brayden nodded. "I can understand how they feel. I have two younger sisters as well as an eight-month-old daughter."

"Aw, can I see a picture of her?"

Happily, he dug his phone out of his pocket and handed it over to me. His screen saver was of a beautiful dark haired, dark eyed grinning baby girl as well as sandy haired little boy with blue eyes. "That's Melody Lane. And that's Jude Paul—he's four."

"Let me guess. Any chance you're an intense Beatles fan?" I questioned with a grin.

Jake groaned beside us. "More like Bray is Beatles obsessed. He likes to think he's Paul McCartney."

Brayden only shook his head good-naturedly at Jake's dig. "I do a lot of song writing just like Paul, and I'm a helluva guitar player."

I smiled at him. "Well, I adore the Beatles too. They're my parents' favorite, so I was raised on them."

"Favorite song?" Brayden asked.

"Without a doubt, *Let it Be*."

He clapped his hands together gleefully. "Mine too! And so written

27

by the fabulous Paul McCartney."

I laughed. "Exactly." I stared down at the picture again. "Your children are absolutely adorable, Brayden. Jude's got future heartbreaker written all over him."

"Yeah, he takes after my wife, and Melody, well, she's the spitting image of me."

"She's already gorgeous at eight months. You're going to be in a lot of trouble in about twelve or thirteen years."

He grimaced. "Tell me about it. I'll be even more over-protective with her than my sisters."

I nodded. "I can only imagine because my dad is even crazier than my brothers. Being the baby girl isn't easy, especially with the age difference. The twins, Gabe and Eli, are twenty-six, and Micah's twenty-eight."

"You must be really spoiled," Jake noted with a self-satisfied smirk.

I shook my head at him. "Yes, but not like you're thinking."

"We'll see," he murmured before winking at me.

I eased down across from the guys in one of the Captain's chairs. "So what's your deal, Angel?" AJ asked.

My brows creased in confusion. "My deal?"

"Why were you at Rock Nation? Were you just checking out the scene to hang out with your brothers or what?"

I opened my mouth to answer when Jake sarcastically replied, "She's obviously in the biz. She came with a guitar, dumbass."

"Well, yes and no on being in the business and hanging out with my brothers. I'm supposed to be headlining with them in the fall. Well, at least with Gabe and Eli. Micah's planning on quitting after he gets married in August."

"Wow, headlining is a pretty big deal," Brayden declared.

I nodded. "Tell me about it. Touring with them the last half of the summer is kinda like a pretest to see if I really want to do it. If not, the boys will just recruit someone else or go on as a duo."

Jake snorted contemptuously at me. "You're getting the opportunity of a lifetime tossed in your lap, and you're not sure you want to do it?"

"It's not that I don't appreciate it. It's just I've spent the past three years studying to be a nurse. I was just about to go through clinicals." At his continued exasperated expression, I added, "In the long run, I think saving lives and helping people might be a little more important than entertaining."

He quirked his pierced brow at me. "Don't you think music saves people?"

"Well, I—"

"A certain song can mean the difference between life and death for someone who is depressed and suicidal. Music can inspire and give hope. It can show adulation and worship and praise love and people." He gave me a pointed look. "Including God."

I blinked several times in surprise at the passion which he delivered his words. "You're right. Music is life-altering and changing."

Jake motioned toward my guitar case. "So play us something."

"Seriously?" I asked, glancing from Jake to other guys.

AJ grinned. "Si, mi amor."

I rolled my eyes. "Enough with the Spanish."

"But I told you how much it turns me on to hear it coming from your lips."

With a wry smile, I replied, "But I'm not interested in turning you on."

A chorus of "Ooohs" rang through the cabin from Jake and Rhys to which AJ only shook his head. "Burn man," Rhys teased with a grin.

"Okay, I think now is as good a time as ever to set up a few ground rules for our bet," I said.

"You're not pussying out, are you?" Jake asked.

I wrinkled my nose. "Ew, I hate that word." When he started to repeat it, I jabbed a finger in his direction. "I will stay on this bus a week and win the bet, but there are going to be a few rules, or I guess I should say some *courtesies* that I expect you guys to follow."

"I agree with Abby," Brayden said.

"You would," Jake grumbled.

"First, you need to respect me and my boundaries. At the moment, I'm not on here to be any of your playthings or hook-ups, so I would appreciate it if you stopped hitting on me."

AJ's jovial expression faded. "You mean you don't think I'm hot?"

Since he appeared almost wounded, I had to rethink my strategy. "AJ, you're a very good-looking guy. I can already tell you have a big heart and a wonderful sense of humor. Any girl would be blind not to want you." When he beamed and puffed out his chest at the other guys, I held up my hand. "But I think we both know at the end of the day, you're not looking for a relationship with me, right? You're just looking to get into my panties."

A strangled noise came from the back of his throat at the mention of my underwear. "Yeah, I am," he finally admitted with a sheepish grin.

I returned his smile as my gaze swept over Jake and Rhys. "So as I was saying, I would appreciate if you would show me some respect by not hitting on me as well as at least trying to tone down some of the language and sexual innuendos. Somewhere deep inside you have the potential to be gentlemen, and you're just waiting to treat women as more than just desirable play things, right?"

With a smirk, Jake countered, "I don't know about that."

"Oh, if your mother was on this bus, you would act the same way you are now?"

He scowled. "No, I wouldn't."

"Good. Then we all agree that you'll try to treat me like a gentleman. Anything you'd like to request from me?"

Jake stepped forward to where he was looming over me, and I had to fight the urge not to cower away from him. "If we're going to act like gentlemen, then you also need to make sure your wardrobe isn't...tempting."

I peered down at my sundress. Since it came below my knees and I often wore it to church, I found his request shocking. "There's something wrong with this?"

When I glanced up at him, Jake's hungry gaze had honed in on my cleavage. I cleared my throat to which he replied, "You're showing

31

way too much skin with the thin straps and the legs, so I'd suggest jeans and t-shirts from now on—the baggier the better."

"Fine. I'll be happy to oblige," I replied.

"And that goes for the sleepwear too. No camis with those booty short things."

I chewed my lip when I thought of what pajamas I had in my suitcase. "Um, okay. I can try. But I might have to make a stop at Wal-Mart or Target before tonight to get some pajamas and shirts.

Jake's face spread into a grin. "I'm glad to hear you're willing to work with us. After all, what good can come out of getting a bunch of horny males all riled up?"

He licked his lips lasciviously, and I gritted my teeth before replying, "Absolutely nothing."

"Good." Jake then turned and brought my guitar case to me. "Now please regale us all with your vocal stylings."

"I'd be happy to." I leaned over and popped open the locks on my case. When I pulled out my guitar, Jake stared at it in surprise. "What's wrong with it?"

"Nothing. It's just I expected—"

"I'll have you know this is a Gibson Hummingbird that cost three grand! I worked my ass off to pay for it!"

He grinned. "Angel, it's a helluva guitar. And what I was about to say before you interrupted me was I just expected it to be all glittery like Taylor Swift's."

Plucking out my pick, I waved it at him and winked. He eyed the shimmering purple before throwing his head back and laughing heartily. "Oh Angel, I'm so glad to see that. You don't disappoint."

Once I adjusted the guitar on my lap, I cocked my head at the guys. "Hmm, so what do you want me to play?"

"Give us what you did for the record execs. You obviously wowed them if they were going to let an unknown headline a tour," Rhys suggested.

I nodded. "Okay, I played a guitar, rather than piano, version of Adele's *Someone Like You.*

Jake's brows shot up in surprise. "Adele?"

From his tone, I could tell he thought there was no way in hell I had a voice that would come anywhere near hers. I pursed my lips. "Yeah, Adele," I countered.

He crossed his arms over his chest and continued giving me a skeptical look. "All right then. Wow us, Angel."

I rolled my eyes before clearing my throat and strumming a few warm-up chords. Then I started the opening melody of the song. "I heard that you're settled down..." I wanted to impress the guys, but I really wanted to knock it out of the park to put Jake's smirking ass in his place. So I did the only thing I knew how to do when it came to performing—I tuned them out. It was about me, the guitar, the music, and the melody. As my voice echoed through the close quarters of the cabin, I closed my eyes, living and breathing the lyrics. I poured my soul into reaching the high and low notes while my fingers picked the familiar chords.

When I finished the chorus, my eyes popped open, and I stopped singing. I continue strumming the chords as I gazed around at the guys. I couldn't help but laugh at their expressions. "So?" I prompted.

AJ grinned. "Tu cantas como un angel."

I snorted. "I sing like an angel, huh? I guess that's a good description since you guys keep calling me that."

When I glanced at Rhys, he was shaking his head. "Damn, girl, no wonder you blew the execs away. You're like a mini-Adele."

Warmth flooded my cheeks. "Really?"

"Hell yeah! Tinier and prettier though." Rhys thumped my back heartily like he would one of the guys. A little too hard because it caused me to yelp. His eyes widened. "Oh, I'm sorry. I forgot you're so dainty."

I laughed. "I'm not that fragile, but I'm not one of you guys either."

Next I looked to Brayden who wore an expression of genuine admiration. "That was absolutely amazing. Not only do you have a powerhouse voice, but the emotion you put into it…" He closed his eyes for a moment. "Just inspiring."

Unable to keep a beaming smile off my face, I gushed, "Aw, thank you."

Finally, I dared myself to look at Jake. He was leaned back against the kitchen counter, arms crossed over his chest. "So?" I finally asked.

His signature smirk curved on his lips. "After those glowing reviews, you really give a shit about what *I* have to say?"

"Of course I do. After all, you're the lead singer of Runaway Train."

"Uh, Bray and I sing too," AJ countered.

I laughed. "Whatever."

Jake rubbed his hand along his chin. "Ever had voice lessons?"

My brows furrowed. "When my brothers made it on to the scene, my parents let me have some training. Before then, we really couldn't afford it. Occasionally, some people from the ministry would work with us."

He bobbed his head. "Just as I expected."

"What?"

"True God-given talent," he replied, with a wink.

His response stunned me, and I just sat there, guitar still on my lap, staring at him. He pushed himself away from the counter and came over to me. "There are people who can spend thousands of dollars on voice lessons and never, ever exude one tiny ounce of the talent you just did on a stinky bus rolling down the interstate."

"Thank you," I squeaked.

"I think you could give Adele a run for her money any day."

A nervous laugh escaped my lips. "Uh, well, I don't know about that."

Jake squatted down in front of me, and I tried ignoring how my body hummed in response to his closeness. I had never, ever experienced anything like it before in my life. It was like every molecule in my body came alive, and the closer he was to me the more I tingled. Whoa. How could I possibly be having a reaction to him? He was an egomaniac jerk!

His gaze went to my guitar. "So you play some ballads. Can you do anything else?"

Pursing my lips at his challenge, I started strumming the opening to AC/DC's *Highway to Hell*. Jake instantly busted out laughing. "Damn, Angel, just when I start to underestimate you, you go and prove me wrong."

Still playing, I teased, "And here I underestimated that you could ever admit when you were wrong about something."

"I normally don't. But I have a feeling I'm going to make an exception for you in a lot of areas." At his wicked grin, I knew exactly what he was meant.

"Dream on," I muttered.

"Fantasizing is healthy, you know. Maybe you should try it more."

Closing my eyes, I kept playing *Highway to Hell*. I licked my lips. "Hmm, yeah, you're right. Fantasizing is nice."

"Whatcha thinkin' about, Angel?" Jake asked, his breath hovering close to my cheek. "Or should I say *who* ya thinkin' about?"

"You," I whispered. My eyes popped open to take in his surprised expression.

"Seriously?"

"Mmm-hmm," I replied a little breathlessly for emphasis. He cocked his eyebrows expectantly. "I'm fantasizing about what it would be like to nail you in the balls again for being such an egotistical jerkwad!"

Laughter echoed around me from the other guys while Jake only shook his head. With a smirk, he replied, "Admit it though. You were still thinking about my balls."

"You're impossible."

Before Jake could give me another witty comeback, my stomach rumbled so loud that it practically echoed throughout the room. Jake's expression became concerned as his gaze honed in on my abdomen. "Why didn't you tell us you were so hungry?"

An embarrassed giggle escaped my lips. "There's kinda been too much going on to pay much attention to my stomach."

"You like omelets?" he asked as he rose to his feet.

"Yeah, I do."

"Then one omelet coming up."

"Um, thank you." My jaw gaped open as I watched Jake head to the kitchen and take out the necessary supplies to make me a late breakfast. I gently put my guitar back in its case.

"You guys want one?" he asked over his shoulder as he began whisking the eggs.

"Nah, I think I'll eat that leftover pizza," AJ replied, sidestepping him to the fridge.

Rhys wrinkled his nose. "You're disgusting." He nodded at Jake. "I'll take one."

"Bray?" Jake asked.

"Nah, I'll fix a sandwich when I come back out. It's almost time for my Skype chat with Lily."

When he started for the bedroom, Jake snorted. "Don't be doing anything raunchy with Lily now that Angel is on the bus."

Brayden whirled around to shoot Jake a death glare. "You know good and well that Jude and Melody are always there for my calls, you jackass!"

37

With a chuckle, Jake went back to working on his culinary masterpieces while Brayden slammed the bedroom door shut. AJ came over to the table with a Dominos box and began shoveling in several cold slices of pepperoni pizza.

"Are you even chewing that?" I asked.

He winked at me and replied, "I got a *big* appetite, Angel."

I wagged my finger at him. "Manners, remember?"

Not taking his eyes from mine, he picked a napkin from the table and daintily wiped the corners of his mouth.

I grinned. "It's not the dirty outside I'm concerned about, perv."

AJ threw his head back and roared. "Damn, Abby, I sure am stoked about having you on the bus with us. You're going to be fun as hell."

"I hope so. I wouldn't want to be a nag." At the mischievous tinkle in his dark eyes, I shook my head. "Don't even go there."

"What do you mean?"

"Don't say some cheesy thing like 'Ooh baby, you can nag me all night long—two or three times!'"

AJ's dark eyes widened as his slice of pizza dropped onto the table. "Okay, it's really creepy how you can read my mind, but then again…fuck! It's so hot that you can think like a dude!"

I laughed. "Older brothers, remember?"

A wide grin spread on his face. "Remind me to thank them someday for raising you right, Angel."

Rhys raked his hand through his unkempt hair. "Speaking of your brothers, I caught part of their show. They're not bad."

"Not bad?" I huffed indignantly.

Pink tinged his cheeks. "Well, you know what I meant…for light rockers."

AJ bobbed his head. "Yeah, when they were introduced, I kinda expected some Jonas Brothers shit. But they're actually hardcore for Christian rockers."

Leaning my elbows on the table, I eyed AJ and Rhys. "My brothers are fantastic musicians! I mean, can you two play multiple instruments?"

"Well, no—" Rhys began.

I smirked at them before crossing my arms over my chest. "Although he's probably the least musically inclined, Gabe is one hell of a drummer, and he can write a song like nobody's business. Micah can play the guitar, bass, banjo, dulcimer, and piano, not to mention he has an amazing voice for harmonizing. And Eli—he plays the bass and the fiddle and sings too. Along with Gabe, they've been writing their own songs and composing their own music since they were ten."

Rhys held his hands up in defeat. "I stand corrected, Angel. Your brothers are complete and total badasses!"

Jake flipped an omelet onto a plate and added, "And their sister is pretty hardcore too."

I laughed. "Thank you—for all your compliments about the general badassery of my family's DNA."

After winking at me, Jake then shuffled over to the fridge and pulled out a carton of orange juice. "I'd really rather have a Coke Zero if you have it."

He ignored me as he poured two large glasses before handing me one. "OJ is better for you."

Rhys shook his head. "Says the dude who has beer with his breakfast most days."

"Shut up, douchebag." Eyeing me, he then said, "You did pass out about thirty minutes ago from low blood sugar, remember?"

"You're right." I took a long swig of my orange juice, and I had to admit it was good. "Thank you."

"You're welcome, Angel."

I huffed out a frustrated breath. "Why do you all insist on calling me that?"

Jake motioned to my dress. "For one, you're all decked out in white."

"But it's just a sundress."

Balancing three plates, Jake then came over to the table and set down our omelets. "Second, you appeared out of nowhere like a fallen angel from the sky."

"How poetic," I snipped.

AJ grinned. "Not to mention, you're a 180 from the girls who are usually on this bus."

"Definitely," Jake replied. Tilting his head, he pinned me with his stare. "And then you've got the most beautiful aura of light about you—pure and exquisite."

I almost choked on my orange juice at the sincerity of his words. "Really?"

"Yeah, you do." After plopping down across from me, Jake added, "And finally, you felt like absolute heaven pressed up against me in bed."

And just like that, the perfect moment was shattered. "Please," I muttered, grabbing my fork. When I bit into the omelet, I closed my eyes from the ecstasy my stomach experienced. "Wow, this is really good."

"I'm good at a lot of things besides singing and playing the guitar," Jake replied.

I popped one eye open to peer at him. "There's some more lovely innuendo in there for me, isn't there?"

Jake grinned as he took my glass to get me more orange juice. "Nope, I'm being a good boy."

"I doubt that seriously."

The table fell into silence as we all gobbled up our food. Brayden came out of the bedroom with a smile from ear to ear. "I guess by your expression your call went well?" I asked.

He beamed. "Melody said 'dada' today and blew kisses at me. She's never done that before."

"Aw, that's sweet," I replied.

Brayden's expression darkened. "I just hate that it's going to be two more weeks until I get to see them. Jude gets bigger and bigger every time I see him."

"Maybe you should think about bringing them along on the tour again," Jake suggested.

I stared at him in amazement. "You like kids?"

He gave me his signature smirk. "Of course I do. I especially like Jude and Melody. I also like having Lily around because she cooks for us and cleans."

Brayden threw a napkin at Jake, hitting him in the face. "My wife is not your glorified cook and maid, douchebag."

"I know that, twatwaffle. But more than anything, I like how having her around puts you in a good mood. When you got your kids around you and you're getting laid often, shit just runs smoother for all of us."

Clenching his jaw, Brayden slammed the refrigerator door. "Somewhere in that statement was something decent and redeeming, but like always you had to trample all over it," he grumbled, bringing his food over to the table.

Raising my arms over my head, I yawned. "Tired of us already, Angel?" Jake asked with an amused grin.

"No, it's just I didn't sleep much last night. Nerves and all. Then I had to get up at the asscrack of dawn to get to the airport for my early flight."

With his expression waxing concern, Brayden leaned forward in his chair. "Why don't you go lie down for a while?"

I glanced around at the guys. "You wouldn't mind?"

AJ shook his head. "Nah, we're probably going to crash again ourselves. We had a week straight of gigs before Rock Nation, so our asses are dragging."

"Oh, okay."

Sweeping his hand to his chest, Jake said gallantly, "And I'll even let you have the bedroom."

"That's awfully sweet of you, but I can always take one of the

42

roosts."

With a twinkle in his eye, Jake replied, "I insist."

"Thank you then."

When I rose out of my seat, he followed suit. Taking my suitcase, Jake rolled it down the aisle to the bedroom. I glanced back at the guys to see their open-mouthed, wide-eyed expressions of disbelief. Putting one foot in front of the other, I trailed behind him. Once Jake wheeled my suitcase inside, he turned around. "All yours, Angel. We'll make sure to wake you for dinner. We'll probably stop a little earlier than normal because those omelets won't sustain us for long, and we're almost out of groceries."

"Oh, okay, thanks."

Jake didn't move out of the doorway, so I had to squeeze past him. Our bodies meshed together, and I fought the familiar tingle that prickled over my skin at being so close to him. It was a feeling I wasn't used to experiencing with anyone. Once I was inside, I turned back to him. "It's very sweet of you to give me the bedroom. The privacy is nice."

He inched closer to me. "Well, just to forewarn you the lock is busted. So if you need me to watch the door while you change into something a little more comfortable, I'd be happy to. You know, so the guys don't get a peek at your goods."

"How sweet of you," I noted as I moved in front of him. Bringing my hand to his chest, I gave him a hard shove, sending him flying out into the hallway. "I'll make sure to put my luggage in front of the door just in case." With a sickeningly, sweet smile, I added, "And thanks again for being so thoughtful when it comes to my goods."

Behind Jake, the guys hooted with laughter. Instead of anger, amusement twinkled in his sky blue eyes. He wagged his finger at me. "I'll get to you sometime, Angel. I'll break down all those goody girl walls you have built around you."

"We'll just have to wait and see then." With that, I slammed the door in his face.

The RV shuddering to a halt jolted me awake. My eye-lids fluttered open. As I took in my darkened surroundings, panic crept over me. Wait, where the hell was I? Gazing around the blackened room, I tried getting my bearings. "Ugh," I muttered when all the events of the day raced through my mind.

When the lamp on the bedside table came on, I jumped out of my skin. Jake perched on the side of the bed, practically on top of me. "W-What the hell are you doing?" I cried, jerking the sheet against me.

He rolled his eyes. "Don't get your panties in a twist, Angel. I'm not here for a repeat performance of this morning." With a wave of a shoe, he added, "I'm sorry to have disrupted your beauty sleep, but all my shit's in here."

"Oh, I'm sorry," I murmured.

"Besides that, we're stopping for dinner, so I figured I'd better wake you up."

"Thanks."

He cocked his pierced brow at me. "Did you know that you snore?"

My eyes widened in horror. "I do not!"

"Yeah, you do."

Covering my mouth, I muttered, "Oh God, I do?"

Jake grinned as he bobbed his head. "It's kinda cute though. Nothing like the loud-as-fuck snores me and the guys do."

"How mortifying."

"You embarrass too easily, Angel. How are you going to make it a week with us if a little snoring gets you so riled up?"

"I'll be just fine thank you."

AJ peeked his head in. "Hey, I need to get my stuff."

"Go right ahead." I threw the sheet back. "Now if you'll excuse me, I'll get my things and go to the bathroom so I can get dressed for dinner."

Jake opened his arms wide before collapsing onto his back on the bed. "Be my guest."

When he didn't move, I grunted in frustration. Just as I started to climb over Jake, AJ flung the closet door open to get out his clothes. Since we were in such close quarters with the bus's bedroom, I couldn't move. To my utter horror, I'd gotten stuck straddling Jake.

When I caught his eye, he grinned and winked at me. My face flushed. "AJ, would you hurry up with the freakin' door!" I snapped.

He peeked around the side and snorted back his laughter. "Whoops, my bad."

I sighed with exasperation. "Any day now, AJ!" The moment I said it, I knew he'd take his own sweet ass time—anything to keep me in the precarious situation of riding Jake.

"You don't have to go, Angel. I'm sure this could be a win-win situation for both of us," Jake teased.

I stared at him for a moment before flopping back on the other side of the bed. I shook my head at him. "Why do you have to do that?"

"Do what?"

"Act like a constant manwhore who only sees women as sex objects."

Jake arched an eyebrow at me. "Oh, I'm sorry. Did I just *objectify* you?"

"Yes," I hissed before narrowing my eyes at him. "Is it too much to ask that we carry on a civil conversation without you always having to make everything between us about getting off?"

Jake's brows creased. "And there's something wrong with that?"

"For me there is." I gave him a pointed stare. "And for our bet."

He turned over on his side to where we were face to face. "I'm not losing this bet, Angel."

"Then start playing by the rules." With the sweetest smile I could muster, I then batted my eyelashes at him. "Or I'm going to start walking around here in my underwear."

His mouth gaped open. "You wouldn't dare!"

"Try me, big boy. Sporting my bra and panties is basically a bikini, so why not?"

Staring at me dumbfounded, Jake drew in a ragged breath. "I'm never going to intimidate you, am I?"

I shrugged. "Nope."

"Damn. I don't know how the hell to take you, Angel."

"Why do you have to 'take me' period? Can't you just talk to me like you would any girl?"

With a sneer, he replied, "If I do that, it won't help us."

I propped my head on my elbow. "When was the last time you actually had a conversation with a female, besides your mother, that didn't involve dirty talk?"

"Hell if I know," he replied.

"I thought as much."

"Wait a sec…" He snapped his fingers. "Actually, it was Tuesday. I talked to my baby sister on the phone."

My eyebrows shot up in surprise. "You have a sister?"

"Well, she's my half-sister. My dad and step-mom each had a kid when they got married. Then they had Allison. She's fifteen and spoiled rotten."

I smiled at the sincerity in his voice when he talked about his sister. "I bet she idolizes her big brother."

Flipping on his back, Jake slid his hands under his head and grinned. "Yeah, she does. I mean, she's always thought I was pretty cool, but even more since I hit it big." His expression slowly darkened. "Some shitheads give her grief about it—like trying to be her friend just to see what they can get from her. I hate that."

"Poor thing. It must be hard sometimes having a famous brother."

Jake frowned at me. "I try making it up to her all the time by giving her shit."

I laughed. "Thus why she's the spoiled baby sister?"

"I guess. Hell, the guys and I are even playing her Sweet Sixteen in a few weeks."

"Aw, that's so sweet of you." I nudged him playfully. "Who knew there was a good guy buried deep, deep down inside."

AJ closed the closet door. "Okay, done."

"Finally," Jake muttered as he got off the bed.

Gesturing to his jeans and polo shirt, AJ said, "Hey, give me some credit. It's not easy changing behind a closet door to protect Miss Innocent Eyes over there."

I laughed as I rose up to a sitting position. "One minute you're trying to get me to see you naked and the next you're protecting me."

AJ winked at me. "Just know I would do anything, and I do mean *anything* for you, mi amor."

I grabbed my dress and cowboy boots off the dresser. "Thanks so much."

***

Chapter Four

JAKE

As soon as Abby disappeared into the bathroom, AJ arched his dark brows questioningly at me. "You better be damn glad it was me and not Brayden who came back here."

"What's that supposed to mean?" I asked as I slid on a clean pair of jeans.

"You said you were coming in here to get your shit and wake Abby up, and instead you're back in bed with her. Hell, she was riding you."

"That was your fault, not mine, opening the closet door like you did."

"Mmm, hmm," he replied, raising his brows suggestively.

I shrugged. "Trust me, she wasn't happy about me being in bed with her."

"But were you?"

I froze half-way in pulling a fresher smelling shirt over my head. Peeking through the neck of the shirt, I shot AJ a look. "Get real, dude. I'm so not interested in Abby."

He grinned. "Keep telling yourself that." He started for the door, but then turned back to me. "So if you're not interested, you mind me making a play for her?"

For reasons I couldn't possibly understand, my jaw clenched at the thought of Abby and AJ. At the same time, my fists tightened at my sides. "She's not stupid. She knows exactly what dogs the three of us are when it comes to women."

"I could try to change her mind."

"Yeah, good luck with that one," I grumbled as I brushed past him.

Using my fist that was still clenched from AJ's comment, I pounded on the bathroom door. "You through in there, Angel? Some of the rest of us would like some mirror time."

"I'm coming, I'm coming," she mumbled as she undid the lock. When she threw open the door, my breath caught at the sight of her. Somehow in the few short minutes Abby had been in the bathroom she'd managed not only to get dressed, but also freshened up as well. Her long, blonde hair fell in waves down her back while she'd also reapplied some makeup. Her full lips glistening with gloss just begged me to reach over and lay one on her.

"What?" she questioned as she swept her hands to her hips.

Trying to cover up for my lustful thoughts, I smirked at her. "Nothing. You just clean up fast."

A giggle escaped those succulent lips of hers. "Yeah, it comes from growing up with one bathroom, six people, and most of the time not a lot of hot water. You should see some of the conditions I've had to get ready in before."

She squeezed past me and then started over to AJ who was messing with the entertainment system. While my gaze instantly honed in on the soft sashay of her hips as she walked down the bus aisle, Rhys sidestepped me into the bathroom. "Oh hell no, dude! I was here first!"

He shot me a wicked grin. "You were too busy ogling Abby's ass to care about the bathroom."

"I was not ogling her ass," I hissed under my breath as I pushed him out of the way.

We began elbowing each other for mirror time when music suddenly blared throughout the bus's speaker system. He and I exchanged a glance before both groaning in unison. "AJ, not that Mexican shit again!" I shouted.

From time to time, AJ insisted on torturing us with the Banda and Cumbia type music he grew up on until we gave him enough hell to turn it off. I poked my head out of the bathroom door. "Dude, seriously, I can't take—"

Before I could give him anymore grief about the music, the sight of AJ dancing with Abby stunned me silent. Well, it wasn't your traditional dancing or the dry humping kind I was used to at clubs or concerts. It was the kind I used to see when I went to AJ's family parties.

AJ could have seriously put the dudes on Dancing with the Stars to shame. He'd been born with a natural rhythm that enhanced his drum playing. Not to mention that when he danced, he had that whole effortless Latin hip swishing and swaying thing that made women's panties melt. But at the moment, I wasn't so concerned with AJ's moves as I was with Abby's. Leaning against the doorway, I watched as Abby danced as effortlessly as AJ. Even with the trickier steps, she kept up, matching his fluid movements. I was treated to quite a floor show considering the hem of her dress twirled provocatively back and forth.

Scratching the stubble along on my jaw, I couldn't help wondering if she could do all that with her hips when she was standing up, what she could do flat on her back.

AJ caught my eye and winked. "She's a natural, isn't she?"

"Oh yeah, she can move."

Forgetting about potentially shaving, least of all fixing my hair, I stepped closer to them. "Where did you learn to do that, Angel?"

Without missing a step, Abby replied, "Over the years, we lived in several places in Mexico—Guadalajara, Mexico City. I was just a kid then, but I went to lots of parties. Everyone wanted to teach the little blonde Gringa how to dance." She giggled. "And since my brothers were older than me and wanted to impress the chicks, they recruited me as a partner. So in the end, you pick up on things."

I crossed my arms over my chest. "I'm seriously impressed. You're a true triple threat—you sing, you play guitar, and you dance."

AJ shimmied Abby across the grungy bus floor. "She's a quadruple threat because she's fine as hell too!"

Abby rolled her eyes, but she still let AJ spin her around and then dip her low as the song came to a close.

As she lay reclined in his arms, I asked, "Tell me, is there anything you can't do, Angel?"

"Hmm, maybe pass my nursing exams or find a decent guy?"

AJ groaned. "You got one right here, mi amor! Say the word, and we can reenact this entire scene later…in the bedroom."

Abby swatted his chest playfully. "You promised to stop with the sex stuff. A gentleman, remember?!"

"Yeah, yeah," he muttered glumly as he pulled her up.

She laughed as she smoothed down her hair and fixed the straps of her sundress. "Honestly, AJ, nothing stops you, does it? I mean, I even pick *Los Caminos De La Vida* out of your Spanish collection for us to dance to because I know it's the least sexy song in the world. It's about a dude worrying about his mother dying for goodness sake."

My chest tightened at the mention of a mother's death, and my hand immediately went to my pocket where my phone rested. "Hey, um, I'll meet you guys outside, okay?"

Abby nodded while AJ said, "I'll round up Bray and Rhys."

"Sounds good." As soon as I stepped off the bus steps, I dialed my mom. She answered on the second ring. "Hey sweetie."

Even though she couldn't see me, a broad smile spread across my face. "Hey, Mama. I just wanted to call and see how your doctor's appointment went." Although I'd never admit it to her, I'd been worried to death about her. Three years ago, we'd faced a crisis when a routine breast exam found a tumor. She had been through the gamut of chemo and radiation, along with a mastectomy. Fortunately though, she had been strong and healthy since then. She just had to go back for routine exams and blood work.

"Oh, just fine. Everything's fine. No need to worry."

"Are you sure? You sound tired."

She laughed. "It's just because some of the girls convinced me to dance again. I overdid it thinking I was twenty, not fifty."

Back in the day, my mom had been a classically trained ballet dancer. Although her dream was to make it into Julliard, she did well traveling and touring with local companies. Once she got too old to dance, she opened a dance studio. It was financially successful for her and successful for me since I met and charmed the tutus off quite a few of the dancers.

I shook my head. Even though she was trying to play it off, I could tell there was more. "I could come home if you needed me."

"Jacob, I'm fine. What I need you to do right now is keep up with your band's obligations. There are a lot of people depending on you."

My mama was one of the few people I allowed to call me by my birth name. "Okay, okay. But you know I'd be there in an instant if you needed me."

I could hear the pleasure in her voice when she replied, "Of course I do. But you know Papa's just down the road and the rest of the family. You just take care of you."

It was then that the bus doors opened up. Missing the last step, Abby came tumbling off the bus, and I had to rush forward to catch her before she fell. She gripped my biceps to steady herself. "Oops, what a blonde moment," she murmured, her face flushing with embarrassment. "Thank you, Jake."

I grinned at her and then winked. "Just glad I could save you from face planting."

Abby gave a small smile before hurrying away from me and disappearing into the passenger seat of the Tahoe waiting to take us to dinner. Rhys and Brayden came out followed by AJ.

"Jacob?" My mother's voice finally brought me back out of my thoughts of how good Abby's hands felt on me and how delicious she smelled.

"Sorry, Mama. Small female crisis."

"Was that Bree?" From just those few words, my mother's tone indicated her disdain for any involvement I had with the dark-haired goddess who traveled from time to time with her dad who was a roadie with the band. Mama hated the fact that Bree showed up all over the country just to be with me.

"No, it wasn't. Her name is Abby. And before you can even ask, she's not a groupie." I then gave my mom a quick explanation.

"She sounds lovely."

I rolled my eyes, but I couldn't help laughing. "Yeah, I'm sure to *you* she does. To me it's a freakin' nightmare—an alleged virgin who isn't going to let me in her pants without the Jaws of Life. She's not intimidated by me at all. Not to mention she has drive and ambition not just in the music world, but with nursing. And to top it all off, she comes from an insanely religious background."

"Jacob Ethan Slater! I can't believe you just talked about getting into a girl's pants in front of me!" Mama chided.

"Sorry," I replied, sheepishly. "I guess I've been with the guys too long."

She laughed. "Please tell me you're not acting like a total animal and that you show some of the respect I instilled in you—especially to this Abby."

"I try…and I'll try with her too."

"Is she pretty?"

Without missing a beat, I replied, "She's beautiful—just like an angel." I winced the moment the pansy words escaped my lips. What the hell was happening to me?

"Mmm-hmm," Mama murmured knowingly into the phone. "She could be good for you if you would give her a chance."

"Come on, Jake!" AJ shouted.

"Mama, I gotta go. We're catching an early dinner."

"Okay sweetheart. I'll talk to you soon."

"I love you," I proclaimed.

"I love you, too," she replied. Just before I could hang-up, she said, "Jacob?"

"Yeah?"

"I'm serious about giving Abby a chance. Fate has a funny way of intervening in people's lives."

I knew what she wasn't saying when she mentioned fate. She meant God. She and Abby would get along really well with their faith—something I had never picked up on, much to my mama's disappointment. "Yeah, whatever."

She laughed. "There's that stubbornness—the worst trait you inherited from me."

"I got a lot of good ones from you too."

"Yes, as well as from your father."

I growled into the phone at the mention of him. Because my mom was an absolute saint, she had been able to forgive the bastard for leaving her for his bimbo of a secretary when I was ten. Me, on the other hand, I still had issues with him and my step-mother.

Our head roadie, Frank, honked the horn, causing me to jump. "Sorry Mama, I really gotta go." After another round of "I love yous", I disconnected and hustled over to hop into the SUV. Leaning forward, I tapped Frank. "So where are we eating?"

He turned back to me and grinned. "The team wanted that pizza place we saw down the road a bit."

I glanced over at the other guys who made faces and wrinkled their noses. We'd been living off pizza and Subway the last few days we were at Rock Nation. Since we'd been out in the desert, there hadn't been shit around for miles, which meant very limited food choices.

"GPS says there's a sports bar/diner about five minutes up the road. A hot spot for tourists and truckers."

I laughed. "If it's a favorite of truckers, then it must be good, huh?"

"I just want a cheeseburger the size of my head," Rhys declared.

AJ licked his lips. "Nah, a big, juicy steak with a baked potato slathered in butter and sour cream."

Catching Abby's eye, I tilted my head at her. "Trucker stop okay for you, Angel?"

Although she tried to hide it, I could tell she was extremely uncomfortable at the thought. At the smirk curving on my lips, she rolled her eyes. "It sounds lovely."

"I'm sure it's not the quality you're used to."

Twisting around in her seat, she glared at me. "You still don't get it, do you? I've eaten just about every animal imaginable, and the quality had certainly not been USDA approved. Once again, the missionary lifestyle is harsh. You don't reach people while staying at the Hilton. It's jungles, backwoods, and slums."

I rolled my eyes. "Yeah, yeah, you've lived a hard knock missionary life. You wanna medal or something?"

"No, I was just making a point that I'm not the prima donna you think I am!"

"Well, you've been stateside since you were twelve. Not to mention, your dad is pastor of one of the five largest churches in Texas—I'm sure he makes a pretty good salary with that many members tithing."

Abby's blonde brows shot up. "How did you know that?"

I grinned at her. "I did a little research on my iPad while we were resting."

"I'm not denying that we have a nice house and nice things *now*. But most everything goes right back into the ministry—even the boys give a lot of their salary. It's how we were raised. But even if my dad had a BMW and my mom was draped in bling, no matter how hard you try, I'm still going to win, Jake. You can bet your sweet ass on it!"

Rhy and AJ dissolved into hearty laughter while Frank tore his gaze from the road to stare at Abby in surprise. Taking one hand from the wheel, he held it out to her. "Can I shake the hand of the only girl I've ever seen put Jake Slater in his place?"

Abby giggled and shook Frank's hand. "I have three older brothers, so I'm used to it."

"We haven't been formerly introduced because these knuckleheads seem to have forgotten their manners. I'm Frank Patterson."

"Abby Renard. I'm very pleased to meet you."

"Likewise." He jerked his head back in my direction. "That little wiseass is like a son to me, but he needs taken down every once in a while."

"Keep talking, Frank," I muttered.

He chuckled as he flicked on the blinker to turn into the diner. As I surmised from the teaming parking lot, it was probably nicer than most of the places we stopped along the road. With all the eighteen wheelers parked in the side-lot along with the gleaming chrome of some motorcycles up front, it also had a seedy flair to it as well. Most of the time, the shittier places were top on our list because we wouldn't necessarily get recognized. There was a lot to appreciate about being able to eat dinner in peace without fans shoving items in front of you to sign or snapping your picture.

Frank pulled into a parking spot but kept the engine idling. "I'm going to head back down the road and check on the boys. Text me when you're ready to leave, and I'll come pick you up."

"Thanks man. Make sure the guys get whatever they want, but watch the alcohol," I instructed.

Frank glanced back and winked at me. "Don't worry. I always do."

I patted him on the shoulder before hopping out of the SUV.

Without even thinking, I opened Abby's door. She tore her gaze from Frank to stare at me in surprise. I held out my hand to her. "I figured after your last little tumble, I should make sure you got out all right. I don't want to be sending you back to your brothers all bruised up." Under my breath, I murmured, "Well, at least not without enjoying it."

She cocked her head at me while the corners of her lips turned up in a half smile. "I heard your insinuation about me getting bruised up through…well, you know."

I laughed. "Now this is me being a pure gentleman like you requested. Wherever your devious little mind goes with my comments is your business."

Taking my hand in hers, she giggled. "Okay then." Once her cowboy boots were firmly set on the pavement, she let go of my hand. "Thank you, Jake."

"You're welcome."

As we started in the diner, I once again held open the door for her. She grinned up at me. "Can I just say a girl could get used to this?"

"Well, that was my mother I was talking to on the phone. She made sure to remind me to act like I had some sort of upbringing when I was around you."

"I haven't even met her, and I already like her." She leaned closer to me, her breath hovering over my cheek. "And deep down inside you, there's the man I'm sure she worked hard to raise. He just needs to come out more often."

"Is that right?"

"Mmm, hmm." Her blue eyes pinned me a stare. "Because when the gentleman Jake comes out, he makes you awfully irresistible"

Something about the way she said those words made a shudder go through me. Trying to recover, my hand went to the small of her back to usher her to a table. "Yeah, well, just don't get too used to it, Angel."

A disappointed look flashed on her face, but she ducked her head before she thought I saw it. Bray had asked the hostess to seat us away from the crowd, and that put us in a side room with a stage and an almost antiquated looking karaoke set-up. I was surprised to see a DJ organizing music.

"Ooh, they have karaoke!" Abby squealed as she eased down in her chair.

AJ grinned at her excitement. "Whattya say you and me do a duet in a bit? Prove to you there's a voice behind the drum-set?"

She bobbed her head. "I'd love to!"

It was then that a very hot, scantily clad waitress with a fabulous rack sauntered up to our table, and instantly my dick twitched in my pants, leaving any ideas of being a good boy in the dust. "What can I getcha?"

Leaning back in my chair, I let my gaze rove over her body. "Hmm, there's a loaded question," I replied suggestively.

She winked at me before saying, "Let's stick to the menu for now, sugar."

I grinned. "Fine if we have to. We'll have five beers—"

"Four. I'll have a Coke Zero," Abby interrupted.

The waitress, whose name tag no lie read Billie Jean, didn't even look at Abby. Instead, she pursed her heavily glossed lips at me. "We don't have Coke Zero here."

Cutting my eyes over to Abby, I could practically see the steam coming out of her ears. "Something else for you, Angel?"

"Diet Coke then," she grumbled.

I cocked my head at Billie Jean. "Angel will have a Diet Coke, and the rest of want beer. Maybe you should just bring us a pitcher or two."

"Anything for you," she replied with a wink. She scribbled down on her pad. "Any starters?"

"Yeah, we'll take a sampling of all your appetizers," AJ replied.

As Billie Jean left to fill our orders, Abby gaped at AJ. "You're serious about ordering after you eat all those appetizers?"

He grinned. "You have to watch out when I'm really hungry, Angel."

"With my brothers, I should expect no less, right?"

"You bet."

Brayden tapped Abby's menu. "Order anything and everything you want. Dinner is on me tonight."

"No, you don't have to do that."

He smiled. "I don't have to, but I want to."

"Okay then. I'll let you this one time," she replied.

Billie Jean returned with our beers and Abby's Diet Coke and began taking our orders. "I'll have the double cheeseburger, fries, and a side order of baked beans," Abby said before handing her menu to Billie Jean.

"You're seriously going to eat all that?" I asked.

She grinned. "I'm starved. I might even order dessert too."

When AJ started to open his mouth to say something I could imagine suggestive about Abby and dessert, she pointed a finger at him. "Don't even go there. It's you, me, and karaoke time."

He laughed. "I'm good with that." AJ swept out of his chair and followed Abby to the stage. Only a few other patrons, mainly truckers, were sitting in our section, sipping beer and eating burgers. They didn't look like they gave two shits about AJ and Abby's performance.

As he started going through the song selection book, AJ grimaced.

"Dude, this shit is like all from the 70's and 80's," he groaned.

"With the looks of this place, did you actually expect some of our stuff to be on there?" I called.

AJ shot me a dirty look before going back to the book of music.

"Ooh, what about this one?" Abby suggested as she pointed her finger at the book.

AJ's dark brows furrowed. *"Islands in the Stream.* You gotta be freakin' kidding me!"

"Please. I love Dolly Parton and Kenny Rogers." She poked her lip out at AJ before saying, "I'm supposed to be part country singer, remember? It's in my blood."

"Well, I love Dolly Parton's—" AJ began before Abby playfully smacked his arm.

"¡La próxima vez que te pegue en las bolas!"

He held his hands up in defeat. "Okay, okay, I'll stop. I don't want you nailing me in the balls, rather than the arm!"

"Thank you."

"So for you, Angel, *Islands in the Stream* it is, but I'm going to be reading off the screen for everything but the chorus."

"That's okay," Abby replied, nodding at the DJ. She then passed AJ a microphone before taking one for herself. "Okay, AJ. Wow me."

He winked at her. "Oh, I plan on it."

The music started up, and AJ peered at the screen to begin singing his opening part. "Baby, when I met you there was peace unknown. I set out to get you with a fine tooth comb."

As his voice echoed through the room, Abby's brows shot up and her mouth dropped, and I could tell she was surprised as hell that he could really sing and hadn't been bullshitting her. She then began harmonizing with him when Dolly's part came on. When they got to the chorus that was familiar to AJ—mainly because we used to jam to Mya/JZ remix *Ghetto Superstar*, he inched closer to Abby. AJ had a gift for improvising, and he was really getting into singing about making love with Abby. She possessed the same gift as he did, and I was impressed with her performance ability, even in the dingy diner's karaoke bar. She had future star written all over her.

Several of the truckers sitting around us took notice of the performance. Well, I guess I should say they mainly took notice of the hot little number in the white sundress intertwining herself with the douchebag she was singing with.

Not enjoying the way I was feeling about what I was seeing, I rose out of my chair. "I gotta go take a leak," I muttered before escaping to the bathroom. What the hell was wrong with me? Why did I give two shits about Abby performing with AJ? I mean, she had made it damn clear she wasn't going to give any of us the time of day. As I washed my hands, I caught a glimpse of myself in the mirror.

"Get a grip, dude. You do not want to get entangled with her," I muttered.

"Huh?" some guy in a stall asked.

"Nothing," I grumbled before exiting the door.

Thankfully, when I came back from the bathroom, Abby and AJ were no longer singing and had rejoined the table. Since the appetizers had arrived, we started attacking them. Abby did a pretty good job putting some away as well. Once they were devoured, we waited anxiously for our main courses to arrive. I cut my eyes over to where Abby twirled the straw in her Diet Coke. A question popped into my mind, and I acted on it. "So Abby, you're twenty-one and legal, don't you drink?"

"No, I don't," she replied, before taking a dainty sip of her Diet Coke.

"So caffeine is your only illicit substance?" I implored with a smirk.

With a shrug, she replied, "I guess so."

"Ever tried a beer?"

She eyed my frothy mug and wrinkled her nose. "No, thank you."

"Oh come on. Just try a sip." I slid my beer closer to her. When she nibbled her lip, I couldn't help goading her some more. "Don't tell me you're afraid to try it?"

Abby snapped her gaze up to mine, and the fire that flashed in her eyes made me shift in my seat. Damn, how was it possible for Miss Priss to affect me with just a look? I could only imagine that with the proper stoking, that flame could be scorching in the bedroom.

Without a word to me, she reached over and grabbed my mug. She licked her lips as I leaned forward, silently daring her to continue. She took in a mouthful before her eyes widened, and she turned away from me to spew out the beer. "Oh.My.God! How do you drink that? It tastes like horse pee!" she exclaimed, swiping her hand across her mouth.

AJ and Rhys chuckled at her response. "You been drinking a lot of horse pee lately, Angel?" I questioned, as I took my beer back.

She scowled at me. "No, I haven't. I haven't even been around a horse since I got thrown from one when I was ten and broke my arm."

"You need to get back in the saddle."

Abby shot me a withering look. "And let me guess. You're the man to teach me?"

I ignored her dig at the innuendo of teaching. "Well, I did grow up on a farm, and I do have six horses—well, my mom and I do."

Abby's disdainful expression slowly faded, and she eyed me with curiosity. "You still live at the farm with your mom?"

"When I'm not touring, it's the only place I want to be."

"No big city, swinging bachelor pad and wild parties?"

I grinned and shook my head. "Nope, give me backwoods bonfires, mudding, and fishing over all of that."

"Hmm, I wouldn't have pegged you for a boonies kind of guy."

AJ snorted. "You won't get any more boonies than where Jake grew up in Ball Ground, Georgia."

Abby's brows furrowed. "But I thought you guys knew each other as teenagers?"

"We did. After my mom and dad divorced, he left and moved to Atlanta. I'd visit him on weekends, and AJ's family lived next door. "

66

AJ nodded. "My family has always been city dwellers. We don't do backwoods. Rednecks aren't real tolerant, ya know?"

I laughed. "Oh please, that's so not true."

"Yeah, right. You don't know how many times I got the 'You're not from 'round here are ya, boy,' " AJ drawled in his best hick voice.

I smacked his arm. "I call bullshit, AJ. My redneck family are some of the best people you know and don't deny it."

AJ grinned. "Okay, so maybe I enjoyed being in the boonies a little too much with Jake."

"Yep, I taught his sissy, city boy ass to hunt, fish, and rope cattle."

Abby's mouth gaped open. "You have cows too?"

"Naw, my Papa does."

AJ nudged Abby. "Did you hear that? Every once and awhile, Jake will slip up and sound like a total country bumpkin."

I rolled my eyes. "Whatever."

Abby smiled. "I like the Southern drawl. I mean, I was twelve when we moved back to the states, so I really can't call myself a Texan but I sure do love it there. My dad's brother has this huge ranch that's out in the middle of nowhere. I could spend days just wandering around the fields and wading through the creeks, feeding the cows, and petting the horses." A little shiver went through her. "I swear that one day I'll conquer my fear about getting back on one."

I stared at her for a moment, taking in the sincerity of her words. I'd never, ever met a girl who sounded like she loved the backwoods as much as I did. "You won't have much time for ranches if you start headlining with your brothers."

Her expression darkened a little. "Tell me about it. They're going to put us on a grueling tour in the fall. I can't even remember how many cities are on it. We'll barely get home for Christmas." She sighed. "That's not the life I see for myself. For the first time in my life, I have some roots, and I want it to stay that way." Her cheeks reddened a little as she added, "Not to mention wanting a home of my own and kids."

AJ chuckled. "You want all that now?"

"As a matter of fact, I do." She cocked her head at him. "You think I'm too young to be married and have kids?"

At the same time, Rhys, AJ, and I in perfect unison replied, "Absolutely."

She rolled her eyes. "Considering the sources, I'll choose to ignore that."

"What's that supposed to mean?" I asked.

Billie Jean, along with another waitress, interrupted the conversation by bringing our food. Once they left the table, Abby leaned in on her elbows and pinned me with a hard stare. "It means that you three are out for nothing but no-strings-attached sex. You can't imagine anyone wanting more than just one night stands or meaningless hook-ups. I'm sure if I asked Brayden, he would feel differently."

Bray winked at Abby. "But I'm probably not the best person to ask. I've always been an old soul. Lily and I married when we were your age, and Jude came a year later." A genuine smiled formed on his lips. "I wouldn't take anything—not the stardom, the fan adulation, or the money—for what my family means to me."

Abby's expression melted at his words, and she practically puddled at his feet. "Aw, that's so sweet." She reached over and patted his arm. "I sure hope I have what you do some day."

"You will. Just be patient. The right guy will come along—one who accepts everything about you and respects your boundaries and your character."

Abby gave Bray a beaming smile. "Thank you."

At the mention of her 'boundaries', there was a question I had to ask. "So Angel—"

She huffed out an exaggerated breath. "Do you all really have to keep calling me that?"

"Fine. *Abby*," I began with a grin. "Is what you claimed earlier really true? You know, about being a virgin, or were you just shitting us to try and steer us from getting in your pants?"

"Jake," Brayden warned.

I held my hands up. "What's wrong with asking a simple question for clarification?"

"Because part of your bet with Abby entailed you being a gentleman, and last time I checked, a gentleman doesn't question a woman's past or lack thereof."

Abby shook her head. "It's okay, Brayden. I don't mind answering the question." She stared straight into my eyes. "Yes, it's true that I'm a virgin."

"Damn," AJ muttered.

"But how is that humanly possible?" Rhys questioned.

Abby laughed. "Mainly because I have a strong belief system, but I also have pretty high standards."

I glanced down at her hand. "So where's your purity ring then?"

Her cheeks flushed a little. "Well, I don't wear one because they mean you're waiting for marriage, and I don't necessarily believe in that."

"You don't?" I pressed.

"I did when I was younger, but for now, it's more about me waiting until I'm in love."

I furrowed my brows. "So all it'll take is for you to fall in love with some dude, and you'll give it up? Just like that?" I snapped my fingers for effect.

"You say that like it's something easy. To fall in love with someone deeply and then have them love you back is truly a miracle."

"Then it sounds like you'll be holding on to your V-card for a while, Angel."

She shrugged. "We'll see. I just know it'll all be worth the wait."

"Good for you, Abby," Brayden said, through a mouthful of steak.

With a disgusted grunt, I replied, "That's all peachy for you, but I gotta say more power to the guy. Me, I could never get it up for a virgin."

Abby gasped and dropped her hamburger. "You liar!"

"Excuse me?"

"Y-You totally were...well, you know, this morning in bed with me," she sputtered.

70

Swallowing a mouthful of my chili dog, I rolled my eyes. "That's because at first I thought you were Bree who is always showing up to bang me when we're on the road."

Poking her finger in my chest, she countered, "Oh no, you kept coming on to me when you turned on the light and saw it wasn't Bree." She pursed her lips. "I may not know a lot, but I do know what *that* was."

The guys snickered to which I shook my head. "Sorry, Angel, but it's still a void point. At the time, I had no idea you were a virgin. Had I known then what I know now, my hard-on would've been withering fast."

AJ snorted. "Oh come on, Jake. That's a bunch of bullshit. Any guy that looks at Abby, virgin or not, would totally get a boner."

"Um, thanks…I think," Abby replied.

With a wink, AJ said, "Just know I would have no problem, mi amor. Any time or any place."

"Or me either," Rhys added. He licked his lips suggestively at Abby.

She let out a frustrated puff of breath. "I cannot believe we're discussing this least of all that I'm about to say thank you, AJ and Rhys, for admitting you could…well, you know, even for a virgin." She glanced at Brayden who widened his eyes.

Holding his hands up defensively, he quickly argued, "I can't comment on this conversation."

Abby's cheeks reddened at his comment. "Oh no, I didn't mean for you to!" She then buried her head in her hands. "This is so mortifying."

Bray shifted in his seat and cleared his throat. "I will say this though." Abby tentatively raised her head to peek at him. "My wife, Lily, was a virgin." He gave a sheepish grin. "We both were."

"Really?" Abby questioned.

He nodded. "It never bothered me that she hadn't been with anyone else."

I grunted. "Yeah, because you were a horny sixteen-year-old dude who didn't know any better."

Bray narrowed his eyes at me. "Yeah, well, there was that year we broke up right when the band hit, and I banged everything that moved, trying to forget how much I loved and needed Lily." A fierce expression spread over his face. "But none of those experiences hold a candle to making love to Lily, and she's only ever been with me. Yeah we might've been two fumbling teenagers back in the day, but nothing was fucking sexier than us discovering it all together."

I stared at Brayden in shock. I'd never heard him speak so passionately about sex with Lily. He usually was very guarded and threatened to kick our asses when we alluded to anything involving them getting it on. His favorite thing to do was to growl, "That's my wife, fucker!" or "That's the mother of my children!" when we made dickhead comments about Lily being a MILF.

"Wow," Abby murmured at Bray's statement.

He grinned at her. "Sorry, I got a little carried away there."

She shook her head. "No, I appreciated it, and I'm sure Lily would, too."

I exhaled noisily. "Regardless of what you three dickwads say, I hold firm to my claim that I wouldn't or couldn't get it up for a virgin." When Abby cocked her head at me, I said, "Fine then. I couldn't *knowingly*, how's that?"

She bit down on her lip and turned her head from me. The table fell into an awkward silence before Abby muttered, "Um, I'll be right back." She practically fell out of her chair and sprinted from the table.

After downing the rest of my beer, I glanced up to see the guys glaring at me. "What?"

Brayden leaned forward so far across the table that his elbows bumped into mine. "You're an utter and complete asshole for hurting her feelings about the virgin thing."

"I'm a dick for telling the truth?"

AJ snorted contemptuously at me. "It's called a fucking filter, man. Try using it from time to time."

When I glanced at Rhys, he narrowed his eyes. "So not cool to make Abby feel bad about herself, especially when she's as smoking hot as she is."

I opened my mouth to argue when the screech of the karaoke microphone being tapped drew my attention to the stage. Gazing out at us, Abby gave me a sickeningly, sweet smile. Immediately my stomach churned, and I knew I was in trouble at being publically called out for being a douchebag.

"I hope you all don't mind me singing again."

The scattered group of truckers whistled and hooted appreciatively, which caused Abby to grin and breathlessly say, "Thank you."

Gripping the microphone tighter, she said, "It's just that I really would like to win a bet tonight, and singing this song is the only way I see being able to do it." Once again her blue eyes locked with mine. "Jake, this one is for you."

She nodded at the DJ who pressed the play button on the music. It took all of two seconds for me to recognize the opening bass thumps. "Oh fuck," I murmured as *Like a Virgin* began blaring throughout the bar. As soon as some of the inebriated truckers realized the song, they hollered and clapped their hands.

From the minute she started singing, it was like Abby sent a direct beam of lust straight to me. I mean, I knew I put on an act when I was on stage, so the fact she was a performer should have made her behavior less believable. But damn was she convincing as a temptress. Every shimmy and shake of her luscious body, every time she tossed her head back and ran her fingers through her hair, every slinky step she took and thrust of her hips was driving me fucking insane.

If I thought I was stunned, the other guys were open-mouthed and wide-eyed at her performance. Out of the corner of my eye, I caught AJ gulping down his beer like a man dying of thirst. Even Brayden was eying Abby in a way I hadn't seen in years—although it was a helluva lot more innocent than how AJ, Rhys, and I were ogling.

Shifting in my seat, I knew it wasn't going to be long before I lost the bet. I glanced down and glared at my traitorous dick. When I peeked up at Abby again, a pained noise escaped my lips as all hell broke loose below my belt with what I saw. Sinking down to her knees, she then began doing the unthinkable. She started crawling towards the end of the stage—never missing a beat or lyric. Sitting below her, I had a straight shot down the front of her dress with an epic view at her fabulous rack. When she reached the end of the stage, she swung her legs around, and for a brief moment, I got a flash of her upper thighs before she let her legs dangle off the edge.

She hopped down and slunk over to our table. Without a glance at the other guys, she gave me a seductive crook of her finger. I shook my head and grinned, trying to make her believe she was having no effect on me, which was a fucking lie. But Abby wasn't having any of it. She strode over to me as she ran her hand over her hips and ass as she sang about being touched for the first time. Her fingers then slid through my hair and across to cup my cheek before playfully smacking it.

Just when I thought she was headed back to the stage, she backed up and straddled me. A hiss escaped my lips as she started moving her ass across my crotch. I couldn't help throwing my head back and groaning. I'd been given expert lap dances in my day from some of the highest paid strippers in the business. Abby was clumsy and didn't know exactly how to ride me to give my dick the most pleasure, but damn, if I couldn't feel her hot, little center burning through my jeans. I had been at half-mast before, but I figured at any minute with her moaning the oohing and aahing parts of the song I would be busting out of my zipper.

Even in her non-existent experience, she knew what was up, no pun intended. With the song still playing, Abby glanced over her shoulder and shot me a triumphant look. "Do you now concede to all the guys that you knowingly and willingly got it up for a *virgin*, or should I continue?"

Although my dick would have enjoyed her continuing the half-hearted attempt at a lap dance, I shook my head. "Okay, Angel, you win."

As AJ and Rhys clapped and cat-called, Abby started to slide off my lap. When she did, I grabbed her arm and spun her around to where she was straddling me again, but this time we were face to face. A startled look flashed in her dark blue eyes. I leaned in closer to her. My breath tickled her earlobe, and she shivered. "So you got me all hot and bothered. Art thou now to leave me so unsatisfied?"

Her chest rose and fell in heavy pants. "You're quoting *Romeo and Juliet*?"

"Why do you act so surprised?"

"You didn't strike me much as the kind of guy who liked to read, least of all Shakespeare."

"I'm full of surprises, Angel." My hands gripped her hips tighter. "Just get to know me a little better."

Abby rolled her eyes. "Did you seriously just use a bad pick-up line on me?"

"Who says it was a line? Maybe I do want you to get to know me better." When she quirked her eyebrows, I laughed. "And not just in the biblical sense."

"With everything you know about me and not having sex, you still want to get to know me?"

For reasons I didn't begin to understand, I nodded. "Yeah, I do."

She stared at me like she expected any minute for me to go, "Gotcha! Just kidding!" But when I didn't, a slow smile spread on her face.

"Okay, I can try to let you get to know me." She nibbled her bottom lip, which did nothing for my hard-on. "And I might as well give you a try, too."

"Good. I'm glad to hear it." I shifted in my chair. "Would you like to get off my lap now? Your little performance has left me needing another bathroom break."

Her cheeks flushed when she thought she got my meaning. "Not very gentlemanly to admit that to me."

I laughed. "I'm talking about dousing some cold water on it, Angel. Give me a little credit not to go jerk-off in some diner bathroom."

Now the pink tinge in her cheeks spread to her neck. "Oh, uh, okay." She quickly hopped off my lap, and without another look at me, eased back down in her chair. Winking at the guys, I said, "I'll be right back." I tossed my phone to AJ. "Go ahead and text Frank that we're ready and settle the check."

"Will do," AJ replied.

I had almost reached the bathroom when someone grabbed the back of my shirt and jerked me hard. "The fuck?" I cried, stumbling backward as I was pulled into a darkened room and the door slammed shut. "Um, what the hell?"

The light flashed on to reveal a grinning Billie Jean. As she leaned back against the door, I heard the distinct click of the lock. She then stepped forward. "I didn't recognize you at first, but now I know who you are."

I quirked my brows at her. "And who is that?"

"Jake Slater of Runaway Train."

"Yep, that's me."

Her gaze left mine to take in the half-mast bulge in my pants. "Looks like you have a little problem." She laughed. "I guess I should say a *big* problem." Her eyes, filled with desire, met mine. "I'd give anything to take care of that for you."

Oh shit. This was so not happening. How was it possible I had a hot babe wanting to screw me not ten feet away from the virgin I'd just asked to give me a chance to be a gentleman? This was all shades of fucked up. As the room closed around me, I knew I needed to get out fast.

When I started for the door, Billie Jean sidestepped me. "Please?"

My cock twitched at her persistence. It had obviously had enough teasing for one evening. Trying to clear my mind, I shook my head. "Yeah, well, my ride is coming in about two minutes, so I don't have time to fuck you."

Her fingers came to the zipper of my jeans. I shuddered as she took my erection in her hand. "I'd be happy just being able to say I sucked Jake Slater off."

"I really need to go," I argued feebly as she sank to her knees. When she took me deep inside her warm mouth, I groaned. There was no more arguing—I just gave in and got off in the dingy storeroom surrounded by extra napkins and ketchup packets.

Any pleasure I'd gotten out of the experience was fleeting in the moments after I came. I actually felt dirty and used for the first time in my entire life, and that was saying a lot. What the hell was I thinking? I wanted to get to know Abby not get blown by some random waitress in a storeroom. My head fell back against a box of salt, and I sighed with disgust.

When Billie Jean rose off the floor, I couldn't even look at her. "Thanks sugar," she said.

"Yeah, whatever," I mumbled as I headed for the door. I was zipping up my fly and adjusting my junk when I bumped into Abby in the hallway.

Warmth flooded her cheeks at my actions. "Oh hey, do you know where the bathrooms are?" she asked.

In that brief instant, she totally misread the situation. But when Billie Jean appeared behind me, Abby glanced between us, and then her eyes widened. It was like a light bulb had gone off in her brain, and she knew without a shadow of a doubt that the hard-on she'd caused earlier had just been taken care of by Billie Jean—the bitchy waitress who refused to speak to her.

Abby stared at me and gave a gentle shake of her head. "You wanted to get to know me, huh?"

"Abby, I'm—"

"Where's the ladies room?" she demanded of Billie Jean.

"Down the hall."

Averting her gaze to the floor, Abby mumbled, "Thank you."

Motherfuckingshit! I had so screwed up.

***

Chapter Five

Abby

When I shut myself into the grungy bathroom stall, I fought to keep my emotions in check. I felt like I was on a defective Merry-Go-Round. One minute Jake is showing interest in me and the next hooking up with some random waitress. What the hell was his deal? I guess the better question was what was *my* deal? Why in the world was I remotely interested in some asshole who would do that? I had to be delusional to think that someone like Jake Slater would actually be interested in me or be willing to give up his manwhore existence.

"I'm so stupid!" I exclaimed.

Once I finished in the bathroom, I drew in a deep breath before heading outside. I half expected Jake to be waiting on me to try and talk or explain himself, but once again, he disappointed me. Instead, he sat at the table with his chin propped up on one of his hands while the other guys talked and laughed.

As I eased down at the table, I didn't dare look over at him. It was too embarrassing. I tried occupying myself with my phone. But I felt his eyes burning into me. Then the heat from his body grew closer as he leaned over, causing me to hold my breath. "Angel, about what happened back there—"

He was interrupted by his phone ringing. One glance at the caller ID and he tumbled out of his chair.

"Dude, what's wrong?"

"It's Sally," Jake replied before he stalked out of the restaurant.

Even though I hated myself for it, I asked, "Who is Sally?"

"His aunt," AJ replied with a grimace. He then downed the last of his beer before adding, "I sure hope that means nothing is wrong with his mom."

I then followed the guys out of the restaurant. Frank hadn't arrived yet, so we stood under the awning waiting for him. Peering into the night, I caught sight of Jake's form. His phone was pressed tight to his ear while he was pacing around the parking lot. With his free hand, he gesticulated wildly. Whatever it was his aunt was saying was obviously very upsetting to him. Just as he finished the phone call, the familiar black SUV came screeching into the parking lot.

"Jake!" AJ called.

Without responding, he came stalking over to us. This time he didn't bother opening the door or helping me inside. Instead, he disappeared into the backseat without a word to anyone.

I hopped inside and then chewed on the inside of my cheek. Should I forget what an asshat he had been earlier and at least check on him? Although part of me wanted to tell him where to get off, I finally bit the bullet and turned back in my seat to look at him. His expression was dark as he stared ahead. "Everything okay?" I tentatively asked.

"Fine," he muttered.

Realizing he wasn't in the mood to talk, I eased around in my seat and looked out the windshield. While the guys were loud and boisterous on the way back, Jake didn't say a word. Once the SUV came to a stop in front of the bus, he hopped out and pounded up the front steps.

"What bug is up his ass, I wonder?" Rhys questioned before getting out.

The boys had all filed out of the SUV when Frank touched my shoulder. I turned back to him in surprise. "Abby, I know Jake, and from the way he was acting, I'm worried that something bad has happened with his family. He doesn't open up easily, but if you can, please try to find out what's going on with him."

"But you saw he wouldn't say two words to me earlier."

"I know. But please, keep trying."

"Fine, I'll try." I got out of the SUV and headed onto the bus. While the other guys were lounging around in the living area, Jake was noticeably absent. I craned my neck around to see if he had slipped into the bathroom.

"Where's Jake?" I asked as the bus driver started up the engine.

"He got his iPod and hit the bed."

A glance at the clock on the microwave showed it was only eight. I couldn't imagine a guy like Jake going to bed so early. I decided I better change the subject. "Speaking of, where will I be sleeping tonight?"

"It's my night for the bed, but I'll totally give it to you," Rhys offered.

"No, no, I don't want any special treatment. I'm serious about the bet and experiencing all aspects of life on the road. I've slept in a roost before, and I can do it again."

AJ grinned. "Let me guess though. You'd prefer a bottom bunk."

I nodded. "Yeah, I like to be close to the ground. A couple of years back I was on the top bunk when we got in a bad hail storm. The bus skidded on the slick roads, and I fell out."

"Then the first bottom bunk is yours, Abby," Brayden said with a smile.

"Thank you."

He motioned to the couch. "We were just about to watch a movie if you'd like to join us."

"Nothing NC-17 I hope?" I teased.

Brayden laughed. "No, maybe a little R-rated Will Ferrell comedy. Would that be okay?"

"If it's Ricky Bobby, you got a deal."

"Great minds think alike."

"Just let me get changed." As I walked back to the bedroom, I paused outside of Jake's roost. "Jake?" I tentatively asked. When he didn't respond, I kept on going. Even though I pushed my luggage and guitar case against the door, I tore off my dress at record speed. I then threw on my ratty Jacob's Ladder's t-shirt and my yoga pants from earlier. I slid my hair into a ponytail and then headed back out.

The opening of the movie was already playing when I eased down beside Brayden on the couch. Even though we'd probably all seen the movie a million times, we were laughing hysterically. I had to admit that it was fun hanging out with the guys sans Jake. His absence seemed to take the pressure off, and AJ and Rhys behaved like brothers, rather than potential lovers.

After they started *Step-Brothers*, the exhaustion of the day, coupled with the lull of the bus, caused me to get drowsy. My eyes grew heavier and heavier until I finally nodded off. When I woke up, the movie was ending, and my head was on Brayden's shoulder. I jerked away from him. "Oh, I'm so, so sorry!"

He smiled. "It's okay. You were tired." He glanced over at the other guys. "We should probably get our asses in bed. Tomorrow is another long day of traveling before the next show."

Once we all took turns using the bathroom, we settled into our roosts. I glanced down at my phone and fielded a few texts from the boys. Thankfully, my parents were at a conference with packed events, so the boys had yet to break the news to them until a few hours before about my mishap. Because it was so late, I didn't get a wrath-filled phone call like I normally would have.

Instead, it was a barrage of heated texts from my dad that if he hadn't been a minister would have equated to "What the hell do you think you're doing on a bus with a bunch of horny rockers?" My mom, who was always the peacemaker, was included in the messages and tried reasoning with my father, which was pretty hilarious considering they were in the same room.

Finally, I went for the jugular by telling him as a minister, he shouldn't be so judgmental. After a lengthy pause, he finally responded with *You're right, Abigail. We know you have a good head on your shoulders. Just make sure you let your conscience and your moral compass guide you.*

I fought the urge to roll my eyes at the epic guilt trip laid at my feet. Instead, I quickly typed back, *Of course I will. I'll see you guys in a week.*

My parents were flying in to see my first performance with the boys. I was supposed to have had this week as preparation, but now I would be heading right off the bus and to my first show. I gulped down the rising bile in my throat at the thought.

After telling them goodnight, I laid my phone down and settled in the cramped quarters. Just as I closed my eyes, a long groan came from close to my head. It took me about two seconds to decipher that I was way too close to Jake for comfort. Each and every time I started to doze off, Jake would make a noise, and I would be wide awake again.

I fluffed my pillow for what felt like the millionth time and tried ignoring the sounds coming from Jake's bunk. Heat flooded my face when the whimpers and groans escalated. *Jeez, it sounds like something off a porno!* With my brothers, I had a pretty good mind what he was doing, and it infuriated me, especially after what had happened earlier with Billie Jean.

They all swore to me they'd be perfect gentlemen if I stayed on the bus with them! I silently fumed. *What kind of sex-fiend maniac is Jake that he needs to do that again after just getting off at the diner? I don't care if he needs to relieve some stress after the phone call earlier. This is bullshit!*

Flopping back down on the mattress, I crossed my arms over my chest before a frustrated grunt escaped my lips.

"¿No puedes dormir, Angel?" AJ's deep voice questioned from behind my curtain.

I flipped back the heavy fabric. He reclined on his bunk, flipping through a sports magazine. "No, I can't sleep with all the racket going on next to me."

He met my gaze and grinned. "Don't get the sexy, lacy panties I dream about you wearing in a twist. He isn't jerking off."

"That's not what I was thinking."

"Yeah right," he snorted with a wink.

As if on cue, Jake let out a long moan. I shook my head. "Um well, if he's not doing *that*, then is he okay?"

"He's been having a lot of nightmares lately. I try to ignore it—let him save face and not look like a pussy."

I rolled my eyes. "Did you ever stop to think maybe you should ask him if something is going on with him?"

AJ quirked his brows at me. "If I started getting sappy and shit like that, Jake would ask me when I grew a vagina."

"Well, I think someone should check on him. I mean, he sounds like he's in both physical and emotional pain."

When AJ didn't move, I heaved an exasperated sigh before hopping out of my bunk. I could not believe after everything I had been through with Jake so far in the last twelve hours that I even had one shred of care left for him. But I had seen something within him— some flicker of decency—that made me worry and care about him, even when I shouldn't.

I shot AJ a murderous look to which he held up his hands. "Look, mi amor, guys just don't do the touchy-feely shit, okay? If I woke up Jake right now to cuddle him, he would get super pissed."

I ignored him and tip-toed over to Jake. With trembling fingers, I opened the heavy curtain to his roost. Jake had the sheet twisted around his waist. A coat of sweat covered his heavily tattooed chest. His brow creased, and his mouth curved up in a grimace. My hand hesitated above his shoulder. Finally, I shook him gently. "Jake, wake up," I urged softly.

His body jerked before his wild eyes popped open and swept across the top of the bunk.

"Shh, it's okay," I murmured.

Jake's frantic gaze swept over to mine while he opened his mouth and gasped for breath.

I gave him a reassuring smile while rubbing his shoulder. "You were having a nightmare."

Jake continued wheezing in air. I eased back as he swung his legs out of the bunk and onto the carpet. Sitting on the edge of the bed, he leaned forward and put his head in his hands. "I'm sorry I woke you," he replied.

With my protective side shooting into overdrive, I scooted closer to him, bringing my hand to his hair. Gently, I ran my fingers through the dark, sweat-stained strands, pushing them out of his eyes. "You didn't wake me. I was worried about you."

His head jerked up as surprise flooded his face. "You were?"

I nodded. "You seemed a little down after your phone call with your aunt. Then with the nightmare." I glanced up at AJ who was curiously watching us. "I know most of the guys aren't men enough to handle emotions and issues—"

AJ snorted. "Those are your words, not mine."

"Anyway, I just wanted you to know that I'm here for you. If you need to talk about something or if you just need someone to sit with you until you can go back to sleep, then I'm here."

With wide eyes and his mouth gaping open, Jake stared at me for a moment like I had grown horns. Realizing I wasn't getting anywhere with him, I held up my hands. "Or I can just leave you alone and go back to sleep. Either is fine."

When I turned to leave, Jake grabbed my hand. "Wait," he instructed in a hoarse voice.

"Okay."

"That's a really sweet offer, Angel. It makes me feel like a real ass. I need to tell you how sorry I am about earlier. That was a real douche move. Not that it matters, but she came on to me. But I should have told her no and meant what I told you."

I was *so* not expecting an apology from him, so it took me a minute before I could even process thoughts, least of all acknowledge what he had said. "Thank you." When he gave me an embarrassed smile, I sighed. "As much as I appreciate hearing that, it's not what's really bothering you, is it?"

He shook his head. "It's just..." He cleared his throat. "My Aunt Sally was calling for my mother. She said Mama didn't want to worry me in the middle of the tour and refused to tell me the truth of what was going on..."

"What's wrong?" I urged.

His chest rose and fell in harsh breaths. "After being in remission for three years, my mom's cancer has come back. Aunt Sally says…" His face contorted in agony. "She says there's nothing they can do this time—no more treatments. She's being given medicine to make her comfortable for her last…few months."

I gasped. "Oh Jake, I'm so, so sorry." I took his hands in mine and squeezed. The expression on his face was one of pure anguish and devastation, and my chest constricted for the pain I could feel radiating off of him.

Tears welled in his tormented blue eyes. "It's just…" He motioned towards the bunks. "You can ask the other guys about what an absolute Mama's Boy I am. After my dad ran off with his secretary and got remarried, I was her world. She's *everything* to me. I can't even think about…" His words choked off with emotion, and then he started crying. Well, it was more harsh, body shuddering sobs. I wrapped my arms around his neck, pulling him to me. He buried his face in my stomach, his body heaving and shaking from his cries.

His wailing brought Brayden from his roost while Rhys staggered out of the bedroom. Both of them stared at Jake in disbelief like he was some alien life form. I don't know if it was the crying or the fact he was wrapped in my arms. When I glanced up at AJ, his expression was shell-shocked, but there was also pain in his eyes. After all, he'd grown up with Jake and knew his mom very well.

I gave AJ an empathetic look. "Not Susan," he said softly. He pinched his eyes shut, and I knew he was fighting not to start crying himself. "Motherfucker," he muttered under his breath.

The next thing I knew I tumbled backward when Jake sank onto his knees on the floor of the bus. Pulling on my hips, he jerked me down beside him, wrapping me in a bear hug. "Shh, it's going to be okay," I crooned into his ear.

He shook his head wildly back and forth. "No, it's not. If it hadn't been as bad as it was, Aunt Sally would never have called." My body shook so hard with his sobs that my teeth clattered together. "Oh God, I can't bear this, Angel. I'll die without her."

Although I'd grown up watching my parents handle emotional parishioners on a daily basis, I felt completely and totally helpless when it came to comforting Jake. I tried to draw on the right words to say to comfort him as I rubbed wide circles across his back.

"Listen, I'll call my parents and tell them to put her on their prayer list. I mean, they don't call my dad's church the God-dome for nothing! And maybe there's another doctor she can see. You know, get a second opinion or something." My mind spun with thoughts as I tried to think of something to do or say to comfort Jake since he continued to sob uncontrollably. As soon as I thought of another one, I blurted, "Hey, one of our church's deacons is on the board of a cancer treatment center. We can get your mom an appointment there."

Jake's sobs started to wane, but he kept his arms firmly around me. His voice, hoarse from his crying, came muffled against my chest. "I appreciate it, Angel. But Aunt Sally made it abundantly clear. The cancer's been back, and there's not a fucking thing I can do but watch her die."

Running my fingers through his hair, I leaned over to whisper in his ear. "I'm so, so sorry. I'd give anything if I could take away your pain."

"Thank you," he murmured. He pulled back to stare up at me. Tears glistened in his blue eyes while his expression still contorted in misery. "You really mean all that, don't you?" When I creased my brows in confusion, he replied, "The wanting to take my pain away and what you would do for my mom."

"Of course I do."

He continued to stare at me with an incredulous look as if he thought at any moment I might disappear—like I was just some illusion. His trembling hand came to rest against my cheek. "You really are an angel, aren't you?"

I smiled. "No, I'm just someone who cares about you and your mom."

"But don't you see. I've never met a girl who really cared about me and not because I'm Jake Slater from Runaway Train."

"Then that's sad because in spite of some of your faults, you really are worth knowing and caring about."

Jake blinked a few times at my words as he ran his thumb across my cheek bone. He leaned up, and just when I sucked in a breath because I thought he was going to kiss me, he planted a tender kiss on my cheek. "Thank you, Abby. Maybe my mom was right when she claimed fate brought us together."

My eyes widened at his statement. "Maybe so," I murmured.

After standing there staring at each other for a few moments, I patted Jake's shoulder. "Are you feeling better now?"

He shrugged. "As good as I can be, I guess."

"Need some water or milk before you go back to sleep?"

The corners of his lips tugged up. "Are you going to offer to read me a bedtime story next?"

I laughed. "No, I was just trying to take care of you."

"You were mothering me," he murmured as sadness washed over his face.

"Well, if you don't need anything else, I guess I'll go back to bed." When I started to my roost, Jake grabbed my arm, pulling me against him. "Sleep with me," he whispered in my ear.

I jerked away, ready to launch into a tirade for him playing on my emotions to put the moves on me when the tormented expression on his face stopped me cold.

He stared pleadingly into my eyes. "I'm still so fucking scared, Angel. I need someone just to hold tonight so I won't be alone."

I had to fight to catch my breath. How was it possible that the broken, vulnerable guy in front of me and the cocky, self-absorbed Jake who infuriated me were one in the same?

"No funny business?"

He shook his head. "I swear."

I drew my bottom lip between my teeth as I weighed my options. After his emotional breakdown, I couldn't imagine being cruel by leaving him all alone. I tried to think about how I would feel if it were my mom. "Okay, I will. If it'll make you feel better."

Leaning forward, he gave my cheek a tender kiss. "Thank you,

Angel."

My heartbeat accelerated so fast that I swept my hand over my shirt to make sure it wasn't going to explode right out of my chest. What was happening to me? One minute I was comforting Jake and then next I was having all these inappropriate feelings about him running through me. Finally, I said, "You're welcome."

Rhys stepped forward. "Take the bed tonight, man."

"No, it's your night."

With a shrug, Rhys replied, "Least I can do and all." His gaze flickered over to mine. "Besides, it'll be more comfortable for Abby."

"I appreciate it, but I don't want pity. Okay?" Jake replied.

Although it was kindness, not pity, that Rhys was offering, he bobbed his head. "Whatever. It's yours if you want it. Just remember that."

"Thanks, man."

Rocking back and forth on his feet, Rhys finally stepped forward. He tentatively put an arm around Jake. "I'm sorry, man. I really am."

Jake patted Rhys's back. "Thanks. I appreciate it."

When Rhys pulled away, Brayden took his place. Jake clung to him, and I could tell he was fighting not to lose his emotions again. "We're here for you, brother. We'll see you through this to the end—to hell and back. Got it?" Brayden said.

"Yeah, I know."

Taking Jake by the shoulders, Brayden looked at Jake almost like a father would a son. "Anything you need, you got it. Tour cancelations or pushing back the album, it's done, okay? No questions asked and no shit taken from the label."

"I can't let you guys down," Jake protested.

"There are other things in the world besides records and concert tickets. Whatever time you need to be with your mom, you have my blessing." He gazed around Rhys and AJ before adding, "And if either one of these fuckers has one thing to say about it, I'll knock his block off."

Rhys held up his hand. "Hey, you guys are my brothers. We're the four musketeers—'All for one and one for all bullshit'. I'm unified in whatever decisions the brotherhood makes, and I'll go toe to toe with the suits if they wanna give us grief. I mean, I did drop out of law school, remember? I can find a loophole in the contract like that." He snapped his fingers for effect.

Tears sparkled in Jake's eyes. "Thanks guys."

I noticed that AJ had been conspicuously quiet. Finally, he hopped down from his roost. He and Jake stood staring at each other for a few seconds before they fell into each other's arms. "Dude, I don't know what the fuck to say. My heart is shattered—for Susan and for you," AJ lamented, his voice muffled against Jake's chest.

"It's okay, man. You don't have to say anything," Jake replied.

"But I want to. I want to say and do all the right things because you've been my best fucking friend since we were eleven years old."

Tears flowed freely down my cheeks at the sight of all the love between the guys. I swept them away with the back of my hands. Jake finally pulled away from AJ and gave a rueful smile. "Okay, enough with the crying—we're acting like a bunch of pussies. I don't know who took our balls, but enough with the bullshit emotions."

At my sharp intake of breath and what I guess was my horrified expression, Jake started laughing. It wasn't long before all the guys joined in with him. Crossing my arms over my chest, I huffed, "Well, I'm so glad I could amuse you guys!"

AJ winked at me. "We needed that, Angel."

"Whatever," I replied.

"Okay, shows over. Go back to bed guys," Brayden instructed.

Rhys yawned and bobbed his head. "Night, guys. Night, Abby," he said before turning back to the bedroom.

"Night," I called after him.

Brayden and AJ made their goodnights and then went back to their bunks, leaving me and Jake completely alone.

As I eyed the crumpled sheets of his roost, I asked, "So how do you want to do this?"

"Can I spoon you?"

My eyebrows shot up. "Can you what?"

The shadow of a smile fluttered on Jake's lips. "You really don't know what that is, do you?"

An embarrassed flush filled my cheeks as I ducked my head. "No," I murmured.

Jake's finger came under my chin and tipped my head up to look at him. "It's okay. I'll show you." On his knees, he edged across the bunk to where he was pressed up against the wall. Then he turned on his side to where he was facing me. He then motioned me with his hand. I sighed. It was now or never time. I eased down beside him.

"Now lie on your side," he instructed.

I quickly flipped over to where I wasn't facing him. My breath hitched when I felt him snuggle up behind me. His arm snaked around my waist to drape across my hip. He then nestled his chin into my neck. His breath was warm against my skin as he asked, "Is this okay?"

I tried to still my rapid breathing. The truth was it felt so good being this close to him. Although it was just to comfort him, it felt dangerous and illicit sharing a bed with Jake.

"Abby, is this okay?"

Jake rarely used my real name, so I knew he was really worried. I reached down to grab his hand in mine. I squeezed it tight before I glanced back at him over my shoulder. "It's fine."

The genuine smile he gave me caused my heart to flutter. "Thank you. I'll never forget this." In a lower voice, he murmured, "I'll never forget you."

I closed my eyes and willed myself to go to sleep. With the heat of Jake's body against mine and the rhythmic rise and fall of his chest against my back, it wasn't long before I was lulled into a deep, contented sleep.

***

Chapter Six

JAKE

Delicious warmth wriggled against me and cut through the levels of my subconscious. I didn't try to fight waking up from this exquisite dream. After all, I'd gone to bed alone, hadn't I? But when my hips automatically bucked my morning wood into the curvy backside pressed up against me, it felt so very real. Without opening my eyes, my hand slid up the dream girl's ribcage to cup her breast. The tiny whimper that escaped her might as well have been a bloodcurdling scream because that's when I realized the girl was *so* not part of my dream, but worst of all, I was molesting Abby.

I jerked my hand away like I had been scalded. Thankfully, she slept like the dead, and my horndog assault hadn't woken her up. Gently, I climbed over her body and escaped the roost. Glancing back, I gazed down at her sleeping form. A tug pulled at my heart. I'd never had a girl comfort me before—well, at least not since I'd hit it big. Girls just wanted a piece of the fame or to be able to say they'd screwed me. With our crazy schedule, it was too much of a hassle to have a girlfriend. At least that's what I told myself.

Pushing the long strands of blonde hair out of her face, I rubbed Abby's cheek tenderly, but she still didn't stir. Instead, she made those cute little snores that would have mortified her if she had been awake.

She truly was an angel right out of Heaven to care enough to dry my tears and comfort me, not to mention sleeping with me when she knew she shouldn't.

Fuck. Why did she have to be so beautiful? It would be so much easier if she was some average or even butt-ugly girl. No, my savior—my angel—had to be any man's fantasy. With a frustrated grunt, I escaped into the bathroom. Even though I was tempted, I would not stoop to jerking off this morning. It wasn't entirely that I had all this integrity—hell, I'd let a waitress blow me the night before in a diner storeroom. It was more about the fact that I knew to get off I'd have to fantasize about Abby.

So instead, I took a cold shower and watched my wood shrivel under the stream. Just as I was about to turn the water off, a riff hit me like a train barreling through my mind. It took me so off guard that I had to lean against the stall for support. Pinching my eyes shut, I hummed aloud what was filling my mind.

Hustling out of the shower, I wrapped a towel around my waist before leaving the bathroom. Normally, I would have gone stark naked to the bedroom for my clothes, but I didn't dare want to run into Abby like that. Once I was dressed, I grabbed my guitar, a notepad, some sheet music, and a pencil and headed to the kitchen. After flipping on the coffee maker, I flopped down at the table.

After scribbling down the riff I'd heard, I worked on the melody. Once it was done, I started hammering out lyrics to go along with it. All of the emotions I'd been experiencing converged on this moment. I only paused in my furious scribbling when my hand cramped from the excessive writing.

I eased my guitar onto my lap and started playing the music I'd written. I erased and changed a few chords before beginning again. Closing my eyes, I focused on the lyrics in my mind as I played.

At the sound of someone behind me, my eyelids popped open.

"Morning," Abby murmured softly.

I glanced back at her and smiled. "Morning. Did I wake you?"

"Yeah, but it's fine."

"Sorry. The muse decided I didn't need any more sleep," I lied. I knew I would freak her out if I told her the truth. Jerking my head over my shoulder, I replied, "There's some coffee if you want some. Of course, you probably need OJ instead." I winked at her. "Don't want you passing out on me again."

Pink tinged her cheeks at my attentiveness. "Thanks. But I'm good for now."

I nodded. "We'll probably stop for some breakfast in an hour or so."

"Okay." She motioned towards the notepad with scribbled lyrics and chords. "How's it coming?"

I grimaced. "Good, but it's never going to work."

"Why not?" she asked as she eased into the bench seat across from me.

"The label wants very specific stuff from us, and this," I waved the notepad at her, "isn't it."

Drawing her knees up to her chest, she rested her chin on the tops of her legs. "You won't know until you approach them."

"Trust me, it's not happening."

She cocked her brows at me "Oh, come on Mr. Glass Half Empty. What's it about?"

With hesitating, I replied, "My mother dying."

Her face fell. "Oh Jake, I'm so sorry," she whispered.

"I know. And thanks." When I started to rip out the lyrics from the pad, she reached over and grabbed my hand.

"No, don't."

I clenched my jaw with determination. "It won't work, Angel. I have to sing about love, relationships, and sex. You know, bullshit like that. A song about my fucking heart being ripped to shreds because my mother is dying isn't going to make an album, least of all a single."

"What about Eric Clapton's *Tears in Heaven*."

I gave her a withering look. "That's Clapton. He could tell any label to screw themselves if they didn't like his songs."

"Fine. Give me a minute here." She drummed her fingers on the table for a few seconds. "Okay what about Alter Bridge's *In Loving Memory*?"

My brows rose in surprise. "You actually listen to Alter Bridge?"

She rolled her eyes. "Contrary to what you think I haven't been in a hole my entire life or jamming to the Jonas Brothers."

I couldn't fight my lips from momentarily turning upwards. "Yeah, well, Alter Bridge's management isn't necessarily marketing them the same way ours is."

"You're honestly going to sit there and give up so easily on something you obviously feel very passionately about?" She shifted her legs to where her elbows leaned forward on the table. "That doesn't sound like the kick-ass and take-names Jake Slater I know."

I scowled at her for a minute before blowing out a frustrated breath. "Okay Miss Fix-It, how do I make it work?"

Tilting her head, she chewed on her bottom lip, lost in thought. "What if you were to choose something symbolic to represent your mother's…" I knew she couldn't bring herself to vocalize the words.

"You can be a big girl and say it. Her *death*." Abby started to open her mouth, but I silenced her with my hand. "Yeah, you're sorry. I know. Now continue on about the symbol shit."

"Like back in the day during the 60's, people sang songs with symbols in them because of the FCC codes. You know, like the Byrd's *Mr. Tambourine Man* was talking about a drug dealer, and I'm sure you know about *Puff the Magic Dragon*."

I shot her an exasperated look. "And you just naturally expect me to know about the songs with the drug references?"

She grinned. "I didn't mean any offense."

I laughed. "I'll have you know that I haven't done drugs since high school, Angel."

"That's good to know."

I made a circular motion beside my temple. "It messes with my creative side, so I like to just say no."

"Hmm, what about the alcohol?" she challenged.

Damn, she had me there. I couldn't help the sheepish expression from filling my face. "Yeah, well, we all have our vices I guess." I then motioned to the notepad. "Okay, you think I should write about

102

my mom's death with symbols—make the emotions sound like something besides death."

"Right."

We sat in silence for a few seconds. When I snapped my fingers, Abby jumped. "What if I made death a person—like a dude I was fighting with for my mom?"

"But make her a girl—the only woman in the world you've ever loved."

"Exactly."

She bobbed her head enthusiastically. "You will totally make the audience believe that. Look at *I Will Always Love You* for example."

My brow creased in confusion. "Whitney Houston?"

"No, Dolly Parton wrote it, but Whitney made it huge."

I grinned. "Angel, you seem to have a bit of a Dolly Parton fetish that's quite disturbing."

Abby laughed. "Actually, it's my mom with the Dolly fetish. She's originally from Sevierville, Tennessee, where Dolly's from. So I grew up with all her albums, and my mom read her book back in the day. In it, Dolly explains that while the song sounds like letting go of a love relationship, it's actually about her severing ties with her business and singing partner, Porter Wagoner."

"What a little fount of knowledge you are," I teased.

"Trust me, when you grow up in places with sporadic electricity or none at all, you learn to amuse yourself. For my brothers and me, it was learning to play instruments and song writing. For my mom, it was books."

Sweeping the pencil from behind my ear, I momentarily nibbled on the eraser. "Hmm, so even if death is the fucker stealing my girl, I still think most of the lyrics I've got will work. They just need some tweaking. And I definitely think the melody will work." I adjusted the guitar on my lap. "What do you think of this?" I asked before strumming a few chords.

Closing her eyes, Abby let the music wash over her. "Wow, that's good. It has a real haunting quality to it."

"You think?"

When she opened her eyes, I peered intently at her. Normally, I didn't want or need any convincing about my creations except from the suits at the label. But this time, I desperately wanted reassurance from Abby. "Yes, I do. Even setting aside what I know about the song's meaning, I want to cry just hearing the music, and you haven't even added the lyrics yet."

"Thank you. Give me a few minutes, okay?"

"Sure." While she went to pour the glass of orange juice I had suggested, I reworked the lyrics. When I was satisfied I had the emotions right where I wanted them, I put my pencil down. I don't know how long I had been focusing on the song. It must have been a while because Abby's glass of juice was empty. She sat patiently in front of me.

"Ready?"

She nodded.

Focusing on Abby, I sang the lyrics with everything I had in me. Tears sparkled in her blue eyes before running down her cheeks. "Oh

Jake," she murmured.

"You think that's it?"

Her hand clutched the place above her heart. "It's breathtaking." We sat there staring at each other for a minute before Abby finally wiped her moist eyes. Then a tiny shudder went through her, and she gasped.

"Are you okay?"

Without answering me, Abby rose out of her chair. "Where are you going?" I asked.

"To get my guitar. It's probably nothing, but I just had an idea."

I grabbed her arm. "No, no, I'll get it."

"But—"

I held up my hand to silence her. "Angel, Rhys is notorious for sleeping in the buff, and I don't think your virgin eyes are quite ready for that."

Crimson splotches dotted her cheeks, and she didn't argue with me. I then hurried down the bus aisle. On his stomach, Rhys snored like a bear while his bare ass stuck out from the covers. Just as I suspected, he would have given her quite an eye-full.

Before Abby got out her guitar, she tore a sheet of paper from my notepad. I couldn't help asking, "Are you thinking you can do it better?"

She shook her head furiously. "No, no, I was thinking of a way to enhance it." At what I could only imagine was my intensely skeptical expression, she added, "It needs both sides of the story—his and hers."

"A duet?"

"Yes. Now be quiet for a minute."

I chuckled as Abby began scribbling down words. "Angel, have you ever even written a song before?"

"Nuh-uh," she muttered lost in concentration. After a few minutes, she finally glanced up at me and gave a sheepish grin. "I've watched the boys do it forever, but I never tried. But for some reason, today it's like… it's just coming to me."

"Like you couldn't stop it if you tried?"

Her eyes widened. "Yes, just like that."

I smiled. "I think the muse has found its way to you."

"Hmm, I dunno," she murmured.

Motioning towards the paper, I urged, "Come on, let's hear it."

Her brow creased as she nibbled her lip. "You won't laugh, right?"

"Of course not."

"Promise."

I crossed my finger over my chest. "Scout's Honor."

"Okay." Bending over, she took her guitar out of the case and adjusted it on her lap. She then mirrored the melody I had written earlier with almost absolute perfection.

Baby, it breaks my heart to have to leave you here—shattered and alone.

With no one to pick up the pieces or ease the ache that you own.

There isn't anything I wouldn't do for you or for your love

Each and every moment I had with you was an amazing gift from above.

I'll wrap the memories around me like a blanket as this winter crushes my soul.

And although I can't stay, I'll keep you with me each and every day.

When she finished singing, she kept strumming the melody. I could tell she was having a hard time making herself look at me. Finally, she dared a little peek.

"That is fucking amazing!"

"Seriously?"

"Hell yeah. We have to record this together."

Her fingers slipped on the chords, making a screeching noise on the guitar. "You're joking, right?"

"No, I'm completely and totally serious. This has chart topper written all over it."

With her blue eyes widening in fear, Abby shook her head furiously back and forth. "But I've never been in a recording booth. This is an important song, so you need someone with more experience who can do it justice."

I leaned forward to take her hand in mine. "I wouldn't have even written the damn thing if it hadn't been for you. As for a better singer, I can't imagine finding one." Giving her a reassuring smile, I added, "Besides, I don't want to do the song unless I can do it with you."

"Really?"

"Yeah, so quit arguing with me about it."

She grinned. "Okay, but only if you insist."

"Why don't we try meshing both parts together now?"

"That sounds good."

As Abby and I ran through the song a few times, the other guys started coming to life. Brayden waved at us before hopping in the shower while Rhys appeared clothed and with his blonde hair perfectly styled.

Without a word to us, he eased down at the table and listened intently. Closing his eyes a few times, I could tell he was imagining how to play his part. "That's kickass, bro," he said when we finished.

I glanced up from my guitar to wink at Abby. She rewarded me with a beaming smile that caused the cutest dimple in her cheek to appear. "You think so?" I asked.

"Oh yeah. Chicks are going to cream the hell out of themselves at the whole angsty thing you got going on about fighting for the woman you love."

"I thought so too. Think the other guys will dig it?"

Rhys bobbed his head. "Bray's gonna want it as acoustic as possible to bring out all the emotions. You know what a sap he is."

I laughed. "I agree—about both the acoustic and Brayden being a pussy."

Before Abby could give me shit about the word she hated most, AJ staggered out of his roost and down the aisle towards us. "What are you douchebags doing up so early?" he asked. His hand, like on autopilot, went to his crotch to do an obligatory ball scratch and then his eyes widened when he realized Abby was at the table too. "My bad," he muttered under his breath.

Although she ducked her head, I caught the grin that fluttered on her lips at AJ's actions.

"It's almost nine. We're stopping for breakfast in a few minutes," I replied.

AJ groaned and rubbed his face. "Nine? Jesus, it might as well be the asscrack of dawn."

Abby laughed. "Let me guess. Not a morning person?"

"Hell no." His gaze then fell on the notepad and our guitars. "Whoa, hold the phone. Don't tell me you guys were songwriting?"

"Yeah, we just wrote a duet. Isn't that amazing?" Abby gushed.

AJ's dark brows shot into his hairline before his eyes locked on mine. Even though I felt like an absolute pussy, I squirmed under the intensity of his stare. Mainly because I knew my secret was about to be out of the bag, and it was going to change things even more with Abby.

With a smirk, AJ crossed his arms over his broad chest. "Oh yeah, it's more than just amazing. It's fucking incredible considering this dude never, *ever* lets anyone in on his writing sessions. I mean, even he and Bray don't collaborate together—each of them just writes his own part and then they merge it together."

Abby stared at me in utter disbelief. "But I...I didn't know. You should've told me you wanted privacy or that—"

"No, it's fine," I muttered, glancing out the picture window as we pulled off the interstate.

"You say that now, but just wait until Bray hears about this," AJ said. He thumped me on the back. "Of course, I can't say I blame you. Who wouldn't want to make music with Angel?"

AJ's words had the same effect as pulling a dark, heavy cloak across my raw and open emotions. Whatever openness and honesty Abby had coaxed out of me automatically shut down. My mother's advice echoed in my ear about giving Abby a chance and how fate could've brought us together. Her words coupled with what had happened last night and this morning made my throat close up, and I fought to breathe. Without another word, I whirled out of my seat and stomped down the aisle to the bedroom. I flung open the door to find Brayden getting dressed. "Where's the fire, man?" he asked.

"Nowhere. We just need to hurry the fuck up and eat so we can get back on the road."

Bray gave me a funny look before leaving me in the bedroom. Once I slid on my jeans and threw on a clean shirt, I didn't go back out into the living room until I was sure we were about to be parked.

When the bus finally shuddered to a stop, I couldn't get off of it fast enough. I didn't say anything to Abby or the guys. I couldn't take being with Abby one more minute. Her very presence had sent tiny fissures through my carefully constructed wall of emotions. She was getting to me too fast and too soon. No woman but my mother had ever seen through to the real me, and I wasn't about to let Abby in.

So I hauled ass down the bus steps and started powerwalking across the parking lot.

"Jake?" Brayden called.

"He must have to piss or something," Rhys replied.

Ignoring them, I threw open the diner door and craned my neck for the bathroom. Once inside, I splashed water on my face and tried to get my bearings. An image flashed before my eyes—one that had an almost identical purity as Abby's. Her name was Stephanie, and she had been my first and only love. I'd been eighteen when I first met her—she apprenticed under my mother at the dance studio. We dated for two years before I made the decision to drop out of college and go on the road with the guys. When I couldn't give her the commitment she needed, she didn't just break up with me—she tore my heart to shreds.

Of course, the songs I wrote from that hellish experience propelled Runaway Train to stardom. I hadn't opened myself up to another girl since then, and I sure as hell couldn't now with everything in my world spinning out of control. I couldn't let the feelings I was experiencing for Abby take hold.

After collecting myself as best I could, I left the bathroom and headed for the breakfast buffet. Filling my plate to the brim, I then turned and went in search of somewhere to sit. At the sight of Abby seated with the other guys, I quickly side-stepped their table to plop down with Frank and some of the roadies. Out of the corner of my eye, I saw Abby's quizzical expression turn almost wounded.

Her reaction caused me to spear my French toast with a little more determination than I should have. Yeah, I was a bastard for ignoring her after everything we had been through the night before and this morning. But I couldn't keep opening up to her and feeling what I did. It had fucking train wreck written all over it.

"You okay today?" Frank asked.

"Fine," I muttered through my bacon.

"Jake…"

"I don't want to talk about it, okay?"

"Okay, son." After taking a thoughtful sip of his coffee, he drew in a ragged breath. "Just so you know, your mom called me this morning."

I choked on my orange juice. After succumbing to a coughing fit, I questioned, "She did?"

Frank nodded. "She knows that Sally called you, and she wanted me to make sure I kept an eye out for you. She's afraid you'll be…destructive."

The agonizing thought of my mom dying once again sliced through to my soul, and I fought to breathe. Nausea crashed over me, and I feared I was about to heave up my breakfast. I knew I had to talk to her again. So I tumbled out of my chair and sprinted out of the diner. When she answered the phone, I demanded, "Why?"

Mama sighed. "I thought it was for the best."

"You thought not telling your only child that you're dying is for the best? Do you know how sick and warped that is?"

"I didn't want to upset you with just a few weeks left on your tour."

A frustrated growl came from low in my throat. "For once, would you stop putting me and everyone else first? This is the time to be fucking selfish. I mean, you're…" Closing my eyes, I still couldn't bring myself to say the words again.

"Honey, there will be plenty of time for us to say our goodbyes when you get off the road."

"Fuck that. I'm coming home now."

"No, Jacob, you're not."

"Look, the guys are all in agreement. Hell, Rhys is even ready to use what little law school he had to go toe to toe with the execs if they give us any shit about it."

"I'm still your mother, and I say no."

A tormented sob choked off in my throat. I gripped the phone tight against my ear as I tried to hold my emotions and sanity in check. "But we don't have that much time left together. How can you be so fucking cruel and deny me one moment with you?"

"Jacob, your language is absolutely atrocious!" she chided.

"Stop it! I don't wanna hear about the wrong I'm doing, okay?"

"Look, these are hard times on everyone, sweetheart. There are a lot of people who work for you and they depend on you and so do their families." When I started to protest, she sighed. "I'm a mess right now, honey—both emotionally and physically. I don't want you seeing me like this. Before I knew for sure if it was terminal, I started treatment again just in case. It's wrecked me. So give me a few weeks, okay?" At her sniffling, I broke down myself. "Sweetheart, I want more than anything to have a month or two just to be your mother and take care of you before you have to take care of me."

Tears streamed down my cheeks when I thought about everything she was going through just to have time to be a mom to me. "Why do you have to be like this?"

She chuckled. "Jacob, it's that stubbornness that we both share, remember?"

"I love you…God, do I love you," I blubbered.

"I know, baby. As high as the sky, remember?"

I was crying so hard I couldn't respond. Even though she couldn't see me, I bobbed my head in acknowledgement of the phrase she had taught me as a child.

You know how much I love you, Jacob?

As high as the sky, Mama!

That's right, sweet boy.

"Jacob," my mother began in the soft, soothing voice she'd used since I was a child. "I know it's hard, but try to put all this behind you. Focus on your music. Find escape in it, and for the next three weeks, give your audiences the best shows you possibly can. And each night you do, rest assured that you're making me proud for your strength and courage."

With the backs of my hands, I tried wiping off the tear-stained, snot-filled mess my face had become. "Okay, I'll try."

"That's my boy. I'll call you each and every day."

"You better."

"I will. I love you, honey."

"I love you too."

And with that she was gone. Doubling over, I rested my palms on my knees. My body heaved and shook as I tried to get myself together.

"Jake?"

Pinching my eyes shut, I willed her to go away. I couldn't deal with her period, especially not like this. "Not now," I muttered.

She snaked her arms around my waist. "Baby, what's wrong?" Bree crooned into my ear.

"Shit that you wouldn't possibly understand. Besides, I just told you I don't wanna fucking talk about it, okay?"

Slinking around me, Bree tucked her finger under my chin and forced me to look at her. "Oh Jake, you look like hell."

"Thanks," I grunted.

"I'm sorry I couldn't make it yesterday. Trust me, if you're going to get like this when I go away, I'll just quit my job," she teased.

"You barely work as it is. It's a wonder you don't get fired as much as you call in."

She laughed. "That's the perk of working for your granddaddy's towing service. It's hard to fire family."

"Whatever."

"Besides, he likes being able to tell everyone that I'm cutting off work to go hang-out with Jake Slater of Runaway Train."

I fought the urge to say that her grandfather was pretty sketchy to enjoy the fact she was a glorified groupie, joining up with me at different tour stops.

Bree's tongue flicked across my earlobe, causing me to shiver. "I could work on you full-time. Cause trust me baby, it's a buzzkill having a real job that keeps me away from you and that fantastic cock of yours," she drawled. The lust in her voice caused my traitorous dick to twitch.

"Is that right?"

"Mmm, hmm." A cat-like smile curved on her lips. "You miss me?"

The truth was I hadn't. Sure, I missed the sex, but there would

115

never, ever be anything stronger between me and Bree. But I desperately needed an emotional escape right now, and the only thing I could think of was screwing my problems out of my mind. "Yeah, I did."

"Hmm, wanna show me how much when we get back on the bus?"

"Yeah, but first I need to get fucked up."

She chuckled. "It's barely ten o'clock, Jake."

"I don't give a shit. Go tell your dad I want his flask—the one with the good stuff in it."

"Okaaay, if you say so." She ran her hands up my chest. "Just don't get too wasted where you can't make me scream at least three times."

I forced a smile to my lips. "Now why would I want to do that?"

***

Chapter Seven

Abby

I could only push around the food on my plate after Jake refused to sit at my table. I tried reasoning that it wasn't really a slight against me. Maybe he needed some space after AJ's dig about our writing session or maybe he wanted time with the roadies and crew. He'd obviously already opened up to me far more than with anyone else, so I guess he needed time to process it all. I had to remember that I would be a total bitch if I laid too much fault with him considering he was going through hell right now with his mother's illness.

We'd barely known each other twenty-four hours, so he didn't owe me anything. But deep down, his behavior pierced through my heart to sting my soul. If I allowed myself, I could really feel something for him—something more than sympathy or compassion. I could even maybe grow to…like him.

When I saw Jake fly out of his chair and storm out of the diner, it took everything within me not to go after him. Instead, I tried focusing on Brayden's stories about his children or how Rhys's parents had almost disowned him after he gave up his Ivy-League background to pursue life with the band. AJ remained conspicuously silent, and from time to time, I would cut my eyes to catch him staring at me.

As we started back to the bus, he grabbed my arm. When I turned back, his expression was pained. "You're starting to like Jake, aren't you?"

"No! Why would you ask such a thing?"

The corners of his lips quirked up in a sly grin. "Call it my Latin intuition."

"Wait, I thought it was supposed to be Irish institution."

"Are you saying we Mexicans can't have it too?"

A relieved giggle escaped my lips. "Yeah, I guess you can."

AJ laughed. "Whatever it is, I meant what I said." When I started to protest, he held up his hand. "You know, it's crazy, but after I met you, I thought I might try to be a one- woman-man for a while. See if your angelic nature couldn't tame me." He winked to which I rolled my eyes but laughed in spite of myself. "But after last night and this morning, I realized there isn't any point." As the wind whipped the long strands of my hair into my face, AJ reached over and pushed it away. "I could go all medieval and fight for you, but there's no point. You and Jake seem to have this magnetic pull."

Before I could stop myself, I gave a mirthless laugh. "Yeah, well, I call bullshit on your little magnetic theory considering he steered right past my table this morning. Not to mention he let that waitress from the diner…" Warmth flooded my cheeks as I realized I'd said too much.

AJ shook his head. "This morning was my fault for giving Jake shit about the songwriting. And the waitress…well, you got him worked up, and I'm sure she was more than willing to take care of it for him because he's Jake Slater of Runaway Train, not because he's Jake this good-looking guy who has a lot of unattractive demons he's dealing with."

Glancing down, I scuffed my boots against the uneven pavement. "Look, AJ, I appreciate your honesty, but I don't think anything is going to happen with me and Jake." Before he could say anything else, I held up my hand. "And nothing is happening with you either. I want us to stay friends, okay?"

"Of course, Angel. Anything you want." He then wrapped his arm around my shoulder and led me to the bus. Frank and Brayden stood in the galley while Rhys was sprawled out on the couch.

"Okay, I'm going to make a quick grocery run, and then we'll get back on the road," Frank said. He glanced around the inside of the bus. "Where's Jake? I thought he might like to go with me?"

"I don't know. I haven't seen him since breakfast," Brayden replied.

Frank grimaced. "Lemme go look for him."

Brayden exchanged a knowing glance with Frank. "I'll come with you."

While they went in search of Jake, AJ glanced at me. "Wanna play some video games, Angel?"

I wrinkled my nose. "No thanks, I think I'm good. I'll do a little studying."

"Suit yourself." AJ shoved Rhys's legs off the couch. "You down to get your ass whipped, dude?"

"Yeah, right, douchebag. You know I wipe the floor with you each and every time," Rhys replied.

As they settled in for a raucous Call of Duty marathon, I headed down the hall to the bedroom. I dug out my giant study packet for my nursing exam along with some of my books from my suitcase. I came back to the living area and plopped down. I lounged on the couch, balancing my opened Anatomy and Physiology book on my knees while AJ and Rhys shouted obscenities at each other's game characters.

Fifteen minutes passed before a red-faced and out-of-breath Brayden appeared. He stalked up the stairs, muttering something under his breath. After flopping down across from me, he jerked up the magazine on the table. With his shaky hands, I could tell he was pissed about something.

It was then Jake staggered up the bus stairs with a leggy, dark-haired goddess. I couldn't help but gasp as pain crisscrossed through my chest. The sight of him with another girl—one that I couldn't possibly compete with when it came to sex appeal—caused me to heave in a few desperate breaths. The knife I felt that was wedged in my chest twisted further at the sight of him so wasted. The Jake swaying to and fro in front of me wasn't the Jake I'd held as he cried or the one who I had made music with this morning. But it hurt just as bad that he had forgotten my very existence. Almost too quickly to believe, he had cemented back up any of his walls I'd managed to break down.

Good one, Abby. You actually thought by comforting Jake and writing a song with him he would magically be a different guy? Fat freakin' chance there. Jake Slater will always only want one thing from women, and that's sex. He's like the Sexual Major leagues, and you're not even a farm team.

I was jolted out of my self-deprecating internal monologue by the goddess's arm snaking around Jake's waist while her tongue licked up his neck. His gaze flickered over to mine before he turned back to the guys. "I call the bedroom."

"You had the bedroom yesterday," AJ argued.

"Easy, grumpy, I won't need it that long," Jake replied, a sexy smile curving on his lips.

"You underestimate your stamina, babe," the dark haired girl replied. I couldn't help the squeak that escaped my lips when her hand left his waist to cup his fly, working Jake over his jeans.

"Take it to the bedroom. There's a lady present," Brayden snapped over his magazine.

When the bulge started to grow, Jake cut his glassy eyes over to me again. I flushed and buried my head in my book. "You're welcome to join us, Angel. Bree doesn't mind sharing me, do you?"

I jerked my chin up. So this was Bree—the groupie he had mistaken me for in his bed.

She eyed me and shrugged. "As long as I get off, I don't care." But her body language told me that she was all about keeping Jake for herself, and she would as soon scratch my eyes out as let me touch Jake.

"Whatta ya say? Want me to break you in real quick? Show you what it's like to be with a man finally?" Jake slurred.

121

I gasped in horror while AJ shot off the couch. A low growl erupted from his throat before he shoved Jake with all his might, sending Jake staggering backwards. "You're a drunken jackass! You're stepping over the line with Abby, not to mention your bargain with her."

"Oh really?" Jake countered.

AJ cocked his brows. "Yeah, especially after last night, not to mention this morning."

The thoughts of what had transpired between us seemed to sober Jake a little, and his smirk faded. A combination of remorse and embarrassment entered his face.

I patted AJ's arm that was shaking from anger. "Stop, it's okay. While I appreciate the machismo ferocity, I can take care of myself." Rising up from my chair, I then stepped in front of Jake. "Thank you so much for your offer, but your vile suggestion of 'breaking me in', as well as the drunken state you're currently in, not only makes me want to vomit, but it makes my skin crawl too. Trust me that you would be the last man on earth I would *ever* let be my first."

Jake glowered back at me before he jerked Bree forward down the narrow hallway and then slammed the bedroom door.

"He can be such a prick," Rhys grumbled from the couch.

Trying not to show how hurt I was, I quickly added, "Yeah, but he's hurting a lot right now about his mom."

AJ threw his hands up in exasperation. "So that excuses him for getting drunk off his ass before noon and for treating you like a sleazy asshole?"

I forced a reassuringly smile to my lips at his skeptical expression. "It's fine. Really."

But then it became very plain that the noises from the bedroom were so *not* fine. Moans and shrieks echoed through the cabin from the bedroom. A warm flush poured over my cheeks and inched down my neck. I gripped the edges of my book tighter, desperately wanting to crawl into a hole and die rather than to hear the sounds of Jake screwing Bree. There was also the fact that the guys seemed totally unaffected by the noises coming from the bedroom.

"Here. These seem to help," AJ suggested, handing me two ear plugs.

I eyed them as Jake gave another long groan. "Oh yeah, suck me harder, babe!"

"Um, on second thought, I think I'll go get some fresh air." I scrambled off the couch and raced down the aisle. The moment I got off the bus I exhaled noisily. Bending over, I rested my elbows on my knees and tried to clear my mind of what I had heard. Once I recovered, I started putting as much distance between myself and the bus as possible.

My mind whirled with out-of-control thoughts. *What was I thinking agreeing to stay on the bus with three perfect strangers and one unimaginable, insensitive, womanzing asshole? I can't do this. I cannot look at Jake again, least of all stay on the bus with him. I'll just give in and lose the bet.*

Craning my neck, I tried to decipher whether this would be a good enough place for me to stay when the bus pulled out. I scowled as I realized we were out in the middle of nowhere and probably miles and miles away from the nearest airport. I seriously doubted taxis came out here either.

A black SUV screeched up beside me. Thankfully the window rolled down to reveal Frank. "Hey Angel, what are you doing out here?"

"Oh, I, um, just needed a little fresh air."

He gave me a knowing smile. "Jake getting frisky with Bree?"

I flushed while ducking my head. "You could say that."

He chuckled. "Come on then. You can go into town with me and get some groceries. I swear those boys go through food faster than I can buy it!"

"Sounds like my brothers," I replied with a smile. "Are you sure you don't mind?"

"It'd be my pleasure."

"Okay then." I opened the door on the Tahoe and hopped inside. After I buckled my seatbelt, Frank gave me a wink. "You know my motives weren't all sincere, Angel."

"Oh really?"

He grinned as he put his foot down on the accelerator. "Yeah, I figure the trip will go faster if I put you to work with the list."

I giggled. "I thought as much."

As we sped out of the bus lot and onto the highway, my curiosity about Bree got the better of me. Fidgeting in my seat, I turned to Frank. "So what's the deal with Jake and Bree?"

He exhaled noisily. "That girl is nothing but trouble, and the last thing Jake needs is more trouble in his life. I mean, a part of me feels sorry for her. It wasn't like she had the best parents in the world."

"Oh?" I asked casually, trying to goad him for more information.

"You haven't had the pleasure of meeting her father yet?"

"He works for Runaway Train?"

"Yep. Lyle's a roadie like me." Frank wrinkled his nose in disgust. "Well, you could say he's only risen as far as he has by using Bree to get to rockers."

I gasped. "Seriously? He like…pimps her?"

Frank chuckled. "Oh Angel, I can't believe you just said that." He glanced over at me. "It's not like he's officially prostituting her. She has always willing gone to all the guys and offered herself. She joins Lyle along the stops—somehow she has the money to travel as much as she does. Lately, she has her eye on one particular rocker, and no one else will do, which couldn't make her daddy prouder."

A knot suddenly formed in my throat, and I hated myself for it. "Jake?"

He nodded. "Of course, Jake really doesn't care about her—he's never cared about any of the girls he's been with since the band made it big. They're just objects for him to fulfill a need." He gave a wry smile. "And does that boy ever have needs."

My mind was assaulted by the horrible flashback of Jake's bedroom antics. "Yeah, he does. Too bad that gets in the way of him actually being a decent guy."

Frank jerked his gaze away from the road to pin me with a surprised stare. "Don't tell me you're falling for Jake's charms"

I squirmed in my seat. "I just said he wasn't a total jerk." Frank obviously cared for Jake, so it wasn't like I could say everything I was feeling about him, which mainly consisted of what a complete and total asshole Jake was. So to curb my tongue I tried focusing on Jake's breakdown last night and our songwriting session rather than his behavior with Bree. "I mean, any guy who loves and adores his mother so much can't totally be terrible to all women, right?" *Obviously he can by the way he just pretended to be interested in you and then tossed you aside for someone who will give him what he really wants—sex.*

"I'm glad you can see through his tough façade to the real man inside. I mean, I love him like he was one of my sons, and I couldn't do that if I didn't know what he was really like."

We rode along the highway in silence for a few minutes before Frank cleared his throat. From the way he fidgeted in his seat, I knew he was about to bring up something that made him beyond uncomfortable. "You know, Jake could really use a girl like you."

I stared at him in surprise. "I would laugh, but you're not joking, are you?" When he shook his head, I mumbled under my breath, "First AJ and now you."

"What?"

"Nothing."

"I'm more than serious about what I said. Jake is going through such a difficult time right now, and what's to come is even worse. He doesn't need darkness like Bree." He turned to smile at me. "He needs light, and damn if you don't have such a beautiful light about you,

Angel."

"Yeah, well, considering he asked me to join him and Bree for sex ten minutes ago, I don't think he truly cares anything about my light unless it's between my legs!"

As his eyes bulged in horror, Frank sucked in a breath. "Oh God," I murmured before ducking my head in mortification. Had I actually just told Frank that? Twenty-four hours on a bus with a bunch of raunchy guys had completely taken over all of the manners my parents had instilled in me. "I'm so sorry. That was totally uncalled for."

"I, erm,…" he stammered.

Warmth filled my cheeks. "What I should have said is that while I appreciate the sentiment, Jake is never going to be interested in a girl like me. We're so different, and we want different things out of the people we date." I winced. "I mean, Jake doesn't date."

Frank took a few moments to absorb my comments. "He could if he was given the chance."

I snorted contemptuously. "Are we talking about the same guy here?"

"Why do I have the sneaking suspicion that your feelings and reactions might have been a tad different if we'd had this conversation this morning?"

Before I could bite my lip or hold my tongue, I blurted, "I'm not being a spiteful little bitch. You don't know how much it hurts that he ignored me all morning and then chose Bree, okay?"

"Aw, Angel, I'm sorry. I shouldn't have mentioned anything."

"It's okay. You were just trying to look out for Jake. But even if he hadn't done what he did and actually gave me the time of day for longer than a minute, I don't know if I could deal with the Brees of Jake's life."

Frank pulled into a teeming Wal-Mart parking lot. After he put the SUV in park, he cut the ignition and turned to me. "Look, when it comes right down to it, I'm just an old fart widower who doesn't know much but the love of my high school sweetheart. But I've seen the way Jake looks at you—" When I opened my mouth to protest, he held up his hand. "And no, it's more than just you're a piece of meat he wants to devour." He smiled. "He's seen past the pretty packaged outside to see the beauty within. I guarantee whatever he was doing with Bree this afternoon was about more than just his needs. He wanted to get you off his mind." At my continued apprehension, he swung the keys back and forth on his finger. "So do an old man a favor and keep an open mind along with an extra forgiving heart when it comes to Jake, okay?"

I fiddled with the door handle, trying to avoid Frank's intense stare. "I can try, but I'm not making any promises."

A wide grin curved on Frank's face. "Good, I'm glad to hear it. And if it doesn't work out, I've got a son not too much older than you."

I laughed. "Do you ever stop with the matchmaking?"

"Nope." He opened his door. "Come on. Let's go get the boys some food."

***

Chapter Eight

JAKE

A long moan erupted from my lips as my eyes rolled back in my head with pleasure.

Bree was riding me like a crazed cowgirl. Her fingers dug into my hips, sending her acrylic nails scratching across my skin. She bounced and jerked on and off of me as I thrust up to meet her frantic movements. "Fuck," I muttered as she tightened her walls around me. If there was one thing Bree knew, it was how to please me and give me the best sex, along with the best head, I'd ever had in my life.

But when I opened my eyes, I didn't see Bree's back arched in ecstasy. Instead, Abby straddled me—her expression one of wide-eyed wonderment. She gazed down at me lovingly, not with eyes hooded with lust like Bree always did. "Angel?" When she didn't respond, I murmured, "Abby," to which she smiled. I rose up to take her swaying breast into my mouth. I suckled the nipple causing her to moan.

"Yeah, do me harder, Jake!" Bree's voice roared through the bedroom.

I blinked my eyes, trying to clear Abby's image from my mind. This time when I looked back, it was no longer Abby, but Bree scratching her fingernails harshly down my chest as she rode me. Shaken by what I had hallucinated, I tried focusing on Bree's writhing form. What the hell was happening to me? I had a sex goddess screwing my brains out, and I was fantasizing about a blushing virgin. A growl escaped my lips as I flipped Bree over on her back and started pounding her hard.

"YES JAKE! Yes, just like that!" Bree cried, smacking my ass.

I sucked one of her nipples into my mouth and teasingly bit it. She screamed and clutched her legs harder around me. But when I raised my head from Bree's breast, Abby stared up at me. "Oh, I've wanted to make love for so long, Jake. I'm glad you're my first."

I blinked my eyes a few times, but it was still Abby smiling up at me. A pleading expression took over her face. "No man has ever made me come before. Please be the first." Hearing those words on her lips was my undoing, and I felt myself start to shudder.

"Abby! Oh God, Abby, yes, yes!" I cried as I came hard into her.

The room became eerily silent. "What the fuck did you just say?" Bree demanded. Before I could finish coming down from my high, she shoved me off of her. "You asshole!"

"What's your problem?" I gasped, trying to catch my breath.

"You called me Abby, you douchebag!"

Oh fuck…I had. I'd not only fantasized about banging Abby, but I'd actually said her name when I came.

Bree shook her head. "I cannot freakin' believe this. I thought I heard you say it earlier, but now I know you did! What the hell, Jake?"

"I don't know why I did that. I'm drunk." I ran my fingers through my hair, trying to still my nerves. It wasn't like I owed Bree an explanation—she was just a groupie I banged frequently. It was more that I was so freaked out myself at what I had done that I wanted to rationalize it.

"That's not an excuse!"

Talking my thoughts aloud, I mumbled, "She comforted me last night about my mom. Maybe that's why I was thinking about her."

"Yeah, thinking about *her* while you were fucking *me*!" Bree shrieked, throwing her dress over her head.

"You're making a big deal over nothing. We're not exclusive, so we're free to fuck or fantasize about whoever we want to." I then narrowly dodged the heel she threw at me. "Are you insane?" I shouted.

"Go to hell, Jake!" she screamed before she stormed out of the room, leaving the black heel that had almost whacked me in the head.

"I need a drink," I muttered before staggering into the hallway.

By the wide-eyed looks of the horror the guys were giving me, I knew they heard what I'd did. Without another word to me, Bree stormed off the bus.

AJ leaned forward. "Dude, did you seriously just call out Abby's name?"

I groaned and stalked over to the fridge. I snatched out a beer and took two long pulls. When they continued peering expectantly at me, I shrugged. "Maybe I did. Don't tell me you've never said something crazy when you were coming."

"I sure as hell never called the girl the wrong name," AJ replied. Brayden bobbed his head in agreement.

When I glanced at Rhys, he gave me a sheepish grin. "In my

defense, it was a three-some. I kinda lost track of who was who."

I rolled my eyes. "Look, it's nothing. Bree's spent the last few months trying to get her hooks further into me. It'll be better if I just find someone else to fuck after the show."

A growl came from low in Brayden's throat. "Pricks like you make me sad for my sweet, innocent baby girl back at home," he grumbled as he headed for the bathroom.

Once he slammed the door, AJ leaned forward in his seat. "So don't you think you might want to take a second to think about why you called out Abby's name?"

Rhys nodded. "Were you like fantasizing about her when you did it?"

I finished the beer and tossed the bottle in the trash. Without hesitating, I grabbed out another one. "Pace yourself, man. We're going out tonight to hear Bray's cousin's band play, remember?" AJ warned.

Ignoring him, I took a long gulp of the foamy beer. When I thought about how I'd pictured Abby riding me and asking me to make her come, I shuddered. How could someone who was so not my type get me so hot?

"So you *did* fantasize about her?" Rhys asked, a knowing smile on his face.

"And what if I did?" I countered.

He snorted. "You're out of your mind if you think you can seduce Abby like Bree or one of your other groupies."

AJ grinned. "Rhys's right man."

132

Closing the gap between us, I asked, "Is that a challenge?"

AJ's expression darkened. "No, it's sure as hell not. And I'll kick your fucking ass if you try anything with her." When I narrowed my eyes, he inched closer to me. "Don't you think after her little performance last night, I might have wondered about what it might be like to get it on with her? To have her legs wrapped around my waist and those lips on mine." He sucked in a ragged breath while a tremble rippled through him. Once he came out of his fantasy, he shook his head wildly back and forth. "But that's all it's ever going to be to me is a thought. Abby is the relationship/marrying kinda girl, and I sure as hell can't give that to her right now. And I respect her too much to try to put the moves on her, and I don't want to see her get hurt."

"Gotta admit that goes for me too," Rhys added.

I rolled my eyes at the two misguided Knights in Shining Armor. "The last thing in the world I want is to start something up with her, got it?" I hissed.

Rhys shook his head. "Keep on telling yourself that, man. You're already drowning in her, and the longer she's on this bus, the deeper you're going to get in."

A shiver ran down my spine at Rhys's words. Was he right? Was seeing Abby while I was screwing Bree some weird double meaning that after a brief twenty-four hours I was starting to like her? My mind flashed back to her holding me while I cried, the tender curves of her body pressed against me, her whispered words of encouragement. No, no, no! This couldn't happen. I wouldn't let it.

"Ugh, I'm going back to the bedroom. Wake me when it's time to

133

leave." Before they could protest, I snatched up a bottle of Jack Daniels from the cabinet—desperately hoping to wipe any sexual thoughts, or any thoughts period, of Abby Renard from my mind.

After downing half the bottle of Jack, I must've passed out because the next thing I knew AJ was standing over me, shaking my shoulders.

"Wake up, douchebag."

I groaned and rubbed my eyes. "What time is it?"

"Six. Cade's set is at seven, so we gotta get hustling."

Glancing over at the digital clock, I realized there would be no time for showering. I'd have to go out smelling like a mixture of booze and Bree. When I swung my legs over the side of the bed, the room spun around me.

"Jesus, Jake. You're completely plastered," AJ lamented as he smoothed on some cologne.

"I am not," I grumbled, staggering to my feet.

When I lurched forward and had to cling to his waist to keep from passing out, he grunted in frustration before reaching out to steady me. "Why do you do this shit to yourself man? Susan would hate to see you like this."

Jerking myself upright, I jabbed a finger into his chest. "Do *not* bring up my mother," I growled.

When I caught a glance at AJ's face in the darkness, he wore a pitied expression, rather than a pissed one. "I'm sorry, man. You know I love her, and I love you," he murmured.

My shoulders drooped in defeat. Christ, I so did not need this right now. Trying to deal with my mother was one thing. Throwing in what had happened with Bree and Abby, coupled with AJ getting all emotional on me, was way too much. "Look, I love you too, but I can only handle so much without absolutely losing my fucking mind."

"Fine. I understand."

"Fuck, my head is about to explode. Did Frank get back from the store with the Advil?"

"Yeah, he and Abby got back a little while ago." At the mention of Abby's name, I tensed as I realized what I had said and done to her earlier with Bree. "Um, did she...you know, with me and Bree?"

AJ quirked his dark brows and crossed his arms over his chest. "Of course she heard you. All your grunts and groans embarrassed the hell out of her, but she finally freaked out and ran off the bus at your 'Suck me harder!' line."

I cringed. I had a special gift for fucking up around Abby that was for damn sure. She probably hated me now. Who was I kidding? She'd hated me from the moment we met, and last night and this morning was all just a pity party. I shook my head. Wait, why did I care if she hated me or not? No, I could not care about Abby—not in any way that wasn't sexual.

With AJ's back turned, I grabbed the bottle of Jack off the nightstand and started chugging. Pinching my eyes shut, I let the harsh alcohol burn a fiery trail down my stomach. My binge was unceremoniously cut off when the bottle was snatched away from me.

"Dammit Jake! You're already a mess! How the hell are you going to go out tonight like this?"

"Fuck off," I grumbled before staggering out of the bedroom.

The aroma of tomatoes and spices hit my nose and caused my alcohol-filled stomach to churn. Someone had actually cooked? I peered ahead of me to see Rhys and Brayden relaxing at the table with empty bowls of what must've been chili in front of them.

When I met Rhys's eyes, he shook his head. "Dude, you look like hell."

"Thanks dickweed. I feel like hell."

Abby stood with her back to me at the stove. The sound of my voice caused her to whirl around. With her hair pulled back in a ponytail, she held a spatula in her hand, which was surprising since I didn't know we had cookware on the bus.

Her blue eyes widened as she took in my appearance, but then she quickly turned away from me. I did a double take because she appeared almost skittish in front of me—something she had never, ever done before.

"What's wrong with you?" I demanded.

"Leave me alone!" she spat from her place at the stove.

"Ah, there's my feisty girl."

Spinning around, Abby's expression darkened. "Don't you dare call me your girl after the things you said and did to me earlier today!"

"You got a problem with me?"

"Wow, you must really be drunker than I thought if you have to ask that!" she snapped.

"Trust me, he's totally hammered. The jackass chased two beers

136

with a fifth of Jack," Brayden replied, shaking his head.

AJ appeared behind me. "Let's not start anything, okay? We have a show to see. Let's just get out the door without any more trouble."

Abby held up her hands. "I'm not the one starting anything. I certainly didn't do anything wrong."

A snort escaped my lips. "Don't you get it, Angel? *You're* what's wrong."

"Jake—" AJ warned.

Her eyes widened as she swept her hand over her heart. "Me?"

"Yeah, you." I lunged forward causing her to take a tentative step back. "It's you with those sexy as hell cowboy boots that I want digging into my ass as I fuck you until you scream my name. And those perfect tits…" I licked my lips at the mere thought of my mouth on them. But in that pause, my cloudy thoughts veered in a different, less perverted direction. "It's the way the dimple comes out on your cheek when you smile really big and the way you blush when I tease you."

I sucked in a breath as a fuzzy memory from the night before crashed over me. "It was the way your sweet, soft hands wiped away my tears, and the way your body just curved into mine when you let me hold you. It all made me feel, for just an instant, that everything really was going to be all right. No one has ever comforted me like that…except my mom." What the fuck? Did I just say all that out loud? I shook my head furiously from side to side as the room started spinning me like a Tilt-a-Whirl at the county fair back home.

Abby grabbed my shoulders to steady me. I blinked my eyes trying to focus on her blurry, but beautiful image. "Most of all, it's that I want someone like you to want me—just for me, not for Jake Slater the singer of Runaway Train." I smacked my hand hard against my chest. "For what's really inside me."

Abby gasped. "Oh Jake, I—"

She never got the chance to say what I hoped to hear because my churning stomach chose that precise moment to lurch, causing me to puke all over Abby's pristine sundress.

***

Chapter Nine

Abby

Reeling from Jake's drunken declaration of his feelings, I never anticipated being drenched in puke. I stood there frozen in horror as Jake retched again. I snatched my hands from his shoulders and fought my gag reflex.

Jake raised his glassy eyes to mine. Pain coupled with embarrassment swam in them before they rolled back in his head, and he started to pass out.

"Motherfucker!" AJ groaned as he grabbed Jake's sinking form.

"He's out cold," Rhys reported.

"Ugh, I vote we throw his smelly ass in the bedroom and let him sleep it off," AJ suggested.

"Sounds good to me." Rhys helped AJ drag Jake back to the bedroom. When they finished, they slammed the door.

"I'm so sorry, Abby," Brayden apologized. He started to take a step towards me, but then crinkled his nose and backed up.

"Yeah, I get it. I reek." As I started for the shower, the guys swept past me towards the bus exit. "Whoa, wait a minute." They paused and turned around. I glanced back to the bedroom and then to them. "You mean you're going to leave me alone with Jake?"

"No, you can always come with us. We'll have an extra place at our VIP table with Jake not going," AJ offered. He gave me a sly wink before adding, "And I'll buy you all the Coke Zero you can drink if you'll promise to dance once or twice with me."

I laughed. "That's very tempting, but I think I better stay here. You know, get a little studying in or clean up this pigsty." I glanced down at my puke-stained clothes. "Besides, you guys need to get going and don't have time to wait on me to cleanup."

Brayden smiled. "We'll make time for you to change, Abby."

"Aw, that's so very sweet. Come here and give me a hug!" I offered with a teasing grin.

Holding his hands up in mock surrender, Brayden replied, "Lemme take a rain check on that one."

"I figured as much. No, you guys need to get going to keep your reservation."

"Are you sure?" Rhys asked before ducking into the bathroom to check his appearance one last time.

"Yeah, I'm sure." I threw another uneasy glance back at the bedroom. "And you're sure Jake will be okay?"

"You mean are you sure *you'll* be okay with Jake?" AJ questioned with a grin.

"No, that's not what I meant."

Rhys chuckled as he stepped out of the bathroom. "It'll be fine, Abby. He'll be out for hours. And I wager when he wakes up, he'll be too hung-over to try anything. Your virtue is safe."

I huffed when he winked at me. "Fine. Go have fun. I'll just be here baby-sitting the drunken, horny douchebag!"

The guys roared with laughter as they clambered off the bus and headed into the waiting SUV. "Men," I mumbled as I headed for my suitcase and a clean change of clothes. When I got into the bathroom, I was quick to lock the door. I didn't want to take any chances of Jake barreling in on me.

Under the scorching stream of water, my mind floated back to what Jake had said before he passed out. I couldn't help the embarrassing flush creeping over my body at what he'd mentioned about us having sex. At the same time, an ache burned its way through me at the thought of what he had suggested, and for the first time, I felt true desire and longing for a guy. It was like nothing I had experienced with anyone else I had liked or dated. And even though I wasn't in love with Jake, I *wanted* him. Bad.

"WHAT?! Have you lost your mind!" I shouted to the shower walls as I raked my fingernails through my hair. I then wildly shook my head back and forth. What was happening to me? No, no, no. I couldn't think about Jake that way. He was a manwhore who only used women. He could never, ever love me or give me what I wanted in life...could he?

But my mind then whirled to Frank's earlier conversation as well as what Jake had admitted after all the naughty stuff. He wanted a girl like me to really like him. It wasn't the first time he had made that statement. He'd made that claim to me after I'd comforted him. Deep down, could Jake want a relationship and more with a girl...with me?

"Ugh!" I grunted as I finished rinsing my hair. I had claimed I wanted to gain some kind of experience of the whole bet situation, and unfortunately, I was getting more than I had bargained for. I'd been on the bus almost thirty-six hours, and my life had already been turned completely upside down.

As I turned off the water and stepped out of the shower, I shivered at the thought of what the rest of the week might hold. Trying to tune out the wild and crazy thoughts flitting through my mind, I worked on drying my hair. I doused myself in lotion to make sure there wasn't the possibility of any remaining puke smell.

Since I had yet to make it the store and my yoga pants and one t-shirt were puke stained, I slipped on a cami and a pair of jersey shorts. After I unlocked the door, I pressed my ear to the frame, listening for any sounds of Jake stirring. I rolled my eyes when I realized how stupid I probably looked. I don't know what I was so paranoid about. It wasn't like Jake would ever try anything. I guess I was more afraid of not wanting to stop him, rather than not being able to.

With a deep breath, I exited the bathroom. Jake was nowhere in sight, and I could only imagine he was still dead to the world in the bedroom. Bringing my hands to my hips, I pondered what to do with my evening. Studying and not getting behind while out on tour was high on my list of priorities, so I dug my books out of my bag. But before I sat down, I surveyed the inside of the bus and wrinkled my nose. These boys were just as bad as my brothers when it came to being slobs. Pulling my hair back in a ponytail, I surmised that there was no way I could concentrate on studying surrounded by all the filth.

Bending down, I grabbed a pair of rubber gloves, cleaner, and

142

sponges out from under the sink. As I started wiping down the counters, I realized it was entirely too quiet. I ambled over to the stereo system and started going through AJ's CD collection. When I got to Michael Jackson's Greatest Hits, I stopped. "Oh yeah, a little old school MJ will do just fine."

The opening 80's synthesized melody of *Beat It* blared out of the speakers. Nodding my head, I started singing along, using my sponge as a make-shift microphone. As I cleaned up the table and chairs, I started shimmying and shaking my ass around the bus. There was nothing like cleaning to good music, and you could say I was a bit Michael Jackson obsessed.

I was halfway through playing air guitar on Eddie Van Halen's solo when a hand on my shoulder caused me to shriek. I spun around, dropping the sponge and cleaner. It clattered noisily onto the floor.

Jake gave me an epic smirk. "Nice moves, Angel, but could you turn that down?"

My cheeks felt enflamed. "Oh, yeah, so sorry," I muttered, hurrying over to flick off the stereo. As I tried stilling my erratic breath, silence echoed through the bus as Jake and I stood staring at each other. "Um, how are you feeling?"

He winced as he rubbed his head. "What do you think? I woke up in Hell with Michael Jackson pounding in my ears."

When I snickered, he added, "Not to mention, I staggered out here to scream at the guys only to see you in that outfit," he motioned to my cami and shorts, "shaking your ass." He cocked his brows. "Totally not within the parameters of our bet, Angel."

Sweeping a hand to my hip, I spat, "Sorry, but I have to have music on while I'm cleaning, and as for the clothes, well, you puked all over my least allegedly provocative outfit."

"Oh Christ," he muttered. It was like the memory of everything that had happened came crashing down on Jake, and he shuddered, falling back against the counter. His weary eyes met mine. He ran his hands over his face and furrowed his eyebrows at the feeling of the crusty, puke stains. "I was so fucked up earlier."

"It's okay. Sit down." My caring instinct kicked into overdrive as I pushed him into one of the captain's chairs. After I grabbed a fresh cloth out of the drawer, I ran it under the warm water while trying not to let my mind wander to which part of our earlier conversation he was most regretful about—the wanting to screw me or wanting me to like him.

Instead, I rinsed out the rag and then took it over to Jake. "Um, would you mind doing it for me since I don't have a mirror?" When I gave him a skeptical look, he laughed. "This isn't a come on, Angel." He held out his hand to show me the slight trembling. "I'm not sure I trust my ass walking to the bathroom."

"Fine then," I muttered. In long strokes, I started washing his face.

He closed his eyes and sighed. "Damn, that feels good." I tipped his head back and scrubbed down his chin. Squinting one of his eyes at me, he asked, "Why are you always taking care of me?"

"You're always a mess," I countered.

"I know," he murmured. Sadness swept across his face. "I think you're a masochist."

144

"Huh?"

"You know, someone who likes pain."

"And why do you say that?"

"Because even though I treat you like a total dick, you're still nice to me and still want to help me."

"You're not always a…" I wrinkled my nose before replying, "dick."

Jake gave me a half-hearted smile. "Mostly I am. Especially to you. And I'm sorry for it. I really am."

I froze in mid-scrub at his apology. It was certainly not what I was expecting him to say, and when I searched his eyes, I saw the sincerity in them. "Thank you. I appreciate that."

Silence echoed around us until Jake cleared his throat. "After everything, you really don't think I'm a total asshole?"

I laughed. "Well, not all the time. You were a giant one this afternoon." At his grimace, I added, "But you've also given me brief glimpses of the guy deep down inside you. You have your redeeming qualities too." I left him to go rinse out the rag again. "And I don't know about being a masochist. But I do know about trying to be the good person my parents raised me to be."

Amusement replaced the anguish in his eyes. "Ah, yes, an allegedly good girl with a heart of gold but who also has the mouth of a sailor."

I couldn't help laughing at his summation of me. "Yep, that's pretty true. But hey, I don't drink or sleep around. I should be able to have one vice, so I guess a potty mouth is it."

I trailed the rag down his chest, swiping the puke off the intricate tattoos inking his skin. "So many tattoos," I murmured.

"You don't like them?"

"No, I do. My brothers have some. In fact, I was thinking about getting one."

Jake howled with laugher. "You cannot be serious."

"Well, I am," I huffed smacking his arm with the rag.

"Oh Angel, I would love to see that."

"Fine then. Maybe you can take me to get one."

A mischievous glint twinkled in his blue eyes. "Are you about to make another bet with me?"

"Maybe."

He shook his head slowly back and forth. "I don't think so, babe. If you go back to your brothers inked up, they'll kick my ass."

I rolled my eyes. "Leave my brothers out of this."

Jake held his hands up in defeat. "Okay, okay, I'll take you to get a tat."

My eyes widened. "Really?" I squealed.

He winced and cupped his ears. "Jesus, ease up with the screeching." When I glared at him, he grinned. "Yeah, I really will. My guy, Adam, is the only one I would trust your delicate skin to. But you better not pussy out on me."

I knew he expected a reaction out of me because he had used a word I hated. But I kept my demeanor calm. "Awesome." I then turned my attention back to cleaning him up.

When I skimmed above the waistband of his jeans, he grabbed my hand. "I can take it from here." He winked at me. "You're getting a little too close for comfort, Angel."

"Oh, um, sorry," I replied. Trying to hide my embarrassment, I whirled around and went back to the kitchen. While I tried busying myself with putting away the clean dishes, Jake rose out of his chair.

"I probably should grab a quick shower."

"Okay."

As he handed me the rag, a sheepish look came over his face. "When I get out, you think you could fix me some of that chili you made for the guys."

"Are you sure your stomach can handle it?"

"Oh yeah, once I puke it all out, I'm usually good to go and starving a few hours later."

"Ew," I murmured.

He grinned. "Sorry. But that's the truth."

"Fine. Go shower, and I'll fix you some dinner."

"Thanks, Angel," he replied before pulling me to him in a chaste hug. When he kissed the crown of my head, I tried not to shudder at the tingly feeling it sent racing throughout my body. My mouth hung open in shock as he padded into the bathroom and closed the door.

"Wonders never cease," I murmured under my breath. I then busied myself with reheating some dinner for Jake.

At the sound of the bathroom door opening, I whirled around. Jake stood there with just a tiny towel wrapped around his waist while water dripped off his body. He glanced down at his lack of attire. "Sorry. My booze-head brain forgot to bring my clothes in with me."

"Um, no, it's okay. I'm just heating up the chili for you. It'll be ready when you get dressed."

"Great."

Even though I shouldn't have, I stood watching him as he walked down the aisle to the bedroom. The fluttering of my heart and churning of my stomach made me realize I was in serious trouble.

I turned my attention back to setting the table for Jake. He appeared a few moments later in a t-shirt that was entirely too small for him because it highlighted every rippling muscle he had along with a pair of ratty boxer shorts.

Frozen, I stood staring at him like he was a vision or something. His hair was still damp, and a few droplets glistened on his face. When he caught me, warmth burned across my cheeks.

"Were you just ogling me, Angel?"

"No, I wasn't."

He chuckled. "I think you were."

I whirled around and swept my hands to my hips. "Fine I was ogling you. Happy now?"

"Actually I am. I like it when you look at me like you want me. Like you think I'm... handsome."

My brows rose in surprise. "Handsome? That doesn't sound like the way you would describe yourself."

With a grin, he asked, "And just how would I describe myself?"

"Hmm, sexy, hot as hell, and panty melting?" I challenged as I handed him a Coke.

"Yeah, you're right. Those really describe me better."

I set a glass of water down. "Make sure you drink all of that and the Coke. You're probably dehydrated."

"Yes, Dr. Renard," he replied, amusement twinkled in his eyes.

"The nurse in me would say for you not to eat anything, least of all chili."

"Trust me, I know my body, Angel."

"Whatever."

After he took in a large spoonful of chili, he closed his eyes and moaned in appreciation. "Damn, this is really good."

"Thank you."

"So you can cook too?"

"A little. My grandmother is a diehard Texan, and that's her secret recipe."

"It's fucking amazing."

I grinned. "I'll be sure to tell her just that."

He snorted. "Yeah, right. Although you have a potty mouth, I can't see you dropping the f-bomb in front of your grandma."

"True, very true."

We sat there in silence for a few minutes while he devoured the chili like he hadn't eaten for days. I couldn't possibly see how he was going to keep it all down or how sick he might be tomorrow, but I kept my mouth shut.

Finally, Jake glanced up at me. "Abby, we need to talk about earlier."

"We do?" I asked, playing with a frayed string on the placemat.

He bobbed his head. "I know I was totally fucked up this

afternoon, and I don't know what all I said to you." He winced like he was in pain. "I have a pretty good idea that I was a disrespectful douchebag to you about Bree. I should have never brought her on the bus with you here. I'm sorry."

I think my mouth dropped so far open it banged against the table at him once again giving me such a heartfelt apology. Just when I thought I couldn't get any more shocked, he continued on. "You've been nothing but caring and compassionate to me even when I didn't deserve it. And trust me when I say it, that I really and truly am sorry."

"Thank you. I appreciate it."

"So are we good? No hard feelings and all that?"

I laughed. "You believe in instant forgiveness and no grudges, huh?"

"Not exactly, but I hope you won't hold what happened against me for long."

"I'll try, okay? I mean, you just can't act the way you did to me and expect me to fall into your waiting arms."

His brows furrowed. "I can't?"

"Um, no, it doesn't work that with me. Maybe with your harem of female admirers, but I'm different."

"You can say that again," he murmured. As his spoon scraped across the bottom of his bowl, I rose up to get him some more. "No, I'm good."

"Are you sure?"

He smiled. "Don't want to overdo it."

I laughed. "I would think even two spoonfulls was overdoing it, but

I don't know your body, right?"

When Jake widened his eyes slightly, I knew I had made a mistake even innocently mentioning his body.

"Listen, I need to ask you something else about earlier." My breath caught at the thought of even remotely revisiting what happened before. "Did I say something embarrassing to you before I puked and passed out?"

"Jake—"

His blue eyes blazed with emotion when he finally met my gaze. "I remember some of it. I know I said I wanted to fuck you, but didn't I say something else? Something more…heartfelt, I hope?"

"Yes," I whispered.

"What was it?" he prompted.

Somehow I remembered everything he had told me verbatim, so I repeated it. Jake's eyes widened, and he sucked in a sharp breath. "But don't worry about the wanting someone-like-me-to-love-you part. I mean, I know you were drunk," I quickly added. I popped out of my seat like a Jack-In-The-Box and grabbed his bowl. After hustling over to the kitchen, I put it in the sink and turned on the water.

I gasped when Jake's body pressed into my back. "Angel," he murmured, his breath hot against my neck. I shivered in spite of the heat. "I meant every word of what I said—the good and the bad."

Spinning around, I stared into his eyes. When I saw the sincerity in them, my heartbeat accelerated. "You did?"

"Yes, I really want to have sex while you're wearing cowboy boots," he deadpanned.

I laughed in spite of myself. I knew for someone like Jake, all the feelings stuff was getting too intense for him, and he needed to lighten it. "That's good to know, but sadly, I don't see it happening any time soon."

"Bummer," he replied. He reached over to sweep a lock of hair out of my face. Once he pinned it behind my ear, he smiled.

The sound of my phone ringing brought me out of the moment. When I glanced at the Facetime request, I grimaced. "Sorry. I have to take this."

"Your parents?"

"No, it's the guy opening for my brothers. We're supposed to be singing a duet my first night and throughout the tour."

"Hmm," was Jake's reply.

As my thumb reluctantly slid across the button, I plastered a smile to my face. "Hey Garrett."

His smiling image reflected back at me. In some ways, Garrett reminded me of a late 20's version of Justin Bieber, although he was a lot more talented. "Hey beautiful. How's it going?"

"Good thanks. You?"

"Just 'good' is all I get? I mean, your brothers told me all about your little adventure on Runaway Train's bus."

I laughed. "Yeah, I'm sure they did. I'm kinda the family black sheep at the moment."

"You're kinda my black sheep too. I mean, I'm going to be denied precious rehearsal time with you for our duet."

I gasped. "Oh no! I totally forgot about that. I'm so sorry. Listen if

152

you don't think I'll be ready, I don't have to do it."

Garrett chuckled. "Abby, I'm only teasing you. I know you'll be fine if we get only one run through."

"Oh," I replied before exhaling in relief.

"I'm just bummed I miss out on all that time with you."

As my cheeks warmed, Jake muttered, "Douchebag," under his breath.

"Excuse me?" Garrett said.

"Oh nothing. Must've been the TV on in the bedroom." Trying to change the subject, I asked, "So are we still on for Sunday night?"

"Hell yeah. I can't wait to have you on stage with me. I mean, *Don't You Wanna Stay* is a hot song, don't you think?"

I nodded my head.

"Maybe as the tour goes on we can add a few more duets in there."

"Sure. That would be great."

"Five minutes, G," a voice came from over Garrett's shoulder.

"I gotta go Abby. I just wanted to call and check-in on you."

"Thanks. But I'm fine. I promise."

His expression darkened a little. "And trust me, if any of those assholes lay one finger on you, they won't just have your brothers to answer to."

At Jake's growl beside me, I quickly added, "Aw, that's sweet. But they've been perfect gentlemen."

"They better. See you Sunday." He gave a short wave to which I waved back. Then he ended the call.

"Ugh, what a tool!" Jake exclaimed.

"He's really being nice letting me sing with him. It's a good introduction to the crowd."

Jake rolled his eyes. "Of course he wants to let you sing, Angel. He wants in your pants."

"According to you guys and my brothers, doesn't every guy?"

He scowled at me. "Trust me when I tell you to watch yourself around him."

I shrugged. "It doesn't matter what his intentions are with me. I'm certainly not interested in him."

"You aren't?"

"No."

The corners of his lips turned up. "Is that because of his epic douchery or because you might be interested in someone else?"

I stared at him in disbelief for a moment. Sweeping my hands to my hips, I asked, "Do you always talk in circles when you're not man enough to make your intentions known?"

"What's that supposed to mean?"

"You really have the nerve to stand there and ask me that?" When he didn't respond, I practically growled as I took a step towards him. "You blow so hot and cold with me that I'm not sure which way is up. It's a wonder I don't need a chiropractor from your emotional whiplash. One minute you're telling me you want a girl like me to be interested in you and the next you're coyly asking how I feel about Garrett." Finally toe to toe, I glared up at him. "You're really good at charming the panties off girls at ten paces, but you can't even tell a girl how you really feel when she's up close and personal!"

Jake's eyes bulged while his mouth opened and closed like a fish out of water. "Abby…I…wow," he finally murmured.

"Excuse me?"

A sheepish grin curved on his lips. "I don't think a girl has ever talked to me like you just did." A shudder rippled through him. "Damn, that was hot."

I shoved him against the kitchen counter. "You're impossible!"

"And you're everything I could ever want."

My mouth, which had opened to lay into him with more insults, instantly snapped shut. Crossing his arms over his chest, Jake chuckled. "Don't tell me I've rendered you speechless, Angel?"

"You keep me in a state of confusion, so I don't know why you would be so surprised," I countered.

"Fine. You ready for this?" He pushed himself off the counter to stand in front of me again. "I like you, Angel. I like you a lot. It's been a whole thirty-six hours, but I like what I see, and I want more. But I'm clueless how to do this, so you're just going to have to be a little patient with me, okay?"

My heart fluttered both at his words and in the way he delivered them. "So we just keep getting to know each other?"

"Yeah, I think so." He scratched his chin thoughtfully. "So I guess normal people go on dates to get to know each other, right?"

"Yeah. Like dinner and a movie."

He bobbed his head. "Well, we sorta had dinner. So how about a movie?"

I grinned. "That sounds great."

"Can I count on you being down for inane comedy rather than a chick flick?"

"If you guys actually have a chick flick movie on this bus, I think we have to watch it."

Jake grimaced. "Yeah, well, Lily might've left a few DVDs behind."

"Oh really?"

"Yeah, but there's Disney shit for Jude too."

"Hmm, let me see what we're dealing with here," I replied before I went over to the entertainment center. It was stuffed full of DVDs along with video games.

As I perused the contents, Jake made a pained noise in his throat. "After the dick way I treated you, you're going to punish me with the video choice, aren't you?"

Glancing over my shoulder, I threw him an innocent glance. "Me? How could you possibly think such a thing?"

"Whatever," he grumbled, collapsing on the couch.

I turned around. "Okay, how does *Dodgeball* sound?" I asked.

His eyes lit up. "Fanfuckingtastic!"

Shooting him a wicked grin, I replied, "Good. We'll watch that after *Tangled.*"

"Seriously?"

I bobbed my head. "Must I remind you that you puked on me earlier this evening?"

"You're never going to let me forget that, are you?"

"Nope. But besides that, you have a lot of work to do to prove to me you're worthy of my time."

"So I have to watch fucking Disney to prove it?"

"It's a small start."

I eased the DVD into the player and grabbed the remote. Without even hesitating, I plopped down beside Jake on the couch. "I still can't believe I'm letting you make me watch a fucking Disney movie," he grumbled.

"You don't have to watch it. You can always do your own thing. But if you really want more from me, than you're going to have to work for it."

He mumbled something under his breath. Although he may have hated the idea, he gave the movie his full attention when it came on. I think something about it having music in it peaked his interest as much as he hated to admit it. When I snuggled closer to him, he glanced down at me in surprise. "I'm cold," I admitted.

"Here," he said, digging in a drawer beside the couch. He pulled out a blanket and wrapped us in it. "How's that?"

"It feels wonderful. Thank you."

"No problem." He then slung an arm around my shoulder, drawing me closer to him.

Halfway through the movie, my eyes grew heavy, and it wasn't long before I nodded off. I don't know how long I was asleep before loud voices and laughter, not from the movie, startled me awake. Rubbing my eyes, I looked up to see Jake begin to come back to life as well.

Back from their evening out, the boys were clambering up the bus steps. At the sight of me and Jake wrapped up in a blanket together, they froze. "What the…" AJ began.

He and Brayden then barreled forward like they were about to protect me from Jake's unwanted advances. I snaked my hand out from under the blanket and held it up at them. "Guys, calm down. Everything is fine."

Brayden glanced between Jake and me before cocking his eyebrows. "Seriously?"

I laughed. "Yes, it is. Jake's apologized for his previous bad behavior, and we're fine now."

With a wicked gleam in his eyes directed toward the guys, Jake added, "Oh we're more than just fine. We're sorta dating."

A collective gasp of shock rang through all the guys. "That's not entirely true," I replied.

Brayden threw his hands up in disbelief. "Excuse me if my mind isn't able to process such a thought. I mean, just how the hell do you make the quantum leap from banging Bree earlier in the day to dating our Angel?"

"We're not really dating—we're just getting to know each other better. He's going to have to prove himself to me before I'll date him," I explained.

Jake bobbed his head. "And I plan on working my ass off to do it."

Rubbing his hands over his face, Brayden replied, "I'll be damned."

AJ's gaze swept from the TV over to us. "He apologized and he's watching *Tangled*. I think Abby brainwashed him while we were gone," he joked trying to lighten the mood.

Jake and I laughed at his assumption. "Nah, there was no brainwashing involved," Jake replied. He winked at me. "She just helped me to see the light about what a complete and total jerkwad I was."

Rhys stood staring at us with a dumbfounded expression on his face. "Dude, I'm not gonna lie and say this doesn't surprise the shit out of me." He then stared at me. "Are you sure you know what you're getting yourself into?"

"No, not really, but then again, does anyone really ever know?" I countered.

"I guess not." He winked at me. "I guess that's why I steer clear of any relationships."

"Sure it is," Jake snorted.

When Rhys opened his mouth to argue, Brayden cleared his throat. "Okay, okay, I think we oughta call it a night. It's been a helluva long day with way too much crazy shit going down, not to mention we gotta show tomorrow night."

"Yes, Daddy," AJ teased.

"Douchebag," Brayden muttered under his breath as he headed to the bedroom.

I unraveled myself from the blanket before making a quick bathroom break. When I got out, Jake was waiting outside my roost. He held the curtain back like a gentleman would a door. "There's that good side showing through again," I commented.

He grinned. "Goodnight, Angel."

"Goodnight, Jake."

Leaning in closer, he whispered, "Thanks for giving me another chance."

"You're welcome. Just make sure you toe the line from now on out, and I'm sure we won't have any more problems."

He chuckled. "You're going to be the death of me."

I blew him a kiss before shutting the curtain. "Sweet dreams, Angel," he murmured. Drawing the covers around me, I fell asleep with the goofiest grin on my face.

***

Chapter Ten

Abby

The next morning we crossed over into Indiana—the next stop on Runaway Train's tour. As we sat around the table eating breakfast, the electricity in the air was palpable. It was amazing seeing the change come over the guys the sooner they got to their next performance. As we got closer and closer to Indianapolis, the more restless they became. The bus could barely contain the four of them. AJ drummed relentlessly on a smaller, plastic version of his real drum set. Rhys's Ivy League background showed through as he focused on playing golf on the Wii. Although Brayden was usually the one who was most level-headed, he paced the floors like a caged animal, occasionally stopping to text back and forth with Lily.

With ear buds jammed in his ears, Jake was the least restless of the guys. I guess he needed the music to tune the others out. He sat across from me at the kitchen table coloring in some sketches that Brayden had made for the band's next album cover.

As for me, I stayed the hell out their way and studied for my nursing exam. It was a little after two when we rolled into the parking lot of the Klipsch Music Center. I'd been reading and trying to tune out the guys' antics. But then Jake appeared in front of me, bouncing

161

on the balls of his feet and held out his hand. "Come on," he instructed.

I cocked an eyebrow at him suspiciously. "Just where are we going?"

He grinned. "You'll see. It's a surprise."

"I'm not real big on surprises. The last one had me getting on the wrong bus and falling into the bed of the notorious Jake Slater."

With a smirk, he replied, "That sounds like more of a dream come true than a surprise gone wrong."

I laughed. "You would say that."

"Come on. Trust me on this one." His tone had become almost whiney.

Pursing my lips, I couldn't help the tremor of excitement that went over me at his hopeful expression. "Okay. Wow me then," I replied, putting my book down.

"Ha! I knew you'd cave. No one can resist my charms."

"Such an egomaniac," I muttered under my breath as I put my hand in his.

As we started down the aisle of the bus, Brayden grabbed Jake's arm. "Where are you going? We got sound checks and rehearsal in an hour."

"I need to do something for Abby." He glanced over at me and smiled. "You know, make up for being such an unimaginable bastard and asshole yesterday."

Brayden's brows lifted in surprise, but he didn't argue. "Okay, man, whatever."

162

After pounding down the bus steps, Frank was waiting for us along with a beefy African American guy who looked like he could bench press me and Jake at the same time.

"Abby, this is Lloyd," Jake introduced, motioning to the guy.

Lloyd glared at Jake. "That's LL, thank you very much."

Jake laughed. "I love to tease him about his real name."

"Yeah and one day, I'm gonna make you pay for it, you little tool," LL threatened menacingly.

I hesitated for a moment before I held out my hand. "Um, nice to meet you."

His dark expression lightened, and he gave me a smile. "Likewise."

With LL trailing behind us, Frank led us into the arena. Once we got inside, Jake held up his hand. "We got it from here."

"I'll hang back, but I ain't leavin'," LL replied.

"No problem."

As we wound around through the darkened back of the arena, I snickered. "Hello Cleveland," I murmured under my breath.

"What?" Jake asked.

"I was just thinking that we seem kinda lost, and I was totally having a *This Is Spinal Tap* moment."

Whirling around, Jake's mouth dropped open. "You actually know that movie."

"Of course I do. I used to watch it with the boys all the time."

He shook his head slowly back and forth. "How is it that you're actually real?"

"Huh?"

Jake smiled. "You're like a guy's wet dream."

Wrinkling my nose, I replied, "Ew, thanks for the compliment."

"Okay, that didn't exactly come out like I wanted it to."

"I'd hope not."

He winced as he ran his hands through his hair. "I just meant that you're a musician's dream girl—a complete and total package. You understand what it's like to deal with the industry and what a gift and a curse the muse can be. Plus you know all about music and singing. To top it all off you're someone a guy could just hang out with and watch stupid comedies. Do you know what it's like to have a beautiful girl in front of me that totally gets you?"

"Thanks," I murmured. My cheeks instantly flamed at his words. When he stood there just staring at me, I finally admitted, "By the way, that was much better on the compliments."

"You're welcome." He took my hand. "Now come on. I have a big surprise for you."

"Once again, I really, really don't like surprises," I protested as he dragged me further back stage.

"You'll like this one."

Finally, we walked through the wings. Instead of stopping, Jake pulled me right on stage. I gazed out at the empty, but huge arena. Tilting my head, I spun around and took it all in. "Wow, this place is intense."

"I love it when it's like this," Jake confided, motioning to the crew who were rushing around with equipment. "It's like the calm before the storm." He bounced on the balls of his feet, and his whole body hummed with excitement.

"The storm that is Hurricane Jake?" I teased.

He laughed. "That would maybe be Tropical Storm Jake and more like Hurricane Runaway Train."

I smiled. "I love the fact you never leave the guys out of the equation. No Adam Levine and those other dudes in Maroon 5 kinda thing."

Jake shook his head. "The label tried that bullshit for a while right after we hit. But it's me and the boys or it's nothing."

Reaching over, I tapped his chest. "Such a good heart in there."

His hand closed over mine, and he pressed it flush against his shirt. "You don't know what it means to me that you're able to see that through all the bullshit."

"I see you a lot better than you'd ever imagine."

"And?" he prompted.

I swallowed hard under the intensity of his stare. "I like what I see. *A lot.*"

He then brought my hand to his mouth and tenderly brushed his lips across my knuckle.

"I'm glad to hear that."

My heartbeat thumped like a cannon blast in my ears, and I was sure Jake could hear it. Just when he leaned closer to me, a voice boomed from below the stage, "We're ready when you are."

His eyes momentarily closed. "The worst fucking timing," he grumbled before turning to the guy. "Thanks Joe. We better get this show on the road."

"Show?" I questioned in a squeak.

Jake turned back to me. "Yeah, last night after your phone conversation with that assmunch—"

"Garrett," I corrected.

"Whatever. Anyway, I thought about how scared and nervous you were at the prospect of not getting much rehearsal time to duet with the douchebag, so I thought I could help."

Suddenly Joe was at my side thrusting a microphone into my hand. "Jake, what's going on?" I asked.

"You're going to practice your duet to where you'll be perfect for Sunday night."

"But how—"

He waved his microphone at me. "We're going to sing it together."

"What?" I practically screeched.

Ignoring my shock, he said, "I know it won't be the same since we're going to have to use canned music. I mean, the guys wouldn't have had time to learn the song, but I know all the words."

I thought back to this morning when he'd had his headphones in, and my heart shuddered to a stop. "You memorized the song?"

"Sure did." He winked at me. "Lucky for you, I'm a fast learner."

"I can't believe it," I murmured.

Jake grinned as he tucked a stray strand of hair behind my ear. "Are you ready to rock this arena?"

If I had any doubts before about the depth of my growing feelings for Jake, they evaporated in that moment. I'd been with him for all of forty-eight measly hours, but somehow I had fallen for him. Wait, how was that even possible? I'd always scoffed at the notion of love at first sight. Stuff like that didn't happen. Sure lust at first sight, but love?

Never.

But now as Jake stood before me, I wondered if it could be true. Well, it was partially true since right after I laid eyes on him it wasn't love, but anger that I felt, especially when I nailed him in the balls.

"Angel, did you hear me?"

"Huh, what?"

"I asked if you were ready?"

"Uh, yeah, sure." I cleared my throat and tried to catch my breath. How the hell was I supposed to sing when my breathing was so erratic?

Jake appraised me with a skeptical look. "Are you sure? Your face has turned green like you're about to puke."

A giggle escaped my lips, and I covered my mouth. "I guess I'm just nervous."

Jake's eyebrows rose in surprise. "Seriously? It's only me here."

You're exactly what makes me incredibly nervous. "I know, but I haven't really done any warm-ups or scales either. I might sound like a sick cow or something."

He waved the microphone in his hand dismissively at me. "You don't need to do any of that. I mean, what are rehearsals for, right?"

"If you say so." I then bobbed my head. "Let's do it then before I lose my nerve."

Jake winked at me before calling, "Okay, hit it, Joe."

Within seconds, the music came blaring through the arena, causing me to jump. Jake brought the microphone to his lips, "I really hate to let this moment go," he began.

I couldn't move—it was like I had been shot with a taser gun and was completely paralyzed. I didn't blink or even draw breath. I just stood staring at Jake as he sang his lyrics with passion and feeling. It was only when he stopped singing that I came back to myself.

"Cut the music!" Jake shouted. Once the song came to a halt, Jake gave me a puzzled look. "What happened?"

"Huh?"

"Um, you didn't chime in with the chorus."

Oh God. I had been so totally enthralled by Jake's voice and performance that I had completely forgotten to sing. "I—uh—I guess it was nerves that got to me, and I blanked," I lied.

With a smile, he reached over and rubbed my arm. "Come on, you don't need to be nervous. Just tune out everything around us and focus on me and the music."

Yeah, right, focusing on you was what got me in trouble to start with! I decided it would be better to focus on the music along with the lyrics I should be singing. "Okay. Let's try it again."

"Again Joe!" Jake called.

This time I was just as into Jake's performance as I was before, but I managed to come in with my part at the chorus. When my voice echoed through the auditorium, I jumped, which caused Jake to bust out laughing. "Hey, you totally messed me up this time!"

He held up his hands in surrender. "I'm sorry. But if you could have seen the look on your face!"

168

"Jake," I growled.

"Okay, okay, I'm sorry." He turned to gaze off the stage. "Sorry Joe. Let's take it from the top again."

This time we made it through without any problems. When it came time for me to sing alone, I kept my gaze locked on Jake's the entire time. The gleam that burned in his eyes made me shudder, but I kept my focus and eventually became entirely lost in the music. The lyrics had so much meaning for what I was experiencing with Jake. I wanted to stay right there in that moment with him for as long as I possibly could.

When the music came to a close, Jake grinned. "You did it, Angel."

"I did!" I squealed. I then proceeded to do a little happy dance on the stage, which caused Jake to laugh.

"Is that your victory dance?" he asked, his voice vibrating with amusement.

As I continued shimmying my hips and high stepping on my feet, I nodded. "Yep, I think it is."

He shook his head and then reached over to ruffle the top of my hair. "You're such a goofball."

"Hey, the very fact I just sang in a huge arena deserves something."

"You wanna try it again?"

"Ooh can we?"

"Sure we can." A wicked grin curved on his lips. "I'm Jake Fucking Slater, and I can do whatever the hell I want."

Rolling my eyes to the ceiling, I huffed out a frustrated breath, which blew some of the stray strands of my hair out of my face. "Just when I think your ego couldn't get any bigger."

"Leaving my ego out of it, this time you need to focus not just on your singing but the delivery as well. Sure you hit all your notes last time, but you were a little stiff."

"I was?"

Jake laughed at my mortification. "I wouldn't say you were robotic, but you need to loosen up quite a bit. Let your body feel the lyrics just as much as your mind does."

"Okay," I murmured.

This time when the music came on, Jake became completely different. It was like he tuned out everything else. His singing was more heartfelt and filled with emotion. If I thought it was hard focusing before, it was even harder this time because I was so mesmerized by him—both as a performer and as my crush.

As I started my solo, Jake stepped closer to me, wrapping an arm around my waist. Since I thought he might be trying to trip me up, I kept my intense focus, but at the same time, I let my body follow with his. When it came time for the chorus again, his hand came to cup my cheek. Closing my eyes, I kept singing as I leaned in to his touch.

When he stepped away from me, I followed him, taking his hand in mine and intertwining our fingers. We finished the song hand in hand with our eyes locked on each other. As the music came to a close, I felt at any minute Jake would be able to hear the thundering of my heart.

"That was amazing—*you* were amazing!" Jake exclaimed.

"So I did better at the performance part?"

He gave a quick nod. "But I would suggest you don't get *that* into it when you're singing with Garrett."

"Why?"

He grinned. "Because you'll make me jealous if you look at him the same way you just looked at me."

I tried not melting into a puddle of emotion on the stage floor at his comment. "Okay then. That's only for you."

"Good. I'm glad to hear it."

The rest of the day was a whirlwind of events. After Jake and I finished singing, the other guys arrived at the arena to do their sound checks and rehearsals. Frank put an Authorized Personnel lanyard around my neck, and I stood in the wings and watched them. Once the sound check was done, we were hustled across the street for an early dinner. I couldn't believe how much food the guys put away. I was too nervous for them to eat, but they packed it all away, including dessert.

Then it was back to the arena to get ready for the show. While Jake and the other guys were ushered for last minute wardrobe fittings and then to the dressing room, I just milled around, watching the backstage rooms fill up with people I'd never seen before. Runaway Train had a *huge* crew and entourage compared to my brothers' outfit. I was trying my best to stay out of the way when my phone dinged with a text.

It was Jake. *Where r u?*

Just waiting on you guys to get ready.

Come back here with us.

I don't wanna be in the way.

U r never in the way. U r with me.

At the sight of his words, I had to take in a few deep breaths. *R u sure?*

Get your fine ass back here now!

I grinned. *You're so bossy.*

Now, Angel.

Yes sir!

As I started across the room to find Jake, a hand reached out and grabbed my arm. I yelped as he pulled me down onto his lap. A lustful gleam burned in his dark eyes. "Hello sexy, where you've been hiding all this time?"

It was then I recognized him as Tyler Mains, the lead singer for Vanquished, the group opening for Runaway Train. His dark hair was already styled to perfection along with his heavy stage makeup. I guess his idea of killing the last few minutes before he went onstage must've included thinking he could molest me.

"I've not been hiding anywhere!" I snapped, smacking his hands away. I started squirming out of his lap when his arms slithered around my waist.

His eyes drank in my appearance. "It's just I don't see your kind around here often. I mean, you're certifiable Grade-A Pussy." He grinned as he fingered the hem of my sundress. "Mmm, this is to die for when it comes to a quickie. You already got plans after the show?"

"Yeah asshole, and they don't involve being your plaything, thank

172

you very much."

He grinned. "Ooh a feisty one. I like that." Intertwining his fingers through my hair, he jerked me closer to where his alcohol-laced breath fanned across my cheek. "Do you fuck as feisty as you talk?"

"Let go of me!" I shouted.

"Get your damned hands off her before I break more than just your playing hand, Tyler!" Jake snarled.

My gaze snapped from Mr. Asshole Mains to Jake who stood towering over us. His fists clenched at his sides while the vein in his neck pulsed in anger. Tyler immediately let me go. "Sorry, Slater. I didn't know she was *your* piece of ass." He smirked at me. "Man, you must really be an amazing fuck if Jake's willing to get so defensive about you. But since I've shared pussy with him in the same night before, you think while he's on stage you could show me what's so amazing between your thighs?"

"You son of a bitch! I'll beat your fucking ass!" Jake snarled as he lunged forward.

"No Jake!" I cried. For a moment, I was pinned between the two of them. I shook my head at him. "It isn't worth it—*he's* not worth it," I argued.

As soon as Jake backed down, Tyler chuckled and murmured, "Pussy," under his breath. Blood boiled within me, and I reached out and slapped Tyler's cheek. Hard. "Don't you dare talk to me or about me like that ever again!" I then scrambled off of his lap. "And for the record, you're the last man on earth I would ever let touch me!"

Without a word to Jake, I stormed off to his dressing room. Jake was close on my heels because I almost slammed the door in his face.

AJ and Rhys looked up from their makeup chairs in surprise at my outrage. "What happened?" Rhys asked.

I was almost too upset to speak, so I sputtered, "T-That asshole Mains tried to molest me and then said things..." I shuddered.

AJ shot out of his chair. "I'll kick his ass!"

Jake held up his hand. "Easy, Terminator, but there's no need. I took care of it." He glanced over at me and grinned. "Well, I could say Angel here handled it on her own."

AJ's brows rose in surprise. "What did you do?"

"I slapped him."

With a chuckle, Jake added, "Yeah and she told him off too."

A wide grin curved on AJ's lips. "Hell yeah, baby girl. You keep on kicking ass and taking names!"

I giggled. "Thank you, I will."

From behind me, Jake's arms snaked possessively around my waist. He nuzzled my neck, and I shivered pleasantly. "I'm sorry you had to go through that. I know he said some pretty vile shit to you."

"He did. But I told him off."

The makeup artist beckoned Jake, and he sighed resignedly as his arms slipped away from me. I eased down on the couch and began watching all the preparation that went into getting the guys of Runaway Train stage ready.

When the guys were almost finished, I heard the roar of the crowd and the opening music for Vindicated. "I hope he falls flat on his face tonight," I mumbled.

Rhys and Jake roared with laughter while AJ glanced at me over his shoulder. "If I could find some good cayenne pepper powder and his change of pants, I'd make sure he didn't enjoy any groupie action tonight."

I laughed. "AJ, that's terrible."

He grinned wickedly as he waggled his brows. "You just say the word. I can always have some roadie go get me some."

"I think I'm good, but thanks anyway."

Once the guys were finished with hair and makeup, they were herded into wardrobe. Jake appeared a few minutes later wearing a pair of skin tight leather pants along with a red shirt that stretched across his muscles. "How do I look?" he asked.

"Wow…you look amazing!"

Jake eyed his pants disdainfully. "These are pleather so we can be politically correct. Thank God I get a wardrobe change halfway through the show because I'd much rather be in jeans."

"Yeah, but those pants are…." I glanced up at him and grinned. "Very, very sexy!"

A wicked gleam burned in his eyes. "Are you saying I need to keep these and wear them for you some other time?"

I laughed. "Now I don't know about that."

Jake reached out to pull me to him when Brayden stuck his head in the door. "Okay, Jake, it's time."

"Always the worst fucking timing," Jake muttered under his breath.

He then took my hand and started leading me to the door. I followed along blindly as we weaved in and out of roadies and

175

technicians.

When we got to the wings, Jake turned back to me. "I thought about getting you into the VIP box, but you'll have a better view here."

"So I can stay here and watch you guys?" I asked.

"Of course." He pulled me against him. "I want you as close as possible."

"Thanks."

"I also told Frank to keep an eye out for Tyler."

"While that's very chivalrous of you, I think I can handle things on my own."

Jake chuckled. "I'm sure you can, Angel, but it'll make me feel better knowing that you're being watched over."

"Fine. Whatever floats your boat," I replied.

As Vanquished made their exit off stage, Jake tightened his arms around me. Tyler only gave us a fleeting sneer before stalking away.

Then the stage lighting changed as Runaway Train's intro music began. AJ entered the stage first, waving to the crowd and throwing up rocker signs with his fingers. From the appreciative whistles and applause he was certainly a crowd favorite. He eased down behind the drum set and twirled the sticks between his fingers several times before beginning an upbeat tempo. I turned my attention from him to where a technician was handing Rhys his bass guitar. He put the strap over his head and adjusted it on his body before jogging out onto the stage, waving manically and grinning like a Cheshire cat. He then joined in with AJ's rhythm. Already outfitted with his guitar, Brayden nodded his head in time to the beat coming from the stage. I didn't know how he knew when to make his entrance since the noise was so loud, but then he entered as the stage lights began to flicker and change colors.

Jake leaned in close to my ear. "Magic time."

As he started for the stage and his big entrance, I grabbed his arm. When I kissed his cheek, he gave me a quizzical look. "That's for luck," I shouted over the roar of the crowd.

A smirk curved at his lips. "Thanks, Angel, but I don't need any of that."

I smacked his arm playfully. "There you go being an egomaniac again!"

He laughed and gave me a wink. The stage lights changed again and blared red as Jake entered from the wings. The already frantic crowd went even more insane. The noise caused a ringing in my ears, and I fought the urge to stick my fingers in them.

When Jake took the microphone off the stand, his signature cocky grin spread across his lips. A thunderous roar echoed through the stadium. "Hello Indianapolis! Are you ready to rock?" Jake asked.

At their response, he glanced over his shoulder at Rhys and Brayden. They shook their heads. "Hang on. I don't think I heard you. I asked if you were ready to FUCKING ROCK?"

If it were even possible to get louder, the crowd did. They stomped their feet, clapped their hands, and whistled and yelled. Jake grinned and nodded. "That's more like it." The lights went down and then the opening beat to their latest hit, "Unravel Me", began playing. The song featured a lot of heavy guitars, and I was amazed by Brayden and Rhys's skills. There was also the fact of the emotion that Jake emitted as he sang. One minute his voice had a hardened, bitter edge on songs like "Unravel Me" or "Twisted Reality".

Then when it came to the ballads, he would instantly change over, and his smooth, velvety voice echoed through the arena. My favorite of theirs was "Never Before You", which I knew from hanging around the guys that Brayden had written for Lily. I closed my eyes and swayed to the music. It was hard admitting to myself just how much Jake's voice affected me emotionally and physically, especially hearing him sing about love.

When the song ended, I opened my eyes to find Jake staring at me. I must've had a pretty serious expression on my face because he winked and then ran his tongue over his lips suggestively. Even though I should've been pissed, I couldn't help laughing. Only Jake would find a way to ruin a potentially romantic moment. I wagged a finger at him, and he threw back his head and laughed.

Next came the part of the show where they brought a fan on stage for Jake to sing to. My eyes widened when an older lady was led up by one of the stagehands. With wide-eyed wonderment, the woman stared up at Jake. When he grinned and winked, she blushed and giggled just like a young teenager as he began his way through "Your Smile."

After a few more fast songs, the show was over, and the guys were coming off the stage, exhausted and dripping in sweat. I couldn't help throwing myself at Jake. Wrapping my arms around him, I let him twirl me around. "I guess that means you liked it, huh?" he shouted

178

into my ear over the crowd.

Pulling away, I stared at his grinning face. "Liked it? Are you kidding me? I *loved* it! You were *amazing!*"

"Yeah, and I'm sweating like a pig now."

I snuggled closer to him. "If I get drenched in your sweat, I can probably make a fortune off this dress on Ebay," I teased.

"Oh, I can think of several more things to do to get me even sweatier." He waggled his eyebrows.

I pushed out of his arms. "No thank you! I think I'll pass."

"You would, Angel." He glanced over at AJ and Rhys who were already surrounded by a throng of girls. "Give me five minutes to change and then I'm taking you to dinner."

I glanced down at my dress. "I hope somewhere pretty low-key."

"I was thinking IHOP or somewhere like that. Nothing too fancy, Angel."

I laughed. "You sure know how to wine and dine me, don't you?"

"Whatever," he mumbled before he disappeared into the dressing room. True to his word, Jake reappeared in less than five minutes wearing faded and holey jeans and a black t-shirt. Of course, he could manage to make a burlap sack look hot and sexy. As we made our way to the exit, he asked, "You mind if Bray joins us?"

"No, of course not." We eased into the Hummer limo. "AJ and Rhys not coming?"

Jake grimaced. "No, they're busy."

Suddenly, I got his meaning. "Oh, I see." Thinking of them with random girls made me nauseous. "If I weren't here, would you be *busy*

179

too?"

Glancing out the window, Jake refused to meet my gaze. "Yeah, probably."

"I'm sorry if I'm keeping you from something."

His head whirled around to pin me with his stare. "You're not keeping me from anything. I'm exactly *where* I want to be at the moment and with *who* I want to be."

"Oh," I murmured.

"You don't sound like you believe me."

"No, it's just I'm surprised that's all."

He arched his brows at me. "That I want to eat pancakes with you over hooking up with some random bimbo?"

I drew in a sharp breath at his summation. "Yeah, pretty much."

Jake grinned. "Well, believe it, Angel because it's the truth. You're all I want or need at the moment."

Turning my head, I tried to hide the goofy grin that spread across my cheeks. Jake Slater wanted to be with me over groupies. That was a pretty amazing feeling.

***

Chapter Eleven

JAKE

Even though I fought hard against it, the next four days moved at warped speed with back-to-back shows. I would have given anything to have stopped the clock, so my time with Abby could have been savored and lasted longer. She was everything I could ever want or need in a girl, and the longer we spent together, the more I realized I hadn't been shitting Abby when I told her I'd never met someone like her.

I mean, what other girl would just sit around with me, talking all hours of the night about music, life, and family? She was the only girl I had ever been able to drag to an IHOP after a show and then go back to the bus for a jam session. We sang duets to crazy songs like Conway Twitty and Loretta Lynn's *Mississippi Woman, Louisiana Man* and then Ozzy Osbourne and Lita Ford's *If I Close My Eyes Forever*.

When Abby managed to one-up me by learning and singing some of our songs, I swore to her that I would drag her on stage with me at the next show. "Oh hell no!" she had replied.

For her last night on the bus, I'd asked Abby to sleep with me again, but this time we had the bed to ourselves. Nothing happened more than spooning, but I was glad to have her by my side.

But all too soon it was Sunday—the day she had to finally meet back up with the boys. We stopped for a somber breakfast at Cracker Barrel—Abby's favorite place to eat. She barely ate though. Instead, she pushed her food around while looking between us and tearing up.

With a frustrated grunt, I dropped my fork, and it clattered noisily onto my plate. "Would you stop that? These people are going to think we've abducted you or are abusing you or something because of how sad you look."

She sniffled and swiped her nose with her napkin. "I can't help it. I'm going to miss you guys." Although she said "you guys", she stared pointedly at me.

"We'regonnamissyoutoo," AJ muttered through a mouthful of pancakes. At her disgusted expression, he poked his lip out. "What can I say? I'm feeling your loss, Angel. I just gotta pack it in because I'm an emotional eater."

His comment brought a fleeting smile to her face, but all too soon it was gone. Once we finished eating, Abby called a cab to come pick her up.

"We can take you to the hotel."

"It's out of your way. I've imposed enough already," she argued.

With a grin, I replied, "Yeah, but you're an awfully cute imposition."

She laughed. "Thanks."

It was then that I hung back and watched Abby go through her goodbyes with the guys. Rhys went first. He hugged her and whispered something in her ear that made her giggle. When Brayden stepped forward, tears shone in Abby's eyes. Taking her hands in his, he spoke softly to her to which she bobbed her head in agreement. She leaned up and kissed his cheek before he pulled her into his arms. He rubbed wide circles over her back as she sniffled. When she finally pulled away, Bray kissed Abby's cheek.

As AJ stepped up to her, Abby couldn't stop the grin that formed on her lips. In a low and tender voice, he started speaking to her in Spanish. She tilted her head and listened to him, sometimes laughing, sometimes tearing up. When he finished, he wrapped her in his arms and squeezed her tight.

The longer Abby lingered in AJ's arms the harder I had to fight the jealousy that ricocheted through me. When he finally released her, he kissed both her cheeks. Then Abby turned to me with tears shimmering in her eyes, and I felt like I'd been kicked in the gut.

This was it. The moment I'd been dreading for days—the moment I actually had to say goodbye to my Angel. Taking her hand, I walked her away from the bus, so we could have a little privacy. When we'd put enough distance between us and the guys, I turned around. Dark circles formed under Abby's eyes, and last night I had felt her sobs even though she thought I was asleep.

Rocking back and forth on my heels, I shoved my hands into the back pockets of my faded and holey jeans. "So…"

"So," Abby repeated lamely.

I cocked my head at her. "It's kinda stupid saying good-bye because it's not like we're not ever going to see or talk to each other again. I've got your number, and you've got mine."

"Yes. Regardless of what happens with us, we'll always be friends."

"Exactly. It's not all ending just because you're getting off the bus. Hell, we're even song collaborators now."

She bit down on her lip to keep the tears that pooled in her eyes from escaping. "Sure."

I took a tentative step toward her. "Angel, what the hell is going on in that head of yours?"

Gazing up at me, Abby gave me a half-hearted smile. "It's just I can't help but wonder if that isn't the line you use with all the other girls. 'Hey babe, it's not good-bye'. Not to mention your epically loaded statement of 'I've got your number'. Kinda thinking there's been a string of girls agonizingly staring at their phones just waiting for a call from you that never came."

My brows creased in anger. "First of all, I'm not giving you some line. When I say I'll see you again and that I'll call, I fucking mean it. And second, there may have been a string of girls leaving this bus like you, but I sure as hell didn't get their numbers."

"You didn't?"

"No, Angel, I didn't." I brushed the silky, blonde strands of hair away from Abby's face to tenderly rub my thumb across her cheek. "Whatever it is that's started between us, I sure as hell don't want it to end."

She sucked in a harsh breath. "So you feel it that strongly too?"

I smiled. "Of course I do. It's like being zapped by a fucking lightning bolt each and every time you're near me. You make me think

184

things...*feel* things I never have before."

"So have you," she whispered softly. Her palms flattened against my chest. "Jake, I'm sorry for what I said earlier. I don't know what to do with all I'm feeling, especially since I have no experience with men."

"And I could argue that we're in the same boat here on being totally fucking clueless about what to do."

Bringing her hand up, she covered mine that was cupping her face. "I know people would tell me that because I'm inexperienced with guys, I'm wrong about what I'm feeling for you." She shook her head. "But I know without a shadow of a doubt the intensity of what I feel for you is real."

I feathered kisses along her hand and fingers. "Mmm, do you now?"

"I've fallen for you, Jake."

For a brief instant, it felt like she had nailed me in the balls again. Her words hit me that hard. After a few calming breaths, I managed to grin. "Well, that's good because I've fallen head over fucking heels for you, Angel."

She laughed. "You have such a way with words."

"What can I say? You bring out the romantic in me."

The taxi pulled up to the bus, and I winced. My chest caved in at the prospect of her leaving me, and I had to fight to breathe. I felt like a complete and total pussy. Dammit, when had I become reduced to a codependent dude who needed a woman to survive? But as much as I hated to admit it, the truth was I needed Abby. She was living and breathing peace to my troubled soul—an angel sent straight out of Heaven. Just a look from her could calm me instantly. With everything happening with my mom, I didn't know how I would make it without her.

Since she could read me so well, Abby threw her arms around my neck, and she pressed herself tight against me. "I wish I didn't have to leave you. I need you desperately, but I know you need me more."

"You're just a phone call away, right?" I asked, hating the way my voice broke with emotion.

"Yes of course. Day or night. If anything happens with your mom or upsets you or if you can't sleep, you can just call me, okay?"

I groaned. "You make me sound like an utter pussy."

She giggled, causing her warm breath to heat my neck. "You just have an amazing, tender heart, baby. Because of that, you're always going to feel more and hurt more than other people." Pulling away, she stared up at me. "Besides, it isn't a sign of weakness to need other people."

"No, it isn't."

"So you'll call me?"

"Oh hell yes, I will." I leaned over to kiss her. Even though I wanted to press her up against the bus and ravage her mouth while running my hands over her amazing tits, I knew I couldn't do that. Not only because I wouldn't dream of disrespecting my girl by giving the cab driver or the guys such a raunchy show, but because I didn't want to move too fast with her. It wasn't just her lack of experience—it was because I wanted to make everything perfect for her…and for me.

186

So with all the restraint I could muster, I brushed my lips chastely against hers. When she sighed in frustration, I pulled away. At her disappointed expression, I couldn't help laughing. Cupping her cheeks in my hands, I asked, "What was your first part of the duet we sang, Angel?"

"Um, it was about not moving too fast and making it last?"

"Nice rhyming, but yeah, that line." When her brows furrowed, I grinned. "I haven't had a relationship with a girl since the band hit big. I'm used to loving in the fast lane, and well, you're the emergency lane at best."

"Hey now," she giggled, smacking my arm playfully.

"So we gotta take this slow. I want to savor what I'm feeling and not ruin it with getting too physical too fast."

Abby pursed her lips at me. "And what if I want some parts of a physical relationship with you? I'm not talking the full deal…well, not yet anyway."

I threw my head back and groaned. "Thanks for trying to kill me, Angel. You've known me a week, and your rules are to be in love with the person, remember?"

She nibbled my bottom lip. "Yeah, well, maybe I'm on my way to falling in love with you."

At the honk of the cab's horn, I let out an exasperated breath. "We both have the worst fucking timing."

"But we'll at least continue this conversation later, right?"

"Yes, we will." I grabbed up her suitcase and guitar case.

"Wait, you don't—"

"Yes, I do. It's the gentlemanly thing to do."

She shook her head and then fell in step behind me. I eased her stuff into the trunk and then closed the lid. "Be careful."

"Thanks. You too."

"And knock em' dead tonight."

"I'll try."

I grinned as I opened the backseat door for her. "You will, and you know I'm always right."

She rolled her eyes but then smiled. "Bye, Jake."

"Bye, Angel."

As she started past me to get into the cab, I stopped her. Sometimes there were just moments you knew you would regret if you didn't follow your heart. Grabbing the back of her neck, I tipped her head up to mine. Then I brought my mouth to hers. This time I let the warmth of my tongue slide her lips open. When she made a little moan in the back of her throat, I tightened my arms around her waist. God, she tasted good. I could've kept on kissing her the whole afternoon, but a symphony of whistles and catcalls interrupted my moment of pure bliss.

I jerked away to see AJ, Brayden, and Rhys standing beside the bus. Warmth flooded Abby's face as I growled, "Thanks a lot, guys."

"¡Agarrale el culo, chica!".

Abby's eyes narrowed before she shouted, "Callete, cabron!"

"What did he just say?" I questioned with a grin.

"Grab his ass, girl," she replied.

"And what did you say to him?"

She grinned. "I told him to shut up and called him an asshole."

I laughed. "I'll make sure to knock the shit out of him for you."

"Gracias," she replied. Glancing at the guys, she shook her head. "I'm tempted to give you all the finger, but I'll just wave instead."

"Bye, Abby," they called in unison.

She turned back to me. "Talk to you later."

"It's a promise."

Without another show of affection, she dropped down onto the seat. "The Hilton, please,"

Abby commanded politely.

"Fine, but just so you know, the meter's been running, sweetie," the cabbie replied.

"It's okay." She glanced up at me and smiled. "It was worth it."

"Damn straight," I replied before closing the door.

Like a love-sick teenage girl, I stood waving at her until the cab disappeared over the hill.

***

Chapter Twelve

Abby

When I arrived at the hotel, all three of the boys were waiting on me in the lobby. I rolled my eyes but grinned in spite of myself. "Don't tell me you were afraid I might get lost and take up with another group of unruly rockers?"

Gabe chuckled as he pulled me into a bear hug. "Nah, we just wanted to do right by you this time and welcome you in person."

"Aw, that's sweet."

Eli's blue eyes twinkled. "There's also the fact we have to be over to the arena in an hour for sound checks and all."

I shook my head. "Just when I thought you guys were playing overprotective big brothers, you crush my dreams."

Micah threw his arm around my shoulder. "I've missed you, Baby Girl." He planted a kiss on my cheek. "Are you excited about tonight?"

Just the mention of performing caused my stomach to lurch. "Yes and no."

He nodded as we swept through the hotel's revolving doors. "I remember the first time I played in front of a packed crowd of tens of thousands of people."

I elbowed him playfully in the ribs. "Not helping, brother dear."

He grinned down at me. We were the matching bookends of the family with our blonde hair and blue eyes. Gabe and Eli were true fraternal twins in the fact that Gabe had about three inches on Eli while Eli was the more muscular of the two. The only matching trait was they had our father's jet black hair while we all shared the blue eyes of our mother. Even if they were my brothers, I had to admit they were good-looking. Of course, Micah had been engaged for six months to a girl named Valerie who worked at our dad's church. Like Brayden, he never even looked at other girls. Now the twins…that was another story.

"You'll be fine, Abster. After all, you're only singing one duet with Garrett and one song with us," Eli said as he held the limo door open for me.

As I flopped inside, I huffed out a frustrated breath. "Oh sure, just two songs. That's two prime opportunities for me to sing off-key, fall off the stage, etc."

Gabe sat next to me. "You worry too much. Just go out there and have fun. Pretend it's like when we were kids."

"Or you could do the old adage and pretend everyone's naked," Eli suggested while waggling his eyebrows.

I nudged his foot with mine. "You're so disgusting!"

After we made the short drive to the arena, the limo pulled up to the back. The boys' head of security, Manny, opened our door and gave me a beaming smile. "Good to see you again, Abby."

I gave him a hug—all 6'5", three hundred pounds of him. "Good seeing you again too." I motioned back at the boys. "You keeping them in line?"

He grinned. "Trying to. It's a hard job."

Giggling, I replied, "I can only imagine."

As Manny ushered us inside, someone outfitted in black with a headset came rushing up to me. "You're wanted on stage right now for your rehearsal with Garrett."

"Oh, okay." I turned back to the guys. "See you in a few."

"Knock em' dead, Baby Girl," Gabe called.

When I got to the stage, Garrett sat perched on a stool with his guitar, doing a run through of his other songs. After finishing the song, he glanced over and caught my eye. His face lit up. "Abby!" he cried before hurrying over to pull me into his arms. We'd only met a couple of times before, but by the way he was acting, you would have thought we were long lost best friends or former lovers. Jake would have gone for the second scenario.

"I see you made it safe and sound."

I laughed. "Yes, I did."

"Great. I'm stoked as hell to be singing with you." He waved at a technician who came to deliver my microphone. "Ready?"

"Sure."

After rehearsing with Garrett, I watched the boys go through their run-throughs before joining them onstage. For the first few shows, I'd only be singing a cover of The Band Perry's *If I Die Young.* Then the guys planned on me taking over some of the vocal leads Micah usually did. Once we went through everything, we were ushered back to our dressing room. While the boys chowed down on the catered food, I could barely down a slice of my mom's homemade pound cake.

The closer it got to show time the more the small space filled up with people. It felt like an out-of-control bee hive with all the conversions buzzing around me. Hair stylists, wardrobe people, management, and roadies streamed in and out. There was no privacy or time to catch my breath with all the madness.

When my mom and dad entered the room, they rushed over to me like I was a hostage who had been released from captivity. It was incredibly ironic considering I had Face-timed, talked, or texted with them every day that I was with Jake and the guys. "How are you sweetie?" Mom asked.

I laughed. "Just as good as I was earlier today when we talked."

"You look fine," Dad surmised.

"Jake and the guys took good care of me."

Mom and Dad exchanged a glance at my mention of Jake. "What?" I asked.

Shoving his hands in his khaki pants pockets, Dad cleared his throat. "Well, your mother and I were just talking about how you seemed to mention this Jake guy a lot when we talked."

I knew what he wanted to say but couldn't. "I like him."

Mom inhaled a sharp breath. "Like a boyfriend?"

With a grin, I replied, "Maybe." I took in the looks of horror that flashed on their faces. "Is there something wrong with that?"

"Uh, no, Abigail, there's not. It's just..." Dad fumbled around.

Mom stepped in for him. "It's just a relationship with a musician is hard. I mean, look at Micah and Valerie."

"Yes, I know. But sometimes you can't help who you have feelings for."

Dad's eyebrows practically shot off his head. "So you might be really serious about this guy?"

"Yes, Daddy. I really like Jake Slater from Runaway Train. Yes, I've only known him a week. Yes, he's a bad boy with tattoos and piercings, and yes, he's your worst nightmare when it comes to the guy dating your little girl." I leaned closer to him. "No, he's not taken advantage of me, and no, he's not going to turn me into a pierced bad girl with tattoos." With a tentative smile, I added, "We're both going to bring out the best of each other as we see where this takes us. Okay?"

Dad's mouth gaped open for a few seconds before he quickly shut it. I think it was one of the first times I'd ever seen him speechless. I turned to Mom who was equally as dumbfounded.

"Abby, we're ready for you," my hair stylist, Renee, said.

"I have to go." I glanced between them. "So we're okay—everything's okay?"

"Sure honey," Mom replied. She sounded a little more convinced than she looked. My dad, on the other hand, still continued to stare at me in shock. I guess I couldn't blame them for being shell-shocked at my declaration. They were going to need more time to absorb it all.

Leaving my parents behind, I headed into the hair and makeup

194

room. The moment I sat down in the chair, my stomach clenched into tight knots. Nervous energy hummed through me. Tapping my boot relentlessly on the floor, I stared into the lighted mirror in front of me as the band's stylist, Renee, made my loose curls bigger and bigger. From the way she was cementing my hair in place with hair spray, I was pretty sure half of the ozone layer was being depleted. Trying to calm down, I took a few deep, cleansing breaths as I sat outfitted in a silky robe.

When I dared to take in my reflection in the mirror, my nerves went into overdrive. Once Renee finished with my hair, Becca, the makeup artist took over and started going all out. I'd never had on so much foundation or blush in all my life, not to mention the fake eyelashes made me feel like a total hooker.

"Are you sure this isn't too much?" I asked.

Becca snorted contemptuously. "Unless you want to look like a corpse under the stage lights, you'll go with the flow."

So I went with the flow, which also included the biggest hairdo this side of a Dolly Parton wig. A roadie poked his head in the door. "Ten minutes, Abby."

"Oh God," I murmured before my whole body started trembling all over.

"Jeez, Abster, enough with the tapping!" Eli growled in the chair next to mine.

Immediately I stilled my foot. "Sorry. It's an anxious tic thing."

"You're going to be just fine," Micah reassured. When I glanced at him through my poofy hair, he smiled.

195

"I know. It's just I'm still scared of forgetting the lyrics or falling flat on my face."

His gaze honed in on my boots. "You scuffed them up pretty good, didn't you?"

"Oh yeah."

"Then you'll be fine."

Renee patted my shoulders. "All right. Time to get you to wardrobe."

I fell out of the chair and followed her through the door. I had yet to see what they had picked for me. I knew the boys never concerned themselves with what they were wearing, and I'd seen the same thing when I was on Runaway Train's bus.

As I started across the hall, a roadie tapped me on the shoulder before shoving my phone at me. "You have a call."

My brows furrowed. "Thank you," I replied before putting the phone to my ear. "Hello?"

"Hey Angel."

Those two words sent a shudder through me, and I skidded to a stop. "Hi, Jake," I replied breathlessly.

"I'm calling you for two reasons."

"Oh?"

"One is to prove that I'm a man of my word when I promised you I would call. And like a fucking love-sick puppy, I couldn't even wait a couple of hours to hear your voice."

Grinning like a fool, I fought to catch my breath. "I'm glad you proved me wrong.

Now what's the second reason?"

"I wanted to call you before you went on stage and wish you good luck. I figured you were pretty nervous."

I chewed my lip to keep from squealing out loud at his thoughtfulness. "I am...and thank you. It's awfully sweet of you to call."

"You have no idea just how sweet I could be for you."

With a snort, I replied, "Just when I'm thinking what an amazing romantic and heartfelt guy you are, there's the real Jake coming through loud and clear to remind me that you're truly a horndog."

He laughed. "I had to give you a little innuendo, Angel, to loosen you up."

"Well, I'm still nervous as hell. My knees are knocking, and I think I might puke."

Jake drew in a deep breath. "Abby, I told you that you've got nothing to be worried about. You have a powerhouse voice inside one hell of a beautiful package. You just go out there and sing your ass off like you did when we practiced."

Just hearing his deep voice say my real name caused my body to shiver. "Thank you, Jake. And I will." With my heartbeat accelerating, I debated whether to say what was on my heart. Finally, I blurted, "I'll pretend I'm singing with you again, instead of Garret. That'll get me through."

Silence came on the other end of the line, and for a minute, I thought I had lost him.

"Jake?"

"I'm here, Angel. And I'm glad to hear it. I wish I could be there singing it with you."

"So do I."

A roadie different from the one who brought my phone said, "Wardrobe is waiting for you in the dressing room."

"Oh, I have to go. But thanks for calling me. You don't know how much it means to me."

"You're welcome, babe. Now go and kick some ass on that stage, okay?"

I laughed. "I sure will."

The roadie then ushered me into a room down the hall. "Here she is, Cari," the roadie said.

A girl with pink hair sized me up. "About time," Cari muttered. Her hands went to the racks filled with clothes in front of her. She jerked out a coral colored dress and shoved it at me. "Here you go."

I quickly stepped behind the partition and slid off my boots. My robe then followed. Since the bodice was strapless, I slid off my bra as well. Huffing and puffing, I managed to stuff myself inside the dress.

"Um, any chance you have a different size?"

"Usually all dresses are custom fit, but you haven't been here to get measured," Cari snapped. Coming around the partition, she zipped me up harshly. Eyeing me, she nodded her head, "That looks hot."

"I. Can't. Breathe," I panted.

Cocking her head at me, Cari rolled her eyes. "Listen sweetie, you're just going to have to deal with it. Maybe I could throw something together for your set with your brothers, but you are out on stage with Garrett in five minutes."

A knock came at the door. "See?"

"Fine," I huffed. I was barely able to bend over and pull on my boots. I feared at any minute the zipper might explode.

"She's decent," the girl called.

Yet another roadie stuck his head in the door. "Five minutes, Miss Renard."

I smiled at him. "Please call me, Abby. And I'm coming."

He nodded and held the door open. Glancing back, I took in my appearance. "Holy shit," I muttered. I didn't even want to think about what Dad would say when he saw my outfit. I'm pretty sure he would have a coronary right at the sight of the dress. It ended way above my knees, and while the applique roses and lacy parts were pretty, my boobs looked like they would come popping out the top at any minute.

I followed the roadie out the door and to the stage. Thank God I had on my trusty cowboy boots and not heels, or I'm pretty sure I would have killed myself. When we got to the wings, Garrett was just finishing his signature hit "Just the Girl for Me". As the stagehands whipped around changing the set, Garrett put down his guitar and took the microphone off the stand.

"So I'd like to introduce y'all to a very special lady. Not only is she the baby sister and potential new lead singer for the amazing Jacob's Ladder, but she's my duet partner tonight for my final song. Would you all welcome Miss Abby Renard!"

I drew in a deep breath and pushed myself forward out of the wings. Throwing on my best megawatt smile, I started across the stage, waving madly at the crowd. Just when I thought my arm might fall off, I reached Garrett.

He whistled into the microphone and then winked at me. "Ladies and Gentlemen, I forgot to tell you how absolutely smokin' hot she was, didn't I?"

"Thank you, Garrett." I paused to let my gaze rove over him. "You're looking pretty fine tonight as well," I replied, trying my best to work the situation.

Turning to face the audience, he grinned. "She's sweet too, isn't she?" They whistled and applauded in response. "Just wait until you hear her sing. You're going to be blown away that not only is she a very beautiful gal, but she has an amazing voice as well."

I waved my hand dismissively at him. "You're embarrassing me with all the compliments."

"So are you ready to wow Des Moines?"

I smiled out into the audience. "Why yes, I am."

Garrett bobbed his head. "All right then. Let's do this."

The familiar melody of *Don't You Want to Stay* echoed throughout the arena. As soon as it came to my part with the chorus, all nervousness faded away, and I gave it my all. With only one quick rehearsal, I didn't know exactly what to expect out of Garrett. And just like I had promised Jake, I imagined it was him I was singing to, rather than Garrett. By the time I got to my solo, Garrett was all up close and personal. He winked at me as if to say, "Let's give them a hell of a show." But then I got the impression he might be actually enjoying rubbing against me or trailing his hands over my arms and back a little

200

too much.

But like the professional I knew I had to be, I forced a smile to my face and acted like I was enjoying it just as much as he was. When we finished, thunderous applause rang around us. "Thank you," I murmured breathlessly into the microphone.

All the loud whistling pierced my eardrums. I could see now why the boys wore earplugs. Garrett pulled me to him and planted a kiss on my cheek. "Thanks for giving our girl Abby such a warm welcome. I'm looking forward to working very closely with her over the next few months." He then winked at me again, and I gritted my teeth to keep from twisting away from his too-close-for-comfort hug.

"Thanks again! I'll see y'all again in the next set!" I called before hurrying off the stage.

Waiting in the wings, the boys launched themselves at me before I could hand off the microphone to the technician. Gabe pulled me into his arms for a big bear hug. "Way to go!"

"Can't. Breathe," I muttered.

"Oops," he replied letting me go.

I grinned at him. "But thanks."

Micah embraced me next. "Nice job, Baby Girl!"

With a wide grin, Eli smacked me on the back and cried, "Abster, you nailed it!"

"Aw, you guys were so sweet to come out and watch me."

"And this time it was all about sincerity. There's two more songs to go before our set."

"What sweethearts," I mused, pinching Eli's cheek.

"Hey now, don't mess up my makeup!" he whined.

"Such a pretty boy," Micah muttered under his breath.

"Speaking of pretty, wowzers that's some more dress," Gabe commented.

"Yeah, I'm changing before our set."

"That's good to hear," Dad said behind me. I whirled around and felt warmth flood my cheeks.

"I so did not have anything to do with this."

He stared at me a moment before a smile spread across his face. "It's not what I would have picked, but you sure look beautiful in it."

"Really?"

Mom nodded. "And you sounded wonderful, honey."

"Yes, you blew us both away," Dad replied.

"Thank you."

It was then Cari, the stylist, strode up to me. "Come on, Abby. I have another dress for you to try."

"Okay." I turned back to the boys. "Good luck. See you in a bit." I gave Mom and Dad a quick hug and kiss before trailing behind Cari to the wardrobe room.

After I saw my new outfit, I decided that Cari was more of a miracle worker than a devil. She had found a slightly longer dress—this time with sparkly, spaghetti straps and a beaded bodice. It was deep purple. "That's beautiful."

"Glad you like it," Cari mumbled as she unzipped my torture-device ensemble.

Now that my first performance was over, most of my nervousness had dissipated. There was only one person in the world I wanted to talk to. "Um, do you know what happened to my phone?"

Pressing a button, Cari spoke into her headset. "I need Abby's cellphone brought to wardrobe. Pronto."

"Oh, it's really not that big of a hurry."

Cari rolled her eyes. "Trust me, honey. You have to talk one way to these roadies and technicians. If you're not a bitch, shit doesn't get done."

As if to illustrate her point, a knock came at the door. "See?" she questioned with a grin.

I hurried into the dress while she went over to the door. Barely cracking it, she took it from the roadie and then brought it over to me. "Thanks!" I called.

Once she had fluffed the dress and adjusted the straps, she sent me on my way. I quickly dialed Jake. He answered on the third ring. "Hey Angel."

"I had to call you and tell you I did it! I sang, and everything went great!"

He chuckled. "I told you that you would. And once again, I'm always right."

"You're always such a smartass," I replied with a grin.

"Deep down, you like that about me."

"Maybe."

"So what are you doing now?"

"Stumbling along backstage before I go on with the boys."

"You aren't still nervous, are you?"

"No, I actually feel awesome—it's like a total adrenaline high. I could so get used to this feeling!"

"That's what performing in front of a crowd will do to you."

"Speaking of crowds, they seriously loved me, and they loved mine and Garrett's duet. Well, I did too except for the fact he got a little too into it."

A growl came on the other end of the line. "Yeah, you tell my man Garrett that the next time he wants to partially feel up my girl and practically dry hump her on stage that the least I'll do to him is break his guitar hand!"

"He wasn't feeling me up. He—" I froze in the middle of the hallway. "Wait, how did you know he did that?"

"Because I saw him."

My heart shuddered to a stop as I glanced wildly around. "Are you here?"

He laughed. "I wish I was, Angel. I would have especially liked to see you up close and personal in that naughty little red number you wore."

"But how—?"

"I had one of the technicians send me a live feed."

"You did that for me?"

"Hell yeah. I didn't want to miss your first performance for anything in the world, especially after our rehearsal."

"Oh Jake…that's so sweet."

"I've tried telling you before how sweet I can be for you," he replied with amusement vibrating in his voice.

"I know."

"You'll think I'm even sweeter when you get back to the bus and find the flowers I sent you."

"Really?" I squealed.

"Well, some of them are from all of us guys, but there's a special dozen just from me."

My heart swelled in my chest to where I feared it might burst right out. "Oh wow, that's so sweet and thoughtful. Thank the guys for me."

"I will."

"You're amazing too."

"I know."

I giggled. "Such an egomaniac."

A roadie waved at me to get my attention. "Five minutes!" he called.

"Oh Jake, I have to go," I lamented.

"Wait, I need to ask you something."

"Sure. What is it?"

"I wanted to see if you would come with me to my sister's Sweet Sixteen party in two weeks. Since the guys and I are playing, we're making a big weekend out of it. Brayden's wife, Lily, is flying in with the kids. Do you think you can make it?"

Oh wow. Jake was inviting me to something that involved meeting his family. This was huge…and fast. *Breathe, Abby.* "Um, yeah, sure."

"If you need to soften the blow with your brothers about running off with me, you can tell them I plan to take you into the studio to record *I'll Take You with Me.*"

"Holy shit!" I exclaimed.

Jake chuckled. "Does that mean you want to come?"

"Yes, I definitely want to come. I just can't believe you still want to record with me."

"Of course I do, and one of my favorite places to record is in Atlanta."

"Wow, this is still so unbelievable."

"Well, believe it. There will be a plane ticket waiting for you back at the hotel. My people have taken care of everything, including the hotel. It's all on me."

"That's too much. I can't let you do that, Jake."

"Yes, you can, and you will. It's my trip, so it's my treat."

"You're so bossy."

He laughed. "Yep and you better get used to it."

"Okay, okay, I'll accept."

"Glad to hear it, Angel."

When the roadie reappeared and beckoned me to the stage, I sighed with frustration. "I gotta go, Jake."

"All right. I'll talk to you later tonight, and then I'll see you in two weeks."

***

Chapter Thirteen

JAKE

Standing in front of the lighted hotel mirrors, I adjusted my black, silk tie. Even though I'd barely had it on five minutes, it was already choking me to death. AJ groaned beside me. "Remind me again why we have to wear suits?"

I rolled my eyes. "Cause this is my baby sister's Sweet Sixteen we're playing, and we're not going to look like a bunch of rocker hoods."

AJ tilted his head at me. "But I thought we *were* rocker hoods?"

With a laugh, I replied, "Not tonight. We're going to blend in with the normal stiffs aka the elite of Atlanta."

Rhys shuddered next to me. "I thought I had escaped all the high-society bullshit when I left home. I swear, if someone tries to 'present' their daughter to me as a suitable marriage candidate, I'm outta here."

I thumped his back. "I think you're fine, man. Sorry for inducing some flashbacks of your horrible youth spent in the country clubs and finest social circles of Savannah."

Rhys scowled. "Okay, so I'm a douchebag for whining about growing up rich, but dude, high-society people are as cutthroat as ghetto people sometimes."

"Whatever," I murmured as my phone buzzed at my side. One

glance at the ID, and I was grinning like a fool.

"Dawww, iz Abby messaging her hunny-bunny," AJ teased.

I flipped him off as I started reading. *Hey baby, I'm ready. Want me to come down and meet you guys?*

Sure. I'll be in the lobby. Can't wait to see u.

Be there in 5.

The last two weeks had been a dizzying flurry of different tour stops and cities. But one thing remained consistent and true, and that was my feelings for Abby. Any downtime I had, I spent with her via text messaging, calls, Facetiming, or Skype. It was long-distance dating in the 21st century at its finest.

"You guys ready? I gotta go meet Abby."

"As ready as I'll ever be to go play to a room with a bunch of screaming, horny teenage girls, most of them if I even look at, I could get arrested," AJ replied with a grin.

"You're a douche," I muttered as I exited the bathroom.

Leaving the guys behind, I strode through the elaborately decorated ballroom. I wanted to get to the lobby and Abby. She had flown in earlier in the day. After meeting up with Lily and the kids at the airport, Brayden had brought Abby back to the hotel. I'd been rehearsing, so I hadn't gotten to see her yet. Although I felt like a giant pussy, Brayden had talked me into sending Abby with Lily to the hotel spa to get her hair and makeup done. Of course any doubts about whether I had balls left or not was short lived when Abby's excited squeal came over the phone when she got my gift.

Craning my neck, I peered through the crowd of people. Like out of a movie, it parted, and there she stood. For a minute, I couldn't breathe at the sight of her. She looked so fucking beautiful that she took my breath away. Her long blonde hair cascaded in curly waves over her shoulders, and she was wearing more makeup than usual.

When she caught sight of me, her face lit up, and she started running as best she could in the sexy-as-hell heels she was wearing. "Jake!" she cried before throwing herself into my waiting arms. I spun her around before sitting her back on her feet. Her blue eyes twinkled as she took me in. "Look at you!" she exclaimed as she ran her hand down the front of my suit. "You look amazing!"

"I look like a real gentleman, don't I?"

She grinned. "I think even my dad would approve of you tonight."

Part of her comment stung, but I covered up my feelings by giving her a cocky smirk. "Yeah, well, what would he have to say about his daughter's attire tonight?"

She glanced down at her dress. "You like it?"

Considering it had flimsy little straps, showed off her fabulous rack and was almost backless, hell yes, I liked it. "I love it. You look absolutely breathtaking tonight."

Abby's cheeks warmed with my compliments. She leaned up to kiss my lips. "Thank you."

"You're welcome."

AJ strolled up to us. At Abby's attire, his eyes widened. "Oh my God, Angel! That is just like the dress Sookie wore in the Season Two finale of *True Blood*!"

Abby rolled her eyes. "AJ, you've got a *True Blood* fetish."

209

He grinned. "Dude, it's basically vamp porn!"

She laughed. "You're impossible."

"Yeah, well, you're beautiful and sexy in that dress."

With a beaming smile, Abby smacked his arm playfully before giving him a hug. "Thank you. You guys are all looking so handsome in your suits," she replied.

I took Abby's hand in mine. "I want to introduce you to someone."

"Okay."

Surrounded by a group of her friends, Allison talked and laughed. When I tapped her on the shoulder, she whirled around, causing her dark hair to fly around her shoulders. "Jake!" she cried before launching herself at me. I hugged her tight. Regardless of how I felt about my dad and step-mother, Allison had always been my baby sister to love and protect.

"You look beautiful," I murmured into her ear.

"Thanks."

"I can't believe you've gone and grown up on me." I pulled away and grinned down at her. "Just promise me you'll keep being my sweet, innocent little Allison."

She giggled. "I'll try."

Turning back to Abby, I said, "I wanted you to meet my girlfriend. This is Abby Renard."

At the word "girlfriend", Allison's dark eyes almost bulged out of her head. "Wow, it's awesome to meet you," she gushed, shaking Abby's hand.

"It's great finally meeting you too. Jake talks about you all the time."

Allison beamed with pleasure. "He's amazing, isn't he?"

Abby grinned. "Oh yes, he is. But we better not say too much. He already has a big enough ego about him."

"Hey now," I argued to which Abby nudged me playfully.

Brayden came up behind me. "Okay, man, it's time."

"Excuse me ladies, but my adoring public beckons, so I'll see you later."

Abby and Allison waved to me as I headed to the stage with Brayden. The plan was for us to play the first thirty minutes of the party, and then the DJ would take over. AJ disappeared behind the drum set while the rest of us suited up with our guitars.

Taking the microphone from the stand, I gazed out into the crowded ballroom. "Good evening, everyone, and welcome to Allison's Sweet Sixteen Party." A symphony of high-pitched, hormonally fueled teenage girl shrieks filled the room along with some hearty screams from the males. "As her big brother, I couldn't be prouder of her at this moment." Meeting Allison's gaze, I smiled. "I hope all your dreams come true, and that you stay forever young."

The guys and I then launched into a harder rock version of Chrissy Hydne's *Forever Young*. We finished to thunderous applause and cheers. I searched through the crowd of faces for Abby who grinned and gave me two thumbs up. I laughed and shook my head before starting "Unravel Me", which got everyone dancing. After playing through two more fast songs and two of our ballads, I handed the mic off to the DJ and headed through the throng of people to Abby.

I was almost to her when my dad stopped me. He gave me a stiff hug before saying, "That was fantastic, son. We can't thank you enough for making this night so special for Allie."

"You're welcome. You know I'd do anything for her."

He nodded. His lips twitched as if he wanted to say something else but was afraid to. Finally, he drew in a ragged breath. "Jake, I'm so very sorry about your mother."

I instantly tensed. "Yeah, it fucking blows when bad things happen to good people."

Dad's expression paled a little. "She's one of the strongest and bravest women I know. I talk to her often, you know. She has the most forgiving of hearts."

I knew Dad was talking about how I couldn't forgive him for the fact he walked out on Mama and me for a piece of ass. Sure, he paid his child support and saw me every other weekend and during the summers. On the surface he was the most attentive and supportive father. But everything changed with us the moment he chose to leave.

"Yes, it's probably one of her only faults."

Seeing he wasn't getting anywhere with me, Dad sighed. "Well, just know I'm here for you, son. Always." His gaze left mine to hone in on Abby who had sought me out. "And who is this lovely young lady?"

"This is my girlfriend, Abby Renard." I slipped my arm around Abby's waist. "And Abby, this is my dad, Mark Slater."

"It's very nice to meet you, Mr. Slater," Abby said politely.

"Likewise, Miss Renard." Dad's gaze roved over Abby, and I

could tell he was surprised. Because even in her sexy little dress, Abby still looked like a good girl, and I'm sure Dad couldn't believe I was actually with someone like her.

As the music turned over to a slow song, I wanted to escape from my dad. Glancing down at Abby, I asked, "Wanna dance?"

"Sure." She smiled at my dad. "Nice meeting you."

"Yes, very nice meeting you as well." He patted my back. "Thanks again."

"You're welcome."

I took Abby's hand and led her out onto the dance floor. As I wrapped my arms around her waist, she pressed against me. Damn, she felt good. I tried tuning out the myriad of disgusting sexual thoughts swimming through my dirty mind.

"Your dad seems nice," Abby said.

"Oh yeah, he's a real stand-up guy."

She pulled away to gaze up at me. "So I was right to come and try to save you?"

When I stared at her quizzically, she smiled, "You're so easy to read sometimes, Jake. I could tell from across the room that you were uncomfortable talking to him."

"The bastard had the nerve to bring up my mom," I muttered through gritted teeth.

"I'm sorry."

"I don't want to talk about him or her, okay?"

"Okay, Grumpy."

Only she could get away with teasing me. I glanced down to find her smiling up at me. "You can be such a little shit, did you know that?"

She laughed. "But you love it."

"For reasons I can't possibly understand, I do." I pulled her tighter against me. "You smell so damn good."

"I have you to thank for that. The spa really helped to clean me up."

"Oh whatever. You always look beautiful and sexy."

"I always want to for you—you and only you," she murmured.

Taking her chin, I tilted her head before bringing my lips to hers. Although I wanted to consume her mouth, I held back. I'd missed her taste, the warmth of her tongue, the way she let her desire drive her body, rather than her insecurities or doubts. When I finally pulled away, we were both breathless. "Damn, I've missed you."

She laughed. "You act like I've been on the other side of the world. We talk a million times a day."

"Yeah, but I don't get to *kiss* you a million times."

"Then I guess we have a lot of lost time to make up for."

I grinned. "I think so too."

The announcement for dinner was made, so we headed off the dance floor and to the table we had been assigned. Just as I suspected, Lily and Abby had become fast friends, and Abby loved helping out with Jude and Melody.

After stuffing ourselves on the three courses, Abby and I sat around talking with the guys. As I watched her holding Melody and cooing softly, I couldn't help the way my heart swelled with love. I'd never thought about marriage or kids before, but something about the way Melody played with the strands of Abby's hair and gazed up at her made me rethink everything about my life. But I wasn't Bray, so I wasn't sure I was marriage and father material.

When Abby glanced up and caught me watching her, she smiled. "Wanna go see Uncle Jake?"

I held out my arms, and Melody happily came to me. I kissed her chubby cheek. "Hey baby girl. You gotta smile for me?"

Melody tilted her head and grinned, showing me her two, tiny bottom baby teeth. "That's my girl."

As I bounced her on my knee, AJ undid the first three buttons on his shirt and ripped off his tie. "I'm ready to dance."

"You've been dancing the entire time we haven't been on stage," I replied.

"No, I mean, I *really* want to dance."

"Ugh," I groaned. "You mean that Mexican shit."

"Jake!" Abby admonished, motioning to Melody.

"Angel, do you really think she hasn't heard worse? We cussed like sailors around Jude, and I promise you his first word wasn't fuck."

She crossed her arms over her chest in a huff. "You're terrible."

AJ leaned his elbows on the table. "Anyway, as I was saying, I'm ready to do some dancing." He waggled his eyebrows at Abby. "And I know the perfect partner. Come on, Angel. Let's show these stiffs how it's really done."

Abby giggled and turned to me. "Is that okay?"

"Sure, go ahead."

215

Squealing with delight, she let AJ pull her up from the chair. He tugged her across the room to the dance floor. I watched AJ lean in and talk to the DJ. After a few head shakes, AJ bobbed his head. Once the other song ended, the DJ grabbed his microphone. "Okay, we've had a request for Paula Rubio's *Dame Otro Tequila*, and according to AJ, he and Abby are going to show you losers how to break it down."

A roar came through the crowd along with a symphony of high pitched female squeals at just the mention of AJ. In his element, he bowed gallantly before the music came on. The upbeat tempo and references to tequila got the crowd going even if they didn't know the words. Then he and Abby began moving effortlessly around the dance floor.

I eased Melody from my lap to my shoulder as I watched Abby dance. Although I didn't want to, I couldn't help the jealousy pricking over my body at the sight of Abby getting so into the motions with AJ. I blew out of a frustrated breath, which Melody mimicked. When I laughed, she grinned. "See that girl," I pointed to Abby. "I think I love her, and it's making me act like a total idiot."

Melody waved her tiny hand at Abby. "Yeah, even you are already in love with her, and you've known her like what, five seconds. She does that to people."

After inhaling a sharp breath of frustration, a nasty smell assaulted my senses. Leaning forward in my seat, I tapped Brayden's arm. "I believe your daughter has a surprise for you."

As I passed Melody to him, he laughed. "Thanks. We'll take care of it."

"Trust me dude, friendship only goes so far, and it doesn't involve shitty diapers."

"Wow, I'm so touched," Brayden replied before rising out of his seat. I snickered at the sight of him with the pale pink diaper bag draped on his shoulder. He bent down and kissed Lily's cheek before heading to the bathroom with Melody "Now that's love," I murmured under my breath.

My gaze once again went to the dance floor to Abby and AJ. "I need some air," I muttered to Rhys. He gave me a knowing smile before bobbing his head. Grabbing two champagne flutes from a passing waiter, I made my way out the side door of the ballroom.

***

Chapter Fourteen

After AJ and I finished our dance, beads of sweat were dripping down my face and back. I was so thirsty that I gulped down a flute of champagne the moment we got back to the table and had started on another. "Ugh, I need water."

Easing down in a chair beside me, AJ asked, "So I assume the way you're throwing it back you've acquired a taste for champagne?"

I wrinkled my nose. "Actually, it just kinda makes me wanna burp. Now these," I picked up a chocolate strawberry off the dessert platter on the table and waved it at him, "These I enjoy a lot."

"Yeah, well, just go easy on getting tipsy. You've got to be at the studio really early in the morning, right?"

"Eight." Then I squealed and dropped the strawberry.

AJ's dark eyes widened at me. "What the hell is wrong?"

"I'm singing in the morning."

"Yes and..." he prompted.

I rolled my eyes. "I've been eating my weight in chocolate tonight, which has dairy in it.

You're never supposed to do that."

At what must've been the absolute horror on my face, AJ patted my leg. "You'll be fine. Flush it out with some water."

"Shit," I muttered as I flagged down a waiter. Once he brought me a glass, I downed it in three long gulps. I then eyed the room for my noticeably absent date. Lily and Brayden were dancing while Rhys sat beside with a sleeping Melody in his arms. I craned my neck around the room. "Where's Jake?"

Rhys motioned to the courtyard outside. "He said he needed some air."

AJ nodded as he eyed Jake's dad, Mark, dancing with Jake's stepmom, Paula. "Even though it's been fifteen years, sometimes Jake still can't take the two of them together."

Rhys snorted. "Yeah, I don't think *them* dancing together was the issue."

When I got his meaning, my heart did a funny little shuddering before I rose out of my chair. "I better go check on him." I hurried out the side door and onto the tiled pavement. In the middle of the courtyard was a huge, circular fountain. It had a giant swan in the middle of it that was illuminated by light.

Jake sat on the edge of the fountain with his elbows braced on his knees. "Hey."

"Hey," he replied.

I eased down beside him. We sat in silence for a few seconds before I nudged him playfully. "I was kinda thinking for a minute there that I'd been jilted."

He glanced up at me. "Sorry. I just needed some air."

Tilting my head, I gazed up at the stars. "It's nice out here."

"Without your dance partner?" he spat.

I couldn't help the smile that curved on my lips. He was jealous of me dancing with AJ. "The only dance partner I want is out here."

"Hmm," he muttered.

Tension hung heavy around us. Trying to ease the mood, I slid out of my killer heels. I groaned in agony. "Remind me to hunt down the person who invented heels."

"Yeah, well, it's your fault for going out there with AJ and acting like you two were on Dancing with the Stars or some shit."

"Jake Slater, I do believe you're jealous."

He jerked his gaze to meet mine. "I am not!"

I grinned. "Pity. I kinda like the idea of you being all caveman possessive sometimes."

"Sure you do."

I scooted closer to him. "There will never, ever be anything between me and AJ. You know that, right?"

"I guess."

"He and I just wanted to dance and have fun."

"And sadly for us, your partner has no rhythm, huh?"

"No, you did just fine before."

He smirked at me. "Just fine?"

"Fabulous? Incredibly sexy moves?"

"Much better."

Taking his chin in my hands, I turned his head to where he had to look at me. "For me, it's always you, and it's only going to be you,

Jake."

The corners of his lips twitched before they curved up in a cocky grin. "I'm glad to hear that."

"I want you think about this for a minute though. That little bit of jealousy you felt over me and AJ. Magnify it by like a million for what it feels like when I think of all the other women you've been with or all the women who want you."

He glowered at me. "That's bullshit."

I shrugged. "Yeah, well, since we're being honest, that's how I feel."

"You're the only one for me, Angel. Hell, you're the only one I'm even bothering to try a relationship with. That should tell you something."

I smiled. "It does, and it means a lot." I cocked my brows at him. "So are we good?"

"We're good."

I winced as I crossed my legs so I could massage one of my aching feet. "Ugh."

"Here let me," Jake offered.

"Seriously?"

A sexy gleam burned in his blue eyes. "You know I would never pass up the opportunity to touch you—even if it is your nasty, sweaty feet."

"Hey now," I replied as I scooted back on the cement foundation. I swung both my legs up to rest my feet in Jake's lap.

"Feel good?" he asked as his hands began kneading my foot.

221

My eyelids fluttered before I closed my eyes. "Mmm, you have magic fingers."

Jake chuckled. "You have no idea, babe."

I squinted one eye at him. "Watch it."

When he dug his hands into the arch of my foot while working the sole as well, I forgot all about his comment. "Oh God," I moaned, throwing my head back.

Scooting over, Jake's body pressed closer against mine. His breath came scorching against my cheek. "Damn, Angel, if I get that kinda response from just massaging your feet, I can't wait to see what happens when I—"

"Don't even go there, naughty boy!" I cried, shoving him away.

Not realizing my own strength, Jake wobbled before crashing backwards. I held on to the sides of the fountain for dear life so I wouldn't go in with him. At the huge splash, I covered my mouth in horror. His legs, that still hung over the concrete side, were the only things dry. He spewed water out of his mouth from where his head had momentarily gone beneath the water. "Oh my God!" I murmured behind my hand.

Propped on his submerged elbows, a stunned Jake stared up at me for a few seconds. Then a smirk stretched across his drenched face. "Besides nailing me in the balls, I think that is the second most epic cockblock you've ever given me, Angel!"

I held up my hands. "I'm sorry. I so didn't mean to do it!"

"You're just too sassy for your own good. I think you need some cooling off." A wicked gleam flashed in his clear blue eyes.

I wagged my finger at him. "Oh no. Don't you dare!" I cried, trying to scramble away.

The next thing I knew Jake's strong hands were gripping my waist. "No don't!" I screamed futilely before he hoisted me up and dragged me over the side. I squealed as the first deluge of icy fountain water pricked over my exposed skin like tiny little knives.

Huffing and puffing, I tried to adjust to the temperature as water cascaded down the front of my dress and other areas. "You bastard!" I cried, splashing Jake in the face.

He chuckled as he rubbed his eyes. "You pushed me first."

"But I didn't mean to get you wet." I glanced down at my dress. "Ugh, I'm soaked through."

He waggled his brows. "I like you wet."

I rolled my eyes. "Of course you do." On wobbly legs, I pulled myself to my feet. "I'm sure this dress is practically see through now."

Jake's hungry gaze roved over me. "Almost." Taking my arm, he jerked me back down next to him. Cupping my face with his hands, he stared into my eyes. "You're so fucking beautiful, Angel."

Leaning in, he kissed a trail across my wet cheek before hovering precariously over my mouth. Tenderly, his lips pressed against mine. Pulling away, he stared into my eyes to gauge if I was okay with what he was doing. "Don't stop," I whispered before bringing my mouth to his.

This time his lips were hungry as they worked against my own. When I gasped with pleasure, he thrust his tongue in my mouth to swirl around mine. The world around me began to spin in a dizzying flurry. I couldn't get enough of him. My fingers raked through the wet strands of his hair. When I tugged them, a low growl came from the back of his throat, causing me to jerk away.

"Did I do something wrong?" I asked.

Jake's hooded eyes opened, and he gave me a crooked grin. "No, baby, that wasn't wrong. I liked it."

Heat warmed my cheeks. "Oh, I'm sorry."

"Don't be sorry for doing something hot." When I started to protest, he shook his head.

"You'll learn, Angel, and until then, nothing you could possibly do would ever make me not want you." His teeth grazed against my bottom lip. "Mmm, you taste sweeter tonight than before."

With my chest heaving under his intense gaze, I panted, "It must be the chocolate covered strawberries."

His thumb rubbed back and forth across my lip. "Regardless of what you've had, I like the way you taste." He then replaced his thumb with his tongue. I couldn't help the whimper that escaped my lips.

Gripping my waist, he pulled me over to straddle him in the water. His hands ran up my back and tangled into my wet hair. Something took over within me, and I began to move my hips. I rose up and then fell back against him. "Oh Angel," Jake groaned into my mouth as he bucked his own hips against mine.

I sucked my bottom lip between my teeth as the friction started to get to me. But I was brought out of my haze of desire when out nowhere beams of light and water shot all around us. On the hour, the fountain put on a show, and we were right in the middle of it. I squealed as the hard streams beat against my back and head.

"Son of a bi-" Jake started before he was doused in the face.

It was then that I began to laugh at the absurdity of the situation. As the water sprayed around us, I doubled over, shaking from amusement. When I peered up at Jake through my drenched strands of hair, he was wiping his eyes both from the water and from laughter. "I think you can mark that as your third most epic cockblock!"

"Damn you fountain!" he shouted kicking up his leg and splashing water. He then wagged his finger at the swan. "Cockblocker!"

I dissolved into giggles and didn't realize we had an audience. The guys stood staring at us. "What the hell happened?" Brayden asked.

"We sorta had a little accident," I replied.

Jake snickered. "You could say that." He put one leg over the side of the fountain and climbed out. He then held out his hand to help me.

Rhys crossed his arms over his chest. "And just how exactly do two people fall into a fountain that isn't more than a foot deep?"

"It's a long, somewhat sordid little tale that involves a foot massage, dirty thoughts, and cooling off out-of-control libidos," Jake replied.

"Huh?" AJ asked.

"I'm freezing. I gotta go get into some dry clothes," I said as I walked past the guys.

"Well, the party is breaking up, so there's no need to worry about coming back down. Plus, you guys have an early morning recording session," Brayden replied.

Jake nodded. "Do me a favor, Bray, and go tell my dad what

225

happened. I'll throw something on and come back down to say goodbye to Allison." He then turned to me. "Come on, Angel. Let's go get changed."

"Wait, my purse with my room key is on the table."

"I'll go get it for you." AJ hustled inside and then returned quickly looking quite comical carrying my satin clutch.

"Thank you."

"Anything for you, Angel," he replied with a grin.

As Jake and I made our way to the elevator, we got quite a lot of funny looks from the other hotel guests. I guess it wasn't everyday they saw two drenched people in formal wear. When we got to my room, I dug around in my purse for the keycard.

Jake leaned one arm against the suite door above my head. "Want me to come in and help you change?" A wicked gleam burned in his eyes. "I'd love to help you out of that drenched dress."

I laughed. "No thank you. I think I'll manage just fine."

"You're killing me, Angel. I think I have the blue balls to prove it."

My eyes widened. "What happened to the 'we need to take it slow and savor every moment' plan?" I asked.

"I realized that plan was fucked the moment I saw you across the lobby tonight."

His words caused my heartbeat to drum wildly. It took everything I had within me not to jump into his arms. "Patience, Mr. Slater. All good things come to those who wait."

He waggled his eyebrows at me. "I just don't want to wait that long to come!"

"Goodnight, Jake," I huffed.

"Goodnight, Angel. Sweet dreams about me."

I glanced back at him over my shoulder and grinned. "And sweet, G-rated dreams about me for you."

He groaned. "You're killing me."

With a laugh, I let the door close behind me.

***

Chapter Fifteen

JAKE

Regardless of how much I wanted to sleep in the following morning, I was dressed and downstairs at eight am sharp for the car to take Abby and me to the recording studio. As she hopped in the backseat, I didn't miss the yawn that stretched across Abby's face. "Sleepy?" I asked as I shut the door behind us.

"A little," she replied with a grin. She then scooted across the leather seats to snuggle against me. "Last night was so amazing, Jake."

I chuckled. "I'm glad you think so."

Her brows shot up in surprise. "Don't you agree?"

Bringing my lips to hers, I devoured her mouth in a hungry kiss. I thrust my tongue against hers, seeking her taste and her warmth. I snaked an arm around her waist and tugged her onto my lap. After several long, delicious minutes passed, she moaned into my mouth before pulling away. "I seem to remember there's someone driving this car," she whispered.

I grinned. "Are you embarrassed or are you afraid he's gonna get off on me making out with my girl?"

She lowered her eyes and then bobbed her head. "A little of both."

"Angel, you're going to have to get used to me wanting my hands and lips on you. It's hard for me to hold back, and frankly, I don't give a shit who sees or what they think."

A shy smile formed on her lips that were swollen from my earlier assault. "Can we at least take baby steps to the whole mauling me in public?"

I threw my head back and laughed. "Sure we can." I rubbed my thumb along her cheekbone. "I never, ever want to do something that makes you uncomfortable. So, I'll try toning it down."

"Mmm, my hero," she murmured before kissing me again. We were just about to get hot and heavy again when the car pulled to a stop in front of the studio.

"Ready to go make some music together?" I asked.

"As ready as I'll ever be, I guess."

I laughed. "You'll be fine."

After I helped Abby out of the car, we headed inside. Pinpoint Productions was a smaller studio than what the guys and I usually recorded in, but it was the intimacy about the place and the production team that I loved. Gio, the head producer, came out of his office and shook my hand. "Good to see you, Jake."

"Good to see you too. This is Abby Renard. She's the one singing the duet with me."

"Nice meeting you," Gio said.

Abby smiled. "Nice to meet you too."

"We're thrilled and honored that you wanted to cut you first duet with us. That was some amazing music you and the guys laid down yesterday for the track."

"Thanks, man."

Gio glanced between us. "So who wants to go first?"

I chuckled. "I would say for Abby to go ahead and get it out of the way since she's so nervous, but I guess I better."

Abby furiously nodded her head. "Yes, you first."

I took her hand and gave a reassuring squeeze as Gio led the way back into the recording and sound booth. "You can sit right here." I motioned to a chair at the soundboard.

"Thanks," she murmured as she eased down. I could tell from her wide eyes she was taking in every aspect and detail around her. I went inside the recording booth and shut the door. After I put on my headset, I waved at Abby. She grinned and waved back. Although the lyric sheet was laid out before me, I didn't need it. The lyrics were emblazoned on my mind.

Gio's voice came through my headset. "Okay Jake, let's try Take One."

"Sounds good."

The opening guitar melody played out in my ears, and I began singing. I closed my eyes and focused on the emotions of the lyrics. When I finished, I opened my eyes to see Abby wiping the tears from her eyes. "Good, huh?" I joked.

She nodded while Gio gave a thumbs up. His voice rang in my ear again. "That was kickass, Jake. You're good, but you're never one-take good. Let's try it again."

I laughed. "No problem, man."

We did about ten more takes to me sure that we had it just like we wanted. When I was finished, I exited the booth and went to Abby's waiting arms. "That was fantastic!" she exclaimed.

"Thanks, Angel. I'm sure yours will be too."

"Ugh, I doubt that," she moaned.

"Come on. Go in there and kick some ass, okay?" At her skeptical expression, I added, "I'll be right out here, okay?"

She gave a brief nod of her head before she stepped into the booth and shut the door behind her. I watched as she reached for the headset next to the microphone. With shaky hands, she put it on. Through the glass, I gave her a reassuring smile and a thumbs up. She bobbed her head before lowering her gaze to the lyric sheet. "Okay, Abby, let's go for Take One," Gio instructed.

"All right," she replied in a small voice.

When the music started in the booth, Abby looked like she might puke instead of sing. She started out evenly, but then when the notes climbed an octave, she missed the note. "Sorry," she mumbled.

"No problem. Let's try it again."

The second and third takes were even worse. Even through the glass, I could see the tears shimmering in her eyes. I leaned forward and patted Gio on the shoulder. "Hold up. Lemme try something."

I walked through the door and into the booth. Abby reached up to take off her headset. "I'm sorry, Jake. I don't know what's wrong with me. I thought I could do it. I'm so sorry."

"We're not stopping."

Her brows rose in surprise. "We aren't?"

"Oh hell no. You're going to sing your ass off right now like I know you can, and we're going to record this song together."

Her face crumpled. "But I can't! You heard me earlier. I'm awful. You need to find someone else."

I took her face in between my hands. "Where is the kick-ass-and-take-names, Abby that I know?" When she shrugged, I shook my head. "The Abby I know wouldn't fall apart right now. She'd sing the hell out of this song just like I know she can."

"You really believe in me that much?"

"Yeah, I do."

She drew in a deep breath. "Fine. I'll do it."

I grinned at her. "Good. I'm glad to hear it." I took her hands in mine and squeezed them tight. "And I'm going to stay right here while you do it."

A determined look spread across her face that was both cute and at the same time sexy. "Okay, let's do this."

I gave a thumbs up to Gio. As the music started, Abby's gaze locked with mine. She didn't even glance down at her lyric sheet. Instead, she sang her fucking heart out to me and only me. When she finished, I blinked a few times in disbelief.

"Holy shit, Angel. I think you nailed it."

She grinned. "You think?"

We both looked to Gio who was making a perfect sign with fingers. He leaned in to the microphone. "That was fantastic, but let's do a couple more just in case."

Abby bobbed her head in agreement. "Think you can do even better?" I asked.

"I sure as hell can try," she replied.

After five more takes, we stayed around the studio listening to them merge our two vocal tracks. "That's a number one right there," Gio said with a grin.

"I never had any doubts," I replied.

Abby's blue eyes widened. "To have my first ever song go to number one would be amazing!"

Gio grinned. "Just wait until this drops. People are going to go batshit, especially with Jake singing a duet. He's never done that before. You couple that with the emotions, and bam, solid gold."

With a squeal, Abby did her happy/victory dance around the studio before jumping into my arms and wrapping her legs around my waist. She then proceeded to lay a hot, lingering kiss on me right in front of Gio. It was in that moment I knew I fucking loved Abby Renard with all my heart.

After we finished at the studio, we headed back to the hotel to join the others for a late brunch. As we sat down, Brayden said, "We waited to order until you got here."

"Aw, that was so sweet. Thank you," Abby replied.

As soon as we had all ordered, everyone wanted to know how the recording session had gone. With animated gestures, Abby filled them in on every single detail—including her freak-out. My heart swelled with pride when she told them how it was me that helped her overcome her stage fright. Leaning over, I planted a kiss on her lips. "You were amazing all on your own. I didn't do anything."

"You did *everything*," she argued.

AJ rolled his eyes. "God, you guys are positively sickening," he groaned.

"You're just jealous."

"Whatever," he grumbled as he raised Jude onto his lap.

Our food arrived, and after we ate, I caught Abby gazing with a wistful look at Brayden and Lily. While Melody slept soundly on one of Lily's shoulders, Brayden nuzzled Lily's neck and spoke softly to her. Lily's eyes closed while a serene smile filled her face. I had a pretty good guess that Abby was envying what she saw of the perfect rock-star family.

When she caught me looking at her, Abby smiled. Motioning her hand towards Brayden and Lily, she asked, "Are they always like that?"

I chuckled. "Pretty much. During the tour, they don't get a lot of time together, least of all alone time. When they finally do see each other, they act like two horny teenagers."

"But they're so in love," she murmured as she watched Brayden rub Lily's cheek. A frown turned on Abby's lips. "Poor things, I bet they don't get much alone time with the kids though."

Shrugging, I replied, "They seem to be doing just fine to me— nauseating as it is."

When her hand came to graze my upper thigh, I almost jumped out of my chair. "Jake, if I asked you to do something for me, would you?"

My heart thudded to a stop before restarting. "Don't tell me watching those two has turned you on, and you want to go upstairs with me?"

"Um no!" she cried.

I laughed at her outrage. "Okay, what is it?"

She glanced from me over to Brayden and Lily. "Would you help me take care of Jude and Melody today?"

"You're joking, right?"

She gave a small shake of her head. "They could have the whole day together—just the two of them. I could even spend the night in their suite and give them mine. You know a whole day of romance."

Crossing my arms over my chest, I asked, "Okay, but why does all that have to involve me?"

Her blue eyes narrowed, and I knew I was in trouble. "I thought you might like to not be a self-centered jackass for once and want to help out both me and the guy who is like a brother to you.

I held up my hands in surrender. "Fine, fine. I'd love to spend the rest of the day babysitting Bray's kids with you."

The corners of Abby's lips quirked up, and I could tell she was fighting not to smile. "Try not to sound too excited about it."

I plastered a fake smile on my lips. "Oh, I'm fucking stoked. Can't you tell?"

She grinned at me. "You're such a tool." Patting my thigh, she said, "Now come on and let's tell Brayden and Lily the good news!"

***

235

Chapter Sixteen

Abby

Brayden and Lily were so touched by mine and Jake's offer. It took about an hour for them to get everything we would need together for a day and night with the kids. Then taking Lily's SUV, Jake and I headed first to the Atlanta Zoo and then we went to the Aquarium. With his dark sunglasses and baseball cap, Jake did his best to blend in and not call attention to himself. While I pushed Melody in her stroller, he carried Jude on his shoulders. Since we appeared to be the model picture of a young family, no one even stopped to look or question whether a famous rocker was in their midst.

After ogling all the wildlife, we then headed back to the hotel for Melody's nap time. "Big boys don't nap!" Jude complained when I suggested he lie down as well.

"Come on, Little Man. You and I will go for a swim while the girls relax," Jake suggested.

Jude squealed with delight and raced into the bedroom. While I got him into his swim trunks and floaties, Jake borrowed a pair of Brayden's swim trunks. When he came out of the bathroom, I drew in a sharp breath at the sight of his bare chest and all his hard, chiseled muscles on display.

Lowering his sunglasses, Jake grinned wickedly at me. "Impressed, Angel?"

I rolled my eyes. "Why do you always have to be so cocky?"

He pulled me into his arms. "And why do you always have to fight your feelings when it comes to me?"

"I'm not fighting anything right now when I say your arrogance manages to ruin more moments."

Jake's hands dipped lower to cup my butt. "Oh come on, baby, you drive me wild with desire every minute, so can't you just at least admit that every once in a while, the sight of me gives you a lady boner?"

I bit my lip to keep from laughing. "A lady boner?"

He grinned. "Yep."

"No, seeing you did not give me a lady boner, but it did get me hot, okay?"

Jake twirled me around. "Finally, you admit it." His lips met mine in a hurried, frantic kiss since we both knew at any moment Jude would be coming out of the bathroom. After he licked a moist trail up to my ear, he whispered, "And as for that lady boner, guess I'll just have to step up my game."

I giggled. "Yeah, you do that."

Jude emerged, and Jake and I reluctantly pried away from each other. After a bottle, Melody went down for a two-hour nap. While she slept, I texted with my brothers and my parents. Jake and Jude arrived back at the hotel suite just as Melody was waking up. Since they were both starved, dinner was our next order of business.

As we gorged ourselves on chili dogs and hamburgers from Jake's favorite Atlanta restaurant, The Varsity, Jude asked, "Are Mommy and Daddy playing somewhere else today?"

When Jake snickered, I shot him a look while wiping the ketchup stains off Jude's face. "Yes, they needed some time alone to do some big people stuff."

That caused another amused snort from Jake. "You're impossible!" I hissed.

A little pout formed on Jude's face. "I'm not a baby. I could do big people's stuff."

"Sorry Little Man, but you're not quite ready for what Mommy and Daddy are up to," Jake said.

Jude crossed his arms over his chest in a huff while I gave Jake a smile. "Now don't worry. Uncle Jake isn't a big enough boy to get to do what your parents are doing right now either."

Stuffing a handful of fries in his mouth, Jake mumbled, "Oh please, I've done it plenty of times. It's Aunt Abby who needs to loosen up." When he winked at me, I tossed the dirty napkin at him, which caused him to almost choke on his fries.

After we arrived back at the hotel, it was after eight. Jake yawned as he collapsed on the couch. "Can you give Melody her bottle while I give Jude a bath?"

He nodded and took the almost sleeping baby from my arms. I then herded Jude into the bathroom. After a quick splash to get clean, I slipped him into his pajamas and read him a bedtime story.

When I finished the book, Jude's eyes were heavy, but he still wasn't asleep. "Sing to me, Aunt Abby."

"Um, okay." I searched my mind for a song and finally remembered the one my mother used to sing to me.

Finally, he nodded off, and I carefully eased myself off the bed. After I closed the bedroom door behind me, I was surprised to find the living room bathed in darkness. Only the flickering TV screen lit the way for me as I walked toward the couch. When I was almost there, I skidded to a stop at the sight before me. Shirtless, Jake lay on his back while Melody slept soundly on his chest. My hand fisted my shirt over my heart as the scene of Jake with a baby wrecked me emotionally.

I drew in a deep breath and continued over to the couch. Gently, I picked up Melody. Sensing the loss, Jake popped open his eyes. "I'll put her down," I whispered.

"Okay," he replied, rising up into a sitting position on the couch.

After I laid Melody down in her Pack-N-Play, I covered her up. Grabbing a t-shirt and a pair of yoga pants out of my suitcase, I went into the bathroom to change. When I finished, I peeked at the kids again before leaving the bedroom. Jake reclined on the couch with the remote in his hand. When he saw me eyeing his naked chest, he grinned sheepishly. "Melody kinda spit up all over me."

"Oh, I see," I replied, as I eased down beside him.

"Jude asleep?"

"Yep." I couldn't fight the dreamy smile that curved on my lips. "I ended up singing him to sleep."

Jake chuckled. "There's not a chance in the world that kid isn't gonna be a rocker just like his old man."

"You're right. He adores music."

With a yawn, Jake turned to me. "I had no idea two kids would wipe my ass out so much."

I laughed. "I know. But they're really good kids."

"Oh yeah, Bray's a lucky man."

At the serious way he was looking at me, I quickly turned my head. Wrinkling my nose at the TV screen, I asked, "Ugh, do we seriously have to watch Sports Center?"

Jake snorted. "If you think we're watching some sappy chick flick, you got another thing coming."

"Well, at least let me see what else is on," I suggested, reaching for the remote.

"Oh no. I don't think so."

When I tried prying the remote out of his hands, it went flying across the living room and bounced onto the floor. Jake and I momentarily eyed each other before we both lunged off the couch for it. Pushing and shoving each other out of the way, I finally grabbed it. "Aha!"

It was a brief victory because Jake flipped me over on my back. After he straddled me, he pinned my arms above my head. "Not so fast."

As he smirked down at me, I tried squirming out of his hold. "Let me go, asshole!"

"Ooh, you get so feisty when you're angry."

"Don't make me knee you again," I threatened.

At the mention of our first encounter, our eyes locked, and in that brief instant, the remote was forgotten. Leaning down, Jake brushed his mouth against mine, caressing my lips with his. I craned my head up, so I could reach him better. The tighter we fit against each other the more feverishly Jake's lips moved against mine. I darted my tongue into his mouth and teased mine against his. His hand abandoned mine and moved to cup my breast. Over my t-shirt, he kneaded my flesh, causing me to moan with pleasure.

Tearing his mouth from mine, Jake panted, "Abby..."

"What?" I murmured as I ran my hands through his hair.

His brows creased in worry. "Are you sure about this?"

"Because of Brayden's kids being in the next room?"

Jake chuckled. "Well, yeah, that's a buzz kill in itself, but I was thinking more about you." He stared down at me with such a mixture of lust and desire in his eyes that I shivered. "I just can't help myself around you. I want you so bad that I can't help but devour you any chance I get. I'm just afraid this is too fast and too soon for you."

My chest constricted at his concern for me. He really was willing to give me the time and space I needed, and that made me love him all the more. When he started to pull himself off me, I knew right then and there that I didn't want him to stop. I was almost twenty-two years old, and I wanted to keep enjoying a frolic on the hotel room floor with the guy I loved. "No!" I cried, grabbing his shoulders.

His eyes widened in surprise. "I want this, and I want you." I tore my gaze from his before adding, "Just not all the way."

"You mean it?" he asked, tipping my chin to make me look at him again.

"Yes," I whispered.

"Thank God," he groaned before he brought his lips back to mine. Kissing me feverishly, he eased my t-shirt up and over my head. Then he snaked his arm around my back. With just a flick of his wrist, Jake unhooked my bra deftly with just one hand and then slipped it off. "Nice work," I panted.

He grinned down at me. "It's tricky, but I've had a lot of practice."

I smacked his chest. "Don't be bragging about your former conquests with me."

"Sorry." As his hand cupped my bare breast for the first time, I gasped. "Would it sweeten the pot if I said you're the only girl in the entire world I dream about conquering?"

"Maybe," I whispered as his thumb brushed across my nipple. It hardened under his simple touch while an ache burned between my legs.

Jake's gaze roamed over my breasts. "God, these are amazing...and real."

I couldn't help giggling at his statement. "Um, should I say thank you?"

He chuckled. "Sorry for the caveman comment. It's just you're so damn perfect everywhere. Including your tits."

His mouth hovered over my nipple. As his breath warmed my breast, I arched my back, encouraging him to stop tormenting me. Happily, he obliged and sucked my nipple into his mouth. "Oh Jake," I murmured. The sensation was like nothing I could have imagined.

While his tongue assaulted my nipple, his other hand continued massaging my other breast. I couldn't help the moans and whimpers escaping me. It felt too good to be quiet.

While he continued giving my breasts attention, I opened my legs wider, allowing him to sink closer between my thighs. My hips bucked up involuntarily to his, and I felt the bulge growing beneath his jeans. He pushed back against me, and I cried out. Grazing my nipple with his teeth, he then began to rock his erection against me.

"Mmm," I murmured, turning my head from side to side. I matched his rhythm lifting my hips to meet his thrusts. Pressure continued to build between my legs as Jake rubbed against me. I bit down on my lip to stifle my cries. If it felt this good now, what would it be like when he actually touched me there or put his mouth there?

The friction was driving me wild, but it wasn't enough. "Jake," I whispered.

He raised his head from my breast. "What do you want, Angel?" he rasped.

"Touch me."

"You sure?"

I bobbed my head. "Yes, please."

Rolling off of me, one of Jake's hands abandoned my breast to trail down my abdomen. When he got to the band of my yoga pants, I sucked in a breath. The back of his hand feathered tantalizingly across my stomach, and I couldn't help but buck my hips up to him. Chewing his lip for a minute, he gazed down at me. "Has anyone ever…"

Warmth flooded my cheeks at his question. "No."

The cocky little smirk that filled his face caused me to smack him. "What?"

"The victorious caveman look you just made at being my first third-base action."

He grinned. "Sorry, but it's new for me too. You know, to be someone's *first*." As his fingers tickled along my abdomen, he asked, "Have you ever touched yourself?"

"What's with the inquisition? Just do it already!" I shouted.

Jake's eyes widened. "Shh, you'll wake Jude and Melody."

Mortification rocketed through me, and I covered my head with my hands.

"So is that a yes or a no?" Jake prompted.

I peeked at him through my fingers. "Yes, I have," I whispered

At my admission, he groaned. "Oh Angel," he murmured before his hand delved beneath my pants. When his fingers brushed against me, I gasped with pleasure. Jake drew in a ragged breath and asked, "When you touched yourself like this, did you come?"

Even though I was embarrassed, frustrated, and even a little angry at his question, I found myself replying, "Mmm, hmm."

He pinched his eyes shut. "You're driving me crazy."

"I could say the same thing about what you're doing to me."

He chuckled as his eyelids fluttered open. "I know." When he gazed into my eyes, desire burned bright in his. "Maybe I should stop asking questions and just kiss you, huh?

"Yes."

As his tongue thrust in and out of my mouth, his fingers delved between my legs. When he finally stroked my sensitive folds, I moaned into his mouth. The pressure continued to build as I rocked my hips against his hand. Beads of sweat broke out across my forehead. I couldn't imagine anything could feel this good.

Jake tentatively slid his finger inside me, and when he started moving it in and out, I went over the edge. "Jake! Oh yes! Jake!" I cried as my walls clenched around his finger. When I finally came back to myself, Jake was staring down at me. "You're sexy as hell when you come."

I quirked my brows at him as I fought to catch my breath. "That's good to know."

He shot me a wicked grin. "I love the way you called out my name. It was so fucking hot." He rose up on his knees while his hands went to the waistband of my yoga pants. "You want me to make you come again?"

"Do you always do this sweet talking with the girls?"

He paused in pulling down my pants. "You don't like it?"

"No, it's just…."

He grimaced. "It's not very romantic, right?"

I shook my head. "No, not really."

Jake sighed. "This is all new for me, Angel. I'm not used to doing the whole emotions with sex stuff. I'm used to fucking and calling it a day."

I winced at his words. "I'm sorry if it sounds like I'm complaining. I did enjoy it—obviously, I mean, I…It's just that…"

"No, I get it. You deserve better, Angel. You're giving me—the most undeserving guy in the world—the most sacred and amazing firsts."

I shook my head. "They're mine to give, and I wouldn't want anyone but you to have them."

He cocked his brows at me. "Even on the floor of a hotel room?"

"If it means being with you, then yes. And even with your dirty talking mouth."

He groaned. Once he pulled off my pants, he kissed a moist trail from my bent knee down across my thigh. His mouth momentarily brushed against my center over my panties before he kissed a trail up the opposite thigh. "Jake," I pleaded.

"Shh," he murmured. His fingertips lazily traced the waistband of my panties. I chewed on my bottom lip until he finally gripped the fabric and slid them off. As he gazed down at me, I suddenly felt very exposed, so I clamped my knees together.

Jake shook his head. "Let me see you, beautiful," he urged, nudging my knees apart. This time he didn't do any more teasing kisses along my thighs. Instead, his mouth sought out my center as he placed a tender kiss on me. I sucked in a breath while Jake blew warm air across my already inflamed core. Closing my eyes, I murmured, "Jake…"

When his tongue flicked across my folds, I cried out. Jake then began alternating between sucking and licking me. Warmth flooded my cheeks and seemed to ricochet over my entire body. It felt like I was consumed by fire. A sheen of sweat broke out along my skin as I rocked my hips against Jake's mouth. I gripped his hair as he slipped two fingers inside me and swirled them around. Then he began to move them in and out of me while still licking and sucking my clit with his tongue. My whimpers and harsh pants filled the room before I finally tensed and went over the edge again. "Jake!" I cried as I thrust my hips up one final time.

From between my thighs, he grinned up at me. I threw my head back and closed my eyes. "Wow…"

He chuckled as he moved his body to cover mine. "That's all you can say is wow?"

I cupped his face in my hands. "It was that good that you rendered me speechless, okay?"

"Mmm, I like the sound of that."

As he lay across me, I felt the hardened bulge in his jeans. While he'd gotten me off twice, he was still in need of attention. My eyes met his as I cupped him over his jeans. When he raised his brows questioningly at me, I bobbed my head. "Show me what to do."

Without protesting, Jake unbuttoned and unzipped his jeans. He lifted his hips and eased his jeans down to knees. My eyes immediately honed in on his erection. Taking my hand in his, he wrapped my fingers around his considerable length. Then he covered my hand with his. Slowly, he worked our hands up and down.

"Like that?"

"Yeah…but you speed it up too," he murmured in a shaky breath.

When I started working my hand over him faster, he gasped. "Oh God, Angel. That's good." My lips met his in a frenzied, hungry kiss. I liked that what I was doing caused him to groan. He raised his hips in

247

time with my long strokes. "Fuck yes," he murmured before his body started to shudder as he came. Hot, sticky liquid spurted into my hand and onto Jake's stomach.

"Um, what do I—?"

With a chuckle, Jake pulled himself to his feet and went over to grab some napkins in the kitchen. He then wiped my hands clean and his stomach. He then kissed both of my cheeks and my forehead before returning to my lips. "Hmm, Angel, that was good," he murmured against them.

To my disappointment, Jake tore his lips from mine to grope in the pile of clothes beside us. He grinned up at me as he slid my panties back on and then he did my yoga pants. "Thanks."

His expression grew serious. "I should be the one thanking you for letting me be the first to make you come."

I exhaled a ragged breath. "I think if we keep going like this, I'm going to want you to be the first in a lot more ways."

When he got my meaning, he groaned before bringing his lips back to mine. Our mouths were waging war on each other when a tiny voice called, "Aunt Abby?"

I jerked my mouth from Jake's and scrambled away from him. Whirling around, I took in Jude's tiny form in the bedroom door. "Y-Yeah, sweetheart?"

He sniffled. "I had a scary dream. Will you come to bed with me?"

"Of course I will. Just give me one second." Smoothing down my ruffled hair, I hopped up, leaving Jake alone on the floor.

Jude held his arms up, and I hoisted him up onto my hip. He buried his head in my neck before he started crying. "Shh, it's okay. It was just a bad dream. It's over now, and I'm here with you."

I laid him down on the bed and then curled in beside him. He snuggled up to me, still snubbing back his tears. "Want me to sing again?"

"Pwease," he whimpered.

After I sang several verses, Jude was fast asleep again. Pulling away from him, I checked on Melody before heading to the door. When I opened it, I froze. Jake was nowhere to be seen. I flipped on the light and peered around the room.

He had left.

I hurried over to the table where my phone was. Sliding my thumb across the screen, I checked for any missed texts or calls.

There were none.

My throat constricted as I fought back the tears. Why would he just leave me? Had he gotten what he wanted and bailed? I shuddered as the used feeling washed over me.

Against my better judgment, I texted a quick *Where r u?*

After a couple of minutes, I typed *Jake?*

Pacing around the suite I waited for his response, but it didn't come. Defeated, I slunk back into the bedroom and crawled into the bed. This time it was me snuggling against Jude for comfort as the tears streamed silently down my cheeks.

***

Chapter Seventeen

JAKE

I was a bastard—a complete and total douchebag for bailing on Abby. I realized that the moment I let the suite door close behind me. Then the feeling persisted as I entered my room and slipped out of my clothes. Butt ass naked, I fell into bed and buried my face in the pillow.

The first reason I left was because Jude appearing freaked the hell out of me. I didn't know how much he had seen, and I didn't want Bray kicking my ass for scarring his kid because Abby was taking care of my needs and getting me off. But then I came to realize that the main reason I had bailed was because I was scared.

Yeah, I didn't know how to deal with all I was feeling for Abby. I knew I loved her at the studio and then when I meshed that with the sexual part, I was fucking floored and obliterated emotionally. So I did the only thing scared men do.

I ran.

And I felt like an even bigger jackass, especially when I got her questioning texts. I mean, I should have texted her right back and lied by claiming I was fine or that I was tired. But no, I was an even bigger asshole because not only did I not reply, but I turned my fucking phone off because I didn't know what the hell to say to her.

And although I was mentally and physically exhausted, sleep evaded me. At two am, I pulled my ass out of the bed and started pacing around the room. Out-of-control thoughts whirled through my mind so fast I staggered on my feet.

There was no more denial. I was truly head over fucking heels in love with Abby.

But deep down, I knew the root of my problem with Abby. I was in love with a girl who was way too good for me. Abby had such a giving heart and a pure, inner beauty that I didn't deserve to taint or destroy. We'd only known each other for three weeks, and I'd already hurt her too many times with my stupidity. Knowing me, I would continue hurting her over and over again. So maybe I should walk away from her. Wouldn't it be better for her in the long run? I could never give her all she deserved. She wanted the fairy tale of a happily-ever-after with a husband and kids, and I didn't know shit about any of that.

Raking my hand through my hair, I thought about going to her in the morning and telling her that whatever we had was over. But just the image of walking away from her caused a searing pain to radiate through my chest, and I had to fight to breathe.

No, I couldn't walk away from her, not when I loved her. I'd never loved a girl as much, and I couldn't imagine ever loving anyone more. I wanted to see where this crazy thing we had started took us. I wanted to claim her as my own in every possible way. Hell, when it got down to it, I could almost envision putting a fat, shiny diamond on her finger.

And then the thought hit me that maybe I'd already screwed up too much and lost her. That's when the walls began to close in around me. I threw on my clothes and headed out the door. Staring at the suite door across from me, I lightly wrapped on the door. "Abby?" I called.

I knew she probably couldn't hear me if she was in the bedroom with the kids, but I was silently hoping that maybe Melody had woken up for a bottle or some shit that babies did. I banged a little louder, but there was still no response. Taking my phone from my pocket, I powered it on. I then sent a barrage of text messages telling her how sorry I was and what a dick I'd been.

My final text read *Angel: I'm right outside the door ready to beg and plead for your forgiveness. If it takes getting down on my knees in a fucking hotel hallway, I will. That's how sorry I am and how much you mean to me.*

Every single one remained unread and unanswered.

Huffing with agitation, I headed down the hall to the elevators. I needed some time to clear my head, and there was no better place than the streets of my second home to do it. I walked a couple of blocks, taking in the sights and sounds. Atlanta was no New York when it came to never sleeping or its crowds, so I didn't have to worry about running into a lot of people who might recognize me.

But no matter how far I walked, peace of mind never came. Finally when I backtracked to the hotel, it was almost five. I knew the moment it wasn't an ungodly hour, I would go to Abby and beg her forgiveness.

I collapsed onto the bed and made the mistake of checking my phone. Every single one of my texts had been read, but there was no response. Tears stung my eyes, causing me to feel like an absolute and total pussy. After exhausting myself with crying, I fell into a restless sleep, and when the first rays of amber sunlight began streaking through the blinds, I woke up.

Checking my phone, I saw there was still no response from Abby. With a ragged sigh, I rose out of bed. While I grabbed a quick shower, I rehearsed in my mind exactly what I was going to say to Abby. I knew some epic groveling was going to be in order for what I had done, and since my mouth usually ruined most moments between us, I wanted to be prepared. I'd just climbed out of the shower and wrapped a towel around my waist when I heard a knock at the door.

My heart surged at the thought that my angel had come to me. I threw open the door. "Angel, I—"

But it wasn't Abby. Instead, Bree stood there with a cat-like smile spread across her lips. "Hey baby!"

"What are you doing here?" I demanded.

A funny look flickered across her face. "I'm here for you of course. Don't I always come along to the shows to take care of my man's needs?" Her eyes trailed down my half naked frame. "Damn, you're looking good enough to eat this morning."

When she started to kiss me, I jerked back. "Look, Bree, I'm sorry, but there's nothing between you and me anymore."

The color slowly drained from her face as she trembled. "You're with someone else, aren't you?"

"Yes, but—"

Her eyes narrowed. "It's that little goody two-shoes whose name you called out when we were screwing, isn't it?"

I ran my hands through my wet hair. "Yeah, it is. So you really need to go."

Bree's tough-as-nails veneer faded a little as she reached out for me. "Please don't do this, Jake. We've been together a long, long time."

"We've been having *sex* a long time, but there was nothing else between us."

"That's not true!" she countered.

"Yes, it is."

Before I could stop her, she threw herself at me, wrapping her arms around my neck and clinging to my body. And because the universe loved to fuck with me, it was at that precise moment that the suite door across the hall opened, and Abby and Lily stepped out.

At the sight of me entangled in Bree's arms, Abby's eyes bulged in shock while her hand flew to her mouth. "Wait, no, this isn't what it looks like!" I argued.

Instead of letting me go, Bree curved herself tighter against me. Abby gave a slight shake of her head before starting down the hallway.

"Abby!" I cried. Trying to control my anger, I pried Bree off of me. "Get out of here right now before I have you thrown out!" I spat.

"Please don't do this Jake!"

I sprinted after Abby. I finally caught up with her at the elevators. "Angel, please listen to me. There was nothing happening with Bree. I swear on my life and my mother's life."

Abby shook her head so fast I feared she might get whiplash. "I can't do this anymore, Jake. I can't keep being yanked back and forth by your emotional immaturity. One minute you're bailing on me and making me feel used and dirty and then the next I find your ex-flame all over you. It's too much."

"But this morning is not what you think! Bree came to see me, and when I told her things were over between us, she lunged at me." At the disbelief that still hung in Abby's eyes, I growled in frustration. "Would you think about what you really saw for a minute? Bree was desperately clinging to me, not the other way around. I wasn't even touching her."

The elevator doors dinged open, and she hopped on. "Please, Angel. You read my texts. You know how fucking sorry I am."

Tears shimmered in her blue eyes. "Yeah, well, sometimes sorry just isn't enough."

"Don't do this!" I pleaded.

She held my gaze until the doors closed. "Fuck!" I cried smacking my palm on the elevator door. A man passing by me tried to hide his amusement at my precarious situation. After all I was out in the hallway in only a towel.

When I stalked back down to my room, Bree was gone. Once I slammed the door, I grabbed my phone. I knew I had to call the other woman I loved for advice. She answered on the second ring. "Mama…"

"Jacob, what's wrong?"

"I'm in love, but I've fucked it all up."

She didn't even bother chiding me about my language. "Oh honey, tell me what happened." I then filled her in on every possible detail. "If you love Abby like you claim to, then you have to keep fighting for her. You can't give up."

"What can I do to make her talk to me?"

"You need to do something sweet for her to prove how much you care."

"But what?"

Mama chuckled. "Honey, I can't tell you that. You have to figure that out for yourself. It has to be from your heart—not mine."

"Thanks a lot," I grumbled.

"All I can tell you to do is fight for her. Don't give up until you've convinced her to talk to you."

"Okay, I'll do it."

"Good luck, sweetie."

"Thanks."

Once I hung up with Mama, I paced around the room, trying to think of some grand gestures. Finally I called a local florist and spent a small fortune on every rose they had in the store. Even though it was mortifying as hell, I rattled on for several minutes about what to write on the card. The guys were texting me about breakfast, so I reluctantly threw on some clothes. I headed downstairs to the hotel dining room where they were waiting on me. When I flopped into my chair, AJ glanced around the table. "Where's Abby?"

Brayden chuckled before winking at Lily. "Don't tell me she needs a day to recuperate from watching our little monsters?"

After shifting Melody on her hip, Lily shot me a disgusted look.

"No, everything went fine with the kids."

Braydon's brow creased. "Then where is she?"

"Why don't you ask Mr. Asshole over there?" Lily snapped.

"Mommy said a bad word!" Jude exclaimed from his perch on Rhys's lap.

"Um, why don't you and I go throw some more pennies in that fountain, huh?" Rhys suggested. As he brushed past me, Rhys whispered, "But I better get the whole damn story when I get back!"

Once Jude was out of earshot, every pair of eyes at the table burned into me. "Okay, so I fucked up pretty bad."

Brayden's brows furrowed in worry. "Maybe you should start from the beginning."

I jerked my hand through my hair and drew in a ragged breath. "Look, last night, Abby and I got a little carried away."

A strangled noise came from the back of Brayden's throat. "Please tell me my son didn't see you guys doing anything?"

"God no! We were done by the time he woke up from his nightmare and came looking for Abby."

Brayden pinched the bridge above his nose. "Would you please explain exactly what happened?"

I squirmed in my seat. "After Abby put the kids to bed, we fooled around a little. When we were done, Jude woke up and wanted Abby. I was embarrassed by him almost catching us, so I bailed. And then I didn't text her to check on her."

"Once again, you're an asshole!" Lily exclaimed.

"Babe, please," Brayden protested.

"Don't tell me you're defending him?"

Brayden shook his head wildly back and forth. "Of course not. What he did was completely and totally uncalled for. He made Abby feel cheap and used!"

I cringed. "I realize that now."

"You're such an idiot!" Lily replied.

"I'm sorry, okay? I'm new to all this relationship stuff. It was a guarantee I was going to screw up."

Lily huffed exasperatedly. "Now tell them what else happened."

AJ's dark eyes widened in disbelief. "There's more?"

"Unfortunately yes." I then explained about Bree showing up and Abby seeing her hugging me.

"Christ almighty, Jake, you sure have a gift for screwing up," Brayden mused.

"Tell me about," I mumbled miserably.

"You gotta make it right, dude," AJ said.

"I've tried. Hell, I just spent a fucking fortune having dozens upon dozens of roses sent to her. She still won't talk to me."

Scratching his chin, AJ replied, "Okay, so it's gotta be something a little more epic than just flowers." He glanced over at Lily. "You're a chick. What should he do?"

She rolled her eyes at him before handing Melody to Brayden. She then sat down next to me. "Jake, I've known you for eight years, and for most of those years, you've absolutely disgusted me with your treatment of women."

"Thanks for the pep talk," I grumbled.

She held up her hand. "Let me finish."

"Fine."

"Even though you made a pretty dick move, I can tell you like Abby a lot. I mean I've never seen you act this way around a girl before." I bobbed my head in agreement. "I'd venture to say that even though it's been a whirlwind the last three weeks that you might even love her."

I swallowed hard under her's and the guy's scrutiny. "I know it's quick, but I've fallen in love with her for sure. And yeah, I like *love* her, love her."

Lily's eyes misted over while Brayden's mouth dropped open in shock. "Seriously dude?"

"Yeah...seriously."

"Have you really told her yet?" AJ asked.

"No, not yet."

"Then you have to tell her," Lily commanded.

"Yeah, well, I'd love to do that, but she isn't talking to me at the moment."

AJ shook his head. "That's why you gotta do something fucking epic to make her see the light."

"And just what would you suggest, Mr. Latin Lover? I bring her on stage and sing to her about how much I love her?"

AJ's eyes bulged as Lily drew in a sharp breath. When I glanced at Brayden, he grinned. "That's exactly what you do."

Both AJ and Lily nodded in agreement. "Like when we usually bring a fan up, I should bring her instead?"

AJ snapped his fingers. "Hell yes!"

"That sounds amazing, but how in the hell am I going to get her to the show? She won't answer my calls or texts or even come to the door."

Lily grabbed my hand in hers. "You leave that part to me."

I didn't reply for a minute. Instead, I became lost in thought about how to make tonight the most amazing I could for Abby. And then it hit me. "Lily, will you take Abby shopping while we're at rehearsal?"

"Do you want me to like distract her or something?"

"No, it's just I need her wearing white like the first time I met her."

Lily expression softened. "Oh Jake, that's so sweet and romantic."

I grinned. "Thank you. I'm glad I have your vote of confidence." I then turned to Bray and AJ. "We're going to need a little extra rehearsal time today to add in the song I want to do."

"You're not doing the usual?" AJ asked.

"No, this has to be completely different and special for Abby."

Brayden cocked his head at me. "And just what song are you planning on doing?"

With a wink, I replied, "It's a surprise I plan to reveal at rehearsal."

***

Chapter Eighteen

Abby

The hem of my short, chiffon white dress swirled around my calves as I struggled to keep up with Lily. The roar of the crowd for Vindicated stung my ears as we weaved in and out of the crowded back stage of Phillips Arena. From time to time, she would glance over her shoulder at me and grin. I couldn't help but smile back at her. After all, I owed everything to her for finally getting me to see the light.

Although I'd turned a hardened heart to Jake when he'd begged and pleaded for me to forgive him, it really only took a few words from Lily to convince me to give him another chance. She'd knocked on the door to my suite shortly after Jake had left, so naturally I'd screamed to leave me the hell alone. Instead, I heard her persistent voice outside. When I threw open the door, she gave me a hesitant smile. "You know I'm on your side in this entire situation. But I just have to say this, and when I'm done, it's totally up to you on how to proceed."

I crossed my arms over my chest. "Okay, I'm listening."

"I've known Jake for eight years, and I've never, ever seen him act this way or feel this much about a girl before. *Ever*. He's a brilliant musician, but he's an absolute screw-up when it comes to matters of the heart. But if he was able to convince me how sorry he was and how much he deeply feels for you, you can bet it's the real deal." At my unresponsiveness, she sighed. "Look, Abby, I was at the same crossroads you are five years ago. I was hurt and angry about some of the really shitty things Brayden had done. He'd screwed up so many times that I didn't think I had it in me to give him yet another chance when he begged and pleaded with me, just like Jake is doing with you. If I kept a hardened heart, I would've missed out on the most amazing man I could ever hope for, not to mention I wouldn't have my two beautiful children."

I closed my eyes for a moment before reopening them. "I'm just scared," I admitted.

She nodded. "I know. I was too, and when it comes down to it so is Jake. But he really has a good heart Abby—one that for the first time in his life he wants to give to only one girl. And that girl is you."

Unblinking and unmoving, I stared at Lily for a moment as I let the depth of her words wash over me. Glancing over my shoulder, I eyed all the beautiful red, pink, yellow, and purple roses overtaking my room. I thought of Jake's countless texts along with his actions at the elevator.

Nibbling my bottom lip, I finally questioned, "So what do I do to make it right with us?"

A beaming smile filled her cheeks before she leaned over to hug me. "Well, first of all, you need a white dress!"

And that's how I came to be trailing behind her as we searched for

Runaway Train, or most importantly Jake. At the sight of Frank talking to some other roadies, I rushed past Lily.

"Where's Jake?" I demanded breathlessly.

His gaze roamed over my attire, and then he smiled. "Want me to take you to him?"

"Please."

"Sure thing, Angel."

He led me through a series of rooms. Rhys, Brayden, and AJ were in the second one, decked out and waiting for their call to go to the stage. When they saw me, they whistled and cat-called. I guess I must've looked like I was on a mission because they didn't try stopping me. "Go on and get your man, Angel!" AJ called.

We'd left the room with the guys when Frank stopped. He motioned to a shut door. "He's in there. Of course, he's left strict orders not to be disturbed." With a wink, Frank then added, "But I'm pretty sure he'll want to see you."

I leaned up and kissed his cheek. "Thank you."

Frank turned and left me alone in the hallway. My nerves caused me to wobble as I pushed myself forward. My hand trembled as I knocked on the dressing room door. "Are you all fucking deaf? I told you I wanted to be left the hell alone, so go away!" he growled.

Testing the doorknob, I found it unlocked. I had to draw in a few calming breaths before opening it. Jake sat hunched down in one of the chairs with a scowl etched across his face. At the sound of the door closing behind me, he jerked his head up. "I said—" The rest of his words died on his lips at the sight of me. His eyes bulged as he shot out of his chair. He just stood there, staring at me with an expression of absolute disbelief.

The corners of my lips twitched in a smile. "Don't tell me that I've rendered you speechless?"

"Angel, you actually came." He then motioned at my dress. "And you're wearing white."

I nodded. "For you."

He closed the gap between us in two long strides. "Does this mean you accept my apology, and you're willing to give a major fuck-up like me another chance?"

I couldn't help the giggle that escaped my lips at Jake's summation of himself. "Yes, it does."

Jerking me to him, he planted a long, lingering kiss on my mouth. "Oh God, you make me so, so happy," he murmured against my lips.

"You make me happy too."

After he pulled away, Jake's brows furrowed. "But what finally changed your mind? I mean, I was about ready to have my mama call you and plead my case."

I laughed. "That might've helped, but it was Lily who helped me see the bigger picture."

"Really? Wow, I'm impressed with her mad skills of persuasion." He grinned. "Damn, I'm glad she came through for me. I guess I owe her big time, huh?"

"No, I don't think you owe her anything. She was just being honest about the person you really are."

"Thank you, Angel," Jake replied with a smile. "Now let me get a good look at you."

With a little twirl, I spun around to give him a view of the dress. Although the bottom was made of chiffon, the bodice had intricate white beading and sequins. With its spaghetti straps, it did an amazing job showing off my cleavage. It was tasteful, but sexy all in the same token.

Jake licked his lips. "Oh Angel...you look absolutely breathtaking."

I grinned. "I'm glad to hear it."

"Jake, it's time," Rhys called from the doorway.

"One sec," he replied.

With a nudge, I pushed him to the door. "You need to go. After all, you can't keep your adoring fans waiting."

Jake's expression grew serious. "There's something I have to say to you before I go out there."

My heartbeat accelerated so fast I felt lightheaded. "Okay," I murmured.

Cupping my cheeks in his hands, Jake stared intently into my eyes. "I love you, Angel."

I jerked back at his declaration. "You do?"

He smiled as he ran his thumb along my cheekbone. "Yeah, I do."

Blinking in disbelief, I continued to stare at him. Finally, I whispered, "Oh Jake," before I threw myself at him. "Say it again," I commanded, my voice muffled against his chest.

"I love you, Abby," he whispered into my ear.

"I love you, too. So very, very much," I replied, squeezing him tight.

"I never thought I'd ever hear you say it."

After he wrapped his arms around my waist, he pressed his forehead against mine. "I could say the same about you."

"Jake!" Rhys called again.

"Fuck, I don't want to go out there. I just want to stay right here with you."

"We'll have time together after the show."

Jake's expression darkened. "It's never enough time, especially since you have to fly back tomorrow."

"We'll figure something out. We always do."

"Maybe next time instead of those douchebags from Vindicated we can have Jacob's Ladder open for us."

I laughed. "That would be awesome."

"I'm totally serious, Abby."

When he used my real name, rather than Angel, I knew he really was. "But—"

He pressed a finger against my lips to silence me. "All I have to do is bring it before the suits, and usually when I go after something, I get what I want."

I shook my head and couldn't keep the smile from forming on my lips. "There you go with that ego again."

"Come on." He then took me by the hand. He led me along the darkened corridors. We reached the stage just as AJ was making his usual grand entrance. Jake pulled me almost to the edge of the wings. "Stay here for the show, okay?"

My eyebrows shot up in surprise. "Right here? I'm practically on the stage," I protested.

He laughed. "I'm serious, Angel." He leaned over and kissed me. Just as his tongue brushed against mine, we were interrupted by the announcer saying, "And lead singer and guitarist, Jake Slater!"

Jerking away from me, he regretfully said, "Gotta go." He then proceeded to smack my ass playfully before strutting out on the stage with more swagger than I'd seen him use before.

Lily wrapped her arm around my shoulder. "So I take it all is well with you guys, huh?"

I couldn't keep the goofy grin off my lips. "Yes, it is. Thank you so much for coming to talk to me."

"You're welcome." She gave me a knowing smile. "I'm pretty good about spotting true love when I see it, and you and Jake are the real deal."

My heart fluttered at her assessment. We then fell silent to watch our men perform. When a technician brought Jake a headset and took his microphone, my brows furrowed in confusion. I didn't know that they had added a different part to the show.

After he adjusted the headset, he turned to me and winked. "So as some of you may know, this is usually the part of the show where I have a fan brought up on stage to sing to. But tonight I want to change things up a bit." Jake paused for a moment like he was trying to find the right words. "Three weeks ago a girl fell into my life. Well, actually she accidentally fell into my bed, but that's another story."

I gasped as the audience whistled and catcalled. "Before her, I may have sung about love, relationships, and being with that special someone, but I really didn't believe in it. But through her physical and inner beauty, she taught me about the gift of giving your heart to someone." Jake drew in a ragged breath, and my chest clenched as I could tell he was fighting his emotions. "In so many ways, she saved me from the hell surrounding me. She is truly an angel—she's *my* angel." Turning to the wings, he met my gaze and smiled. "So come out here, Angel."

Frozen, I couldn't blink, least of all move. Lily had to nudge me forward, or I would have remained rooted to my spot. On trembling legs, I strode across the stage to where Jake stood beckoning me. At my appearance, the crowd went wild, causing my ears to ring from the noise.

A wide grin curved on Jake's lips as he took my hand in his. He brought it to his lips and gallantly kissed my fingers, which caused the audience screamed in approval. "Atlanta, this is Abby, but to me she's Angel."

In a weird, out-of-body experience, my gaze swiveled out to the crowd, and I gave a lame wave with my free hand. "And while I could've written a song that would have captured everything you are to me, I feel like this one pretty much says it all." Glancing over his shoulder, Jake said, "All right boys, let's hit it."

AJ started in with a drum beat before Brayden began a melting guitar intro. Almost instantly I recognized the song and gasped. It was Aerosmith's *Angel*, and it was all for me.

"I'm alone, and I don't know if I can face the night…" Jake sang into the microphone on his headset. I gazed into his eyes and saw the emotion reflected in them. Without a guitar or microphone to hold, his hands were free to roam over me. As he sang, his eyes never left mine. Warmth spread over my cheeks and throughout my entire body at the devotion he used singing the lyrics. At the second verse, he spun me around and pulled my back against him, wrapping his arms around my waist. Closing my eyes, I swayed to the love song while he crooned into my ear. Well, even with the microphone, it felt like he was singing just to me when actually he held a crowd of fifty thousand in rapt attention. I barely realized when Brayden harmonized with him.

In that moment in time, there was nothing in the world but Jake performing those amazing lyrics just for me. When it got to the part where he repeated "Come and save me tonight", he turned me around. Pulling me flush against him, Jake cupped my cheek before bringing his lips to mine. I could've cared less that we were in front of thousands and thousands of people. It felt like it was just the two of us, and I couldn't get enough of him. Wrapping my arms around his neck, I pressed myself against him and deepened the kiss. My tongue danced tantalizing around his as AJ chimed in with Brayden to finish the lyrics for Jake. We didn't break apart until the music ended, and the screams and whistles interrupted our moment.

I stumbled away from Jake before turning my wild gaze to the crowd. Jake chuckled into the microphone at my reaction. "So what do you think, Atlanta? Can you see now why this amazing girl has stolen my heart?"

Wincing, I waited for a round of boos and hisses to come at me for

269

being the bitch who stole Jake from his adoring female harem. But surprisingly I heard nothing but cheers and more whistling. "And you know something else? She has a kickass voice, and not only did we just record our first duet, but we wrote the song together too. Would you like to hear it?"

Although the fans went wild, I couldn't help grabbing his shirt and protesting, "No, Jake!"

He leaned over to whisper in my ear. "Don't argue with me, Angel. Even though you don't want to believe it, you're ready for this moment. All you have to do is tune everyone else out and just look into my eyes. We'll sing to each other just like always."

A ripple of pleasure ran through me at his words. Pulling my shoulders back, I finally nodded in agreement. It was a good thing because a technician appeared out of nowhere with an exact replica of my guitar.

"But how—" I began as other technicians raced around placing stools on the stage and adjusting the microphones.

With a wicked grin, Jake's only reply was a wink. He handed off his headset and then turned back to the crowd. We both eased down onto the stools and adjusted our guitars on our laps. I made sure to smooth out my dress to ensure I wasn't flashing half of Atlanta.

"All right, this is a very special song, and it's called *I'll Take You with Me*."

Jake began strumming the introduction, and then I joined in. Instead of singing to the audience, he swiveled on his stool to where he could look at me as he sang. Once again, his performance was so heartfelt and strained with emotion that I found tears stinging my eyes. We sang the chorus together, and then it was time for my solo. I didn't take my eyes off of Jake the entire time. A shadow of a smile played on his lips as he strummed his guitar.

When we finished, I leaned over to kiss him. "I love you, Jake," I murmured against his lips.

"I love you too, Angel."

He rose off the stool before taking the microphone off the stand. "Thank you Atlanta! My hometown crowd, you've been amazing as always. See ya next year!" Taking my hand, he then led me off the stage. As soon as we were in the wings, he swept me into his arms. Sliding his hands under my butt, he hoisted me up, and I wrapped my legs around him.

Our lips raged against each other until Brayden cleared his throat behind us. After I reluctantly pulled away, I glanced over my shoulder at him. With a smile, he asked, "I guess this means you two are good now?"

Kneading my butt cheeks with his hands, Jake gave me a wicked grin. "I'd say we were more than great."

I tugged the strands of hair at the nape of his neck hard. "Stop manhandling me in public, Mr. Slater."

"Angel, you're going about getting me to stop the wrong way. Pulling my hair is a hell of a turn-on for me," he whispered in my ear. I shivered at both his words and the warmth of his breath.

"Hmm, so if I let you take me back to the bus and fool around a bit, will you bail on me again?"

A determined gleam burned in his eyes. "Never. You're mine, and you're not getting rid of me."

I grinned. "Good, I'm glad to hear it."

Frank, along with LL, came up to us. "We've got a pretty large crowd outside waiting for you guys. Lots of stuff with them to sign."

"Okay," Jake replied. Reluctantly, he eased me back down onto my feet. He still kept an arm around my waist as we started out the backdoor of the arena while the guys followed behind us. At the sight of Jake, a ripple of screams and shouts erupted in the throng of mainly girls and women.

As the fans swarmed at Jake and the guys, I grinned at him. "I'm going on to the bus."

He smiled and then kissed the crown of my head. "Frank," he called.

Frank nodded and put a protective arm around my shoulder. "Come on, Angel."

The fans barely acknowledged us as we weaved past them. They only cared about seeing Runaway Train—but most importantly it's lead singer.

Unable to keep the goofy expression off my face, I glanced up at Frank. "Did you see what Jake did?"

He chuckled. "Oh yes. I saw and heard." He winked at me. "And I couldn't be happier that he's finally wised up and fallen in love with an amazing girl."

I giggled deliriously like I could only imagine someone with a few shots of liquor in them would, except I was stone cold sober. Well, extremely high off life at the moment. Twirling out of Frank's embrace, I walked backwards for a few moments to face him. "I cannot believe he took me out there and sang to me in front of all those people—that I'm really *his* angel." I swallowed the lump in my throat. "And that he loves me."

"I gotta admit that even for a gruff old fart like me, it was downright touching and so damn romantic."

The piercing squeals of girls screaming interrupted us, causing both of us to glance over Frank's shoulder. The boys seemed cornered by all the fans, and Jake's wide-eyes swept over to us. Frank pulled his phone out of his pocket and called for more of the security detail.

"I can make it from here. Go on and help Jake out."

"Okay, Angel."

I twirled the hem of my dress back and forth while I felt like I was walking on air. I'm sure if anyone saw me they would swear I was tripping on some elicit substance. I had to bite on my lip to keep from grinning. Jake really and truly loved me. It was an amazing feeling.

Just as I turned the corner to the bus, someone grabbed my hair, yanking me back. I cried out just before my head was smashed against the side of the bus so hard that I saw stars before my eyes. Considering some of the rough areas I'd lived in, my parents had made sure I was enrolled in every self-defense class imaginable from the time I could walk. Of course, nothing quite prepares you for being taken off guard and having your thoughts jumbled by the pain of your head cracking against steel.

Fingers twisted further into my hair while my head kept being smashed against the side of the bus. Regaining my footing, I whirled around to launch two harsh punches at my assailant's face, causing them to stumble back momentarily. In the dimly lit parking lot, I squinted my eyes. "Bree?" I questioned dumbly.

Her harsh voice echoed through my disoriented state. "You fucking bitch! It wasn't enough he called out your name when he was inside me, but no, he has to go and sing to you?" She shook her head wildly. "If you think I'm going to give up on Jake so easily, you've got another thing coming!!"

I tried blocking her next hit, but she grabbed both of my shoulders and then smacked my head again, causing me to cry out. "What have you done to him? Jake never, ever would have gone for a girl like you. Now you got him singing songs to you and professing his love. He's supposed to love me!"

"Yeah well, I'm sorry, but he doesn't. It's me he loves," I protested.

Bree released my hair, but before I could get my bearings, she punched me in the mouth, sending blood spattering across the both of us. When I deflected her next two hits, she then kicked me hard in the stomach. I doubled over in pain as she kicked my back. Collapsing to the ground, I tried to disable her next kick, but it just ended up nailing me in the ribs.

"JAKE!" I screamed with what strength I had left.

"Yeah, let's see how much Jake wants you when I'm finished with you," Bree taunted over me.

A metallic rush filled my mouth, and I sputtered out a stream of blood. "Jake!" I whimpered again.

Just as everything started to go dark around me, I heard Jake's voice, "ANGEL!" And then pitch blackness enveloped me.

***

Chapter Nineeen

JAKE

When I saw Frank heading back to me, I finally exhaled the breath I'd been holding. The last time we'd been mobbed like this I'd lost my shirt, a shoe, and my junk had been grabbed multiple times. I don't know where the fuck the rest of the security team was, but their asses were going to get jacked up for leaving us with barely enough coverage, not to mention having to be saved by a roadie.

"Can you sign these?" a busty blonde asked as she jerked the collar of her shirt down and thrust her boobs up at me.

"Yeah, sure."

She grinned. "You sign one and AJ signs the other."

AJ chuckled. "I think this may be the last pair of tits our ol' boy Jake signs, ladies. He's officially been taken off the market."

With my Sharpie, I scribbled my name across her skin. "I think I have to agree, man."

The blonde pouted as AJ leaned in to sign. "His loss. This is an extra nice pair." AJ winked as his pen lingered a little longer than it had to, which caused the girl to giggle. Leaning over, he whispered something in her ear. Her eyes widened and then she bobbed her head furiously.

I opened my mouth to argue that if he thought he was getting the bedroom tonight to bang this random chick, he could think again. I planned on some heavy third-base action with my girl but nothing more since I wouldn't dream of degrading her by taking her virginity on the bus. No, she deserved rose petals and thousand count sheets and nice shit. "AJ—" I began but the sound of a scream cut me off.

"What was that?" Rhys asked, craning his neck around the throng of fans.

Then another bloodcurdling scream came—this time calling for me. It cut me right through to my soul because I knew that voice. "Abby!" I cried, dropping whatever the last fan had shoved at me to sign. I started pushing and shoving people out of the way.

"Move dammit!" I didn't give a shit that I was manhandling fans. Abby needed me.

Once I was out of the crowd, I started sprinting through the parking lot. Frank and AJ were close on my heels. When I rounded the side of the bus, I saw Abby crumpled on the ground, her once pristine, white dress stained with mud and grease, but worst of all blood. Bree stood over her, kicking her repeatedly.

"What the fuck are you doing?" I shouted running over to them. "Get your damn hands off of her, Bree!"

When she didn't even falter at the sound of my voice, a growl erupted from deep within me as my fingers molded into Bree's shoulders. With everything I had, I jerked her off of Abby. I slung her against the side of the bus so hard that I heard the unmistakable crack of bones breaking. Although Bree screamed in pain, I ignored her. My only focus was on Abby.

Crouching down, I nestled next to her and could see the extent of her injuries. Blood flowed like a crimson river from the large gash on the back of her head. Angry red welts were forming on her face, and her lip was busted and bleeding. Her hand clutched her abdomen while her head turned from side to side as she moaned.

My chest twisted so tight in agony that I found it hard to breathe. "Oh Jesus, Angel!"

Her eyelids fluttered open. "Jake?" she questioned hoarsely.

"I'm here now. You're safe. No one is going to hurt you ever again."

When Abby's eyes closed, I glanced up at Frank. "Get the car!"

Without even answering me, he sprinted away. As gently as I could, I gathered Abby into my arms. When I pulled up to a standing position, it jostled us, and she cried out. "I'm sorry, baby. I'm so, so sorry."

Her eyes widened as her brow furrowed in pain. "Jake…hurts…so bad."

I grimaced. "I know, Angel, and I'm sorry. But we're going to get you to the hospital just as quick as we can."

Cradling her to my chest, I hustled to the curb just as Frank came screeching up. AJ opened the door for me, and I eased Abby onto the seat. She shrieked and clawed at my chest from the pain. Tears stung my eyes as I murmured "I'm so, so sorry," over and over again. Once I was seated and had pulled her back onto my lap, she just whimpered, rather than cried hard.

LL hopped up front with Frank while AJ slid in beside me. As I

278

held Abby to my chest, I watched her eyes close. "Try to stay awake. Don't go to sleep." I didn't have any medical training, but I knew from how damaged her head was that she probably had a concussion.

But no matter how hard I tried to keep her awake, the pain must've been too intense, and she passed out. We screeched up to the ER at Piedmont Hospital on two wheels. How Frank got out so fast I don't know, but he was there to open the door for me. When we busted through the ER doors, every person in the waiting room turned to stare at us.

It took all of five seconds before someone shrieked, "Oh my God! That's Jake Slater!"

"And AJ Resendiz too!"

Ignoring them I hustled up to the front desk where an ER clerk stared wide-eyed at me. "My girlfriend has been beaten pretty badly, and she needs medical attention." When she momentarily hesitated, I shouted, "Right now, did you hear me?"

"Y-Yes, sir."

The automatic "Authorized Personnel Only" doors buzzed open, and I rushed through them. Two nurses came forward to usher me into a room. Once I deposited Abby onto the gurney, they pushed me to the door. "No wait, I want to stay with her!"

"I'm sorry, sir, but—"

I jerked my hand through my hair as tears of frustration scorched my eyes. "You don't understand. I *love* Abby, dammit! There are only two women in the entire world I love, and one is already dying. I can't lose Abby too!" I cried.

"I'm so very sorry, but it's against hospital policy to have friends or family members back here while we assess a patient's condition."

My fists clenched at my side as I shouted, "Yeah, well, fuck your precious policy!"

While one nurse began cutting away Abby's dress, the other put a hand on my shoulder. "Please do as we ask. You'll be no good to her if you're in lock-up from security being called."

"You promise you'll take care of her and won't let her die?"

Her expression softened. "We'll give her the best possible care, but I can't promise you any more than that."

Exhaling a defeated sigh, I stomped out of the door. I watched it close behind me while the nurses worked on Abby. The sobs that had been building overtook me. Just as I was about to sink to my knees, Frank's strong arm came around my waist. "Come on, son."

With my eyes blinded by tears, I let him lead me past the Authorized Personnel Only doors and back into the waiting room. Collapsing down into a chair, I put my head in my hands as my body shook with sobs.

"She's going to be fine, Jake. She's just banged up real bad," AJ reassured.

"I can't lose her," I muttered.

He thumped my back. "You won't, man."

"Should we call her brothers or her parents?" Frank asked.

Digging my phone out of my pants, I thrust it at Frank. "Micah's number is in there. They're all together tonight. They had a show in Tennessee or Kentucky."

"Okay, I'll go call."

I shuddered at the thought of Abby's parents and brothers finding out what happened. It was bad enough I wasn't high on their list of favorite people, so the very fact she lay battered and broken in the emergency room because of me wasn't going to cement our relationship.

Raising my head, I swiped away the tears. To my horror two people across the room started snapping pictures. Unable to control my emotions, I whirled out of my seat. "Do you have absolutely no fucking shame? My girlfriend was almost beaten to death not thirty minutes ago, not to mention my mother's dying of cancer! So you think you could give the fucking photos and gossip a rest for one moment?"

Their eyes widened in shock while AJ grabbed me around the shoulders. "Let it go, man." Dragging me over to the registration desk, he asked, "Is there somewhere more private we could wait?"

The lady nodded. "Sure, come right on through here."

As the Authorized Personnel Only doors buzzed opened again, AJ, along with Rhys who had appeared a few moments earlier, ushered me inside a small room that had a few plush chairs. Chewing my ragged thumbnail, I refused to sit down. Instead, I paced around the room like a caged animal. "Why don't they come tell us something?"

"They have to check her out first, Jake," AJ argued.

Standing in the doorway, I caught of glimpse of Bree limping past the door with her father, Lyle. Rage burned within me, and I raced out into the hallway. Before I knew it, I'd grabbed her by the shoulders and was shaking her so hard her teeth were clattering. "You conniving little bitch! How could you do that Abby? She never did a damn thing to you!"

Rhys grabbed my waist and jerked me away. "Don't touch her, man!"

"Touch her? I want to *kill* her!"

Rhys's breath warmed my ear as he spoke in a low voice. "Look, I can understand that you want to break her neck right now, but you have got to think clearly. You physically assaulted her tonight too, and she and Lyle could sue the hell out of you. Give him one hell of a severance package and send them on their way."

"What about Bree attacking Abby? Is she just going to walk away from all of that?" I hissed.

"It's the bigger picture, man. Trust me."

I slung him off of me. "Fine."

Tears streamed down Bree's face. "I'm sorry, Jake. I really am."

"Don't give me your bull-shit apologies. It's Abby you should be telling you're sorry."

Lyle wrapped his arm around Bree's shoulder. "I hate that it had to end this way."

"Just pack your things and go. I'll have the lawyers get you a settlement." My eyes burned into Bree. "But I better never see her at any show of mine ever again, or I'll press charges!"

Bree broke down in sobs as Lyle led her into one of the rooms where a nurse waited to asses her sitation. Brayden and Lily appeared then. Their expressions were ashen and filled with worry. "Heard anything yet?"

"No," I muttered miserably.

It seemed like an eternity passed before a middle-aged doctor in a pristine white coat entered the room. "Which one of you is Jake Slater?" she asked.

Swaying on my legs, I tried not to pass out. "I am," I croaked.

She gave me a reassuring smile that sent relief ricocheting through me. "I'm Dr. Mitchell, and I'm in charge of Ms. Renard's case."

"How is Abby?"

"I won't lie when I say that she suffered some pretty extensive injuries. The CT scan along with some X-Rays confirmed she has some bruised and fractured ribs, a fractured clavicle, and a concussion, but fortunately, there's no internal bleeding or hemorrhaging."

In one long, exaggerated whoosh, I finally exhaled the breath I'd been holding. "So she's going to be all right?"

Dr. Mitchell nodded. "She's going to need quite a while to recover though. Fractured ribs can take up to eight weeks to heal, and they can be very painful. After stitching her up, we've sedated her and are moving her to a room. We'll keep her overnight and then probably release her in a day or two depending on how she's doing."

"Can I see her?"

Dr. Mitchell hesitated. "Well, we currently have her heavily sedated for the pain, so she probably won't wake up."

"I don't care. I still want to be there for her. In fact, I don't plan on leaving her alone one minute. I want to be right there when she wakes up."

With a smile, Dr. Mitchell patted my arm. "She's very lucky to have such a caring and loving boyfriend."

I fought the urge to say, *Yeah, well, it's all because of me thinking with my dick that Abby's in the broken and bruised condition she is.*

"Give us about thirty minutes, and you can go up to see her. She'll be on the fourth floor."

Extending my hand, I shook Dr. Mitchell's. "Thank you so much, and thank you most of all for taking such good care of my Angel."

"No problem," she replied before she left the room.

"Need me to stay with you?" Brayden asked while Rhys and AJ nodded in agreement.

"No, I'm fine."

"Are you sure?" AJ questioned.

"Yeah, you guys go on home."

Brayden stepped forward to give me a hug. "Frank told us that Abby's family should be here in the morning. They were going to have to drive since they couldn't get a flight out."

Inwardly, I cringed at that statement. "Okay, thanks for letting me know."

After AJ and Rhys gave me a brotherly hug, Brayden said, "I guess we'll head out for now and come back to check on Abby in the morning."

"Thanks guys."

While I waited to go up to see Abby, I called my mom. She was devastated to hear what happened. And because she was the most amazingly giving and caring woman, she told me to bring Abby back home to the farm for her recovery. The thought of having the two women I loved most in the same place made me very, very happy.

I had just hung up with my mom when a nurse came out to tell me that Abby was upstairs and I could see her. The entire elevator ride up I waged war on myself for what had happened. I played a thousand "what-if" scenarios in my mind of why I hadn't ensured there were more security or insisted that Frank walk Abby all the way to the bus. Most of all, I wondered how I ever let someone like Bree weasel her way into my life and my bed.

When I got to Abby's room, I hesitated outside of the door. I couldn't help but be afraid of what I might find once I got inside. Guilt continued crisscrossing its way through my chest. The sins of my past had come barreling into my future and almost destroyed my perfect happiness. With a gutted feeling, I pushed open the door.

The room flickered in shadows as only the dim light over Abby's bed lit the room. Even in the dark, I could see the extent of her injuries. Just the sight of the angry purple and green bruises along with Abby's swollen face made me feel like someone had kicked me in the balls. Bending over, I braced my hands on my knees and tried stilling my out-of -control emotions by taking several deep breaths.

At Abby's whimper, I jerked my head up. "Angel?" I questioned before striding over to her bedside. I took her hand that was bandaged with IV's in mine. "Angel, I'm here, and I love you."

Her eyes stayed pinched closed, but her brows furrowed. "Just rest, baby. You're safe now, and I'm not leaving you."

At her continued restlessness, I considered calling the nurse's

285

station and asking for more pain medication. But then an idea flashed through my mind, so I acted on it. Drawing the chair close to the bed, I eased down. I then began singing *Angel* again to Abby just like I had earlier. Almost instantly, she calmed and began to rest more peacefully.

I continued singing different songs to her until my voice was hoarse, and my eyelids drooped in exhaustion. Laying my head down on the side of the bed, I fell asleep with my head nestled against her hip.

Rays of amber sunshine bursting through the window blinds stung my eyes and woke me from my sleep. Raising my head, I looked at Abby. Some of the swelling had gone down in her face, but the bruises were just as bad. I was about to go to the bathroom when she moaned. At the fluttering of her eyelids, I leaned forward. "Angel?"

Her eyes flew wide open. She turned her head to look at me and winced in pain. "Jake…"

"Are you hurting? Let me get the nurse for you."

"No, that's okay. I just feel woozy and really sore."

I nodded. "You're in the hospital. Do you remember what happened?"

"Bree tried to kill me," she replied hoarsely.

"Yes."

"But I'm okay?"

I filled her in on everything Dr. Mitchell had said. Then taking her hand in mine, I squeezed it tight before bringing it to my lips and bestowing kisses across the back of her hand and fingers. "I'm so, so sorry for what happened to you, Angel."

"But it wasn't your fault."

"Yes, it is. If I hadn't ever been involved with Bree, she would have never gone after you like that." Ashamed of the remorseful tears burning my eyes, I buried my face on the side of the bed. "I ruin everything for you."

"No you don't."

Raising my head, I stared sadly at her. "Yes, I do. I'll never be good enough for you."

"Stop it, Jake. I don't want you beating yourself up over this." She reached out to run her fingers over my cheek. "You gave me the most romantic night of my life—you told a crowd of fifty thousand people that I was the girl you loved most in the world and that my love had saved you. Nothing that happened will ever take that moment away from me."

I groaned. "You go and say shit like that and make me realize for the millionth time that you're way too good for me."

Abby gave a slight shake of her head. "You stayed with me last night?"

"Of course."

She tried to smile at me, but the stiches in her lip made it more of a grimace. "Just when I think I couldn't love you more than I already do, you go and prove me wrong."

"Listen, Angel, you're going to have a long recovery ahead of you—maybe six weeks. I want you to come to my farm and let me take care of you."

Abby's eyes widened. "No, Jake, I can't let you do that. You have too much going on with your mom."

I shook my head. "This isn't up for discussion, Angel. I'm not letting you out of my sight. I intended on seeing you through your recovery every step of the way."

"But what about your mom?"

I grinned. "It was her suggestion in the first place." When Abby started to protest, I replied, "She and I both want to do this very much, Angel. Besides, she knows all about my love for you. In fact, she was the one who told me to keep fighting for you after I screwed up."

"Really?"

"Yes, so there's no point in arguing, okay?"

Happy acceptance entered Abby's eyes. "Thank you. I would love to spend that time with you."

"Good, I'm glad to hear it." I rose up to tenderly kiss her forehead. It was one of the only places that wasn't bruised or cut. With a grin, I added, "Since we're off tour for a while and recording the album, you can let me know which songs are good or which ones suck."

"I highly doubt any of them will suck."

"That's debatable." I brought her hand to cup my cheek. "Maybe we can work on some more collaborations?"

"I'd like that a lot." Her fingers brushed against the stubble on my skin. "I like anything that means I get to be with you."

"Right back at ya, Angel," I replied with a smile.

Our beautiful moment came to a screeching halt when the door burst open, and Abby's parents rushed in. "Oh Abigail sweetheart!" her mother, Laura, cried as she practically elbowed me out of the way to get to Abby. Tears streamed down her face as she hovered between wanting to hug Abby and knowing better. Finally, she grabbed Abby's hand.

"Mom, it's worse than it looks. I'm going to be just fine."

"We just spoke with the doctor, and it seems pretty bad to me," her father, Andrew, replied. His expression hardened as his gaze honed in on me. His dark eyes narrowed at the sight of my t-shirt stained with Abby's blood along with the tattoos peeking out from under my sleeves. Without even a hello or an introduction, he demanded, "How could you let this happen?"

My hand automatically flew up in surrender. "Mr. Renard, I'm terribly sorry for what happened to Abby. I never meant for her to get hurt because of me," I replied as sincerely as I could.

Apparently my words had little effect on him. He abandoned Abby's other side and rounded the bed towards me. "It's no secret that my wife and I are less than pleased about this infatuation that Abigail seems to have with you. Your reputation as a womanizer and heavy drinker certainly makes you the last young man on earth we would want our daughter being associated with."

"Daddy!" Abby admonished. Raising her voice caused her to grimace from the exertion.

"Stop it! You're upsetting her!" I shouted as I came to stand toe to toe with him.

"Don't you tell me what to do! Abigail is *my* daughter, and I know what's best for her," Andrew countered. He took a step forward to where we were practically nose to nose. "The moment she's released from the hospital I intend to take her back to Texas where she belongs. Hopefully, when she's far, far away from you, she'll forget this silly infatuation and come to her senses."

I opened my mouth to protest, but Abby beat me to the punch. "Daddy, stop being such an asshole to Jake! And I'm not leaving with you!"

Andrew's brows shot so far up in his hairline they practically disappeared. "Excuse me?"

Abby softened her expression. "I'm sorry, but you're being disrespectful and rude to the very guy who stayed all night in an uncomfortable chair while I was out cold to make sure I was safe and not alone." Abby sighed. "But most of all, you're breaking my heart by being so cold and thoughtless to the man I love."

Both Andrew and Laura's mouths gaped opened at Abby's statement. "You two have been the best parents, and all my life you taught me not to judge people and to give everyone, no matter the circumstances, a chance. Now how is it that you're completely trampling upon everything you instilled in me?"

"Abigail, it's just that—" Laura began.

"No, you're stereotyping and judging Jake by rumor and what you think you see. But he's so much more than just a rocker. He has a tender heart and a giving soul. If you only knew the love and affection

290

he has for his mother, his bandmates and even the crew who works for him, you would see that he is someone you should like and respect."

Andrew ran a shaky hand through his hair while Laura stared wide-eyed at me. Just like Abby, she nibbled her bottom lip when she was nervous and was waiting for the courage to say what she needed. "Do you truly love Abby?" Laura asked.

"Yes, ma'am, I do. I love her with all my heart and soul. I intend on working my ass—" I cleared my throat at my language choice, "Uh, I mean, butt off the rest of my life to prove that I'm worthy of her and her love."

"Oh that's so sweet," Laura gushed to which Andrew only grunted.

"Daddy, you know that I love you both, and I'm not going to do anything to hurt you or disappoint you. Just like I told before to you about Jake, I am an adult, and I have to live my life. And right now I chose to spend my recovery time with him."

Her words sent a beaming smile to my lips. I was so fucking proud of her for being so strong. I couldn't have loved my girl more for standing up for me and herself.

"But Abby, we want to be with you while you're healing. I can't bear the thought of just abandoning you."

Tentatively, I reached out to touch Laura's arm. "You won't have to do that. You and Mr. Renard are more than welcome to stay at my farm for as long as you like."

Laura's expression warmed at the thought. "Really? You wouldn't mind?"

"Of course not. Abby needs her parents around her." I gave a pointed look at Andrew.

After a few seconds of staring each other down, he finally sighed resignedly. "I do apologize for any wrong doing on my part." He held out his hand to me. "I believe we were never formally introduced. I'm Andrew Renard."

"Jake Slater," I replied as I pumped his hand up and down.

Although I knew he hated it, a smile filled his face as he added, "It's a pleasure meeting you."

"Likewise."

"You guys really make me happy," Abby said.

"Anything for you, sweetheart," Laura replied.

Abby winced. "Good. Because I *really* need some more pain medicine."

Even though I wanted to, I held back and let Andrew punch the button for the nurse. I figured it was just another set of baby steps along the way to building our relationship.

***

Chapter Twenty

Abby

For the next month, I spent my recovery at Jake's farm. Although I was wrecked physically, I don't know when I'd been happier emotionally. Sure, I didn't necessarily want to almost be beaten to death by a psychotic, jealous ex-lover of Jake's, but in the same token, it meant I had time to spend with him and with his mom. The first week my parents stayed in the guest bedroom while I stayed next door in Jake's bedroom. Although the barn boasted a finished loft that was as nicer than any apartment, Jake refused to sleep far from me, so he either slept in the chair beside my bed or on the couch in the living room. I'd offered to let him sleep with me, but he was too afraid of accidentally hitting or kicking my wounds during the night.

That first week I was smothered to death by Jake, my parents, and Susan. Even Rhys, Brayden, Lily, and AJ hovered over me. Don't get me wrong. It was nice milking my injuries for my favorite home-cooked meals of my mother's or little gifts from the guys. But after a while, it got really old being spoiled. I couldn't even sneeze without everyone freaking out and rushing to my bedside. It was sweet, but it was also incredibly annoying.

Once I was literally back on my feet again, my parents reluctantly left to go back to Texas. They'd spent ten days away from their jobs to make sure I was on the road to recovery. They still weren't happy with me recuperating at Jake's, but they had resigned themselves to the fact that I was an adult and made my own decisions. We had a teary goodbye where I promised to come home at the end of the month.

Some days Jake would reluctantly leave me with Susan, so he could go to Atlanta with the guys to work on the new album. I had to admit that I enjoyed the time with her. She was truly an amazing woman of strength and courage. Physically, she had her good days and bad days, but emotionally she was upbeat each and every day. She was also really funny. When I felt up to riding in a car again, she took me to her dance studio and showed me around. Jake's family came in droves to meet me and to bring home-cooked meals to Susan and to Jake. I'd never felt so much love outside of my own immediate family.

One afternoon after Jake got in from the recording studio in Atlanta, he found Susan and me on the front porch each reading a book. With a beaming smile on his face, he beckoned me with his hand. "I have a surprise for you."

Wrinkling my nose, I replied, "You know I hate surprises."

"You'll like this one. It's a special gift from my grandfather." It didn't escape me that a knowing look passed between Susan and Jake.

Reluctantly, I pulled myself out of the chair and walked down the length of the porch to meet Jake. He took my hand in his and led me across the yard to his barn. When he opened the door, a fluffy ball of a Golden Retriever puppy came galloping over to me.

My eyes widened in shock. "You got me a dog?"

"It's a gift from my Papa. She's the pick of his new litter."

I squealed with delight as I went to pick up the puppy. "She's beautiful," I murmured as I rubbed my face into the soft fur.

"Does that mean you like my surprise?"

I grinned. "Oh I *love* this one."

Jake tipped back his baseball cap off his forehead and eyed me. "So what are you going to name her?"

"Hmm, good question." I stared into the puppy's warm brown eyes. "What should I name you, sweetheart?" As she opened her mouth and yawned, it hit me. "Angel. She can be my angel."

"But you're *my* Angel," Jake protested.

"I think there's room for two Angels around here."

"Whatever. She's your dog."

I couldn't help my brow creasing in worry. "But what happens when I have to leave or go back on the road?"

Jake shrugged. "She'll just stay here with all our other dogs until you get back."

My heartbeat hammered so loud I feared Jake would hear it. I didn't know if he realized that by saying my dog would always have a home at his house, he had just alluded to a massive level of commitment between us. "Are you sure that wouldn't be an imposition?" I finally asked.

"Of course not. I mean, we have all these fenced in acres for her to run around and frolic in."

I giggled. "Did you just say frolic?"

"Yeah, I did, smartass," he replied with a smirk.

Setting Angel gently down on the floor, I then put my arms around Jake's neck. "Thank you so much for the sweet and thoughtful gift. You made my day."

He grinned. "You're welcome."

I leaned in and gave him a lingering kiss. Since the night I had been beaten by Bree, Jake had been gun-shy about kissing or touching me. More than anything in the world, I wanted his mouth and hands on me again like the night in the hotel room. I slid my tongue against his lips, urging him to open to me. When he did, I thrust my tongue against his. Surprisingly, Jake ran his hand down my back and cupped one of my butt cheeks, jerking me against him.

As our tongues danced around each other, I brazenly rubbed myself against the bulge growing in his jeans. I hiked one of my legs up and wrapped it around his hip, giving him part of his former wish to have my cowboy boots digging into his ass. Since I wanted to give him and myself the full experience, I melted against Jake, silently begging with my body language for him to raise me up. Fortunately, he appeased me by cupping my other butt cheek and hoisting me up to wrap my other leg around his waist. I arched my center against his crotch, causing him to groan into my mouth. "Angel," he murmured as he kissed a scorching trail down my neck.

When his hand moved up my ribcage to cup my breast, I cried out. Thinking it was from pain, not pleasure, Jake froze. My vocal reaction had the same effect as pouring a bucket of ice cold water over Jake. "Oh fuck," he muttered before gripping my hips and unwrapping my legs from around his waist. Once he sat my feet back on the ground, he

296

ran a shaky hand through his hair.

"Jake, please don't stop!" I protested.

He shook his head. "You're not fully healed. I hurt you."

"No, you didn't. I cried out because I liked what I was feeling."

He stared at me for a minute. "It doesn't matter. We shouldn't be making out anyway."

Cupping his cheek, I argued, "But I want to make out with you. You're my boyfriend, and I love you."

Staring down at Angel playing at our feet, Jake refused to meet my gaze. "No, we don't. Not now and not any time soon," he muttered before stalking out of the barn. Angel started after him, but then she came back to me. I pulled her into my arms and let the tears rolling down my cheeks dampen her fur.

I didn't see Jake the rest of the afternoon until Susan called us to dinner at seven. To say that you could have cut the tension in the air with a knife would be a mild understatement. Susan chattered along, and I tried keeping up with her while Jake sat in a broody silence, shoveling in his food. Our plates were half-eaten when he sprang out of his chair. When Susan and I stared up at him with our mouths open in surprise, he muttered, "I'm going to the barn to work out."

Angel followed him out of the dining room, but her whines echoed throughout the foyer when he slammed the front door. With an anguished sigh, I dropped my fork onto my plate, causing a noisy clatter. "Sorry."

She gave me a sympathetic smile. "Sweetheart, you don't need to apologize to me. Instead, you should be marching yourself right on out to the barn to sort things out with Jacob."

My eyes widened at her suggestion. "Y-You know things are strained between us?"

"Oh honey, I know I'm dying, but seriously, I would have to be blind not to notice that." Easing back in her chair, she eyed me for a moment. "He's afraid to touch you, isn't he?"

I gave a brief nod. "Since my accident, he acts like I'm some fragile piece of glass that will break at any minute. I know he loves me—he shows it in every way possible."

"He's conflicted about the guilt he feels for what happened to you. In his mind, Jacob thinks that by keeping you at arm's length he's somehow atoning for what he feels are his sins for your accident."

"That's so wrong!" I protested.

"I agree."

"So what should I do?"

A mischievous gleam burned in Susan's blue eyes. "You're going to have to figure that one out on your own, honey. But I think your best strategy to clear the air and end all the tension is to force Jake to touch you again."

I gasped as warmth flooded across my cheeks and down my neck. "Are you suggesting what I think you're suggesting?"

Susan held up her hands. "I just said that you needed to go out to the barn and fight for your man." She rose out of her chair. "If anyone needs me, I'm going to take a bath and turn in early tonight." With a wink, she walked out of the dining room.

Chewing on my nails, I let Susan's words sink in. I knew what I wanted to do, but I didn't know if I had the courage to do it. After all, the cards seemed stacked against me for anything about my plan to work out right. I was twenty-one years old, in love with a womanizing rock star who was going through emotional hell because of his mother's illness and the fact a psychotic ex-girlfriend had beaten me, and my idea of making things better between us was to give him my virginity. Surely that made me crazy.

But when it all came down to it, it wasn't just the desire pumping through me whenever I looked at Jake or when we were close to each other. No, I was crazy in love with him. I'd been in love with him before my accident, and after the last month with him, I was even more in love with him than ever before.

So it was now or never. I loved Jake, and I wanted to be with him. Who knew what the future held for us? But deep down, I would always regret it if the first man I loved wasn't the first I slept with.

"Alrighty then," I muttered before rising out of my chair. I stalked down the hallway and locked myself into the bedroom. My mind was now made up. Susan had planted a tiny seed, and I was going to act on it by going to Jake in the barn and seducing him.

I knew the first thing I needed to do was arm myself with the necessary tools. I had to look like sex to him. Well, I guess that wasn't exactly true since the last time we had almost had sex I was wearing an old t-shirt and yoga pants, not to mention the fact we'd gotten pretty frisky this afternoon when I was wearing jeans and a sweater.

Regardless of what had happened before, Jake needed to know just by looking at me tonight what I wanted.

I snapped my fingers and made my way over to the closet. Digging in my suitcase, I pulled out the white baby doll nightie I'd bought when I got the white dress for Jake. I slid on the glittery thong before shimmying into the nightie. Gazing at myself in the mirror, I turned left and right, appraising my reflection. I guess I looked sexy. The pearl and sequined encrusted bodice barely held in my cleavage, and it felt like at any minute my boobs might pop out of the front, which was probably a win-win situation considering how much Jake professed to like my boobs.

Pulling my hair out of my ponytail, I then brushed it until it to where it cascaded over my shoulders in waves. I reapplied a light coating of makeup, and when I finished, I rolled some shimmering colored lip gloss across my lips.

I slid my robe over my shoulders and stepped into my boots. Cracking open the door, I poked my head out and surveyed the scene. Susan's door was shut tight, so I tip-toed down the hallway and then closed the front door quietly behind me. The full moon overhead lit my way across the yard to the barn.

Although Jake had six horses, they weren't housed in the barn. Instead, they were down the hill in the stables. The 'barn' was more of a finished house or his bachelor pad, so to speak, where he had work-out equipment, a living area to relax in, and then the loft upstairs to sleep.

With gangsta rap blaring out of the stereo speakers, Jake didn't even hear the door close. Over and over, he pummeled the punching bag as sweat dripped off his head and onto his shoulders.

"Jake," I shouted.

The sound of my voice caused him to still instantly. His arms reached out to steady the swaying bag before he turned around. "What are you doing out here?"

"I need to talk to you."

"About what?"

I crossed the gap between us. I was sure he could hear the knocking of my knees as I feared my wobbly legs wouldn't hold me up. Without taking my eyes off of his, my trembling fingers went to the sash of my robe. I untied it and then slowly slid it off. When it dropped to the floor, it felt like the sound was so deafening that it echoed around us.

Jake's blue eyes widened as his gaze trailed over the negligee. He licked his lips several times and swayed on his feet before he finally spoke. "Angel, what are you doing?"

"Seducing you."

The corners of his lips twitched, and I could tell he was fighting not to laugh. "You came out here in some racy get-up to seduce me?"

"I-I want to be with you. I want you to make love to me."

Jake's eyebrows shot up before he quickly shook his head. "I told you no earlier, and I still mean it."

My mouth gaped open in surprise. "That's your response to *this*?" I motioned to my jacked-up cleavage.

His Adam's apple bobbed up and down a few times as he

swallowed hard. "Yeah, it is."

He then bent over and snatched my robe up off the floor. "Now put this back on and go to bed."

"Jake, I'm not in pain anymore. I'm healed, and I can do this—I *want* to do this."

"No."

Tears stung my eyes, and I bit down on my lip. "You seriously don't want me?"

With a grunt, Jake replied, "Oh my dick wants you more than anything in the world right now. But for once, I'm going to think with the head on my shoulders, rather than the one below my waist." Jake gripped the edges of my robe so hard his knuckles turned white. "Trust me, Angel, I'm the last man on earth you should want to give yourself to."

"But I do want to be with you. I bought this a month ago when Lily convinced me to wear a white dress. I realized that day I wanted to be prepared because I knew sometime soon I would want to make love to you."

My statement caused an agonized groan from Jake, but he didn't respond. Instead, he paced anxiously around the room. Finally, he whirled around and threw up his hands in defeat. "After everything that happened with Bree and your recovery, I've been doing some thinking—hell you could even call it soul searching."

"So have I, and I—"

His blue eyes blazed with fury. "Don't you get it, Angel? You deserve a hell of a lot better than me, both in and out of the bedroom."

"Not that bullshit again. I'm so sick of hearing how you think you aren't worthy," I protested.

"It's the truth, dammit! You're this beautiful, pure spirit, and I'm corrupted and tainted from my past. I won't put that on you."

Taking a tentative step forward, I took his hand in mind. I brought it to my lips and kissed along his knuckles. "You're not able to see yourself like I do. You're deserving of my love, and I want to give it to you in all ways."

His expression darkened. "But I haven't made love since I was eighteen years old—if I even did it then. I only know how to fuck girls, and there's no way in hell I'll fuck you!"

Frustration and anger swirled within me. I swept a hand to my hip. "So just because you have a past and I don't that means we can't have sex?"

"Yeah, that's right."

"Well, that's not fair."

Jake tossed the robe at me. "Life's not fair, babe. Get used to it."

I threw the robe back at him, smacking him in the face with it. "No, I won't. I'm not taking no for an answer!"

He smirked at me. "And just what do you plan to do? Rape me?"

"No, I intend on making love with you." Stepping forward, I slid my arms around his neck and then pressed my body flush against his. Jake instantly tensed. Before he could push me away, I said, "Even though you don't believe it, I know you, Jake. I understand that feeling and expressing emotions off the stage is hard for you—I've seen you screw-up way too many times, remember? More than anything I

303

understand that now with everything that is going on with your mom and what happened with me, that you're gun-shy, scared, and unsure of what you're experiencing and feeling."

I rubbed the back of my hand across his cheek. "But I want you to listen to me. I love you, Jake. I've never loved another guy in my entire life. I've given myself over to you emotionally, and I'm more than ready to do that with my body as well. So I don't care whether I make love with you, have sex, or even fuck."

His eyes widened as big as saucers at my using the F word. I smiled reassuringly at him. "I just want to be with you." I pulled his head down to where our foreheads touched. "Not only have you told me over and over again that you loved me, but you've managed to *show* me just how much you love me too. I don't care if you've been with a thousand other women—that was the past. We're the present and the future—right here and right now."

Jake made a pained noise in the back of his throat. "Can't you see I'm fucking drowning in all this guilt?" He smacked his hand against his bare chest. "It's because of me that you were almost killed. I don't want anything else on my conscience, so I won't ruin you by taking your virginity."

I couldn't help rolling my eyes. "Would you stop talking like I'm some fragile flower or something? I may be fifty percent angel, but I'm fifty percent hellcat too." I curled my fingers into his sweat slickened strands of hair. "I'll be your holy water—I'll purify you and wash away the past. Just don't deny me this."

"Angel, I don't ever want to deny you anything. I'd give you the world if I could. It kills me inside to have to tell you no." He wrapped his arms tight around me. "It's just I'm so afraid that my love can never be good enough for you."

"Don't ever think that, Jake. It's all I need—all I want." I gazed up at him. "Besides, you may be with me and decide I'm not enough for you."

He shook his head. "I fucking doubt that."

"But I don't know what to do…to you know, please you."

Jake grinned down at me. "Please me?"

I felt my cheeks warming. "Get you off?"

His thumb rubbed across my cheekbone. "Babe, I doubt you'll have any problems getting me off. You did just fine last time."

"But you were helping me. I just want to be everything you could ever need and more both in and out of the bedroom."

Jake then brought his lips to mine and silenced any remaining doubts. His tongue slid against my lips, and I opened my mouth, inviting him in. I wanted to taste every inch of him tonight. Our kisses deepened as our tongues danced and fought against each other.

With our mouths and arms entangled, I used my hips to nudge Jake toward the loft steps. I wasn't going to give him another chance to talk me or himself out of this. When his butt knocked against the stairs, his lips pulled away from mine. His signature cocky smirk spread across his lips. "Ladies first."

I giggled. "Why do I think this is less about you being chivalrous and more about getting to see my ass in this thong?"

He banged his head back against the railing. "Christ almighty, that sexy-as-hell-get-up has a thong too?"

"Mmm hmm."

A sexy grin stretched across his face. "You're killing me." He then stepped aside for me to start up the stairs. With every step I took, I could feel his eyes scorching into my bare skin. It caused heat and moisture to grow between my thighs.

When we reached the landing of the loft, I started to wrap my arms around Jake, but he stopped me. "Wait, Angel, I'm all sweaty from working out, and I stink."

I leaned in to inhale his bare chest. "You smell good to me."

Jake chuckled as he pushed out of my arms. "If we're doing this, we're doing it right and when I'm not stinky."

"If you say so," I replied.

Tugging my hand, he pulled me to the bathroom. Just like everything in the barn, it was breathtaking with its marble tile and granite countertops. Jake turned on the shower knob, and a steady stream of water came jetting out. With his hands on the waistband of his shorts, his lips curved in a smirk. "Did you plan on joining me or just watching?"

"Um…" Did I want to shower with him? That threw me for a loop since that usually came after sex, right? Ugh, this was all happening wrong and not like I pictured it. And I sure as hell didn't think it would be romantic to watch him shower. The sight of Jake lathering up while I stared at him sounded like something out of a bad porno. "Uh, I can just wait in the bed." I then started inching back from the shower.

He was sliding his shorts down when I quickly turned to go. I didn't make it far before he grabbed my arm and spun me into him. I squealed as the water drenched my hair and soaked my lingerie. "Don't go, Angel. I want you to stay."

At the desire and love that burned in his eyes, I found it hard to breathe. When I could finally speak, I replied, "Then I'll stay."

Jake glanced down at my wet nightie that was now molded to my body like a second skin. "You really bought this for me?"

"Yes," I replied as my arms went around his neck. "Do you like it?"

"Hmm," he murmured as his hands came up to cup my breasts within the bodice. "It's beautiful—you're beautiful in it."

I smiled. "I thought you would like it because it was white, and you always say—"

"You're an angel in white."

"I'm *your* angel."

Bending down, he gripped the hem of the nightie and pulled it over my head. Closing my eyes, I leaned my back against the shower stall as he took in my appearance. When he didn't reach out for me, I opened my eyes.

Jake was staring right below my chest. When I glanced down, I gasped. Somehow in my nervousness and enthusiasm, I had thrown my negligee on over my chest wrap. My hand flew to cover my eyes. "Oh God, I'm such an idiot! What a way to ruin a moment," I moaned.

With a chuckle, Jake pulled my hand from my eyes. "I assume it comes off just like the lingerie, right?"

"Yes."

He winked at me. "Then stop worrying. I'll just take it off." Bringing his fingers to the clip, Jake then started unwrapping the bandage. I began to twist from side to side to help him get it off quicker. With a wicked grin, he said, "You know, this makes me think of that scene in the movie *Shakespeare in Love* where Will unbinds Viola's breasts."

I laughed. "The very fact you know that movie is very swoonworthy, Mr. Slater," I teased.

"Hey, don't be acting like I'm not a romantic. I was quoting *Romeo and Juliet* the first night we were together."

I cocked my brows at him. "Right after I had to prove that you could get it up for a virgin."

Jake winced. "I was such a douche to you."

I leaned in and kissed him. "I've forgiven you for all your douche moments in the past."

"Thanks, Angel," Jake replied with a grin. Once he finished taking off my bandage, Jake's expression darkened, and he sucked in a harsh breath. I knew he was surprised by how bruised I still was. Most of them had faded, but there was still a yellow and green discoloration all around my ribcage and abdomen.

I cupped his cheek and shook my head. "Please don't do that. I promise you they don't hurt."

Dropping to his knees, Jake began feathering tender kisses along my ribs and across my stomach. "I'm sorry," he murmured, his breath warming my already scorching skin.

I gripped the strands of his hair and gently pulled his head back to look at me. "Stop apologizing for something you couldn't help. You're not the one who did this to me, and I will never, ever blame you."

He rested his cheek against my stomach. "I love you, Angel."

"I love you, too, Jake."

As his fingers grazed the waist band of my thong, he glanced up at me. I gave a short nod of my head before he tugged it down my thighs. We were both totally naked together for the first time ever, and I shivered with anticipation.

"Are you cold?"

"No, I just want you."

A pained noise came from the back of Jake's throat. He kissed my inner thighs before nudging my legs further apart. Staring up at me, he held my gaze as his tongue flicked out to lick across my folds. I sucked in a breath and let my head fall back against the shower wall as his warm tongue worked over me. He lapped and suckled at my clit to where I was rocking my hips against him. He took one of my feet and pulled it up to rest on his shoulder giving him better access. The moment he thrust his tongue inside me I came apart and cried out his name.

Once I came back to myself, I figured he would stand up, but instead, he remained on his knees. He pulled away momentarily to tease my opening with one finger before pushing it inside. He added two and then three to swirl and move within me. With his free hand, his fingers skimmed over my stomach before coming to cup one of my breasts.

I was on sensory overload as my nipple peaked under his attention.

His hand then snaked over to the other breast to bring it to a hardened nub as well. All the while he kept plunging his fingers in and out of me while his thumb made my clit feel like it was going to explode.

Gripping the strands of his hair, I cried out his name over and over again as I came. If it were possible, I think I had experienced an even stronger orgasm that time. When I gazed down at Jake with hooded eyes, he frowned.

"What's wrong?"

"Baby, you're so tight. I'm worried about hurting you."

"I'll be fine," I panted.

"Are you sure?"

"Yes, dammit, now take me to bed and make love to me!" I demanded.

Jake chuckled. "Boy, you get bossy when you come, don't you?"

"Please?"

"Well, I never actually took a shower." When I started to protest, he grabbed the body wash. Pushing my hands together, he squirted some into my palms. "Wash me, Angel."

Bringing my palms to his chest, I worked my hands over his pecs, down along his heavily tattooed arms, and then to his rock hard abs. As my hands skimmed above his waist, his stomach tensed while his erection bucked up against my hand. Eying it, I couldn't help but start to feel some of the anxiety Jake had earlier. I pressed myself flush against Jake to reach around to wash his back before I let my hands dip down to grip his butt cheeks.

With our bodies so close, Jake began to slide his erection against my folds. I gasped and rocked back against him. Just as I began to get carried away again, he stopped. In a ragged breath he said, "We need to get to the bed."

"Okay," I replied.

When we stepped out of the shower, Jake didn't even bother with a towel. He swept me off my feet and then proceeded to carry me to the bed. Gently, he deposited me on the side of the mattress. Drawing my knees up, I wrapped my arms around my legs while I watched as Jake opened the top nightstand drawer. He pulled out a condom and a bottle of something I didn't recognize. At what I guess was my questioning expression, he replied, "It's lube. It'll make this first time easier for you."

"I see." I tilted my head up at him. "So you have a whole drawer of sex goodies in there?"

"It's not what you're thinking, Angel," Jake replied as he ripped open the foil wrapper.

"And just what am I thinking?"

"That I use this loft as my swinging bachelor pad where I bring all my conquests and bang them."

I hated myself for being that easy to read. "Are you sure, or are you just giving me a line so I won't bail on you?"

He grinned. "I keep this out here because it's the one place that's off limits for Mama and her cleaning lady. I would prefer to keep this aspect of my life private."

"Yes, it would break the poor cleaning lady's heart to find out you were such a naughty boy."

With a shudder, Jake replied, "Not to mention my mama."

My laughter died on my lips as Jake began putting on the condom. Even though I wanted to look away, I couldn't help being fascinated by the sight of him sliding it down his extreme length. When he finished, his eyes met mine, and he nudged my shoulder gently with his own. I then scooted on my butt to the center of the mattress. On his knees, Jake crawled along the bed until he was looming over me.

He kissed me tenderly before plunging his tongue into my mouth. Although I hadn't kissed a lot of guys or men, I knew good when I experienced it, and Jake was very, very good. As he ravaged my mouth, I felt moisture growing between my legs again. Jake's hands managed to be everywhere all at once. They were kneading my breasts, caressing my buttocks, or slipping between my legs to stroke me. I shivered in spite of the beads of sweat breaking out along my skin from the heat building within me.

As Jake settled himself between my thighs, I couldn't help but tense up. This was it—the big moment, and I couldn't help being nervous. I had to draw in a few deep breaths to calm me down and keep from going into full on panic mode.

When his erection nudged at my entrance, I pinched my eyes shut, bracing myself for the pain.

"Don't close your eyes," he whispered, his breath fanning against my cheek. My eyelids fluttered open to take in Jake's intense stare. "I love you, Angel."

"I love you, too."

As he pushed inside me, tears stung my eyes both from the

physical pain and the emotional enormity of the moment. "I'm so sorry, baby," Jake murmured as he kissed away the tears that had escaped in salty streaks down my face.

"It's okay. I want this...I want you," I replied as I tried inhaling a few deep breaths. Once Jake felt like I was accustomed to him, he withdrew and thrust back into me. This time it was both painful and pleasurable. "Mmm."

"Better?"

"Yes."

He then began to move within me. After a few minutes, the pain evaporated, and I began to feel like raising my hips to meet his thrusts. That caused Jake to moan with pleasure. As we moved in perfect sync together, Jake brought his lips to mine and began to kiss me passionately. His tongue plunged into my mouth and mimicked his movements inside me. A hot flush ran over me from the top of my head down to my toes, and I couldn't help tearing my mouth away from his to pant and moan with pleasure.

Although it felt so very, very good, I knew I wasn't going to come like I had before. When I felt Jake's body tensing, I wrapped my arms around his back, drawing him closer to me. "Oh Abby!" he cried as he shuddered with his release. I rubbed circles over his back as he continued to tremble within me.

When Jake pulled his head away from my shoulder, I smiled up at him. "That was so amazing, baby. I love you so much for giving it to me."

"I love you too, but..." His brows furrowed.

"What's wrong?" I asked.

"You didn't come."

My cheeks warmed at his comment. "No, but I think that's kinda normal for girls the first time." When Jake didn't respond, I took his face in my hands. "I did twice before though."

"Yeah, but…"

I smiled. "Baby, you just gave me the best experience of my entire life."

He scowled. "You have nothing to gauge it by. I coulda been lousy as hell, and you'd think it was rainbows and unicorns."

"Are you trying to ruin my making love for the first time just because your ego is bruised because I didn't come?" I snapped.

His expression softened. "No, that's not it."

"Well, that's what it sounded like to me." I snatched my hands away from his face. "I've been waiting and wondering my entire adult life what sex would be like, and for me, you blew away all my expectations. So what if I didn't come when you were inside me? It was my first freakin' time, and for the first part, it hurt like hell!"

When I started to climb off the mattress, Jake wrapped me in his arms. "I'm sorry, Angel."

"Yeah, well, you should be. Asshole!"

He chuckled. "Trust me, I am." With his fingers, he tipped my chin up to look at him. "You were right. I was being a complete and total dick because I thought I had totally fucked up your first time because you didn't come." He tenderly kissed my cheek. "It's hard for me getting used to the all the emotions with sex. It's overwhelming being your first."

"So what you're trying to say is you were under a lot of pressure?"

"Yeah, but it was worth it. It was fucking amazing." He grinned. "*You* were fucking amazing."

"Really?" I asked, my voice rising an octave.

Jake propped himself up on one elbow to stare at me. "You know what made it for me? It was the look in your eyes as you were experiencing every range of emotion from the physical pain to the emotional connection. Your eyes are so expressive, and I felt like I was really, *really* inside you."

My heartbeat raced at his thoughtful words, and for a moment, I could only reply, "Oh wow." I cocked my head at him. "So does that mean you like making love better than fucking?"

Jake chuckled as his finger came to trace my lips. "Such a dirty mouth you have, Angel."

"You're avoiding the question."

"I plan on continuing to make love to you as well as introducing you to fucking."

I grinned. "I look forward to that."

"Now come here and let me spoon you again."

I happily snuggled up to him. After all, who would argue with that?

*** *** ***

Chapter Twenty-One

Abby

Sunlight streamed across my face, warming my cheek. Yawning, I started to stretch when I realized I was imprisoned by two muscular, tattooed arms. When I tried squirming away, Jake tightened his hold on me. "Where do you think you're going, Angel?" he murmured drowsily.

"Nowhere," I replied. Glancing over my shoulder at him, I grinned. "I'm not used to waking up naked with a guy."

Jake's closed eyes popped open. "Hmm, that's right. Since I've got you naked and in my arms, I think I should make the most of the moment. Don't you?"

"What did you have in mind?"

"Showing you just how much I love you," he replied as he pushed me onto my back. He then began nibbling a moist trail over my shoulder, up my neck, and then finally after what felt like an eternity, his lips met mine.

Realizing I hadn't brushed my teeth, I jerked back and covered my mouth. "Oh God, do I have morning breath?"

Jake rolled his eyes. "Angel, me and my morning wood couldn't give a shit about whether or not you have morning breath."

I giggled. "If you're sure."

"I'm sure, but maybe I should put my mouth somewhere else."

I inhaled sharply as his lips closed over my nipple. I arched my back, allowing him to take more of my breast into his mouth. Swirling his tongue over the hardened peak, he then gently nibbled it, causing me to gasp. "You like that?"

"Mmm, hmm," I murmured.

He chuckled as he kissed a trail over to my other breast to give it the same attention. "Let's see how wet you are for me," he said as he brought a hand between my legs. He stroked and caressed me until my hips were arching off the bed. "You like that too, huh?"

"Yes, Jake!"

But when he thrust two fingers inside me, I cried out from pain, rather than pleasure. He grimaced before withdrawing his fingers and tenderly kissed my cheek. "I'm sorry, Angel. I should've realized you would've been too sore this morning."

"Ugh, this sucks!" My breaths came in harsh, frustrated pants. "I really wish it didn't hurt because I do want you again. Very much." I cupped his face in my hands. "I can't tell you enough how last night was the most beautiful experience of my life, and I can't wait to make love to you again."

His genuine smile made my heartbeat accelerate. "We will. But I think we better give you a little while to recuperate."

I grinned coyly at him. "If you just didn't have such a big penis, I would be fine."

Jake threw back his head and laughed. "Yeah, right. You wouldn't know big from small."

Sliding my hand between us, I cupped his erection in my hand. "I dunno. Seems pretty gigantic to me."

"Hmm, now you're just being a smartass and getting me riled up even more with no hope of getting off."

When he tried to push my hand away, I shook my head. "Just because we can't do it, do it, doesn't mean I have to leave you unsatisfied."

"And just what did you have in mind?"

I gave him a flirty wink as I sat up in the bed. "Taking care of my man." I then rose up to straddle him. Ignoring the ache of both pain and pleasure at the position, I began kissing and licking my way down Jake's tattooed chest. I boldly flicked my tongue out and circled both of his nipples, causing him to moan. Then I worked my way down his well-defined abs to that delicious V. Just before I got to his erection, I stopped. He whimpered in disappointed. "Patience, baby."

"Don't 'baby' me when you're torturing me!" he argued.

With a laugh, my hand feathered across his abdomen and between his legs. I took his length in my hand and stroked it like he had taught me before. Gripping him tighter, I bent over to teasingly lick my tongue over the tip. I met Jake's gaze, which burned into me with desire, before I slipped the head into my mouth.

"Oh fuck me," Jake muttered as his head fell back against the pillow.

I grinned as I tried taking him further into my mouth. Fighting my gag reflex, I worked him in and out, stroking him with my hand as well. "Angel...Abby. Oh yeah, keep doing that. Damn, it feels so good," he groaned, his hips bucking off the mattress.

Although I'd been mortified to get sex advice from Lily, I remembered she'd said to give a guy's balls lots of attention. With my free hand, I cupped them gently, working them between my fingers. Jake grunted in pleasure, so I kept up my ministrations. One hand twisted into my hair while the other fisted the sheet. "Oh Angel, I'm gonna come."

When he tried moving me off of him, I murmured, "No," against his penis. I wanted to do everything I could for him, and that included letting him come in my mouth. My acknowledgement caused a low groan from deep in Jake's throat before he began shuddering. When he came, it took me off guard for a minute, and I jumped, but I kept him in my mouth until he was done.

After swallowing hard, I let him fall from my mouth. I glanced up at him to gage how well my first blow job had gone. A lazy grin etched across his face. "Angel, do you even have to ask?"

I giggled as I snuggled against his side. "Yeah," I replied.

"Fanfuckingtastic." He kissed the crown of my head. "You're good at everything you do, so I don't know why you would doubt your sex abilities."

I shrugged. "Because it's all new for me, and you're so experienced. I don't want to be a disappointment."

He brought his fingers to my chin and tipped my head up to meet his intense gaze. "The past is the past, remember? All that matters is you and me and the future. And I have no fucking complaints about anything, got it?"

"Okay, Mr. Bossy, I got it."

He grinned. "Good, I'm glad to hear it." He had just begun to kiss me again when I heard Susan's voice from inside the barn. Jake jerked his lips away from mine.

"Jacob?"

"Yeah?" he called breathlessly.

"I'm cooking breakfast, so make sure you and Abby pry yourselves away from each other for some fortification, okay? I'll expect you down in fifteen minutes."

"Okay, Mama," Jake replied.

"Oh God," I gasped as mortification rocketed through me. Even though Susan had practically pushed me out the door to be with Jake, I was still horrified that she knew exactly what we had done and what we were still potentially doing.

Jake snickered at me. "Quit worrying, Angel. Mama isn't going to be mad or shun us for what we did. Hell, she's even cooked breakfast for us."

"If you say so," I murmured.

He then tugged me up from the bed and led me into the bathroom.

After a quick shower and one mind-blowing orgasm later from Jake's magic mouth, I slipped into my robe and hurried across the yard to the house. I threw my partially wet hair into a ponytail before I slipped on a pair of jeans and shirt. I then padded down the hall to the kitchen. Susan was taking out a pan of homemade biscuits from the oven while Angel played on the floor. At the sight of me, Angel yapped happily and ran to my waiting arms.

"How's my baby girl?" I asked as Angel licked my face.

"She's better this morning, but last night, someone abandoned the poor thing, and she came scratching at my door," Susan replied as she took a plate of bacon and sausage to the table.

"Oh no! I'm so sorry."

She winked. "Don't worry honey. You had bigger things on your mind last night." When my cheeks flushed, she laughed. "Besides, I enjoyed having her with me. She makes a wonderful bed buddy."

"I'm glad to hear that."

Jake arrived then, and we sat down to eat. I would be lying if I said my exertions the night before along with this morning hadn't made me starved. I ate until I felt like my stomach would explode. When we were finished, Susan stared intently at me before turning to Jake. "Jacob, why don't you do the breakfast dishes and give Abigail and me some time alone for a few minutes?"

"Sure. I might as well do something for you since you cooked it," he replied good-naturedly.

I followed Susan down the hall to her bedroom. When she closed the door behind us, she smiled at what must've been my apprehensive expression. "You're not in trouble, Abigail. The reason I brought you in here is that I wanted to give you something."

I followed her over to the dresser. She raised the lid on a glass jewelry box that had a ballerina etched into the top. The theme to *Swan*

Lake began to play. Her fingers delved inside, and she took out a strand of expensive looking pearls. "My parents gave me these to me for my high school graduation along with this jewelry box. I've worn them through so many major events in my life." She held them out to me. "I want you to have them."

My eyes widened as I shook my head furiously back and forth. "No, I couldn't. You should leave them to Sally or your nieces."

She patted my cheek. "But I don't want to leave them to anyone but you. There are some other things I want you to have as well, but these, along with the jewelry box, are the most special to me."

Realizing how serious she was, I finally relented. "Susan, you can't imagine how touched I am that you want me to have them." Although I tried fighting them, tears burned and blurred my eyes. "They're beautiful, and I'll treasure them always."

"Good. Maybe someday you can pass them on to my granddaughter."

At my gasp, she laughed. "Don't think that I can't see you for exactly who and what you are. I'm thrilled that Jake has found a girl he can marry and raise a family with."

"I would love nothing more," I answered honestly.

"Then let me say this as well. I know Jake is hardheaded and stubborn, and I know he's going to make some mistakes in the future like he has before. But promise me that you'll give him a chance and try to forgive him?"

Even though it was hard, I bobbed my head. "I will."

"Good. Because when it comes down to the end like it has for me, you don't want to live with the regret of not forgiving the man you loved with all your heart and soul."

I furrowed my brows. "But I thought you had forgiven Jake's father?"

A flush entered Susan's pale cheeks. "This is a secret just between you and me, but Mark wasn't the love of my life."

"He wasn't?"

"Although he gave me the greatest gift of my life, Jacob, I could never feel for Mark what I did for Yuri. He was a dancer in one of the traveling companies I was in. We dated for years, and when I refused to marry him because I thought we were too young, he went out and slept with another dancer to hurt me. Although he apologized for weeks and months, I was stubborn, and I wouldn't forgive him. He finally gave up and moved on, and I've regretted it all this time. A couple of years after Yuri is when Mark came into my life." She gave me a wry smile. "Jake's never been able to understand how I could forgive Mark for leaving me, but the truth was I just didn't love him like I should, so it didn't hurt as much."

Speechless, I could only murmur, "Wow."

She smiled. "So in the future when there are times you want to strangle Jacob or he's tested your love, just remember that forgiveness is so much easier than regret."

"I will. You have my word."

She pulled me into a tight embrace. Both her words and her emaciated frame caused tears to prick my eyes. She rubbed wide circles over my back. "Sweet Abby, you're an answer to a prayer. My

Jacob is very, very lucky to have you. Don't doubt for one second that I won't constantly remind him that for as long as I have left."

With tears streaking down my cheeks, I couldn't reply at first. Finally, I choked off a, "Thank you."

As she pulled away, she cupped my chin. "Do you know there's an old saying that for every tear you shed for someone else's grief, it takes one off of their suffering?"

"Really?" I hiccupped.

She nodded while swiping the tears off my cheeks. "So you've just managed to take a few off of Jacob."

"I'm glad. I'd do anything for him," I replied.

Susan smiled. "But no more tears, honey. Let's just enjoy the time we have left together. Okay?"

"Okay," I agreed.

"And speaking of time, I'm pretty sure it's time to go check on how many little 'presents' Angel might've deposited in the house."

I laughed. "Let's give that job to Jake since it was his idea to give me a puppy."

Susan's eyes widened. "Oh honey, I do like your thinking!"

***

Chapter Twenty-Two

JAKE

Lounging on an old patchwork quilt, I reclined my head to get a better view of the blackened sky encrusted with twinkling stars. With her back against my chest, Abby signed with contentment. "Gosh, that is so beautiful," she remarked.

"You're so beautiful," I murmured into her ear.

She rubbed my arms that were wrapped tightly around her before tilting back to bestow a kiss on my cheek. "Aw thank you baby. You say and do the sweetest things for me."

"So you like this surprise?"

Glancing over her shoulder at me, she grinned. "Yes, this was another good surprise."

It was our last night together before Abby had to leave, and I had intended to make it as special as I could. I wanted it to be just the two of us—no friends or crowds. So I had decided on a twilight picnic down by the lake on my grandfather's property. It was miles and miles off the main road, and you had to get to it either with an ATV or a Jeep. Nestled within a few rolling hills, it boasted breathtaking views of the mountains.

We had already finished the dinner I'd gotten from Abby's favorite restaurant, Longhorn's. We were just making a dent in the dessert—

my mama's homemade Strawberry Shortcake—as the sun began making its decent in the horizon. I'd nestled Abby in my arms so we could experience our first sunset together. Now that it was over we were stargazing as light flickered around us from the votive candles lining the blanket's edges.

"Want some more cake?" Abby asked.

"Sure." I eased my grip on her so she could reach the plate.

Taking the fork, she cut off a piece and swiveled in my lap to bring it to my mouth. She in turn took a bite as well. "That's sooo good," she murmured. As I chewed, I took my finger and dipped it into the cool whip lining the plate. I then covered Abby's top and bottom lips. Leaning in, I kissed her deeply, licking and tasting the sweetness off her mouth.

"Now that's good," I murmured against her lips.

"Mmm, hmm," she replied dreamily before she turned around to rest her back against my chest.

Pulling the long shroud of her hair back, I kissed a moist trail down her neck and across her shoulder. When I got to her sundress strap, I tugged it down, causing part of her breast to spill over the cup. I nibbled on her shoulder as my fingertips feathered over the exposed part of her breast.

Abby's laughter caused her body to vibrate against mine. Glancing over her shoulder at me, she shook her head. "Jake Slater, I'm beginning to think you're an insatiable sex fiend."

I grinned against her shoulder blade as I thought about our rather raunchy escapade a few hours ago. When I'd come out of the barn to the sight of Abby bent over the picnic basket with her tits practically hanging out of her sundress, my dick had twitched in need. I'd waited until after she had placed everything into the back of the Jeep before I'd had taken her hand in mine and tugged her into the barn. "Jake, what are you—" she began. But then her eyes widened at what had to be the lustful gleam burning in mine.

Before she could protest, I'd shoved her back against the wall. After wrapping one arm around her waist, I'd used the other to jerk up the hem of her sundress. With one quick tug, I'd left her panties in shreds.

Abby gasped at the sight of her ruined underwear hitting the barn floor. With a sheepish grin, I replied, "Sorry, Angel. I'll get you another pair."

"Why bother? I mean, you'd probably just tear them up as well, you horndog!" she huffed.

I threw back my head and laughed at her mock outrage. She smiled as she brought her lips to mine for a fiery kiss. After all the times we'd been together since that first night, I knew she still needed preparation to take me. Using one hand to unbutton and unzip my fly, I used the other to stroke and tease Abby into a frenzy. Closing her eyes, she had bit down on her lip before arching her hips in time to my hand.

When I had her dripping with need, I momentarily pulled away to push down my pants and dig a condom out of my pocket. Then I had grabbed her by the ass cheeks, hoisted her up, and impaled her on my dick. "Jake!" she'd cried, and I'd almost blown my load right then and there. It was so fucking sexy the way she had said my name coupled with the fact that she was finally starting to be able to come when I was inside her.

Wrapping her legs around my waist, Abby finally fulfilled one of my longest fantasies about her by digging her delicious cowboy boots into my bare ass. I pounded into her hard and fast while she gripped my shoulders to hold on. Her tiny pants along with my grunts of pleasure had echoed through the barn. "Are you close, Angel?"

"Yes, oh yes," she had moaned. It was only a few more moments before her walls clenched around me, causing me to come.

Even though it had been the hottest sexcapade I had ever had with my girl, I still wanted more from her. I could never get enough of her sweetness, and then there was also the fact she was about to leave me bereft of her delicious curves.

My hand snaked inside the bodice of her dress to cup one of her breasts. Abby sucked in a breath as my thumb flicked back and forth over her nipple, causing it to harden. When I pinched it, her head fell back against my shoulder as she moaned. While I kneaded her breast, I kissed her cheek and over to her ear.

"Rise up," I commanded.

Fumbling, Abby rose up on her knees before staring at me expectantly. When I started pulling up the hem of her dress, she swatted my hand away and widened her eyes. "Not out here."

I couldn't help chuckling. "Baby, this is private property, and we're out in the middle of nowhere. I promise that no one else is going to see your sexy bod but me."

Nibbling her bottom lip, she asked, "Are you sure?"

"Positive."

She didn't reply. Instead, her fingers came to the buttons on my shirt. In almost record time, she was stripping me of it, and then her hand went to my belt. She helped me out of my jeans.

At the sight of me without underwear, she shook her head. "Commando?"

"You know it."

She rolled her eyes but grinned in spite of herself. Since I knew she was modest, I let her keep her dress on until I was totally naked. Then I lifted it over her head. "So beautiful," I murmured as my hands went to cup and knead her breasts. Our lips found each other, and we began kissing passionately. I lay back on the blanket and urged Abby to straddle me. I knew she loved riding me because it gave her more pleasure, and it was hot as hell for me to watch her swaying breasts and her body bouncing on and off of me.

As she rubbed her wet center across my dick, I groaned. "Wait a minute." I furiously dug a condom out of the back pocket of my discarded jeans and then slid it on. Abby rose up and then started easing down on me inch by inch. Placing her palms on my chest, she then set an agonizingly slow rhythm rising almost off of me and then bringing herself slowly back down. After a few minutes of breathless panting from the two of us, I gripped her hips tighter and started working her harder and faster against me. Our pants were replaced by the sounds of grunts and groans and skin slapping together. "Oh Jake," Abby murmured as she came. I kept raising her hips and jerking her hard down on me, but with her clenching walls, I didn't last much longer before crying out her name and spilling myself inside her.

Collapsing onto my chest, Abby began sniffling. "I already miss you."

I chuckled. "Angel, I'm still inside you."

"I don't care." She rose up to shoot me a death glare. "And don't joke at a time like this."

"I'm sorry. It's a defense mechanism." I brushed her long blonde hair out of her face. "Trust me that I feel just as desperate about you leaving. But we're going to make this work."

"How?"

"With Mama, it's not going to be an option for me to come to you, so I've been thinking that I'll just fly you out here on the days you have off between tour stops."

Abby's eyes widened. "Do you know how much that would cost!"

I shrugged. "So."

"Jake, it's awfully sweet, but I can't let you do that."

"It's not up for discussion, Angel. I want to be with you, I have the money, so you might as well not argue with me since I always get my way."

Rolling her eyes, she replied, "You're such an egomaniac."

I ran my fingers over her bare back, causing her to shiver. "But in spite of all my faults, you still love me, right?"

"With all my heart and soul."

"Good. Because I feel the same fucking way." Flipping us over, I settled myself between her thighs. "Ready to show me once again just how much you're going to miss me?"

***

Chapter Twenty-Three

Abby

One Month Later

"Love ya, Austin and see ya again next year!" I cried into the microphone. As I started off stage, I waved at the boisterous crowd. Unlike the guys, I didn't stop at the dressing rooms to change. Instead, I headed straight for the bus. My hulking bodyguard followed right at my side and didn't leave me until the bus doors closed and locked behind me.

Once I was in the safety of the bedroom, I dug out my phone and called Jake. While our long-distance love arrangement had been running smoothly, I'd been worried about him the last few times we had talked. In the weeks after I'd left, Susan's health had begun rapidly deteriorating, and it was wreaking havoc on Jake emotionally. I wanted more than anything to bail on the tour to be with him.

He answered on the third ring. "Hey Angel, how was the show?"

"Good. It was a pretty big venue, and we sold out."

"That's awesome. I miss you like crazy."

His words caused a fluttering in my chest. "I miss you too. How's Susan?"

Jake inhaled a sharp breath, and I could almost feel his anguish through the phone. "She's okay I guess. She's having more bad days than good."

My heart ached for him, and I would have given anything to be able to wrap my arms around him and comfort him. I knew he needed a distraction, and after more girl talks with Lily, I knew she had admitted that she often resorted to comforting Brayden's emotional heartaches with physical love.

After gnawing on my bottom lip, I finally decided to go brazen. "I bought something for you today."

"You did?" Jake questioned absentmindedly.

"Actually, it's for me, but I think you'll enjoy it."

A hissing noise came from Jake. "Whoa, wait a minute. What did you buy?"

I giggled. "I'm glad I have your full attention now, Mr. Horny."

He groaned. "Fuck, did you buy some lingerie?"

"Mmm, hmm."

"Show me."

"Nope, not until this weekend."

"*Yes*! Go put it on and take a picture for me!" he commanded in a voice that made me instantly all hot and bothered.

"Nope. Patience, Mr. Slater. You'll have a nice surprise this weekend."

In an almost helpless, pitiful voice, he asked, "Please?"

I couldn't help grinning at his change in tone. "All right, all right. Give me five minutes."

"Thank you, baby. You don't know how happy that makes me. Of course, I'm already hard just thinking about you getting undressed."

"Jake!" I cried as heat filled my cheeks.

He chuckled at my outrage. "Okay, go change."

After I hung up, I peeked out of the bedroom. The boys still hadn't made it back to the bus. I locked the door and then slipped on the black and white checkered bra and thong. With white bows along the edges, it had an extremely naughty school girl look, especially when I slid on the white, lacy garters. Innocent, but sexy. Once I was outfitted, I stood in front of the mirror and snapped a few pictures from different angles. Then I texted them to Jake. I'd barely finished sending the last one when he called me.

"Are you trying to kill me? You're even wearing garters!"

I laughed. "Does that mean you like it?"

"Oh fuck, Angel, I'll explode before Friday." He sucked in a ragged breath. "Are you still wearing it?"

"Yes," I replied warily. I had a feeling where this was going, and I wasn't sure I was ready for it yet.

"Wanna make love to me over the phone?"

I snorted. "You mean, 'Let's have phone sex'."

"Anyone can make it sound dirty," he teased.

Fiddling with the lace on my garters, I asked, "Are you in your bedroom?"

After I heard some muffled noises, Jake replied, "Yes, I'm in bed now—naked and hard as a fucking rock because of your pictures."

A thrill went over me at the image that formed in my mind. Closing my eyes, I focused on the familiar sight of his lean muscles, his tight abs and all his tattoos. When heat burned between my thighs, I got a little more courage. "Do you want me naked?"

"Just your bra first."

I reached around and unhooked the snaps. Once it fell free, I fought the urge to cross my arms over my naked chest.

"Is it off?"

"Yeah..."

"Put me on speakerphone."

"Jeez, you sure are bossy," I muttered as I put the phone on the bed and punched the button.

"Cup your breasts." Just as I was told, I brought my hands to my chest. "Are your nipples hard yet?"

"No," I murmured.

"Pinch them."

Against my better judgment, I did as I was told. "Does it feel good?" Jake asked.

"Yeah," I murmured truthfully. Okay, maybe I could get into this a little bit.

Jake's long moan echoed throughout the room. "Oh baby, I wish I was there. I would have my mouth and hands all over your breasts."

"I wish you were here too." Biting my lip, I hesitated before I asked, "Are you touching yourself?"

"Oh yeah. But I'm imagining it's your hands on me or I'm sliding in and out of your warm mouth."

While slightly mortified by his dirty talk, a shudder went through me at his words. The dull ache between my legs began to grow. "Do you want me to take my panties off now?"

"Mmm, yeah. But keep on the garters."

I slid off the thong and then buried myself under the covers. "Okay, I'm naked."

"Are you wet?"

Warmth entered my cheeks as the reality crashed down on me again of what I'm doing. "Jake…"

"Come on, Angel, tell me."

"Yes," I whispered.

"Mmm, I love how wet you get for me. Now stroke yourself nice and slow," Jake ordered. Once again, I did as I was told. Closing my eyes, I pictured him and his delicious fingers touching and probing my center. "Now faster." When I sped up my tempo, I couldn't help gasping with pleasure. "Oh baby, that's right. Let me hear you."

Even with the TV on, I still didn't want to be too loud in case the boys came in. So instead, I bit down on my lip, stifling some of my cries. "You're holding back," Jake panted.

"Yeah, well, I'll let go if you let me hear you," I countered breathlessly.

At the sound of his grunts and groans, I felt myself building closer and closer to coming. "Oh Jake!" I cried as I went over the edge. Just as I started coming down, Jake's breathing grew even more ragged. "Angel, oh fuck!"

I lay there for a moment, trying to catch my breath. It was a few seconds before either of us spoke. "That was fucking fantastic!" Jake exclaimed.

A giggle escaped my lips. "Yeah, it was. Now you've even taken my phone virginity."

"I love that you did that for me, Angel. But most of all, I love you."

My heart thumped wildly in my chest. "I love you too. I can't wait to see you Friday."

"Will you promise to wear the lingerie under your clothes?"

"Of course I will. I'd do anything for you."

"God, I love you, Angel."

"I love you more."

***

Chapter Twenty-Four

Three days and two performances after my infamous phone call with Jake, I lounged in a giant hotel suite the label had provided for my brothers and me. I was counting the hours and minutes before I could see Jake again.

At the sound of a Mariachi ring tone echoing through the room, I grinned and picked up my phone. "Hello, AJ, what's shaking?"

"Hola, Abuela, como estas?"

My brows furrowed as I pulled the phone away to make sure it was really AJ. Then I replied in Spanish, "Um, I think you have the wrong number."

Still in Spanish, AJ replied, "Yeah, I got the right number. I just can't speak freely at the moment. That's why I'm talking in Spanish."

I gasped. "Is it Jake? Is something wrong?"

He drew in a ragged breath. "He's in bad shape, Angel. He's totally shut down, and I don't know what the hell to do."

"But why? What happened? I just talked to him last night." My mind spun frantically as I tried to remember anything unusual about our conversation. He'd mentioned the nurse was worried Susan's pneumonia might be getting worse, but Jake hadn't told me much more.

"The pneumonia took a greater toll on her system than the nurse and hospice people thought. She's been practically comatose all day."

My stomach churned, and I fought the urge to throw up. "Oh God...poor Jake...poor Susan," I murmured, gripping my phone tight as tears burned my eyes.

"Even though he won't say it or admit it, he needs you. Can you come?"

My mind whirled with the next few days of shows. The logical answer was I couldn't go, but there was no way in hell I was leaving Jake alone when he needed me most. "Of course I can. I'll get the next flight out."

"Good. I'll come pick you up, okay?"

"Thanks. I appreciate it."

"See you soon."

"Bye."

Surprisingly, my brothers and parents didn't protest about me leaving. They believed my place was with Jake and Susan. I was able to get a flight two hours later, and true to his word, AJ was waiting to pick me up. After he filled me in on everything that was going on, we spent most of the drive in silence.

Cars were parked everywhere along Jake's driveway. Since it was raining, AJ dropped me off closer to the door and then went back to park. With a shaky hand, I rang the doorbell. I half expected a nurse or one of Jake's relatives to answer it. Nothing could have prepared me for Jake throwing open the heavy mahogany door. At the sight of me, he did a double take. The color drained from his face before he demanded, "What the fuck are you doing here?"

I jolted back at the harshness of his tone. It took me a moment to find my voice. "AJ called me and told me about Susan. I came as soon as I could to be with you…and her."

He stood there still staring at me. My heart ached at his appearance. Rough stubble covered his face from where he hadn't shaved, and his usually styled-to-perfection hair was unkempt. Dark purple circles formed under his eyes. He wore a ratty Runaway Train t-shirt and a pair of holey jeans. While he had yet to ask me in, I threw myself forward, wrapping my arms tight around him. "Oh, baby, I'm so, so sorry. I'm here for you, and I love you."

He didn't hug me back. In fact, his arms lay limply at his sides. I pulled away to tenderly kiss his cheek. "Talk to me, Jake," I implored.

His body shuddered for a moment before he shook his head. Without a word, he pushed out of my embrace. Taking my hand, he jerked me further into the foyer and down the hallway. I thought we might be going to Susan's room, but instead, he ushered me into his room and slammed the door.

"Jake, what are—" He silenced me by crushing his lips to mine. The kiss was demanding and harsh, nothing like I was used to experiencing with him. Taking my shoulders, he whirled me around and shoved me back against the door with such a force I cried out. His hands raked over my body as I tried getting away from him.

"Stop it!" I cried against his mouth.

When he pulled away, his fingers went to the button on his jeans. When he started to undo them, I shook my head. "What are you doing?"

"I'm gonna fuck you. That's what you came here for, right?"

My mouth, bruised from his earlier assault, fell open in shock. "No! How could you think such a horrible thing? I came to be with you because I love you and you need me."

With his blue eyes blazing, his hips pinned me against the wall again. His lips curled into an angry smirk. "All anyone ever wants is a piece of me—a way to further themselves through me. That's what you want too, right? You're Jake Slater's girlfriend—the one who finally tamed the notorious womanizer."

I shook my head wildly back and forth at his accusation. "I'm your girlfriend because I *love* you—not because of who you are or what anyone thinks." I brought my hands to cup his cheeks, forcing him to look at me. "I know you, Jake. I see every single imperfection you have, and I still love you. There's no one else in the world for me but you. And when you're hurting, I want to be with you. When you're broken and shattered like you are right now, I'm going to help you pick up the pieces. That's what love is, baby." I leaned over to whisper against the coarse stubble on his chin. "Trust me when I say that I'd do anything to be able to take away the terrible hurt you're feeling right now. But you have to let me in a little."

He grabbed my wrists in his hands and shoved them above my head. "You'd do anything for me, huh?"

"Yes," I murmured, fighting the urge to cry out from the pain of his grip.

"That's a fucking pity. Because all you've done is become my whore."

My head jerked back like he had slapped me. It was as if a total stranger had taken over Jake's body. I'd never seen him act this way, even his infamous drunken bus escapade paled in comparison. "Jake, please don't do this! Don't shut me out now." Tears burned my eyes. "I know you're hurting, but I know you love me and you need me."

With a cruel sneer, his hands left mine to slide down my body and rest on my hips. "I'm sorry, Angel, but that's where you were mistaken. You were just another piece of ass to conquer—although yours was a little more of a challenge. But I have to admit how surprised I was that some romance and a profession of love had you parting those sweet thighs faster than I ever thought."

"That's a lie! I know you loved me then, and you do now. You're just twisting everything around because you're mixed up inside." I gripped his shoulders. "You have to fight this, Jake. You can't give over to the darkness. That's not what Susan would want either."

A stormy mix of emotions flickered in Jake's eyes. "You can think what you want to, but I know what I'm saying about screwing you. I'm glad I got to break you in because you were meant for fucking. The way you cried out my name and came so hard on my tongue when I went down on you...Mmm...baby that was hot."

"Stop it," I protested feebly as tears of frustration and hurt streamed down my cheeks.

"Now don't cry, Angel. It was an honor to be your first. And I promise I'll remember you as one of the best fucks I've ever had—the innocent little angel who let the Big Bad Wolf inside her tight-as-hell walls."

The frayed strands of my emotions snapped in two, and before I could stop myself, I brought my palm hard against his cheek, causing a loud crack to reverberate throughout the room. Any hurt within me gave way to white hot anger. "You unimaginable asshole! Don't you *ever* talk to me like that again! I know your mother is dying, but that doesn't give you an excuse to spit and trample upon everything we are. You better wake up fast and realize what you're saying. You need to get it through your thick skull that I wasn't just a piece of ass—that I was everything you ever dreamed of, but you fucked it all up because you had to push me away when you needed me most!"

With that, I turned away and sprinted out of the room. As I raced out the front door, AJ called my name, but I ignored him. Not even thinking of where I was going or how I would get there, I ran headlong off the porch and into the blinding downpour.

I got halfway down the gravel drive before I heard Jake's voice cutting through the rain. "Abby! Please wait!"

Whirling around, I jabbed a finger at him. "Leave me alone now, Jake. I may have made a promise to Susan to try and give you second chances when you screw up, but you're testing my sanity right now…"

My voice trailed off as Jake sank to his knees in the mud. His chest rose and fell with harsh sobs as he buried his face in the hem of my

343

dress. "I'm sorry. Oh Christ, Angel, I'm so, so sorry."

Unblinking and unmoving, I stared at him in shock. I didn't know what to say or do. He had hurt me so deeply that part of me wanted to kick him off of me. "Jake, I—"

"I'm sorry. I'm sorry. I'm sorry," he repeated, clutching the backs of my knees. "I didn't mean any of it—I swear to God I didn't. I made AJ promise not to call you or get you to come because I couldn't bear the thought of you seeing me like this." He shook his head forlornly. "When you showed up, I thought I would die, and I couldn't think of anything but driving you away. So I said and did all that shit just to hurt you, so you'd run away. You're right when you called me an unimaginable asshole."

When I gasped, he stared up at me, tears shimmering in his eyes. "But the moment you slapped me, it was like I saw everything so clearly again. I couldn't imagine not having you in my life, and I hated myself for doing that to you."

"Oh Jake," I murmured.

"And I swear to God that I do love you—I've never loved any girl like I have loved you. You are the most amazing thing that's ever happened to me in my life. It's just...I don't know what to do with all this," he smacked his hands against his drenched chest. "I barely know how to be with someone when I'm whole. How the hell am I supposed to be with you when I'm so fucking broken?"

Any anger I still harbored for him melted in an instant. I ran my fingers through the wet strands of his hair. "Baby, that's what love is. Standing by someone in the good times and the bad."

"You deserve better than what I've got to give you. I should've walked away from you a long time ago rather than being selfish and trying to keep you with me."

I shook my head. "You couldn't have kept me away. I love you too much. That's why I'm here now."

His face contorted into a mask of agony. "She's going to leave me. Please say you'll stay—even though I don't deserve you."

"I'm not going to leave you." I eased down onto the ground to wrap my arms around him. "I'm going to be here for you every step of the way. Just lean on me," I whispered in his ear. He began sobbing again, clutching me tight against him. "It's okay, baby," I murmured, running my hands over his back.

The rain continued beating down on us as Jake wept uncontrollably. When he finally started coming back to himself, he sighed raggedly. "I'm sorry, Angel."

I eased out of his embrace to stare into his eyes. "No more apologies, okay?"

He nodded before rising to his feet. Offering me his hand, he pulled me up. Wrapping his arm around my shoulder, he drew me to him as we started the walk back to the house. When we got inside, I was once again overwhelmed by all the friends and family filling the rooms. Jake ushered me inside his bedroom. AJ had brought my bag inside, so I quickly changed my drenched clothes while Jake did as well.

I was drying my hair when Jake appeared behind me in the bathroom. "Come with me to see Mama." I quickly shut off the hairdryer and followed him across the hall. A hospital bed now sat in the room where Susan's massive four-poster bed had once been. Her frail form seemed dwarfed in the bed. Her sister, Sally, and some of her nieces sat on the couch in the corner while her father perched in a chair. They acknowledged my presence with sad smiles.

Jake motioned for me to have a seat in one of the chairs pulled close to the bed. I eased down as I watched him sit down across from me. Jake took Susan's hand in his and kissed it. "Mama, I'm here," he said softly.

I don't know how long we sat like that—still as statues and waiting for some kind of response from her. I gasped when Susan's eyelids finally fluttered open, and she gazed around the room. I knew exactly who she was looking for. Once Jake reached forward and grabbed her hand, a beaming smile stretched across her face. "Jacob.'"

"Yes, Mama?"

"Do you remember the story I used to tell you about why you became a musician?"

Jacob's brows furrowed as if he was confused by her question. "Um, yeah, I do, but what—"

She shook her head and then turned to me. "I've always teased Jacob that he owes all his success as a singer and guitarist to me."

I smiled. "Does he?"

"Oh yes. Because of my studio and teaching dance lessons, he was surrounded by music while I was carrying him. He got hours of the greats like Mozart, Beethoven, and Brahms. I always felt him kicking the most when I was teaching a class. It was like he was letting me know he felt the music already."

"That's such a sweet story."

Susan drew in a ragged breath. "You know I was never supposed to be able to have children. After four miscarriages, I had given up on ever giving birth to a child of my own. Mark and I had begun to look into adoption when I got pregnant again. With all the other pregnancies, I'd been so careful to stay off my feet in the early days and weeks, but this time I didn't let myself get attached. Instead, I did everything I usually did—rode horses on my dad's farm and taught dance classes from morning until night. I didn't let myself believe that I could really be pregnant. But after another month passed and I was still pregnant, I began to hope and pray that this time it was for real. And when I got into my second trimester—weeks after I had lost the other babies, I knew I was finally going to have my miracle."

She turned her head to gaze at Jake. Tears streamed freely down his cheeks, and he didn't bother wiping them away. "My sweet son, you've always been the sunshine in my life—"

Pinching his eyes shut, Jake pleaded, "Don't do this."

"I have to say goodbye, honey, and you have to let me do this."

His chest rose and fell with harsh sobs as he buried his face onto her chest. When her hand stroked the top of his head, I couldn't hold my emotions back any longer, and I began to weep. At my sniffling, Susan smiled. "Abby, after I'm gone, I want you to remind Jacob of the story of his birth. When he gets so down and low that he cannot stand or when he thinks there isn't any reason to go on, tell him the story. Remind him that he was a miracle and the most precious gift I ever received."

Tears spilled across my face and dripped onto my lap as I leaned forward to take her hand in mine. "I will. I promise I will." I brought her hand to my lips and kissed it before pressing it to my cheek. "I promise to make sure that he never, ever gives up, no matter how much he wants to."

"I thank God he has you, sweet girl. You'll take good care of each other." She smiled as tears shimmered in her eyes. "You two are going to be so happy together and make the most beautiful grandchildren for me."

Her words made both Jake and me cry even harder. "Oh Mama," Jake sobbed. He reached up to tenderly kiss her cheek.

"You have to let me go, baby."

He shook his head wildly back and forth. "I can't do it. Please don't ask me to do that."

She rubbed her hand along his face. "It's not goodbye for forever. We'll see each other again. And until then, you live a full, happy life and make me proud."

"I will."

Susan smiled. "Now tell me goodbye."

Jake's anguished expression broke me, and I wept openly. His chest rose and fell with harsh breaths. "Goodbye, Mama. I love you so much."

"Thank you, sweetheart. And I love you too." Susan's gaze then turned to me. "Abby, do you remember that angel song from *Oh Brother Where Art Thou?*"

We'd watched the movie together probably three or four times when I was recovering from my beating. She loved the Cohen Brothers films as much as she loved George Clooney. "Yes, *Angel Band*. I know it."

"Sing it to me, please."

I didn't know how I could breathe through my sobs, let alone sing, but somehow I steadied myself and tried to draw on strength I didn't know if I had. "My latest sun is sinking fast. My race is almost run," I began.

"That's it. So beautiful," she murmured. She then closed her eyes while Jake kept his arms wrapped around her. As I kept on singing, a gentle smile formed on her lips. Her breathing grew more and more labored. When I got to the last verse, she drew in one last breath.

And then she was gone.

Jake fell apart, burying his face on Susan's chest and crying hysterically. A symphony of wailing echoed throughout the room as Sally and her daughters began crying as well as Jake's grandfather. I stepped around the side of the bed to wrap my arms around him. "I'm so sorry," I murmured over and over.

Just when I thought he would collapse from exhausted grief, Jake jerked his head up. He unwrapped my arms from him. "I have to get out of here," he muttered before he sprinted out the room. I met AJ in the hallway. "Go to him," he urged.

I nodded and then hurried after Jake. When I got to the porch, I glanced left and right before running to the barn. "Jake?" I called. Silence echoed around me. Whirling around, I then ran down the hill to the stables. I peeked in several stalls until I saw him standing in one.

With tears still streaming down his cheeks, Jake was saddling up a towering black horse. Sensing my presence, Jake said, "I have to get away from here. I need to take a ride."

I stepped back as he led the horse out of the stall. "I'll go with you."

He glanced at me in shock. "You don't ride horses after you got thrown as a kid," he reminded me.

A shiver went over me at the memory from all those years passed, but I shook my head. "I'll ride them for you."

Jake stared at me for a minute before taking my hand. He pulled me over to the horse. "This is Lennon." He gave me a sheepish grin. "Brayden might be a Paul McCartney fan, but it's all about John Lennon for me."

"I like it."

"Ready?"

"As I'll ever be."

Tension and unspoken words hung heavy between us. I was at a loss for what to say to comfort him. He'd just experienced the worse loss of his life, and I was afraid I might not be enough to fill the void. Maybe there wasn't anything I could say—maybe all he needed was me by his side, showing my love and support.

Jake brushed the wet strands of hair out of my face. "You can hold tight to me. I won't let you fall, Angel."

"And I won't let you either." I wrapped my arms around his neck and pressed myself against him. I gave him a lingering kiss. "We'll ride this storm together, Jake. Forever and always."

His warm breath fanned across my cheek. "And you'll always be my sweet angel—my saving grace and the love of my life."

***

Epilogue

JAKE

A deep, regretful sigh escaped my lips as I stared down at the bronze marker memorializing my mother. Although I had gone all out to get her the best there was, it still seemed like an inadequate representation of how amazing a woman and mother she was.

Abby's arm encircled my waist, pulling me to her. She leaned her head on my shoulder. "Are you sure you don't need a minute alone?"

"No, I want you here." I kissed the crown of her head. "I always want you with me."

"And I always want to be here for you."

I smiled down at her. "Besides, Mama would want you here. She loved you like I do."

Abby's chin trembled. "And I loved her too. I always will."

At the sound of crunching leaves behind us, Abby and I turned around. A tall, lean man came striding toward us. His arms were laden with dozens of pink roses. When he got almost to us, he stopped abruptly. His dark green eyes scanned our faces. "Excuse me, are you part of Susan Moore's—I mean, Susan Slater's family."

My brows shot up at his thick Russian accent. "I'm her son."

A hesitant smile formed on his lips. "Of course. I see the resemblance now." His gaze left mine to take in my mother's grave.

Regret filled his face. "I'm so sorry I didn't get here for the funeral. I didn't know she was sick. I would've liked..." He drew in a sharp breath like he was trying to control his emotions. "I would have liked to have seen her again."

"How did you know her?" I asked.

"We used to dance together many years ago."

Abby's arm jerked from my waist to cover her mouth. Her eyes had widened as big as saucers. "Oh my God. You're Yuri?"

He smiled. "Yes, but how did you know?"

"Susan told me about you."

"Wait, what?" I asked.

Ignoring me, I watched as Abby closed the gap between her and Yuri. She leaned up to whisper something in his ear. An agonized sob escaped his lips. When she finally pulled away, tears streamed down his cheeks. "Really?"

Abby nodded.

"Thank you," he murmured. Swiping his cheeks, he turned his attention to me. "May I have a moment with her?"

"Sure. We really have to be going anyway," I replied.

"Nice meeting you," Yuri said.

"You too," Abby replied while I nodded.

As we walked away, Abby took my hand in hers. "Who the hell is that guy and what did my mom tell you about him?" I demanded.

"It was something she wanted just between us—a girl's thing."

I skidded to a stop. "Please tell me that dude isn't my real father or something like that!"

Abby's blue eyes widened. "No, no, of course it's nothing sordid like that!"

"Tell me," I growled. When she shot me her infamous 'Don't you dare use that tone with me, Jake Slater', look, I grunted in frustration. I hated begging, and she knew it. "Please."

"Okay, since you asked nicely, I'll fill you in on the way to the concert."

The idea of a benefit concert in my mother's memory had been Abby's idea. She wanted it to be a hometown crowd for those who knew and loved my mom as well as me. All proceeds would go to cancer research and the American Cancer Society. She organized everything from having us perform in the park behind the high school where both my mom and I went to school. It would also be the opening of our newly billed act, The Crossroads Tour, where Jacob's Ladder and Runaway Train teamed up together for a North American tour.

After performing with her brothers, Abby and I would be singing several duets before Runaway Train came on, including *I'll Take You with Me*. It had been bittersweet when the song shot to number one on the Billboard Top 100 the day of Mama's funeral. Although everyone was heralding it as the most emotional break-up song of the year, I knew the truth. It was about immense heartbreak and suffering—just not the kind they thought.

Since we were performing in a park, we had to get ready in our tour buses. My first order of business for our upcoming tour was to ensure that Abby and I had our own bus, so we could be alone without interruptions. Always thinking of someone else, Abby had insisted that we share it a lot with Brayden so that he and Lily could have more family time. Until then, I planned on christening every square inch of it with her when we got on the road. Tonight, however, there was no time for funny business.

Besides organizing the venue and bands, it had also been Abby's idea for everyone to dress-up, so to speak, in respect for my mama. The guys from both bands were wearing black dress pants, black shirts and black ties. A single pink ribbon for Breast Cancer awareness was pinned to our lapels. Although strapless, Abby's black dress came to her knees and met the tops of her black cowboy boots. Wrapped around her neck were my mother's pearls. She wore them often, and every time she did, it made my heart ache with both pleasure and pain at the bond the two amazing women in my life once shared.

A stylist was still working on my hair when they came to escort Abby to the stage. After what had happened with Bree, I insisted on two bodyguards each and every time. She leaned over the chair to kiss my cheek. "See you in a few, babe."

"Bye Angel," I replied.

As soon as I was finished, I headed to the wings so I could watch Abby perform. I never got tired of watching her work a crowd. She was truly amazing in every aspect of her life. After singing several songs of her brothers' hits, Abby sat alone on the stage with her guitar. "This song is for all of you out there who know the pain of loss and the anguish of grief." She then began strumming the opening of Pink's *Beam Me Up*. Her voice filled the stadium and warmed my soul. It meant so much that I had someone to share my grief with. Abby hadn't known Mama long, but she still loved her. Having my Angel stand by me in the darkest, most hellish times of my life meant everything in the world.

Glancing over my shoulder, I grinned at the guys. "Damn, she's amazing, isn't she?"

With one arm wrapped around Lily's waist and Melody in the other, Brayden smiled. "She gets better and better every time I hear her."

AJ nodded. "But I still don't know what the hell she sees in you."

"Douchebag!" I shouted before ruffling his hair.

"Hey man, don't be hating on the hair!" he countered smacking my hand away.

Rhys rolled his eyes at our antics and went back to texting on his phone. I knew he was fighting his nerves because his parents were in the audience. They'd flown up in his dad's corporate jet. Like the true angel she was, Abby had called to invite them. She had also gone on and on about what an amazing son they had and how proud they should be.

As Abby finished up the song, I adjusted my guitar on my shoulder, so I could head out to join her. We'd planned to sing several duets together, including *I'll Take You with Me*. But Abby surprised me by abandoning her stool and handing off her guitar to a technician. She then went over to the piano and sat down. "There's one more song I'd like to do tonight before Jake joins me. It's another song by one of my favorite and most inspirational singers, Pink. It's called *The Great*

356

Escape, and it's for anyone who has hit rock bottom and is thinking about making an escape." She glanced up from the microphone and met my questioning gaze. "But most of all, this one is for you, babe."

Her fingers effortlessly flew over the black and white keys as she began the song. Leaning against the side of the stage, I listened intently to the lyrics. Even though I tried fighting them, tears stung my eyes, especially the part about how the passion and the pain would keep me alive someday. The song captured so much of the desperately dark emotions I'd been experiencing in the past two months since Mama's death. I knew there would be more desperate times ahead, but I wouldn't be making any escapes. I had Abby by my side, my bandmates and brothers, and the new love of Abby's family to get me through.

When Abby finished, I strode out on stage and pulled her up from the piano bench. After I wrapped my arms tight around her, I murmured into her ear. "Thank you, Angel."

"You're welcome." She kissed me on the lips, which caused the crowd to go wild. Working the moment, Abby took a microphone from the technician and asked, "I guess you guys are ready for us to sing together now?"

Whistles and catcalls filled the air. "Well, all right then." The set was changed to where two microphones sat between two stools. Abby and I adjusted our guitars on our laps.

The first song we did together was a cover of Tim McGraw and Faith Hill's *I Need You*. Perched on the stool across from me, Abby grinned when I changed the lyrics from riding across West Virginia to

West Georgia and the part about cowboys going out like that to rockers. We finished the song to thunderous applause. I bobbed my head at Abby to do the next introduction. She grinned and winked at me. "We want to thank everyone who has made *I'll Take You with Me* a hit. It means so much to Jake and myself because we wrote the song together. In fact, it was the first songwriting I ever did. So here it is."

Even though the song was emotional hell, I never got tired of performing it with Abby. Each time she brought something different to it—either emphasizing a new word or whispering part of a line. She kept me on my toes on stage just like in the real world, and I loved every minute of it.

After the applause died down, I leaned in to the microphone. "So for our last song together, we wanted to do another cover. Hopefully this time next year we'll have written more material together. But for now, this song captures so much of what I feel for Abby, or my Angel. Here's Paul McDonald and Nikki Reed's *All I Ever Needed*."

Throughout the song, Abby and I kept our eyes locked. Although we were separated by our guitars and the microphone stand, we inched as close as we could. Like the lyrics, she was my shelter in the storm and all I would ever need.

When the last verse echoed throughout the park, Abby leaned over the microphone to kiss me passionately. The crowd loved it, and the applause and cheering became deafening. Abby started to rise off of her stool to make her departure from the stage, but I stopped her.

Her brows furrowed in confusion. "Jake—"

I tried stilling the rapid beating of my heart. I knew what I was about to do was huge, and I wanted to make sure it was absolutely perfect. Speaking into my microphone, my voice cracked as it echoed over the crowd. "Two of the songs we sang together mean everything to me, Angel. You're all I've ever needed, or I could ever want. There's nothing I want more than to spend the rest of my life making you happy."

I rose off my stool and dug the small jewelry box out of my pocket. When I cracked it open, the enormous emerald cut diamond caught the stage lights, and it sparkled, causing Abby to shriek with shock. "Oh my God...Oh. My. God!" she exclaimed. Her hands came up to cover her mouth.

With a grin, I knelt down on one knee before her. The crowd started screaming and whistling so loud I could barely hear myself think. I'd gone over and over in my head a million times what I planned to say. I wanted it to be heartfelt and meaningful. I was a songwriter for fuck's sake, but in that moment, it all flew out of my head.

So I gave up and took Abby's hand in mine. "Angel, will you make my life complete and whole by marrying me?"

Tears shimmered in Abby's eyes as she hopped off of her stool. I barely had time to prepare before she threw herself into my arms, almost toppling me over. "Yes! Yes, I'll marry you!"

At her acceptance, the crowd once again went crazy while the guys played a rocker remix of the Bridal March. Wrapping Abby in my arms, I stood up and spun her around. As a self-respecting dude, I'd never believed in fairy tales, but in that moment, I did. I'd found my angel to live happily-ever-after with.

A message from Katie Ashley:

Please do me a tremendous favor by leaving a review on Amazon, Barnes and Noble or Goodreads. If you're not comfortable with leaving a review, find one that you think expresses your feelings and like that review. You don't know how much it means to Independent Authors.

Find Katie online at:

http://www.katieashleybooks.com

http://katieashleybooks.blogspot.com/

Facebook:

https://www.facebook.com/katieashleybooks

https://www.facebook.com/katie.ashleyromance

Twitter

www.twitter.com/katieashleyluv

***

About the Author

Katie Ashley is the New York Times, USA Today, and Amazon Best-Selling author of The Proposition. She lives outside of Atlanta, Georgia with her two very spoiled dogs and one outnumbered cat. She has a slight obsession with Pinterest, The Golden Girls, Harry Potter, Shakespeare, Supernatural, Designing Women, and Scooby-Doo.

She spent 11 1/2 years educating the Youth of America aka teaching MS and HS English until she left to write full time in December 2012.

She also writes Young Adult fiction under the name Krista Ashe.

***

Acknowledgements

Thanks first and foremost always go to God for his love and abiding support, for speaking peace to my often troubled soul, and for exceeding my expectations of unanswered prayers. To my church family for always giving me love and support when I needed it most and being supportive of my alter-ego Katie.

Michelle Eck: Even as a writer, words seem inadequate to say how grateful I am that God brought you into my life. You're a daily blessing as a friend, a hardcore supporter, a Stream Team Captain extraordinaire, and the best eagle eye editor a girl could ever ask or hope for. I don't know what I would do without you, your love and care, your straight forward honesty, and your willingness to fight long and hard to make my books and my career better. I couldn't navigate these crazy waters without you at the helm! Love and hugs always!!

Cris Hadarly: Thank you for being one of the sweetest, kindest, and most caring people I know. We're truly soul sisters divided by oceans and continents! I can't thank you enough for all your support, pimpage, long and grueling hours working on book tours on my behalf, and overall book love. Most of all, I thank you for your friendship, for your prayers, and for having a smile for me when I needed it most. I pray God blesses you with the desires of your heart that you so richly deserve.

Marilyn Medina: You mean so much to me girlie and have so many places in my heart. You're my fellow Golden Girls goddess, my "twinsie and sista from another mista, my Latin lover, my eagle eye editor and book lover and supporter. I can't imagine writing a book if I didn't have you to support me and help to make it better. Thanks also for helping with all things Spanish for AJ. Thanks for always having your eye for me—I know I can count on you to shank any haters!

JB McGee: Thank you for being one of the kindest, sweetest, and most generous people I've been blessed to get to know in the business. Your courage and your ability to smile in the good and bad times are truly an inspiration to me. Thank you for all things design related and most of all for being the most kickass formatter (including being willing to do it last minute!).

Yesi Cavazos: Thank you so, so much for all your book love and support. I appreciate all your help with Music. Thanks for making sure AJ and Abby were speaking Spanish in the right tenses and using the right Spanish curse words!! LOL I love our marathon dinners together with JB and Michelle, and I'm going to miss them so much!!

Lisa Kane: Thank you so, so much for your willingness to be an early reader. The insight and enthusiasm you brought to Music made it such a better book. I'm forever in your debt. Big hugs always for the support of all my books.

Raine Miller: Thank you lady for being a part of my life. I will always see our friendship as divinely brought about! You're a true inspiration. Thank you for always being there for me to provide laughter, support, advice, and guidance. You are truly my Mama

Raine!!

Heather Gunter: Thanks to the most amazing margaritas, Mexican food, and tattoos partner in crime! Thanks for giving me a shoulder to cry on as well as an ear to piss and moan in! Your support has meant so much to me over the last few months. You're a true soul sister! Love ya lots, girlie!!

Andrea Riley: Thanks for your love and support, cuz! I appreciate the constant writing support and encouragement all the way back to when you read that first draft of The Road to Damascus many years ago. We were raised like sisters and have weathered the tough times together. I love you very, very much.

Sara Wolf: Thank you for being such a wonderful and inspiring writing buddy all these years. You've been there encouraging me through the good times and the bad, and I'll never forget you for it. Thanks so much for lending your eye to early drafts of Music, for encouraging and lifting me up with your enthusiasm

Paige & Enzo Silva: What can I say to two of the most amazing, supportive, enthusiastic and giving friends a gal could ever ask for? Most of all, I give thanks that you both have been a part of life for all these years and have hung in there with me through the very, very dark times. Your love means the world to me.

To all the ladies of my street team Ashley's Angels: Your support, enthusiasm, pimpage, humor, and general amazingness makes me very humbled and honored to have you in my corner!! Special shout-outs to Shannon Furhman & Tamara Debbaut for their AMAZING Music of the Heart inspired fan art and quotes. You rock, ladies!! And also thanks to Amber Vaughn for your pimpage of my fanpage as well as all the amazing fan art. Plus it was pretty amazing seeing The Proposition in the sights of Ireland! You're amazing!

To the **Book Avenue Review, Kim Box Person, Ana's Attic, Aeastas Book Blog, Flirty and Dirty Book Blog,** and **Literati Literature Lovers** for being a supporter of my books from the very, very beginning. Your pimpage and love means so much to me. There's so many other blogs I owe thanks to like **Shh Mom's Reading, Three Chicks and Their Books, Into the Night Reviews, My Secret Romance, Smitten's Book Blog,** and **Reviews by Tammy and Kim** along with sooooo many others!!

Emilie Grey for you overwhelming enthusiasm and support for my books along with making all the fabulous Jakeisms on Pinterest!! You are a true ray of sunshine!

To Amazing new writer buddies: **CC Wood, RK Lilley, Jasinda Wilder, Tara Sivec, Amy Bartol, Georgia Cates, Jenn Sterling, Nyrae Dawn, AC Marchman, Jami Mac, Jenn Foor,** and **Michelle Leighton.** You ladies rock my rocks with your talent, your support, and your laughter!!

To the ladies of the Hot Ones: **Karen Lawson, Marion Archer, Amy Lineaweaver,** and **Merci Arellano**: You ladies are too amazing for words. I love how our first book chat went for three hours. I could Skype with you guys every day and still not talk enough! Your support and enthusiasm for my books is such a blessing, but it's also the fact you care so much about Katie/Krista as a person that means the most. Big hugs and love!

To reader buddies who inspire me with their love, support, and fangirling: **Ricki Wieselthier, Kimberly Sutherland, Andrea Gregory, Angie Hocking, Aimee Packorek, Donna Soluri,** Amanda **Orozco, Missy Mealer, Jennifer Singh, Donna Kilroy,** and **Stephanie Tolsky.**

To my IRL besties **Kim Benefield, Kristi Hefner, Gwen McPherson, Brittany Haught, Jaime Brock, Erica Deese,** and **Lindsey Cochran.** Thanks for being there for me in the good and bad times. Your support of my writing has meant the world to me, but it's your friendship that I truly treasure. I wouldn't take anything for the years of laughter, tears, and craziness we've all shared together. Love you lots.

Gene & Yvonne Norton & Jimmy & Joy Stephens: Thank you for being a blessing and light in my life since the day I was born. Your love and dedication to me and my family has mean so much in the good and bad times. Thank you for your constant prayers, encouragement and love and for standing by me in the storms of life when those we all loved and adored were taken from us.

And big, huge, tremendous hugs to all my readers and bloggers!!

***

WITHDRAWN
Monroe Coll. Library

23108273R00198

Made in the USA
Lexington, KY
28 May 2013